Impossible Standards

A Novel

Christiana Harrell

Copyright © 2009 by Christiana Harrell

This is a work of fiction. The author has invented the characters. Any resemblance to actual persons, living or dead is purely coincidental.

All rights reserved. No part of this publication may be reproduced or transmitted in any form or by any means, electronic or mechanical, including photocopy, recording, or any information storage and retrieval system, without permission in writing from the publisher except for the use of brief quotations in a book review.

Edited By: Christina Cosse', Bianca Oscar, Sherrill Harrell

Poem by:**Natasia Easley aka Flow2Eazy**

Email the author: wordsRmylife86@yahoo.com

First Edition

Visit: **christianaharrell.com**

ISBN-13: 978-1480165502

ISBN-10: 1480165506

Preface

      I had an ex that would always say that women had "impossible standards" and I had to think to myself if I was in fact one of those women. I also had to think to myself that maybe the jerk only said it because they themselves did not have much to offer any woman. I went with thought number two and after ten months that relationship had run its course.
      Although the game of love was over, the words "impossible standards" stuck in my brain and I thought to myself that it was a catchy title. We've all read about difficult women so what's one more right? I decided to mix two of my worse relationships together to make one bad experience because I know that there are women out there who can empathize with what I went through. I figured that maybe I could help someone realize the signs before they get caught up with a cheater and a liar and then afterwards still be who they are and allow the right person to love them.
      In this book you will find a woman who is all out of love (Eliza) but there is man who will help her realize that she never gave her love away at all (Emmanuel). It is a true tale of love and triumph if you're into that sort of thing lol.
      There was no real research done for this book. The only thing I had to look inside of was myself and now I'm sharing it with you.
      There is no such thing as having your standards too high. You are who you are and you want what you want, but just remember to be able to offer all that you ask in return. I hope you enjoy this book!

Now with that said I'd like to thank my two wonderful ex's Cricket and Mole, is what we'll call them, for being disasters, but leaving me with a story to tell.

And to the beautiful people who showed me that love does not have to be complicated I love you very much.

To my mother Tammy who wrote me a letter that changed my life after the last time I had my heartbroken, you are a true warrior in life and love and I don't know what I'd do without you.

Dedication:

To the battered, the broken, and the bruised…you are good enough.

To the nice guys that finish last, let the bad men have the trash.

Table of Contents

PROLOGUE — 1

FLASHES OF THE PAST — 5

REKINDLE — 29

APRIL SHOWERS — 39

MAY ~~FLOWERS~~ — 55

QUICK REMINDERS — 67

THE DISTRACTIONS — 77

CROSSING PATHS AND THE MAJORITY — 87

NICE JOB, NEVER BEEN MARRIED, AND NO KIDS? — 103

OPTIONAL, BUT SEXY TATTOOS AND OWN PLACE — 119

CONSIDERATE — 135

GOD-FEARING AND FUNNY — 143

MAKES THE FIRST MOVE, GREAT KISSER, GREAT.... — 155

DANCING — 165

LOYAL	181
PASSIONATE AND ROMANTIC	189
LOVES TRYING NEW FOODS	199
LOVES TO READ, LOVER OF ALL THINGS ART	207
MISERY LOVES COMPANY	221
HURRICANE SEASON WITH MR. INTELLECTUAL	231
~~SECURE AND CONFIDENT~~	241
LOVES TO TRAVEL	247
THIRTY DAYS AND THIRTY NIGHTS	273
SECOND CHANCES	287

Prologue

"It's about damn time you answered the phone. Are you okay?" Madra asked.

"I feel a lot better." I said sitting in the middle of the bed recovering from my cemetery breakdown.

"Are you sure?" she asked again.

"Yeah I'm sure. I'm just ready to get back into my routine."

"Well, before you do that, do you think you could have a little fun and come to a card party tonight and let Paul and I whip you and lover boy in some spades?"

"I think I just might do that."

"Good, you and Emmanuel can bring the paper plates and stuff."

"Does Emmanuel know already?"

"Yeah, Paul told him. The original plan was to just bring you here against your will."

"I've been forced to do a lot against my will the past couple of months. I don't think a card party would have killed me." I smiled.

"I'm just happy to hear your voice. I was worried."

"Don't be Emmanuel has been wonderful."

"Well you and Mr. Wonderful better get here before seven."

"We'll be there." I laughed then we said our goodbye's until later. I hung up my cell and stretched. I had slept all day while Emmanuel ran errands. I smiled and thought about how great of a man he really was.

The front door opened as thoughts of him crossed my mind and there he was, "Hey sleepy head." He said.
"Hey." I smirked.
"You talked to Madra?"
"We just got off the phone a minute ago."
"Well why aren't you up getting dressed?"
"I'm getting up."
I hopped out of bed and got dressed. It would be good to get around some good people and have a few drinks and few laughs. I had isolated myself long enough. I needed to call my mom and dad when I got a chance, because they had called the most since I went away. I just still wasn't ready.
I dressed and Emmanuel and I headed to the store to get our items for the party. We pulled up to the dollar store and went in.
"I'm going look for cards." Emmanuel said.
"I'm sure they have cards. It's a card party."
"I don't trust people. They can rig the deck." He said then headed off.
"Whatever, I'm going find the plates and stuff."
I walked off into the opposite direction. I walked down to the last isle and turned to my left. I stopped in my tracks when I saw Tavis stocking shelves. I tried to turn around so he wouldn't see me, but I didn't move fast enough. He stopped what he was doing and walked over to me.
"I texted you, did you get it?"
"Yeah I have just been real busy…"
"Busy ignoring me?"
"It's not like that."
"It's cool. I understand. I just wanted you to know I was sorry for your loss…"

"Well thanks…"
"You can call me if you ever need to talk."
"That's probably not a good idea."
"Why not?"
Emmanuel yelled out my name just as I was about to answer Tavis' question. He turned at the other end of the isle and saw Tavis talking to me. He was calm as he walked in our direction. He bumped Tavis out of the way.
"You got the plates?" he asked.
"They're right there." I pointed at the plates on the shelf.
He grabbed a pack and looked Tavis up and down then grabbed my arm and pushed me toward the register. I was saying a silent prayer in my mind as Tavis walked to the front of the store watching our every move. I hoped that we could leave in one peace. Tavis was the double standard guy. He could do whatever he wanted with whomever he wanted, but the thought of me with someone else killed him and I was sure he recognized Emmanuel's face.
We checked out and got into Emmanuel's truck.
"Shoot!" I said smacking my lips.
"What?" Emmanuel asked.
"We were supposed to get napkins and forks too."
"I'll go back in and get them."
"No, let's just go somewhere else." I placed my hand on his arm as he swung his door open and one foot dangled out.
"I'm not worried about your ex Eliza."
He wasn't, but I was and the moment he said that Tavis was out the door and walking full speed in our direction.

"Yo Eliza, so this the simple Simon ass dude you've been seeing? He the reason you don't love me anymore?!" Tavis yelled and headed for Emmanuel.

Emmanuel turned to step out of the truck, but before he could get all the way out Tavis ran up to him, pushing the door as hard as he could slam it.

"Tavis no!" I screamed.

Before I could stop it Tavis slammed the door on Emmanuel's leg. He slammed it so hard I heard the bone in Emmanuel's leg crack…

Flashes of the past

Eliza

"Human Resources this is Eliza, how may I help you?"

"Hello Eliza...."

The familiar voice sent chills through me. It had been an entire year since I heard from my once upon a time lover, well not exactly once upon a time more like one year and five months ago. Tavis was the third man in my life that I had allowed myself to have feelings for and although they weren't those dangerous deep forever feelings, they were enough to keep him in my life for over...wait let me count...five years if you don't count the break-ups in between.

"How did you get this number?" I asked knowing the answer, but needing the confirmation that he never really let me go or forgot anything about me.

"It's still programmed in my phone."

"Okay then I guess what I need to be asking is why are you calling me after all this time?"

"I just needed somebody to talk to."

"And you chose me, your ex?"

"Well, you know me better than anybody and you always know what to say to me."

"I don't have time for this Tavis." I said knowing I had nothing but time.

The sound of Tavis' voice always made me smile no matter how long it had been since I heard from him. He was the one man that I could talk to about anything, because before he and I got romantically involved he was a best friend to me. I was dating one of his male friends and before you judge me keep reading.

His friend's name was Jarrod Sampson. I was head over heels in love with that half man, half animal fire sign. Now he and I shared a dangerous kind of love. I gave him seven long years of my life. He got me when I was young and dumb, emphasis on the dumb. The first time that I laid eyes on Jarrod was in a high school talent show that we were both in. He was performing an original rap song that he wrote. It was a bold thing to do in the cruel world of teenagers. He was chubby and mysterious, just the way I liked them back then, because I had always been a sucker for the boys that nobody else wanted. He was my first real crush.

I sat on the sideline at his audition beside my best friend Madra, giggling like the high schooler that I was, because I loved to hear Jarrod talk. He had a New York accent and he wasn't shy about telling us Southern New Orleans folk exactly where he was from. He was aggressive and no matter what time of the day it was he had a smile on his face.

I stalked him in the day light. I knew his locker number and all his classes. All the boys wanted to be like him, the girls wondered about him, and I just wanted to be with him. It took me an entire year to say two words to him, but even then it still was nowhere near "would you go out with me". I just didn't want to seem fast. He was transferred before I could dig my nails into him and I was crushed.

My mother couldn't pick me up from school one day and she told me I needed to ride the bus home. I hated the bus. I hated the loud children that got on there and went straight to the back as if Rosa Parks didn't fight for the right to sit up front, and I hated the smell. The ride was always long and annoying, but that day the stars were aligned for me and my long time crush.

  I had to take two buses just to get to my house since I lived in a different parish from my school and really wasn't supposed to be a student there. I used my Aunt's address to look legit, but that's a story for another day. I sat in the terminal awaiting my next bus since the buses in my parish ran less often than any other parish. I decided to catch up on some history notes while I waited. I pulled my book out of my bag to read it and highlight whatever I felt would be important for a test. I looked down and looked back up and there he was inches taller, slimmer, and way hotter than I remembered him. He still had that smile.

  "Hey don't I know you?" he asked with that beautiful smile that I loved so much.

  "Yeah you went to school with me; we were in a talent show together." I gave him a friendly reminder.

  "Eliza?"

  "You remembered my name." I smiled.

  "I don't forget pretty faces." He flirted.

  I looked away blushing. "What school are you at now?"

  "Ehret," he said and I suddenly felt stupid for asking that question when it said it on his blue shirt clear as day.

  "Well it was nice seeing you again Jarrod." I smiled.

  "We should keep in touch." He suggested.

  I bit my bottom lip trying to keep my cool and stop myself from smiling so hard. I pulled my notebook from my bag and jotted down my number handing it to him and telling him to use it whenever he wanted to.

I went home that night and I sat by the phone. He called me the same night and we talked until it was time for school. He told me so much in so little time, but the one thing that I remembered was him telling me that he was a boy that was not afraid of his own tears and he would cry anywhere if he felt the need to and he didn't care what anyone had to say about it. I was in love before dawn and I vowed to keep all his secrets. I was in love with him before I had even known him completely.

Jarrod respected me more than any guy ever had. He never brought up sex and I was intoxicated by his kisses wishing they never had to end. I could be my whole self with him.

He and I were inseparable for a while until the disappearing acts started. He told me his mom was in the military and he had to take a lot of trips back and forth to New York to be with his dad. I was so stupid I believed him. He wouldn't call for weeks at a time and I would cry myself to sleep wondering where he was and if he was okay. He would eventually pop back into my life and call like he never stopped. He wrote me long love letters and sometimes songs since he loved rap so much. Jarrod would suggest books for me to read and he often challenged religion, which made me do the same. I believed in everything that he believed in.

He stopped existing in my world eventually, standing me up for homecoming and then prom or any random date that he planned using the excuse that he had a terminal illness that had to be treated and kept him in the hospital for weeks at a time. I still could recall past plans where he would call and tell me to get dressed so we could go out and I would get excited time after time, dressing to impress only for him to never show as I sat on my sofa for hours. It hurt like hell, but for some reason his excuses were always good enough and forgivable. My mother hated him, but I loved him and I wouldn't be without him no matter how long he could be without me. Things got better once we were out of high school. I gave my body to him sealing the deal in my mind that he would be with me forever. That was a lie.

He disappeared again and this time he came back with another woman who was carrying his baby. I cried hard, but I took him back because he said he didn't love her and loved me. This cycle went on and on for years. There was always another woman. I stopped trying to figure him out and just dealt with it, because I loved him. Yes I know. I was pitiful.

Jarrod tore me down overtime, making me feel that I was less than nothing. I got to a point where I wouldn't eat and I had lost so much weight that I didn't recognize myself. I stopped looking in a mirror because I felt ugly and I stopped dressing myself up. The 150 lb frame that I was used to was now a frail 115 lbs.

Soon Jarrod needed a way to do his dirt and keep me distracted, that's when I met his good friend Tavis. When I got my first job Tavis would pick me up on the days that Jarrod couldn't. He would take me to eat and we'd share some laughs and he'd try to figure out what I was doing with Jarrod, but I never had an answer.

If you let him take me from you by Beyonce' had become an anthem for me. I loved Tavis' company and on top of that he was definitely something to look at. He and Jarrod both stood at 6'1", Tavis light-skinned and Jarrod dark. Tavis had a muscular body and Jarrod had an average one. Tavis was the kind of man that a woman lusted over, but I was so blinded by my love for Jarrod that I never saw him that way. I always ignored his obvious flirting too. Tavis wasn't really my type, but Jarrod he was exactly what I looked for. I'd even take a caramel man, but a high yellow one was out of the question.

I still don't know until this day if it was Tavis' plan to have me, but he got me the moment that I found out about yet another woman. Jarrod had been living a double life. He was living with another woman, making plans with another woman, making love to another woman.

Tavis called me in a tone I had never heard before. I didn't even remember when we had become so close that he could call my phone anytime of the day and night. It was 11:58 pm when he told me that he needed to tell me something. I wasn't ready for whatever it was, but I knew that it was something I needed to hear.

"Eliza I really don't want to tell you this, but I can't just keep it to myself. You've become such a great friend to me and I can't sit and watch a good woman go through this."

"What is it Tavis?" I asked worried.

"I really don't want to tell you this..."

"Don't sugarcoat it. You know I hate that."

It was then that he shattered me, but in the same breath he began to pick up the pieces of me, confessing his undying love and admiration, telling me I deserved better, telling me I deserved him and like a twenty-two year old dummy I sucked it up.

I had not broken it off with Jarrod, because I needed him to feel what I felt and Tavis seemed like the perfect revenge. Tavis filled the void that Jarrod left behind, listening to me breathe late nights and sending me sweet text messages to start my day. Tavis didn't have much else to offer me driving his mother's car, living with his mother, grandmother, his brother who flirted with me often, and his sister with the butt chin who liked me when it was convenient for her. I called them the pig noses because that's exactly what they looked like. He only had a part-time job, and despite all of that his attention and affection made up for it.

Tavis eventually got tired of sharing me and he wanted me to choose. I wanted to know what it was like to finally be able to have a relationship with someone who was physically around and didn't make excuses but it was a hard decision leaving my love for possibility.

 The decision was made for me when Tavis and I were riding around one day and I missed one too many calls from Jarrod. I couldn't ignore him all day so I picked up automatically placing him on speaker phone. Jarrod was furious; he cussed at me, calling me out of my name for the first time since we had been together and questioning me about my whereabouts. It seemed the shoe had been on the other foot for a change. Tavis snatched the phone from me.

 "You need to kill that noise," he said in an angry tone.

 "Tavis?" Jarrod asked confused.

"Yeah it's me."

"Put Eliza back on the phone!"

 "Nah, whatever you gotta say to her you can say to me."

 "Hold up, so you kicking it with my girl now? After everything I did for you?"

"You wasn't giving her what she needed. I'm doing you a favor." Tavis said taunting Jarrod.
"Both of y'all are dead." Jarrod said then hung up the phone.

Of course, Jarrod never followed through with his threat. Instead he called telling me I was making a mistake. He apologized for every wrong thing he had ever done. He admitted that he wasn't perfect and he promised that Tavis would be much worse than he was.

Tavis and I spent our first night together as an official couple that night. I felt free. I woke up the next morning happy to belong to someone that belonged to me too. I played with his lips as he still slept soundly, then his eyes fluttered open and he smiled at me saying, "You look like somebody in love."

His words were like a dart, because I felt as though he meant it in a way that said I was about to be in love alone, again.

It had not even been a good month that Tavis and I had been together when the shit started to hit the fan with him too. I received an anonymous message from someone telling me that Tavis was not who he claimed to be and that he too was a dog. I ignored the message being that the sender didn't even have the guts to reveal themselves. I told myself that I trusted my man.

The trust was questioned when he suddenly had a female best friend who was well known in his family and came over quite often. He drove her car, dropped her off to work, and whenever I was on the phone she never spoke to me. I figured maybe she was just territorial and jealous like most female best friends were so I trusted my man.

I received another anonymous message and this time they gave me Tavis' license plate number and an address that led me to the house of the best friend. I was upset at first, but since he came to the door and he was fully dressed and not panicked I didn't make any assumptions. I still trusted my man.

Eventually it came out that he and his best friend had a thing long ago and she still had a crush on him. He promised that they had never had sex and he cut her off not to put our relationship in jeopardy and it made me feel good that I meant just that much.

Tavis put a ring on my finger asking me to be his wife. I didn't question why he asked so soon since he and I had been friends so long, I figured maybe it was just meant to be. I cried crocodile tears as he bent down on one knee and told me how much I meant to him. It was the best feeling in the world, one that I had not experienced with Jarrod. I felt that I had made the right choice.

My confident, good feeling about my decision faded about two months down the line when a play "sister" popped out of the sky. I can't recall exactly how he said he knew her, but it turned all bad when I found over twenty-five love letters she had written him and learned that the code to his cell phone was her birthday. At that moment I stopped trusting man.

He begged and he cried and threatened to end his life because of what he did to me with his lie. I was a sucker for his tears and like a damn fool I forgave him.

Tavis fell on hard times and I was all he had. I moved out of my mama's house and into my first apartment and moved him in too. I got him a cell phone in my name and allowed him to go back to school while I worked. I took online courses to get a degree in Human Resources. The raise in income allowed me to get us a new apartment and me a brand new car without a down payment. I worked two jobs for a long time making sure that Tavis and I were well taken care of. I paid all of the bills on time and saved any spare money I had.

Eventually I got Tavis a job working with my brother's brick laying business where he was making fifteen dollars an hour and getting a pretty decent tan. Most of his money went toward school and the rest toward partying and shopping. I never paid much attention to the fact that he never did much for me because I would get distracted by nice random gifts and the ring I wore on my left hand.

He and I were solid for a good two years and then he showed more of his true colors once he got really comfortable. There were rumors of him taking other women on lunch dates and when I approached him about it, he'd say they worked with him. The only women I knew that laid bricks wore men's clothing and found me more appealing than Tavis. I never asked my brother because I didn't want to put him in the middle. The rumors died down and he came clean and for his honesty I forgave him.

Next our cell phone bill had come in the mail and it read $1704.32. I knew damn well it wasn't me who ran the bill up that high. I had never in my life read a cell phone billing report, but that day I took a ruler and a highlighter and went over every single line. There was a reoccurring international number that had been dialed and a few more area codes that I had not recognized.

The fighting started from there. Tavis told lie after lie about woman after woman. He had dropped out of school and didn't even tell me. He was using my car to go and see another woman when I was at work. I found that out when he forgot to sign out of his MySpace page. He told her that he wasn't happy and that all he wanted was to be happy. That was our first break-up. I packed his shit and sent him on his way.

    He cried and begged his way back in and this time he brought family drama with him. His mother hated me and didn't know a single thing about me. She told him that I thought I was better than him and she called me a bitch often. He never defended me, but the moment that I defended myself all hell broke loose. His sister was convinced that I was doing him something after he returned home after our break-up; God only knows what he said about me to that girl. His grandmother would call constantly checking on him because she too was now convinced that I was evil. I knew it was all Tavis, but I didn't want to believe he'd slander my name. I got harassing phone calls from his family and his mother went as far as creating an internet profile to call me names and tell me what she thought of me. I surely returned the favor. I didn't give a damn who she was. I had to defend myself if Tavis wouldn't.

    The next fight came when my sister came home from college with her best friend and needed a place to crash for the summer. I let them both stay and he came onto my sister's best friend and lied and told me she had come on to him. I packed his shit again, but he didn't leave. He sat on the porch then apologized to us all for his lies with tears streaming down his face. This guy could seriously be an actor the way he could cry at the drop of a dime.

The fight escalated from there once my sister and her friend were gone. Tavis punched holes into the walls of our apartment and I would call the police worried that my face was next when I could hear the sheetrock shatter behind it. I sent him over the top when I threatened to leave. Twice he wrapped his hands around my neck, trying to remove all of my air, because if he couldn't have me then no one else would.

I should have left him the day he chased me around the apartment with a knife and then outside where all our neighbors stood with their mouths wide open. I hopped into my car and when he ran out in the street with the knife I hit him. He was the one caught with another woman and I was the one being chased. The nerve…

He tried his hardest to be honest with me after that because he knew he'd get caught every time. My own stupidity kept him because I had convinced myself that as long as he told the truth I could deal with it. At least he wasn't like Jarrod with his double life and silence for periods of time. I had just gotten used to him and I didn't want to let him go. I wasn't sure I ever would let him go. He knew my entire family and all of my secrets and even if life for us was hectic, it was ours.

The last straw came when I found out about yet another woman. I was sick and tired of being the main chick. I wanted to be the one and only, but it was clear that was never going to happen. He tried his hardest to make me feel special telling me story after story of women that he met and turned down because he loved me but the one that stuck out the most was the girl he met at the barber shop with the tattoos and piercings. He claimed she looked like a clown to him and that it was the guys in the shop trying to push him on her. I'm sure you can guess what hap pened next right? Yes, he was talking to her behind my back and the way I had to find out killed me. It was Jarrod who saw them together and weather it was love, history, or vengeance that made him tell me I was grateful.

The clown was all the way from Texas, but had friends in Louisiana so she partied here often. She clearly had no job if she could come here so often to be with a man who was barely taking care of himself.

I stole Tavis' phone and found the girl's number from a text she had sent him and I told her to come get him. She never did, but I sat all his things outside and got the locks changed all before he was off from work. It was the best seventy-five dollars I had ever spent. He beat the door down and I just wanted him to leave. We had been a part ever since. I heard rumors that he had moved in with the "barber shop" girl in Texas and that was fine with me.

Now here it was a year and five months later and he was calling like nothing had ever happened.

"Eliza…"

"Huh?" I snapped back to present day.

"I want to see you."

"I don't know about that…"

"Why, You in a relationship or something?"

"No, but you are and aren't you in Texas now?"

"No and that's over, let me come see you."

The stupid woman in me had arisen, "Where Tavis?"

"We aren't strangers E, just let me come over tonight. I promise not to try anything."

I swallowed back hard, "fine, but I'm not letting you inside."

"Okay whatever makes you comfortable."

Emmanuel

I laid back on my sofa as I watched Desiree float around my studio apartment, cleaning and organizing while she had the music channel on full blast. It had been a long time since I sat around the house doing nothing. I was usually at work restoring cars or just creating false paperwork for myself so I wouldn't have to come home and be bored out of my mind. Don't get me wrong Desiree was good company, but we had fallen into a routine and I couldn't find a way to tell her I was tired of it.

Every now and then I'd express how I felt to her, but things would only change temporarily. I had the option to break-up with her, but I convinced myself that committed pussy was better than no pussy at all. Excuse my French. I could easily be one of these cats out here smashing everything that walked, but with the way diseases were spreading nowadays it was best to just find one clean woman who wasn't stingy with it. Desiree was very giving in the bedroom. Her charity was probably what kept her around for so many years, especially since I had vowed to focus on my career and nothing else.

She and I were never supposed to be anything serious. When I first met Desiree, she was pulled over on the interstate with her hazard lights flashing and her car on lean. I guessed she had a flat tire. I had just gotten off from a sixteen hour shift and I was tired. I wanted to just

pass her by, but the man in me just wouldn't stand for a woman sitting on the side of the road that late at night. I pulled up behind her and hopped out.
"Hey you need some help?" I yelled to her over the passing traffic.
"Yeah, but I don't have a spare."
Lucky for her I was a technician and had access to several tires. I pulled my truck bed down, pulling out my jack and four-way, and the spare tire I never used. I rolled it over to her car and did what I do best.
"Thank you so much I really appreciate this."
"It's no problem." I said looking up at her face and realizing just how beautiful she actually was.
Desiree stood back until I was finished then she pulled forty dollars from her purse and tried to give it to me.
I pushed her hand, "now what kind of man would I be if I took that from you?"
She smiled, "a typical one. Hardly anything is free anymore. You're either paying with money or services." She laughed.
"That's true, but I'm not that kind of dude."
She offered me her hand, "Desiree."
"Manny...I would shake your hand, but mine is dirty."
"I think I could stomach a dirty hand, my day has been much worse than that."
I smiled and shook her hand.
I looked Desiree up and down, "You better get off the interstate now, someone could be worried about you."
She looked around then laughed, "If someone were worried about me they'd be here and I wouldn't be

20

stranded." She reached into her purse and pulled her business card out and handed it to me, "here, call me sometime."

I smiled and slid the card into my pocket then walked her to her car and watched her drive off safely. I hopped into my truck and headed home to shower and relax.

I was skeptical about calling Desiree because I had been avoiding women at all cost. I just couldn't deal with them after so many bad experiences that landed me in bad mental states.

I started at half-crazy with Ariel, my first love. She and I had grown up together then dated from middle to high school. Our relationship lasted a little bit past high school, damn near into her second semester of college and then she decided she was tired of my young ass and went on to date some dude who was older and played sports. To her I was just a dirty old country boy with a dream and a love for cars. I was hurt for a minute, but not completely broken apart since I was soon distracted by this short yellow, dark-haired, and thick female named Sophia.

Ariel and I remained friends. She forced me to try college and every now and then we got it in, in the bedroom for old times' sake. She was still dealing with ole boy, but I just didn't know it. She complained about their sex life and lied and told me that it was over between them just to get the "D". You could imagine what that did to my ego. Yep, blew it up.

Ariel had always wanted me to be a different man. She wanted me to be soft and sensitive. She would make me listen to R&B music, complaining that rap was the reason I was so "thuggish". I never saw myself as a thug. I saw myself as a man who handled business by any means necessary.

    College had changed Ariel and I learned it the hard way when I let her stay at my place for a summer while she was out of school. All she wanted to do was hit the club and try to stop me from anybody she thought I was dealing with. The love that was once there had finally faded away and I just wanted her to go.

    Ariel was furious when she found out about my association with Sophia. She tried to fight her when she saw us together in a club. It was her first time seeing me with another woman that wasn't her. Sophia found it funny standing there patting her weave while Ariel's friends held her back from attacking.

    Ariel ran back to her college boyfriend, throwing their relationship in my face, but at that point I didn't give a damn. I was swimming in new water.

    Sophia had a baby boy named Sean who I took to for awhile until he started calling me daddy and she started pawning him off on any friend and family member that she could push him on so that she could party. She drove an old beat up, navy blue Caprice, but I fixed it up so she could get to work and bring Sean to daycare. Sophia was good to look at, but in bed all she did was lie on her back and complain about how much the dick hurt when we tried different positions. I tried everything to make her comfortable and keep it interesting. I was good to her, allowing her and her son to sleep over at my place whenever they pleased and in return she'd cook for me and paid a light bill here and there when I didn't ask her to. I helped Sophia get back into school, paying forward what Ariel had done for me. Eventually all I was to her was a paycheck and a babysitter for Sean. On top of her sucking me dry she was bisexual going back and forth between me and chicks who dressed like men. I was hurt and pissed when I found out I was being two-timed. Sophia had knocked off the half and just left me crazy. I was tired of having feelings and being the man only good enough to use until they found who was more suited for them man or woman.

 I needed a breather and I needed somebody who could throw the ass back after all the manual labor I put in with Sophia only to get nothing in return. I hooked up with Marie, Natasha, Kendria, and Naomi for on-call night caps, depending on my flavor of the week. Marie was my blackberry, Natasha was my chocolate, Kendria was my cocoa, and Naomi was my apple because of her fat ass.

 Of course dealing with all those different women didn't last too long, because I was not the type of man to date so many women at one time, knowing damn well they would eventually want more. I liked spending time with one woman. I liked being in relationship, but with the sad choices of women these days I settled for whatever I could get to keep me from a bad case of loneliness and blue balls.

 Marie was the only one left before long. We never got into an official relationship, but we spent a lot of time together. She would bring me lunch at work and she took every inch of me like her body was designed just for me and for a bonus she gave me head without me having to ask for it and without expecting anything in return. I could live with that.

 After a few months she stopped being the only one, because I knew myself. I'd start having feelings for her solely because I was dealing with her exclusively and she just wasn't a woman I saw myself with in the long run. Her feelings started to get involved and she thought I didn't notice, but I was no fool. I was a lot of a things but a fool wasn't one. She tried to play it cool, because she wanted to keep kicking it and for awhile I played stupid, but in the meantime I started to get to know someone else.

    Her name was Danielle. Danielle was a stallion with her long caramel legs, perfect teeth, and stacked body. She was exotic. I jumped head first in lust with Danielle, taking her on dates and staying up late at night on the phone with her as she quoted bible scriptures into my ear. It made me feel like she was a woman of substance and I didn't just need to look at her body. She stopped me in my tracks and had me ready to be better to her than I had ever been to anyone.

    Danielle taught me the definition of the phrase "Devil in Prada". Her exotic look came from her being an ex-stripper, but wait there's more. I moved her into my place after learning that she was homeless. I took her on a shopping spree to get her wardrobe up to par, because no lady of mine was going to be without, yes I said lady. The instant she was a resident of my apartment I made her mine. I figured I was doing the right thing.

    I never asked her to get a job or to pay a bill and for the first five months or so everything worked out. I would come home to a clean house and a cooked meal. She made a man feel like he was supposed to feel. She even put it down in the bedroom. She had me blinded. So blinded that I never saw her drug addiction, ignored the fact that she stayed in constant contact with her ex, ignored the medicine bottles in our bathroom filled with prescriptions for mental illness, didn't complain when she stopped cooking and cleaning, didn't complain when her mother used me to fix her car for free, but hated my guts, and didn't complain when the sex became rare and slightly boring. Instead I fed her habits of weed and cocaine and cooked and cleaned myself and continued to pay the bills.

I learned the hard way that being a good man to a woman who didn't deserve it only made me broke and landed me in jail for a night while my mama had tears in her eyes. My mama had to empty her bank account to get me out.

I came home one day to find Danielle in our apartment with another motherfucker. She had pushed something behind the door to keep me from getting in. I yelled through the door and she pretended not to hear me. I was pissed. I punched the window beside the door, shattering it and letting myself in. Danielle was sitting on the sofa alone, pretending that nothing was going on. The good thing about most apartments was that there was no back door, so there weren't too many places for you to run or hide. I knew whoever she had in there had to be hiding so I cased the place and just like I already knew the punk bitch was hiding in the bathroom. He raised his hands in surrender when I kicked the door down to show he didn't want any trouble with me.

I didn't lose my cool like I usually would; instead I got in my truck and left, because she said she was calling the police. I called my mama to tell her what happened and she told me to go back and wait for the police so I could tell my story.

My story didn't mean shit when the red and blue lights pulled up and saw a woman with a cast on her arm and a black man with a cut up hand. She even had the punk bitch stand as a witness for her as if I really put my hands on her. The moment they put the cuffs on my wrist I really wished I had beat the shit out of her. I was going to jail for nothing. I sat in jail for a night and I was banned from the complex. At that point crazy had become psychotic. There was nothing a woman could say to me.

  I knew that I was just upset saying I wasn't going to deal with no women, because I wasn't the kind of dude that allowed females to make me bitter. Instead I showed them what they were missing by treating the next woman ten times better. Danielle had taken a lot out of me though.

  She called and called, crying and begging on my voicemail, telling me how much of a good man I was and how much she missed me, she claimed to have a job and a car, and that her system was drug free, but after that stunt she pulled I'd never go back. She even said she'd drop the charges and I still didn't care to breathe the same air as her ever again.

  I did the bachelor thing for maybe six months until I met Desiree and it was getting old quickly. At first the only reason I dialed Desiree's number was to soothe the loneliness. She complied with my offers of emotionless sex as two consenting adults and filled the void but overtime Desiree had become my friend and then lover. I confided in her in and I was content. She was a decent woman and simple. She didn't come with the extra BS that most women did and I liked that. After Danielle, Desiree was exactly the speed of woman that I needed. It didn't matter too much that she wasn't spontaneous, because I had had enough action with the women of my past. I had enough adventure with working as a technician and then finally getting my own shop. I was comfortable.

Rekindle

Eliza

"Look at you, still as beautiful and as classy as I remember you." Tavis said as he attempted to hug me, but I rejected him.

"What do you want Tavis?" I placed my hand on his chest to keep him at a distance.

"I missed you."

"After a year and five months?"

"I would have come around sooner, but I wasn't sure you wanted to see me or hear from me."

I folded my arms, "right."

"You seriously aren't going to let me come inside?"

"Why should I?"

"Because it's cold out here."

"Well you should have worn an extra layer of clothing then."

"You're real cute when you being flip."

"Cut the crap Tavis, why are you here? Where is your little tatted up freak of a girlfriend?"

"I left her."

"Is that right?"

"Yeah, the bitch was crazy."

"If I didn't know you so well I might believe that."

"I mean it, she really was, she stabbed me E."

I dropped my arms by my side and the façade that I was putting on vanished, "are you serious?"

"Yeah, struck a nerve and had me limping for months."

"Oh my God, I'm sorry to hear that." I placed my hand against my face, "why did she do that?"

"Because I tried to leave her; she stabbed me then left me there. I had to crawl to a phone to call 911. They told me I was lucky, because I could have bled to death."

I stood shaking my head in disbelief.

"How did you get away? Did she come visit you at least?" I had so many questions.

"No, her friend came and told me I needed to lie to the doctor because she already had enough warrants out for her arrest."

"And you lied?"

"Hell yeah, her friend might have finished my ass off right there in the hospital if I didn't."

"Hmm you sure know how to pick them."

"Tell me about it."

"So, did you go back and get your things?"

"I went back and she threatened to stab me again, making jokes of it and shit. I was really scared of that broad man."

"Tavis? Afraid of a woman?" I laughed.

"Man yeah."

"Well, how did you leave?"

"Told her I needed to go out of town with a family member for an emergency, of course she didn't believe me because all my shit was packed." He laughed.

"That was real genius."

"I know, so I just took one bag and gave her the keys to my car and told her to drop me off at the bus station. After she did I called my mom to come pick me up and I haven't seen her since."

"So you left all your clothes and your car?"

"Yep, my job too, I'm starting over."

"Doesn't she know where your mom lives?"

"Yeah, but she won't go over there because she knows I told my mom that she stabbed me, but anyways I didn't come here to give you a sob story."

It was nice to see Tavis' face even after all the bullshit. He seemed so different. I was thinking to myself *that's what your ass gets* as I looked him in the face, but I didn't say it out loud, nobody really deserved to be stabbed but you reap what you sew.

"Can we please go inside?" Tavis asked.

I stepped back turning the knob and keeping my eyes on him as he walked toward me. I knew exactly what was about to happen and I wasn't going to resist. I liked the comfort of his skin and even though I wouldn't say it out loud I missed him. I missed his scent. Suddenly all the bad memories went away and I remembered the good feelings we did share sometimes.

~~*~*

It only took three months for Tavis and I to pick up right where we left off. Go ahead call me stupid. Funny thing was that I didn't feel stupid at all. I honestly felt that Tavis was different. We spent a lot of time together, going on French quarter dates to every festival in town, catching matinees, and having late night pillow talks. It seemed that his horrible experience made him appreciate what we had. He told me more about what he went through with his ex, telling me about other guys he found out about that she was seeing behind his back and talking to online, the drugs she was on, and her best friend that was prostituting from their apartment and paying them to do it and keep quiet because she had a man. He told me that he finally understood how I felt about his mother because his ex's mother hated him and didn't make a secret of it, disrespecting him often and calling him trash.

Tavis stared off into space as I sat on top the folding counter in the laundry mat, breaking conduct rule number six that hung up on the wall. Tavis and I were just getting back into the hang of things. It was almost as if we had never been apart, well at least for me.

"Where is your mind?" I asked him as he continued to stand in a trance.

"I don't know…"

"You've been spacing out a lot lately. What's going on?"

"If I tell you, you might get upset…"

"Try me."

"I don't know…you know how you are."

I sighed. I knew that I could be a difficult person and sometimes even hard to communicate with, but usually if I was pre-warned I was easier to deal with. "I promise not to get mad."

"It's about my ex."

I stood silent for a ment. "Do you miss her?"

"No, it's not that. I just hate that I left so much behind."

"We can go get your things Tavis."

"Nah, I don't want to start any mess."

"How is mess going to get started if all you want is whatever you left there?"

"She might try to stab me again, especially if she finds out me and you are back together."

"What do I have to do with this?"

"She was so insecure about you," he shook his head, "you know with our history and all. The tattoo on my back didn't help either."

"Nobody told you to get that anyway. You only got it out of guilt, we had only been together what? Three months?"

"Yeah I know..." he stood still. "Her best friend hit me up on Facebook."

I laughed, "You have a Facebook?"

"Yeah got it to keep in touch with a few people."

"Uh huh so what did the friend say?"

"Nothing much, just told me that her friend misses me and she knows we'll get back together, it's just another fight."

"Were you and her that serious?"

"To her we were, she was telling people I was her fiancé."

"And you weren't calling her your fiancé?"

"Hell no, I had lost the woman I wanted to marry."

I looked down at the ground and smiled.

"What if I asked you to marry me again, what would you say?" he asked.

"I don't know. I probably wouldn't take you seriously."

Tavis dug in his pocket and pulled out the ring I threw at him during one of our many fights. "You remember this?"

"You kept it?"

He nodded his head yes. "Would you take me seriously if I said marry me this year. I'll even pick a date?"

"Tavis are you serious?"

"Dead ass, I don't ever want to lose you again Eliza."

"I…" he stopped my words by kissing me then placed the ring on my finger. I looked down at it and got that feeling I had the first time that he asked me. It was really going to happen this time. Tavis had changed.

~~*~*

After we loaded all of our clothes up into my car we headed over to my mom's house. She had cooked a big dinner and wanted me to come over. I didn't tell her Tavis was with me, because I already knew what she would say.

We pulled up and Tavis looked over at me not moving as I opened my door. "What's wrong?" I asked.

"You know your mom hates me."

"She doesn't hate you."

"Hate, dislike it's all the same thing."

"My mom isn't like your mom Tavis, if she does dislike you she won't show it and besides the only reason she doesn't like you is because of all the stuff you did in the past and the Christmas before we broke up she gave you fifty dollars. You know that lady tight."

Tavis laughed because he knew it was true. "Think I should give her the fifty back?"

"I already did, now get out of the car."

I hopped out and shut the door. Tavis was still reluctant walking slowly as we headed to the door. The door swung open before we could get to it and my big brother Eli gave me a big smile. I ran into his arms and jumped on him. I never felt too big to jump on my brother. I gave him a hard kiss on the cheek. "What did mama cook, it smells good up in here."

"She made your favorite, chicken and dumplings."

Eli looked behind me at Tavis who was only midway up the walk-way, "what is he doing here?" he asked in a low voice, placing my feet back on the ground.

"We're back together."

My brother looked down from his 6'4" frame into my face and raised one brow.

"Just be nice okay?"

Eli switched his expression, perking up as Tavis approached. He gave Tavis daps. "What's up blast from the past?"

"Nothing much, what's up man?"

"This food that's what," He said and we all went into the house laughing.

I had never told Eli the whole story of me and Tavis, but he did know the worse parts. He wanted to fire him after we broke up, but Tavis fired himself, because he just stopped coming.

My brother always intimidated Tavis. Eli had that "don't mess with me" look. He almost never smiled unless he was around family and his arms were covered in tattoos. He always wore a hat pulled down over his eyes and he always looked over his shoulder. The streets and the military had him messed up.

We all walked into the kitchen where my mother was pulling out dishes and my sister Ella was sitting at the table playing on her phone. I walked over to my sister and hugged her and kissed her cheek. She was also nothing like me. She wore her hair in front of her eyes and it was jet black. She had her lip pierced on both sides at the bottom and had a tattoo on her wrist of an infinity symbol. She was also taller than me and way more developed. We had taken on genes from two different sides of the family. Where I was more hips and ass, she was all breast and belly.

My sister hugged me then looked up at Tavis and rolled her eyes. She was never discreet when she didn't like somebody.

"Hello Ella." Tavis said to Ella, but she ignored him and continued to play on her phone.

I walked over to help my mom with the dishes. She gave me a smile and turned to see Tavis. Her expression went sour, but quickly faded once he looked at her. I laughed to myself.

"Boy you speak when you walk in people's house." My mama spat atTavis.

"Good evening Ms. Campbell." He smiled and hugged her.

We all sat down at the table and shared a few laughs, everyone but Tavis. He was spaced out again and I couldn't help, but be concerned and start to feel doubts about the ring he had just placed on my hand for the second time.

After dinner we all went into my mother's living room to watch Shaquille O'Neal's All-star Comedy Jam. Tavis laughed but he still was not there completely. I shook it off. I went back into the kitchen where my mother was cleaning and I helped her.

"You know something is wrong with that boy right?" My mama said not cutting corners with me.

"Mama please don't start."

"I wasn't going to say a word until I noticed that ring…"

I looked down at my hand with nothing to say. That woman didn't miss a beat.

"You know I don't get involved in none of y'all relationships, but that boy is shady." My mother stated.

"And how do you know that?" I asked.

"I'm shady! I know a shady person when I meet one."

I laughed and shook my head. "I appreciate your concern mama, but we'll be fine this time. I love him and we have history."

"History is just that baby history, things that can't be changed and time that you'll never get back. I just want you to be careful."

I nodded my head yes and my mother hugged me.

Tavis and I left after the immediate family gathering was over. We joked in the car and then jumped in bed once we were home. I wanted to take heed to what my mother said, but my heart wouldn't let me be careful.

He and I sat up in bed that night, making plans for the wedding and picking out the colors. He planned a date for June 23rd. He wanted to be involved in the whole process. We sat up on my laptop, picking out colors, registering on websites, and creating a guest list. He was here to stay for real this time.

April Showers

Eliza

April 10th

    Cameras flashed as family and friends snapped picture after picture at the birthday bash I had put together for Tavis. He walked over to me placing his hand at the back of my waist and kissing me on my left cheek. "Did you really have to do all this?" he asked.

    "Well you said that you wanted to do something major for your birthday this year, since you're getting old."

    "I don't remember the getting old part."

    "Okay I added that," I smiled as I turned wrapping my arms around him. I was going to eat him up when the party was over if I wasn't too tired. I laughed as I stared into his eyes, remembering when we met and how I wasn't attracted to him at all. I ran my hand across the top of his faded head then planted a kiss on his lips.

    Tavis pulled back grabbing my left hand and holding it up. "I can't believe you'll be my wife in two months."

    Tavis and I were engaged for two years of our relationship the first time, so for me this was a victory.

    My birthday was three weeks after his and setting a date was the best early present ever. It sucked that it was such short notice, but I was getting as much as I could done in the time that I had. I even made personal calls from work.

    I heard a throat clear as Tavis and I held each other, "get a damn room for all that shit this is a party!"

my brother Eli yelled over the music and I turned to smile. "Damn let the dude breathe sis."

I rolled my eyes at my brother as he gave daps to Tavis. "The big two eight!" my brother smiled.

"Yeah I'm getting old as shit." Tavis laughed.

My baby sister Ella joined us in our little corner of the party. "Hey sorry to interrupt, but I just wanted to tell the birthday boy happy birthday before I left."

"Where are you going?" I asked with an attitude.

"I'm meeting up with one of my guy friends."

"Why can't he come to the party?"

"Eliza don't start with me tonight okay?"

I rolled my eyes and shook my head. My baby sister was just like my mother, running after man after man, sleeping with them and never getting anything in return, but calling it love. I wanted to let her learn from her own mistakes, but it was a hard thing to do when you were the older one that had been there and done that.

"Enjoy y'all night," she smiled and walked off.

I turned to Tavis, "I'm going to get a drink." I said then headed to the bar leaving him and my brother to their silly guy talk.

The bartender walked right over to me ignoring everybody else that waited. "Amaretto and pineapple," I said then waited. I wasn't really much of a drinker, because I hated the way alcohol made me feel afterwards. Tavis would always tease me about my fruity drink choices whenever we would go out.

"Girl you are wearing that BeBe dress." I heard a voice say behind me. I swung around and wrapped my hands around my best friend Madra. Madra was taller than me so I had to reach up to hug her. She wore her hair short like Monica and she had beautiful chocolate skin. To say she had two kids she maintained herself well and she was always so full of life, but I didn't expect to see her at the party.

"I didn't think you were coming!" I screamed as I held her tight then released her.

"Girl I needed to get out of that house. I left the boys with Paul. They'll be okay." She smiled and I motioned for the bartender to make one more of what I was having for Madra. I tipped the bartender then headed to the dance floor with Madra in tow. I danced to the music with my drink in the air as Madra did the same. "I can't wait to do this all over again in a few weeks!" Madra yelled over the music.

"I don't know what Tavis has planned for my birthday!" I yelled back.

"It better be nice! You rented out a whole club for his ass." we continued to dance.

I had done a lot more than rented out a club. I rented a limo to drop him off, paid for the expensive ass fit he was wearing and I had put away money to get him courtside seats to the Celtics VS Heat game when the season started. I'd be his wife before then, so everything was looking up.

~~*~*

April 23rd

I rolled over in the bed and smiled. Tavis was already out of bed. I could hear his spoon hitting the glass bowl in the kitchen. I stood out of bed and joined him in the kitchen. "You better not be eating my *Captain Crunch*."

"Nope I'm eating *Smacks*."

I turned and headed for the fridge and noticed two black bags sitting by the door in the living room of our apartment, "Where you going?"

"Out of town with my mom, did you forget?"

I threw my head back, "I did, when will you be back?" I asked pretending to act like I cared because I really didn't. His mother hated me. She was a female truck driver who switched boyfriends like she switched underwear. I had never done that woman a single thing, but she hated me. I figured it was due to the fact that I took Tavis and made him the man that she should have. I also considered the fact that I was beautiful and shapely whereas she was just a shape and had the face of a pig. I could see her hating me if I was taking all of Tavis' money and separating him from his family, but I wasn't. I was building him.

"Monday morning."

"Oh, well have fun." I said as I prepared my cereal.

After breakfast Tavis and I both dressed and parted ways; him on his road trip and me to work.

It had been almost three weeks since the party and I was relieved that there was one event I could cross off my list. Now all I had left was my birthday in seven days, my wedding, and the honeymoon. I didn't know which one I was more excited about. I sat at my desk scrolling through wedding photos and smiling at the happy brides and grooms thinking to myself *that's going to be me in two more months.* There were still a few decisions that needed to be made before it got too close to the wedding, but Tavis had been so tied up I could barely catch him and now he had this damn trip. I figured he was doing something major for my birthday so I didn't bother him too much, but come May 1st his ass was mine.

"Eliza I need you." My boss's voice came through the speaker on my desk phone. I hurried to minimize the window on my computer and stood to walk into his office. I walked in and stood in front of his desk.

"How are we looking on overtime this month?"

"Actually better, since it's a slow season there is almost no time being used other than over night."

"What's going on overnight?"

"They're short staffed."

My boss sighed, "Any applicants worth looking at?"

"I pulled fifteen if you want to go over those."

"You can sit them on my desk; I have to get to this meeting."

"No problem." I said as he stood and grabbed his coat and put it on to head out.

I returned to my desk and gathered the information that my boss asked for then decided to go ahead and do some work, so I could get back to making eyes at wedding photos. I opened my desk drawer to see if Tavis had called or texted. I had one unread message.

Tavis: I can't believe this is you on my phone.

I held my phone confused then texted him back.

Eliza: huh?

I waited for a response, which took longer than I cared for.

44

Tavis: I was just looking at your picture and thinking about how beautiful you are.

I still felt thrown off.

Eliza: Have you made it to your moms?
Tavis: Yes

I scrolled back to the first message reading it over and over. It was too random for me.

Eliza: who was that original message for?
Tavis: you baby, who else
Eliza: Ok...
Tavis: it really was silly

Something in me didn't believe him.

~~*~*

April 24th

1:35 AM

My eyes popped open and I sat up in my bed and looked over at the clock. I had fallen asleep at 8:15pm, which was early for me, but not early enough for me to wake up in the middle of the night. I turned and looked behind me. I let my eyes linger on the frames that were filled with photos of me and Tavis. A feeling of uneasiness came over me as I remembered that the reason I went to bed early in the first place was because he had not called me and when I called him it went straight to voicemail. Our text conversation was the last of our communication that day.

I gave him the benefit of the doubt that perhaps he was just distracted since he was out of town with family for the weekend. I tossed the covers to the side and stood from my bed to walk around in the darkness. I bumped my leg against the corner of my mattress as I walked and waited for my eyes to adjust. The uneasy feeling remained as I opened my room door and headed to the kitchen. I opened the fridge and squinted my eyes as I reached for a half drank bottled water. I sipped just enough to wet my throat then I shut the door and headed into my living room. I drug my feet across the carpet then opened the front door to look around. It was quiet, which was unusual for most parts of New Orleans. I shut the door and returned back to my room to force myself to sleep.

    The instant I laid my head on my pillow *Destiny's Child's Girl* rang throughout my room. I sat up and walked over to my desk to answer the phone with a confused look on my face. I skipped the hello. "Madra? What are you doing up this late?"

    "Girl Caleb has a bad cough and I needed to get him something for it, but that's not why I'm calling."

    "Oh then what is it?"
    "I just saw Tavis."
    "Saw him where?"
    "In Wal-Mart."
    "Tavis is out of town with his family, maybe it was somebody who looked like him."
    "Nope, it's him."
    "Well, what was he doing?"

"Walking with some girl and they were carrying a bag of pillows."

I stood silent for a minute not wanting to think what I was thinking. Tavis had never had his own room at his mother's house. He had a bed in a little area in a room that looked like a dining space and it didn't have pillows on it or sheets. He would just sleep on it with a blanket. It was amazing the things men could survive with.

I stood confused, "what did the girl look like?"

"I didn't get a good look."

"Where are you now?"

"Still in the parking lot."

"No, I need you in Wal-Mart!"

Madra had been my best-friend since middle school. She was that friend that I could call for anything, I mean ANYTHING, bust out some windows, slash some tires, put sugar in a gas tank, and then sit in jail with you later, whatever it was, she was down. I listened as Madra's feet moved frantically through Wal-Mart, looking for Tavis and whoever it was that he was with. I wanted to scream, but something was keeping me calm for that moment; for confirmation. My supposed-to-be fiancé was parlaying around town with some trick while I was at home sleeping alone and thinking he was with family.

My heart stopped when Madra said she spotted them walking out of the opposite exit door.

She yelled out Tavis' name and I held the phone waiting. My heart was beating fast in my chest.

She explained to me the look of guilt on Tavis' face when he turned around and noticed her. I knew that look all too well. I had seen it for years, each time he got

caught. I was picturing it in my mind that very moment. Madra engaged in brief conversation with Tavis.
"Eliza has been looking for you, she said she's been calling you, but the phone has been going straight to voicemail."
"Oh my battery died." I heard him say.
"Tell him I'm on the phone."
"Well, she's on the phone." She repeated.
"Tell her I'll call her."
"So you don't want to talk?" Madra said more agitated than me.
"Nah…" he simply said.
"Oh, that's what's up." Madra said.
"What's happening?" I asked. I could barely hear what was happening, but I could tell there was another woman there. My body started to shake as this situation turned out to be exactly what I didn't want it to be. "Who is that girl?" I asked. "What is she saying?"
"She's asking Tavis if he's just going to disrespect her like that."
"Give him the phone Madra!" I heard silence, guessing that she had attempted to reach him the phone.
"He said he'll call you later." Madra's voice vibrated in my ear as my blood boiled.
"He doesn't want to take the phone." Madra was heated. "You want me to handle this because I can handle it."
"Tell him to take the damn phone!"
"He won't take it."
"What does the girl look like that he's with?!"
"She has the same brown complexion as you, she's wearing long brown weave, and it looks old, she

has tattoos all over, and a facial piercing, definitely not prettier than you."

"That's his ex!" I didn't need to see a picture to know who his ex was. I wasn't slow. I dropped the phone and screamed to the top of my lungs. I had felt that something was wrong all day and my best friend had just confirmed my ill feelings. I cussed and I knocked things over in my room. I yanked his pictures from my wall as tears ran down my cheeks. Destroying my room wasn't enough as I stormed into the living room to release more emotions. How could I not even be worth picking up the phone for?

Madra must have hung up the phone because her ringtone started to echo in my room again as I smashed picture frame after picture frame on the floor. I ignored the phone wishing she had never called in the first place. Ignorance was truly bliss. I fell down on the sofa and my body convulsed as my crying was now at a point where I could not control it. I had forgiven Tavis so many times in the past using the excuse that we were young, but what excuse could I use now that we were only two years from thirty. He humiliated me.

Madra had stopped calling and now *six foot seven foot by Lil Wayne* blared. She had called my big brother. I walked to my phone and picked up my phone. I couldn't say hello as I choked on my tears.

"Eliza?" my brother asked in a disapproving tone. "Madra called me, just say the word sis and I'll handle that for you."

I wanted to say a word, but I couldn't get one out. I tried to slow my breathing and calm myself down.

"Sis, do you hear me? I'll handle it."

"I don't even know where he is!" I screamed into the phone. I tossed my phone across the room and it hit the wall hard, falling into several pieces. "LYING MOTHERFUCKER!" I screamed to the top of my lungs. I continued to destroy the apartment we shared. Happy early birthday to me...

~~*~*

April 25th

The sun rose but my apartment remained dark from the curtains that covered the windows. I had managed to piece my phone back together and instantly regretted it since my brother and Madra blew it up all night. They had even come over and knocked on the door, yelling my name but I didn't move. I sat on the sofa, not blinking, barely breathing, and thinking of where to stab Tavis first when he walked through the door, if he walked through the door. I had never been the violent type, but after the pain that I had felt I was contemplating murder. I had not slept, didn't even nod off, just sat there staring into myself at the blackness that had settled because of this betrayal that I never saw coming.

All night I asked myself question after question. *Who was this girl? Was she more important than me? How? Why?* My questions went without answers as I got well acquainted with the wall in front of me. I wanted to sleep but I just couldn't. Tavis' face popped into my head each time I closed my eyes. He was kissing and touching her the same way that he kissed and touched me. The images made my eyes just pop back open and the entire phone conversation played over and over and over again in my mind.

    I sat thinking about everything that happened before last night and wondering how I didn't see it coming, especially after the odd text messages and frequent spacing. I felt it in my heart, but I didn't want to believe it. How could I be so stupid?

    I went as far as getting on my laptop and creating a Facebook page to find Tavis. I found him too, easily. I found him, his pig nosed mom, and his butt-chin sister. His sister's page had sabotage written all over it. His mom was a truck driver and from what the sister posted they rode to Texas to pick up the hoe-skank. What type of woman is a truck driver anyway? She needed to come out of the closet already. The sister called the hoe-skank her sister-in-law. Tavis knew all along and he lied. He lied about the mom not liking her and everything. The spacing out suddenly made a lot of sense. He wasn't thinking about the bad things, he missed her. He was reconsidering; he was doubting. I was just his way of making it while he was back home without a car and a job and now he had both; one at my expense.

    That one incident triggered every wrong thing he had ever done to bring me pain. In five years there had been numerous women, but it had never gotten to this point. I was always number one. I was "wifey". I wanted to cry, but my tears were dried out by rage.

    I was happy that it was Saturday. At least I didn't have to go to work in the state that I was in, which was a mix between shocked and half-crazy.

Emmanuel

1:35 AM

    I stared at the clock with my arms wrapped around Desiree wondering why I was so restless. I had a beautiful woman in my arms, but I could not get comfortable and just doze off. I had been feeling empty lately. I thought about calling my mom, but I already knew what she would say. Desiree shifted in my arms.

    "Are you awake?" I asked like an idiot.

    "No," she said in her raspy voice.

    "How did you answer me then?"

    "It's my subconscious."

    I laughed.

    "Why do you sound wide awake?" she asked.

    "I never dozed off…"

    Desiree turned and pushed her face into my chest, "something on your mind?"

    "It's nothing baby go back to sleep."

    Desiree huffed against my chest then pulled away and sat up, leaning her back against my headboard. She took a breath and wiped her sleepy eyes, "what's on your mind Manny? You haven't slept the entire week that I've been here."

    I turned over on my back and looked up at the ceiling, "Dee you love me right?"

    "Of course I do."

    "Are you *in love* with me?"

    "This again?"

    "You asked."

    "I don't know Manny, yes, no…what does it matter?"

"It matters a lot…"

She sighed hard, "You know most men wouldn't even care about this."

"I'm not most men," I said and sat up. "I don't want to die and never experience being in love. I'm 28 years old, most black men aren't even lucky enough to live this long."

Desiree kissed my lips then lay back down, "I'm going back to sleep."

"But we're talking…"

Desiree sat back up, "Manny I love you and that's it."

"Do you see yourself marrying me and having kids with me?"

Desiree sighed again, "Are you gay?"

"What? No, don't ask me that shit!"

"I'm just saying all these questions are so suspect. I should be asking you this. I don't really care. We have a good life baby and if it's not broke don't fix it." Desiree laid back down.

I took a deep breath, "Dee I don't want to be with you anymore."

"What…"

"I want out of this relationship…"

Desiree turned over and stared up at me. She bit down on her lip and looked out of the side of her eye. "Are you serious?"

"Yes…"

She nodded her head then got out of bed. She grabbed her bag and packed up all of her things as I watched. What the hell was wrong with me? I wanted to stop her, but I couldn't and I wouldn't.

"If I leave Manny, I'm not coming back."

I didn't say a word as Desiree showed me her disappointed face then her back.

~~*~*

I woke up the next morning and looked over to see if last night was a dream and I was just tripping. Desiree was gone and so were all of her things. I grabbed my cell phone from the stand beside my bed and I had a long text from her.

> *Desiree: Good morning Manny, I thought about what you said last night and you were right. As much as I didn't want you to be you were. A part of me wanted to sit around for another two years and wait for us to fall in love. I was comfortable with you and I didn't want to let that go. I guess now I have to, but I'm not upset because I realized that I was just standing in your way of true love and happiness and God knows I'd never do anything to cause you pain. You are a good man and you deserve a woman who wants to be with you, marry you, and give you as many babies as you'd like. I'm just not that woman. I really pray that you find who or what it is that you are looking for. I love you Manny. <3 Dee*

I smiled and sat my phone down so that I could get ready for work. I had made the right decision and I felt good about it.

May flowers

Eliza

Monday had come and gone. I called my boss Sunday night to let him know I would not be coming in to work. I wanted to be right there when Tavis showed up, but he never did. Even though time was passing I felt like I was frozen in place as I called in day after day waiting for him to walk through that door. I was forced to take a leave of absence.

I had spent my birthday feeling sorry for myself and sipping on wine. He never came home, didn't text, and didn't call. His silence was the answer to all of my questions, but I still found it hard to accept what had happened. He could have given me a reason. I deserved that much. The most I had done in seven days was create a playlist filled with songs that made me want to stab myself in the heart. It couldn't hurt if it wasn't beating.

I sat in my destroyed apartment still ignoring everyone's attempt to contact me and currently blasting Jazmin Sullivan's *in vain*. Each line over the somber beat shot through me like a bullet. *Hope she's everything you wanted*...POW! *Hope she's everything I wasn't*...POW POW! *Hope she gives up more than I*...POW POW POW! *Hope she keeps you satisfied*...BOOM POW! *Cause if you sacrifice everything, it better not be in vain*...FLATLINE.

Heartbreak triggers the craziest things. You start to remember what life was like before you knew what love was at all. I sat thinking about when I had no worries. I wanted to be a little girl again. I wanted to erase Tavis from my existence. Could there be anything worse than betrayal? I thought I knew who Tavis was, even the worst parts of him, perhaps I did know him, but somewhere along the lines of our forever he may have become a stranger to me. Love was most definitely blind if in five years I had not noticed he was changing on me right before my eyes. Maybe he wasn't changing at all, this was who he was all along and it took me five years to see it.

It's so bad because I sat waiting to fall out of love, while he clearly had already left me alone in it. He was one step ahead of me for the first time in our relationship. He was just waiting for the perfect moment to cast the pain on me. I had always been a rip the band aid off kind of girl. If you love me say that you love me and if you hate me then say that shit too. I prided myself on being able to take the truth well no matter what it may be. I soaked words up like a sponge even if they hurt. He never gave me a chance to handle the truth. He lead me to believe that we were okay when in fact he was okay with someone else and pretending with me. I looked down at the ring on my left hand and decided I needed another drink.

  I stood from the sofa that I had been laying on for days without sleep because I couldn't bear to lay in the bed he and I shared and walked into the kitchen. My feelings about drinking was about to go out of the window. I opened the liquor cabinet and I was all out. Tavis had probably packed up all his liquor to share with his bitch. *Figures.*

  I walked into my bedroom and grabbed a blank CD so I could burn my depressing music and carry it with me in the car. I popped it into my laptop and started the burn as I slid my feet into slippers then walked in circles and I waited. Once it was finished I popped it out and grabbed my purse and keys. I walked down the stairs and into the parking lot and hopped into my silver Hyundai Sonata. All I needed was a corner store to grab a few bottle of vodka or anything that burned.

I pushed my CD into the stereo and *Mariah Carey* hit me with *Hate U.* I already hated Tavis, next. Paramore's *all I wanted* played and I sunk in my seat. It was a murderous list. I had passed several stores just letting lyrics cut through me: Tony Braxton's *Stupid,* Brooke Valentine's *laugh til I cry and dying of a broken heart,* Syleena Johnson's *Another relationship,* Dawn and Que's *Broken promises,* Robyn's *every heartbeat,* Melanie Fiona's *it kills me,* Rihanna's *photographs,* Meshell Ndegeocello's *fool of me,* Aretha Franklin's *hurts like hell,* Mary J's *missing you*…this was not my life.

I finally pulled up at a store. I hopped out of my car and all eyes were on me as the loitering drunks out front stared. My hair was all over my head, my clothing was layered, and I was sure I smelled worse than they did, but I didn't care. I walked straight to the isle filled with liquor. I grabbed two bottles of Grey Goose because I liked the way the bottle looked. I handed my drinks to the cashier who was silently judging me in her mind then I handed her my credit card and ID. She swiped it and I snatched my bag to head back to my miserable and empty apartment. I started my CD over.

I parked to head back inside.

"Eliza!" I heard someone yell, but I kept walking. "Eliza!" Madra ran up on me. "I've been calling you for days, I was worried.

"Well, I'm fine as you can see."

Eliza covered her nose, "no offense E, but when was the last time you brushed your teeth or showered?"

I shrugged my shoulders and continued to my apartment. Madra followed me. "E, talk to me and what's in the bag?"

"Juice," I lied and Madra snatched the bag from me. "Give it back!" I yelled for the first time in days.

"Alcohol Eliza?! You don't drink!"

"I do now."

Madra snatched my keys from my hands and opened the door to my apartment. She paused as she observed things scattered all over the floor. I walked past her and kicked things out of my way to flop down on the sofa. I stared at the floor.

Madra walked over to me and kneeled down in front of me, "He never came home did he?"

I looked into Madra's eyes and all the tears that were covered by rage had finally fought their way back as I shook my head no. Madra grabbed me and held me tight. "Shhhh," she said as she rubbed her hand across my tangled mane. "It's going to be okay."

"No it's not," I sobbed. "What did I do to deserve this?"

"Nothing, he's just a bitch ass mother... let me calm down; I have kids. I shouldn't talk like that." Madra stated angrily. Madra released me and grabbed my hands, "I want you to sit right here. I'm going to run you some bath water and attempt to clean up this mess in here. You have to pull yourself together E. He's not worth losing yourself over."

"We were getting married in two months."

"Well, it's better this happened now rather than after you said I do. You are so much stronger than this

Eliza. Just go look at yourself. My best friend is a beautiful independent woman who can have any man she wants, not some bummy broad who sits on a sofa crying crocodile tears behind some low life. I need you to be my best friend." Madra squeezed my hands and hugged me one more time before standing. "Where are your garbage bags?"

"In the cabinet beside the stove, at the bottom." Madra walked away.

I watched as Madra pulled out several garbage bags, then headed into the bathroom and ran water. She came back into the living room and started to pick up anything that was lying on the floor. If she thought this was bad she definitely didn't want to see my bedroom. She didn't even ask me what anything was; she just tossed everything in a trash bag.

Madra sat the garbage bag down and walked over to me and grabbed my hand, "come get in the tub."

I stood reluctantly and went into the bathroom. I started to disrobe. "Are you going to watch?" I asked.

"Tramp I've seen you naked, now get in the tub."

I eased into the steamy water and sunk down as low as I could get.

"We need to wash that hair."

I nodded my head then Madra stepped out, closing the door behind her. I looked down at my naked body through the clear water. Tavis had always complimented my body. I thought about how his hands ran across my brown skin. He loved my thick thighs, but he loved my corpulent ass even more. I placed my hands on my 36 C's and squeezed them the way Tavis used to then I felt sick to my stomach as I imagined him doing the same thing to the woman Madra had described to me over the phone. Without noticing I started to bite my nails and the door swung open.

"Where is your dumpster located?" Madra looked down at me. "I know you're not biting your nails again."

I snatched my hand away from my mouth, "umm it's at the end of the gate to the right." I said as I placed my hand beneath the water.

Madra gave me an ugly look then shut the door. I grabbed my towel and Dove soap and began to wash away the funk. I hoped the pain would go with it.

After washing myself at least six times and re-running my water to keep it warm I was finally back to feeling fresh. I hopped out of the tub and wrapped a towel around myself. I went into my bedroom and froze in place as I stared at the closet. Tavis' things were still in there. I walked over to the drawer near my window and opened it to pull out some panties and a t-shirt. I still didn't want to put on any clothes. I slid into some sweats and put my slippers on. I walked around the room, picking up all the pictures of Tavis that I had pulled down. I put them in a shoe box and slid them beneath my bed.

"You look much better." Madra said from the doorway, startling me.

"I feel a little better."

"Good," she turned to walk away.

"Madra…"

"Yes?"

"Can you get me some boxes?"

"With pleasure," She smiled.

I swung the closet door open and pulled all of Tavis' things out and tossed them on my bed. I walked

into the living room to retrieve my phone so that I could call my brother. He answered on the first ring.
"You okay?"
"I will be."
"You need anything?"
"Yes, call all of your male friends and tell them to come over to my place. I'm selling all of Tavis' stuff for ten dollars, everything must go."
"I got you sis."
We hung up.
I went back into the bathroom to grab my shampoo and conditioner then I headed into the kitchen to wash my hair. Madra returned with boxes the moment I was done and had my hair wrapped in a towel.
"I hate you," Madra watched me as I pulled the towel from around my hair.
"Why?" I asked detangling my hair, combing up from the ends to the roots.
"Because I'd kill to have your hair and all you do with it is wash it and put it in a ponytail."
I laughed for the first time in days, "I think you rock that cut pretty well and it's more manageable than mine."
"Umm hmm whatever, come grab a box."
Madra and I separated all of Tavis' things into boxes: shirts in one, jeans in another, and so forth and so on.
My brother showed up with just enough men to clean out everything. They shopped around like they were in a mall, wide-eyed at the expensive things I was selling for ten dollars.
"Hey sis how much you want for these clippers?" Eli asked.

"Ten dollars," I said.

"You could get at least fifty for these. They've never been opened."

"Well, I tell you what then, you can get them on a family discount of free." I smiled.

Eli shook his head and smiled as I collected ten dollars from one of his friends for a pair of diamond earrings. Nothing was left behind as Eli's friends called more of their friends to come have a look at my bitter woman sale. I got rid of everything except his boxers and t-shirts. I figured I could sleep in those and it would be kind of trifling to sell his under garments to other men. I didn't get back all of the money from his birthday bash and limo rental, but it put a nice dent in the balance and made me feel a lot better.

Madra and I sat on the sofa exhausted once everyone had left. "I want to kill him," I blurted out.

"He's not worth the jail time."

"No, but I'd be at peace."

"No, you'd be giving up that yoni to bitches bigger than Tavis for the rest of your life," Madra laughed and I picked up a decorative pillow and threw it at her.

"You've been here all day, shouldn't you be home with your husband and kids."

"They know where I am. You know I take breaks as often as I can."

"See I knew you didn't care about me, you just wanted a break."

"It was a little bit of both," Madra smiled and looked at her phone. I do need to get out of here though, so I can grab something quick to eat and put the kids to bed." Madra stood. "You are going to work tomorrow right?"

"I still don't feel like it. I think I'll take one more day, maybe I'll make a spa appointment."

"Well do what you need to, but no more moping or vandalizing your apartment." Madra laughed, "You know what you should do?"

"What?"

"You remember all those stories you used to write?"

"Girl I haven't written anything since high school."

"Write Eliza, you're good at it and it'll help you deal with all these emotions."

"I'll try," I stood to hug Madra, "what would I do without you?"

"Murder Tavis."

We both laughed then she was on her way and I was left alone with my thoughts again.

Emmanuel

I rummaged through the mail on my desk, shaking my head as I recognized the label from the government. I was behind on my taxes and they made sure I knew it as month after month went by. I had to do something and fast, but I didn't really have the money to do much with. I tossed the mail in a bin with all the other unopened mail. I'd deal with it eventually.

My office phone rang as I sat back and took a moment to myself. "Shop, Manny," I answered.

"Well, good morning to you young man."

"Good morning mama, how are you?"
"I'm good baby, just making my rounds."
"What rounds mama, you only call me and messy ass Devina."
"Boy watch your mouth."
"I'm sorry," I smiled. My mama's voice always washed my worries away.
"What's the matter?"
"Nothing, why you asked that?"
"Because I know my child, I can hear it all in your voice, now stop lying and tell me what's going on."
I sighed, "I broke up with Desiree…"
"Good."
"What?"
"I said good, y'all we're never too good of match anyway."
"But I thought you liked her."
"I did, but not for you, there wasn't any real chemistry. Hell you're at that shop more than with her and that should have told you something. Ain't no man finna be at work all the time with free coochie at home."
"Mama I'm sitting the phone down."
She laughed, "Don't act shy, I know you have sex."
I shook my head; this lady just didn't care what came out of her mouth, "what am I going to do with you?"
"Nothing, I'm too old to change." She laughed. "So tell me what else is wrong."
"Nothing."
"Boy you better stop lying to me, I had you at 15. I'm still young and can box your ass up."
I laughed, "I got another notice."

"Aww baby don't stress about that, your business will be fine."

"I feel like I should have waited another year or two. You know the government wants their money and they can take it too. And on top of that I owe the bank on the loan they gave me just to help start it."

"I've always told you to pray and not worry, so if you're going to worry I suggest you don't even talk to the man I serve. It's going to be alright."

"I hear you mama."

"Now let me go, Devina is beeping in. I love you."

"Uh huh love you too."

We hung up.

Quick Reminders

Eliza

    My insides were still in complete disarray, but I had finally managed getting back to work before my boss decided he didn't need my services anymore. Even though Tavis had done what he did I still had to live and make a living. I sat at my desk getting reacquainted with my duties as my computer loaded.
    I had 435 unread emails; half business, half personal. I clicked on my inbox and all of the wind felt like it was knocked from my chest as I was hit with wedding reminders. Tavis and Eliza flooded my screen with the date June 23rd. I turned away from the screen and took deep breaths. I could check my email later. I just needed to make it through the day.
    I sifted through the paperwork on my desk to see what I could start with first. Payroll was all over the place since I had been out. My boss didn't even bother with it. I shook my head as I looked at the missed punches, overtime reports, terminations, early-outs, and so on. I hated being the assistant of a Human Resources Director. I did all his work while he got the corporate pay. Not that I wasn't making good money I just felt I should be on the same level as him and driving a Benz.
    My cell phone vibrated in my desk drawer. I opened it and Madra's face flashed on the screen. "I'm fine Madra." I answered because she had been calling damn near every hour everyday to check on me.
    "See I wasn't even calling to check on you."
    I sighed relief, "good, then what?"
    "How do you feel about blind dates?"
    "They are for desperate women."

"No they aren't, look Paul has this friend and he's kind of dealing with what you're dealing with and I just thought you two could distract each other."

"Oh my gawd are you kidding me?"

"I'm so serious! You need to do something with your time or you're going to fall back into a depression."

"No I won't I'm just fine."

"Have you called and canceled the wedding yet?" Madra asked.

"No…"

"Then you're not fine. Just go on one date with him and if he doesn't do the trick, we'll just move on to plan B."

"Plan B? You have put some serious thought into this. I've only been separated a few weeks and you're pimping me out to everyone on match.com."

"E I'm just trying to help. You already know how this goes. You get mad and bitter, you stop believing in love before weighting your options, and then you end up with the next jerk."

I sighed, "I know," I shook my head. "What's his name and when is this date supposed to happen."

She hesitated, "actually I told him where you work and he wants to do lunch."

I put my hand up to my forehead, "just give him my number Madra, bye." I hung up. I was going to get this over with quick. I dropped my phone back into my desk drawer and looked at the time on my comp. I had three hours before lunch.

~~*~*

"Madra told me you were beautiful, but damn." Blind date guy said as he kissed my hand, pretending to be a gentleman like most men did when they first met a woman.

"Thanks…" I pulled my hand back and joined him at the table he had reserved.

"Anyone ever tell you that you resemble Stacey Dash?"

I laughed, "yeah and she's a Republican so I'm not sure how flattered I should be." I looked over the menu not thinking that I could have offended him with the Republican comment. He could be one for all I knew. Not all Republicans were bad people. But sister girl was endorsing Mitt Romney. I shook my head at my own thoughts.

The smiled he had faded, "order whatever you like."

He didn't have to tell me twice. My appetite was finally somewhat normal after my drama so I was about to go in. I ordered an appetizer, a salad, a main course, and a drink. There was no way I was about to act cute in front of this man when I had no intentions on ever seeing him again.

Mr. Blind date sat across from me and talked about his ex-wife who left him for a younger man and their three kids. At some point I just knew he was going to burst out into tears. I wondered how old he was if his wife was tired of him and he had three damn kids. That was too much baggage for even me. He didn't need a distraction, he needed therapy.

After lunch I thanked him, allowed him to kiss me on my cheek, then programmed his number into my phone as *do not answer*. I made a mental note to look up bug-a-boo for a ringtone for him.

When I got a moment to myself I called Madra back. She picked up and I could hear water, "hello?" she said.

"What are you doing?" I asked.

"Washing dishes, how was the date?"

"You are so wrong for hooking me up with that man. He has three kids!"

"I didn't know that."

"Did you not get all the details about him when you and Paul had a meeting about my love life?"

Madra laughed.

"It's not funny, that man looked old enough to be my daddy. I probably went to school with one of his kids."

Madra continued to laugh, "I'm sorry E, I really thought y'all would hit it off."

I shook my head and held the phone.

"Well, this next one..." she started to say.

"Next one? How many are there?"

"I just called a few friends who know some single men."

"I'm not ready to date Madra. The wedding date hasn't even passed yet. I have to deal with the flood of emails I'm getting, my family, my other friends...I appreciate what you're trying to do but..." Madra cut me off.

"I understand all that and I'm going to help with whatever I can, but in the meantime you need somebody to eat with and catch a movie or something or your mind will keep traveling to a dark place, trust me I've been through this. Just be honest with them and nothing will happen that you don't allow."

I sighed heavily, "I have to get back to work; I'll call you later," I hung up.

~~*~*

I never called Madra back. I just wanted to be alone. The microwave beeped three times, letting me know that my frozen dinner was hot and ready. I walked into the kitchen and pulled it from the microwave. I sat the little plastic plate on the table then grabbed a bottle of water from the fridge. This was my new life. I felt lonely and empty. "How could you Tavis," I said out loud then dug into my food.

I thought about my lunch date from earlier. It was nice to eat with someone even if I didn't particularly care for anything he had to say or offer. I just liked not sitting alone like some sort of pedophile at a park looking for a kid to make my victim. Right now Tavis would be sitting to the left of me telling me about his day. I looked over at his empty chair.

I thought about what Madra said about my thoughts traveling to a dark place. She was right. I had not been sleeping and I barely ate much of anything when I was alone, because all I could think of was Tavis and all the bad things I wanted to do to him. Then there was the softer side of me that loved him and just wanted him to come home, apologize, and marry me. How was I going to tell everyone the wedding was off? When Was I going to tell them? I just couldn't. I couldn't hear I told you so.

If Madra was going to play the love connection game, she at least needed to know what I liked. If I was going to have a distraction, it was going to be an appealing one. I stood from the table and went into my room to get a tablet and a pen from my desk. I returned to my food and jotted down "Standard List" at the top of the paper. I tapped my chin as I thought about all the things I would want in a man. "God-fearing duh," I said out loud to myself then wrote it down.

It took me damn near thirty minutes, but I had a list that I was proud of with maybe a few things missing:

God-fearing	*Family Oriented*
Opens Doors	*Tall*
Courteous	*Parents have to like me*
Nice job	*Nice car*
Own place	*No kids*
No ex drama	*Dresses well*
Loves all things art	*Knows how to dance*
Loves movies	*Loves food & trying new ones*
Educated	*Intellectual*
Honest	*Faithful*
Funny	*Romantic*
Passionate	*Great kisser*
Loves to travel	*Makes the first move*
Loyal	*Communicates well*
Never been married	*Secure and confident*
~~*Good*~~ *Great in bed*	*Tattoos (optional but sexy)*

Considerate   *Keeps up with politics*

Doesn't flirt   *Loves to read*

    Madra was going to have her work cut out for her finding a man that was everything on this list. The thought of how difficult it was made me laugh. Even Tavis wasn't this man. I pushed my list to the side and held my pen over blank paper. I wanted to write. It came so easily in high school, but now I saw nothing. I slammed the pen down on the notebook and went into my bedroom, pulling my laptop from my desk. I opened it and logged on. I went straight to the folder where everything I had ever written was stored. It was all undone short stories. All I had ever given was a taste of me. I made a promise to finish at least one of those stories. I had to.

Emmanuel

    Desiree walked into my studio wearing a long black jacket as I sat up in bed reading a business magazine. I sat it down and looked over at her.

    "How'd you get in here?"

    "I didn't leave my key." She said in a low sexy tone.

    "Okay what are you doing here?" I grinned.

    She pulled the straps to the jacket a loose and dropped it to the floor, exposing her naked body that I had been so familiar with. She bit down on her bottom lip then clicked off the light and walked over to the bed. I felt my man grow as she moved closer now crawling toward me on the bed. She straddled me and wrapped her tiny arms around my neck, pushing her lips against mine. I allowed our tongues to dance then I moved her back. "We broke up Dee."

"I know that, but I was horny and I thought maybe since we were two single consenting adults who knew each other so well then we could still please each other." She pushed her moist lips back against mine and I almost couldn't resist her offer. Desiree moved her hand down to the seam of my shirt and pulled at it, "take this off." She whispered.

I lifted my arms to assist her with pulling off my shirt then she grabbed my hand and placed it between her legs so I could feel her juices, "see what you do to me," she whispered.

I grabbed her and turned her on her back ready to give her exactly what she came for as I leaned up and unbuckled my jeans. I pushed them down just enough to expose what she wanted so badly. I was ready to be inside of her. I positioned myself back between her legs so that I could slide into her and hear that first moan.

"I love you so much," she said as she lifted her arms to reach for me.

Her words brought me back to reality. All I was about to do was get sucked right back into the routine we had been stuck in for years. I'd do her good then feel nothing after I got a nut which was really all I wanted. I stopped, pulling her arms from around me and easing out of the bed. I grabbed for the shirt beside her, "I can't."

"You can't what?"

"Do this. I can't lead you on."

"How are you leading me on if I want this?"

"Dee we just broke up, you still have feelings."

"And you don't?"
"Not the ones that you have, I want something else."
"No you want someone else! I'm not stupid."
"Don't put words in my mouth."
"Forget you Manny," she said as she slid from my mattress and picked her coat up from the floor.
"You said you understood."
"I do. I get it, crystal fucking clear. I'm out." She said as she wrapped her coat back around the body I almost invaded. She stormed out of my life once again.

I hung my head looking down at the bulge in my pants. "You gon ask me if I'm gay too?" I said to my man then stretched my hands above my head. I needed a cold shower and some self-love with my right hand.

The Distractions

Eliza

    Madra and Paul had managed to dig up five more heartbroken men after the first one who was in need of company. I felt like I was being pimped out by the two of them, well more so Madra. I knew Paul had nothing much to do with it and was probably being bullied by my best friend. I told her she was two steps from lesbian with how aggressive she was.
    I didn't bother remembering much about them, because it was too much to remember and I really didn't want to embarrass myself by missing information. I really only cared about what they matched on my list. I gave them all numbers so I knew who I was answering the phone for.
    Distraction one had already crossed three things from my list being God-fearing, dressing well, and loving all things art. Our first date was at a museum and I was actually impressed by his knowledge of painters and the history of the works. He wasn't exactly my type, because when I put heels on I hovered over him by at least two and half inches and that to me just wasn't sexy. I made it a point to wear flats anytime he asked me out so that I wouldn't look like a big sister next to my kid brother. I guess now you need to know why he needed my company. Mr. One had walked in on his wife cheating. He drove off and never went back. He didn't even beat the guy up or anything. I found that slightly noble and disturbing. I would have said or done something if I walked in on my wife in my house where I paid the bills with another man in my bed.

Moving on to Distraction number two; he had major personality. I loved a man that could make me laugh, so even if he lacked five things on that list, being funny made up for them. He was kind of shy at first, but he eventually came out of his shell and we hit it off pretty well. He took me to a comedy club downtown where there were some independent comedians on Wednesday nights and he even surprised me by getting on stage himself. I had tears in my as he told joke after joke. It was hard to believe that someone would want to break funny man's heart, but it happened. Mr. Two was left for another woman, now if that wasn't a joke he could tell for life I don't know what was; the irony of it all.

Distraction numbers three and four didn't even make it after the first date. They both were nice looking well-dressed men, but they were also controlling older men who didn't think women should have much of an opinion on anything. Don't get me wrong I'm a sucker for somebody old school, but even that was too far back in time for me. They'd probably take away my right to vote and lessen my pay. I wasn't feeling that. They had seven ex wives between the two of them and I wasn't surprised and didn't care why each one ended because I had a pretty decent idea.

Now distraction number five, that brother foine, yes F O I N E. He was a fitness instructor. I felt like I needed to pray the first time I saw him. It had to be a sin to look that good. He was tall and his skin was chocolate. I just wanted to bite him. I understood at the moment I saw him how men felt when they saw a woman with a fat booty. I imagined every inappropriate thing I could about that man as he stood behind me helping me lift a ten pound weight. I hated to sweat, but I made an exception that day. Mr. Five was still bitter about a high school love and admitted to running from any woman he thought he'd fall for, but he found something special in me. I was sure that special thing was my hips and ass, but I'd still be happy to mend his broken heart and run before he could, because after Tavis I never wanted to hear the word love again. Mr. Five made me forget everything when I got caught his lustful presence. I had forgotten about my list. I forgot about my wedding day...

~~*~*

June 23rd

The alarm clock on my phone rang loudly and I fell off the sofa, hitting the floor hard. "Ouch..." I said as I stretched then pushed myself from the floor. My eyes were barely opened as I searched for my phone to shut off the annoying sound. I saw it lighting up in the kitchen and went for it. I looked at the screen and it read *wedding day!!!* It was instant caffeine for me as my eyes popped open and I ran into the bathroom to brush my teeth and wash my face. The day had snuck up on me. I had not canceled a single thing still holding on to false hope that this was all a nightmare and Tavis would be back any day now. I had lied to myself. I had to get down to the church.

I tossed on some jeans and pulled a shirt over my head. I slid my feet into some slippers, grabbed my phone and keys, and ran out of the door. The heat hit me hard as I ran. It was just too damn hot in this city. On top of New Orleans being hot it was also humid and the two did not mix well for skin or hair. I hopped into my car putting the air on full blast then I sped out of my apartment.

It was Tavis' idea to have an early morning wedding and now I had to be the one to disappoint everybody. I pulled up to the church and parked right in front. Everyone had already arrived. I walked around back and Madra pulled me into the room with the rest of my bridesmaids which included my baby sister.

"What's going on Eliza, I thought you told everybody?" Madra gave me a disappointing glare.

I stood silently looking around at all the bridesmaids dressed so beautifully in all white with red bows in their hair. My sister walked over to me.

"Eliza what's happening, why aren't you getting dressed."

My body started to shake and a tear fell from my eye. I stuttered, "t-t-there isn't a wedding today. It's off." I struggled to get the words out.

"What, why?" my sister Ella asked.

"Uh," I fidgeted with my hands, "Tavis left me and I don't know where he is."

My sister grabbed me and pulled me into her arms as the other bridesmaids whispered and sighed.

"We have to go tell everyone," Madra interrupted and I shook my head in agreement then headed for the door. My bridesmaids walked behind me all with expressions like they were the ones who had been abandoned. We heard talking as we approached the front. The voice sounded familiar.

"I'm sorry to deliver this news to you all today, but my name is Shana. I'm the mother of the groom and…"

I ran into the church and punched Shana before she could finish her sentence. She fell to the ground dramatically. I had wanted to do that for a very long time. That woman had disrespected me in the worse ways, calling me out of my name when I wasn't around and encouraging her son to find someone new. I knew she was partly responsible for the presence of his ex because of his Facebook. She drove to pick the bitch up. She jumped up and attempted to charge at me but my bridesmaids moved in front of me and restrained her.

I turned to the shocked crowd filled with my family, friends, and ex-in laws. "Good morning everyone, I know that I should have done this sooner, but the wedding is off. I pulled the ring from my finger and tossed it to the ground where Shana stood held up by two of my bridesmaids. I stormed out of the front of the church and my parents followed. "Mom, dad, I don't want to talk about it."

"You need to tell us something Eliza, you just punched your mother-in-law." My mother said.

"Ex mother-in-law. She hates me mom."

"What if she presses charges?" my dad asked.

"Then let her! I did so much for her and her raggedy ass son and this is what he did to me! He left me here alone with all these thoughts and feelings!" Tears started to run down my cheeks as I lost it, "now I'm humiliated twice! First Madra catches his cheating ass and now I have to stand here and tell everybody it's over and I have to be the one who answers why when I don't even know why!" My knees buckled beneath me and my mother caught me and wrapped her arms around me. My father stormed off back into the church. I could hear him yelling from outside, asking Shana where Tavis was. I wanted to hit her again. I wanted somebody, anybody to feel this pain.

"I need to go…" I sniffed as my tears dried and I released my mother. I hopped into my car with my sappy CD and sped off back to the safety of my apartment.

Madra called me as soon as I stepped through the door. "Hello…" I answered.

"You okay?"

"I will be…"

"You need me to come over?"

"No, I have a date with distraction number two later, that should get my mind off of everything."

Madra laughed, "You started numbering them?"

I cracked a smile, "yeah, I'm not trying to learn their names."

"You still comparing them to that retarded list you made?"

"Yep and my list is not retarded it. It has weeded out a lot of stupidity."

"How many dates have you been on with number two?"

"This will be out third date."

"I can't believe he made it to date number three."

"Shit me either, but hey I'll call you later okay. I want to go back to sleep before I have to head out."

"Okay, talk to you later."

I hung up and snuggled with my pillow until I dozed off.

~~*~*

Madra had spoken too soon about Mr. Two as I sat with my face twisted up and ready to run the hell out of that damn restaurant as he rambled." This was the first attempt we had ever had at a serious conversation and I really wish he had stuck to be funny.

"I know God's not real and if he is he is one sick dude watching down on all of us and giggling as he makes people suffer. How can you call nations your children and some are doing better than others, shouldn't we all be equal."

"What would be the point of life if we were all equal, how would we know happiness from anguish or triumph from failure?"

"We would just know." He said.

"Okay so, if you don't believe in God what do you believe in?"

"Myself, I control my own destiny. Why give glory to someone when I did all the hard stuff?"

"What about the unexplainable things that happen every day; you don't think that's God?"

"No it's nature," he said as if he knew for sure.

This dude was making no sense. He was so full of idiot logic that I had to laugh out loud. He thought he was just being amusing, but all he was doing was getting himself deleted. I didn't know where Madra was finding these men.

As number two continued to talk it started to rain outside. The lightning and thunder made my heart jump in my chest. I needed to get home. "I think you're making God mad." I said as thunder roared.

"I'd have to believe in him to give a shit." He laughed.

I was done entertaining him, "statistics show that men are twice as likely to get hit by lightning than women are, so be careful on your way out," I stood and headed for the exit. He didn't have to believe in God, but I bet those stats put something on his mind. He would walk home shaking, because not only was the weather bad, but I was his ride.

Crossing paths and the majority

Emmanuel

"Manny what up boy?" Paul gave me daps then handed me his keys.

"It's time for an oil change already?" I asked.

"The oil is probably still good in that car, but you know how the wife is, once it hits the mileage she reads on the sticker she wants it done." Paul joked.

"I understand, well give me about thirty minutes, I got one or two ahead of you."

"No rush man."

"Cool, so how are the kids?"

"Bad as hell, but I'm good with that because boys should be bad."

"I feel that." I said as I punched numbers into the computer.

"Hey what you got going for the fourth?" Paul asked.

"Nothing, I usually barbeque at my moms, but she's going out of town with her friend instead."

"You should roll by the house then. The kids will be gone so we doing something for grown folks. Bring your girl with you."

"Me and Dee broke up."

"Damn for real?"

"Yeah…"

"When that happened?"

"Few weeks ago, I just wasn't feeling it no more. I don't know what the hell is wrong with me." I shook my head.

"You crossed that line between man and boy, that's what. You ready to be like me."

I laughed, "I won't go that far, nigga you drive a Minnie van." I joked.

"Man forget you," he laughed. "But seriously stop by, they'll be some single ladies there."

I nodded my head not exactly sure if the single ladies would mean much when I wasn't even sure what it was that I was looking for. "I'll slide through." I grabbed his keys and headed out to the shop.

Paul was one of the best friend's that I had. I used to envy him because of the life he had with his greeting card family. I used to want that for me and Desiree, but over time that dream got lost and I stopped seeing her in my future.

I imagined her pregnant and didn't see her as a mother. I figured maybe after a year of being married to her I'd be stepping out on her with the first young chick that threw the ass on me. I was starting to notice other women with Desiree. She just wasn't keeping my interest anymore.

I thought about the night before and the desperation in her eyes when she popped up at my place wanting sex, but still craving my love. It just wasn't there. I wanted to feel bad for hurting her, but I was honest. Women say they want an honest man then tell us fuck us when we give them the truth. I shook my head at the thought. I was ready to embrace the life of a bachelor and face the reality that maybe that was all I was ever meant to be.

Eliza

The seven stages of a break up started all over again as I ignored all my distractions and shut down from the thoughts of my canceled wedding. I sat in the middle of my bed ripping up pictures of Tavis and me, shaking, crying, and from time to time yelling at the pictures as if it were Tavis standing before me.

I was doing the exact opposite of what people said not to do when dealing with a bad break-up: freaking out, minimizing the situation as if it were no big deal and we could fix it if he came back, isolating myself from family and friends, calling out of work again, attempting to act on my hate for Tavis by thinking of everything that could be done to ruin his life, bargaining with myself that if he just came back I'd listen and forgive him because things could be worse (or could they), falling victim, and binging on food.

I was doing everything, but accepting what was happening. It was over and I needed to get over it. Madra's ringtone blared, snapping me out of my trance.

"Hello?"

"E what are you doing?" Madra asked as if she already knew the answer.

"Just sitting in bed…"

"Glad to know you're sleeping in the bed again."

I sniffed, "yeah no use it letting a Temper Pedic just sit in here."

She laughed, "Well, I was calling to invite you to the barbeque me and Paul are having for the 4th."

"I won't be able to make it…"

"Lies, your family doesn't do shit on holidays so run that bull to somebody else, I'm not taking no for an answer."

"What about hell no?"

"I'm not taking that either, you've gotten back to sitting in that damn apartment. I hate to say this to you Eliza, but as your best friend it's my job," she sighed, "Tavis is gone and he's probably never coming back. Time is just going to pass you by. He's probably somewhere with his bitch smiling and laughing while you're in tears. Suck it up baby girl."

Tears ran down my face and not from pain this time, but because she was right. I gathered all of the ripped pictures and swept them into the shoebox that I kept them hidden in from myself and Madra. I needed to get rid of them once and for all before I really went crazy and attempted to tape them all back together. I needed to forget about Tavis the way he so easily forgot about me.

"So I'll see you at the barbeque right?" Madra asked.

I dried my tears with my hands, "yeah." I forced a smile.

"Now if you don't show, I'm going to pack up the party and bring everybody over to your place."

I laughed, "I'll be there."

~~*~*

My heart beat fast in my chest as I pulled up to Madra's house. There were cars all over the place. I wanted to park somewhere that I couldn't get blocked in so I could show my face and leave. I drove around to the

side of Madra's house and found a vacant spot. I parked then checked myself one last time before hopping out.
 Cupid shuffle rumbled through the neighborhood and I could see the smoke from the grill as I approached the opposite side of the house. There were so many people. I took a deep breath and opened the gate. There were tables and chairs set up. People were eating and mingling. I was happy that Madra had convinced Paul to get that cover over their patio, because we'd all burn the hell up.
 "Eliza!" Madra yelled from across the yard.
 I lifted my hand and waved as she ran over to me with excitement. She pulled me into her arms and squeezed.
 "You look so good." She pulled at me. "Come say hey to Paul and meet his friend."
 I rolled my eyes already aware of what she was doing as she drug me over to the grill where Paul stood with his friend. "Hey," I said as I hugged him and kissed his cheek. Paul was always easy to spot in his tacky clothing and white socks that he wore with everything. He was a good man though with an even better heart and Madra loved him.
 "Hey there miss lady, how have you been?" Paul asked.
 "I've had better days?" I responded.
 Madra cleared her throat and Paul looked at her from the corner of his eye. I laughed on the inside at this bad communication. "Oh, this is my boy Manny." Paul said pointing his spatula.
 I shook Manny's hand, "nice to meet you." I gave him an uninterested smile.

I scoped him from head to toe, from his neat fade and clean shave to his fresh white tennis shoes. He was well put together in his fitted jeans that sagged just a little bit. He wore a plain white t-shirt and a silver watch. Both of his ears were pierced and the diamonds in them shined as he turned his head. Manny was fine. I could see his muscles through his shirt as he stood straight up holding a beer in his hand. I guessed that he was about 5'11", 190lbs, solid muscle. I had seen plenty of attractive men in my life, but this copper colored brother made me want to place his profile on a penny and carry him around in my pocket. He was all man with his thick eyebrows and full Tyson Beckford lips. His neck was even sexy.

I moved down his body and noticed that he was bow-legged. I loved bow-legged men. They reminded me of the cowboys I used to watch in the movies my mother played over and over again. I wanted to see him walk. His hands were large and so were his feet. I just couldn't stop scanning him. I thought to myself *bring on the distraction*, but then again I had more than enough. He was probably another walking problem and I had more than enough of those.

"Nice to meet you too," Manny said.

"I'm going to go and get something to drink." I excused myself and Madra followed.

Emmanuel

I watched as Madra's friend walked away. I tried hard not to look, but she was thick in all the right places as her jeans hugged her hips and ass. I had always been a sucker for brown skin women and she was a beauty. Her eyes were empty and she had a discouraged stance, but she was still beautiful though. Her ponytail let me know that her hair was real and I instantly imagined what it looked like if it were down around her shoulders. I had even taken a glance down at her feet; those were just as perfect at her manicured nails.

Paul elbowed me in the chest, "quit staring."

"Shit it's hard not to." I turned my head.

"Madra's best friend right?"

"Yeah that's E, but stay away she carrying bags."

"What you mean?"

"She got issues, emotional ones."

"Is that ole girl whose boyfriend was caught at Wal-Mart?"

"Yep."

"Damn, no wonder she looks like she doesn't want to be here."

"Madra's been trying to get that girl out of a funk for weeks. I told her let her be."

"She's just being a good friend, leave the girl alone."

"She being too damn good, leaving me at home with the kids at night. We could be getting it on. I don't get it that often as is."

I laughed, "You know that's married life, get used to it." I said as I stole another glance at Madra and her friend.

"I can see you out the corner of my eye. Stop staring."

"Watch the grill man. I'm just taking in her pretty face that's all, I'm not trying to holla."

"Good because she is damaged and there is nothing worse than a damaged woman."

"I wouldn't know, never dated one." I said as I sipped my beer.

"Alright then think of her as a car, she's at that mileage where she starts giving you problems. It might be better to just trade it in."

"Don't insult my intelligence man, you know I love cars, even a totaled car can be repaired if you're willing to put in the time and money."

"Whatever you say dude."

Eliza

"So what do you think?" Madra said as I opened an ice chest and grabbed some water.

"He's nice looking."

"Nice looking? Girl he is FOINE!"

I laughed, "I've seen plenty of fine men and umm you are a married woman quit looking at that man like that."

"Wasn't nothing in my wedding vows that said thou shall not look and lust."

"First off *thou* is tagged to ten commandments and secondly lust is a sin." I laughed as Madrà continued to look at Paul and Manny, but more Manny than Paul.

"Then take me to hell because that man looks delicious."

I popped Madra's arm, "so that's why you were hell bent on getting me to this barbeque."

"Of course not, you needed to get out of that apartment," she smiled to hide her lie. "This is my first time seeing Manny. I've talked to him several times on the phone because he works on our cars, but never met him."

"Uh huh, well I appreciate the effort but I'm going right back to my depressing cave. I just came to show my face and make a plate. I have enough distractions and I'm tired of them all already."

"Even Mr. Five?"

"Him too."

I chatted with Madra a little while longer then grabbed some food to go, said my goodbyes to Paul, and headed to my car. I sat my things on the passenger seat and attempted to start my car, but it wouldn't turn over. I grew frustrated as I tried over and over again. I cussed out loud then headed back to the yard.

Madra walked over to me,

"What'd you forget?" she asked.

"Nothing my car won't start?"

"Wait, let me get Paul." She walked off and I stood aggravated.

Madra returned with Manny instead. "Let's go see if we can figure out the problem." He said then headed for the gate. I followed and Madra stayed behind.

"You coming?" I asked her.

"Nope," she smiled and walked away swiftly. I shook my head and walked to the gate where Manny waited holding it open for me.

I showed him to my car then he reached out his hands.

"What?"

"I need your keys?"

"Oh," I said handing him my keys and moving out of his way.

He tried to start my car, "you hear that clicking?" he asked.

"Yeah, what does it mean?"

"It's your battery."

"That battery is new."

"When did you get it?"

"About a month ago."

"Batteries are hardly ever new depending on where you purchase them, they take the old battery back for a reason."

"This is bullshit." I said as Manny handed me back my keys.

"I'm sure AutoZone is still open. I can take you to get a new one and I'll put it on for you."

I felt like a damsel that was just rescued. "I'd really appreciate that."

Manny popped my hood then walked away. He returned with two silver tools and removed my battery from my car.

"Come on, my truck is in the front."

I followed Manny to his truck and he opened the door for me then walked around to his side. I smiled as I realized it was the second door he held for me. *How cute* I thought to myself and laughed on the inside because I was sure that Madra had probably hinted to him some things that I liked from the list I created. I didn't believe that she didn't purposely invite him just to hook him up with me. This was a joke and so was he.

He drove a blue Titan and it was nice. I looked around like a kid, wanting to touch everything since I never really rode in trucks. "So Eliza, how old are you?" he asked.

"Twenty-eight, you?"

"Just made twenty-eight in February." He said.

"You have any kids?" he asked.

"No, why?" I said defensively as I felt he was surveying me to ask me on a date. I didn't need another distraction that I'd be ignoring in less than a week.

"It's just a question."

"Really, just cut the crap. What's your pity story?"

"What pity story?"

"I know this isn't just some big coincidence and Paul and Madra are just trying to distract me with yet another man with no good sense and a sob story of some broad doing him wrong."

Manny started to laugh, "You really need to chill out, and nobody is trying to hook us up. I don't need my friends to hook me up with anybody, when I want something I get it." He shook his head. "I'm just making conversation."

I had egg on my face as I sat there thinking of a comeback. I made the drive awkward with my assumptions as we rode in silence now.

We pulled up to AutoZone and walked up to the cashier. I gave her the year, make, model, and engine size of my car and she went and pulled a battery. Manny handed her the old one and his AutoZone card then lifted the new battery and headed for the exit as I paid. He waited and still held the door for me despite my attitude. I looked down as I passed him. He walked past me to open the truck door again and then I really felt bad.

"Look I'm sorry for snapping like I did."

"It's cool." He said then shut my door and walked over to his side placing the battery behind his seat like he had done the dead one.

I couldn't shake my embarrassment and felt the need to validate my reaction, "Madra has been hooking me up with all these different men and I'm just overwhelmed. She won't just let me grieve."

"Grieve? Somebody died?"

"I wish," I laughed, "it's a long story."

"Bad break-up?"

"Yeah…"

Manny had no more words as we drove back to my car.

He pulled up right beside my car then hopped out and walked around my side and helped me as I stepped down out of his truck. I gave him a half smile then watched him as he walked to my car to replace my battery. It took him less than fifteen minutes. He tossed me my keys and I got in and started it right up. I was relieved. "Thank you so much," I reached for my purse. "You have to let me give you something."

"Nah you good, just go home and grieve so you won't be snapping on people tomorrow," he joked. He laughed and walked back to his truck and pulled off.

I smiled, shut my door, turned my sappy music up loud, and headed back to my apartment.

~~*~*

I stood in front of my movie case looking for *Pride and Prejudice*. I loved movies that were set in the 1800's, *why couldn't men be more like those men*, I thought to myself. I pulled the movie from my shelf and headed into my living room to pop it in. I grabbed ranch dip, ruffle chips, olives, and sliced cheese from my cabinet as the previews played. I carried it all over to my sofa and plopped down on it, waiting for the movie to start.

My cell phone rang. I knew it was Madra, she was starting to aggravate me now. I loved my best friend, but I really needed to be alone.

"Yes Madra?"

"Don't give me that tone, what are you doing?"

"Watching a movie."

"Let me guess *Pride and Prejudice*, then you're going to watch *Love Jones, Disappearing acts, The Notebook, Bed of Roses, While You Were Sleeping, Sleepless in Seattle, Diary of a Mad Black Woman, The Lake House,* and *What's Love Got to Do with It*?"

"How do you figure?"

"Umm maybe because every time that piece of shit Tavis does something to hurt you, you repeat the same routine. Bet you have a chip in your hand."

I looked down at the chip in my hand and tossed it back into the bag. "Nope see how much you know and I'm watching *Boyz in the Hood*." I lied.

"Sure you are. I was calling to find out what you thought of Manny."

"He was nice."

"Just nice, you didn't get his number?"

"No Madra, and I wish you would stop trying to hook me up with people to get my mind off Tavis. I completely embarrassed myself today because of you."

"Well damn, I'm sorry. I just don't like to see you down."

"I know and I appreciate your caring, but I just want to be bitter for awhile…"

"Alright then I'll leave you be…for now." She laughed.

"Bye heifer," I laughed and we hung up. I stopped the movie and ejected it. I didn't need to be watching love stories. I needed something that would make me feel better. I stood and went back to my movie shelf. I was glad I didn't give away Tavis' porn collection.

Nice Job, Never been married, and no kids?

Eliza

Tears fell down my cheeks as Tavis entered me slowly, kissing the tears that fell from my eyes. My body shook as he stroked me. I released my pain through my finger tips and dug my nails into his back as he whispered "I'm so sorry baby" into my ear. This was all I needed; now everything would be alright as he went deeper into me, pushing his weight onto my body. Tavis knew exactly how to drive me crazy as he held his dick inside of me and my pussy pulsated against each vein. "I'll never hurt you again," he whispered and I was ready to let go all over him. I couldn't let him do this.

"Get off of me," I sobbed as he gripped my thighs and danced his dance between my legs. "No, Tavis stop," I choked on my tears as I pushed his chest. He was stronger than me. He silenced me with his lips against my lips. I pushed him away. "Tavis no!" I said now frantic as I thought about him being inside of another woman. I kicked and I screamed now as he bit down on my neck and restrained my wrist. I pushed my pelvis, still fighting against him. "STOP IT!" I screamed as loudly as I could and Tavis fell from the bed pulling me with him.

I hit the floor hard, wrapped up in my sheet. I sat up and looked around. My heart was beating fast as the flick still played on my TV screen. I took a deep breath and stood to stop the DVD, no more porn before bed for me. I grabbed my cell phone and looked at the time. I had two hours before work. Going back to sleep was not an option after that dream, so I decided to take a shower

and take myself to grab some breakfast from waffle house.
    I hopped into my car after showering and started my car up. The battery light was now on. I cussed and called Madra.
    "It's five in the morning girl what do you want?"
    "Do you or Paul have what's his face's number?"
    "You're going to have to be more specific."
    "The guy from the barbeque."
    "Oooh Manny, I knew you were feeling him, hold on let me get Paul's phone." I could hear Paul groan as she rolled over. "It's 504-282-0208."
    "Thanks." I said as I saved his number then hung up and called it.
    "This is Manny." He said wide awake.
    "Hi Manny this is Eliza, from the party yesterday…"
    "Hey what's up?"
    "I'm having an issue, my battery light is on."
    "Did you car start?"
    "Yes…"
    "Then it's probably your alternator."
    "How do you know that?"
    "I'm a mechanic. You think regular dudes just drive around with tools, but look, nobody is at my shop right now, so bring it to me and I'll test it for you."
    "Where is your shop located?"
    Manny gave me the address and I punched it into my GPS then hung up and headed his way. I prayed to Jesus that nothing happened while I drove.
    Manny was standing outside waiting when I pulled up. He directed me to a garage door then told me to shut off my engine. "Pop your hood!" he yelled and I

did as I was told as he walked over with something I guessed was used to test my alternator. It only took him a few minutes then he walked over to my window. That alternator is definitely bad.

"How much do those things cost?"

"For this car, I'd guess about 130."

"And labor?" I asked cautiously since I was still rebuilding my funds from that big bash for Tavis.

"Two hundred, but you do have another option."

"Which is?"

"This is a brand new car, so I'm guessing it's still under warranty, bring it back."

"I think that's what I'll do."

"You're draining it the more you drive it though, so unless you're bringing it right now I'd leave it parked."

"I have to go to work." I said frustrated.

"Calm down lil lady. Look, I only came in to do some paperwork. I can drop you off at work."

"You've already done enough."

"What can I say I'm a sucker for a damsel in distress, just let me get my keys."

"Alright fine, but at least let me treat you to breakfast."

"Will that make you feel better?" he smiled.

"It really would and I'm kind of still feeling the need to apologize for snapping and embarrassing myself."

He laughed, "Well in that case, breakfast it is."

I hopped out of my car and walked over to Manny's truck as he grabbed his keys. He opened the door for me and we headed off to waffle house.

It was close to empty when we got there. Tavis let me choose which side of the booth I wanted to sit in before he sat down. I grabbed my menu and looked over at him as he scanned his. I sat my menu down. "Can I ask you something?"

"Yeah what you got?"

"Is this just an act?"

"What?"

"The door opening and just courtesy in general?"

"Why would it be an act?"

"Because most men…"

"Uh uh don't you dare compare me to other men."

I smiled, "I'm sorry, it's just most…"

"Look, you're about to do it again."

I fell out laughing, "I can't help it."

"See that's where women mess up at. They put all men in a box expecting us all to be the same. There are a few exceptions you know."

"And I guess you're one of them right?"

"I sure am."

I laughed, "Okay I hear you."

There was silence for a moment. "Now that I think about it women just have a comparison issue period."

"Now what makes you say that?"

"Because y'all even compare yourselves to other women, especially when y'all get cheated on."

I put my head down and tried to mask my discomfort at the word cheat, but he noticed anyway.

"Oh damn my bad, I didn't mean to strike a nerve or anything."

"It's fine, I'm dealing."

Manny lowered his head to the level of mine, "are you?"

"I don't know."

"You want to talk about it?"

"Not really, I don't think it'll help much."

"I think it would, try me. Maybe I can give you the male perspective."

I laughed, "Unless you want to sit here patting me on the back while I gag on tears I suggest you change to the subject."

He smiled, "alright fine new subject then." He sat back in the booth, "what do you do for fun?"

"That's such a typical question."

"So, answer it."

I sighed and looked up, "well, I love to bowl and skate even though I suck at both, I love to go to poetry clubs, and that's about it."

"You are so boring." He laughed.

"I am not!" I smiled widely.

"I'm kidding, that's cool. I love doing all that stuff. I don't think there is anything that I don't like to do."

The waitress finally came over and took our order. I hadn't even noticed that it took her forever because I would have been showing out. Manny was good company.

"So what else do you like to do?"

"Are you seriously going to make me think?"

"We can talk about something more interesting."

"Okay then let's do that."

"Tell me about these distractions you brought up last night."

I laughed as the waitress sat our drinks down and walked away, "you don't want to hear about that."

"Yes I do, now tell me."

I twirled my drink around with my straw, "it's just something Madra came up with to keep me busy. I was really depressed after my ex."

"And how did this work exactly?"

I rolled my eyes and smiled, "well, Paul has all these lonely ass desperate friends apparently, excluding you obviously," I smiled, "and Madra introduces me to all of them I guess because we have misery in common."

"Are you miserable?" Manny asked me in a serious tone and it knocked the wind from me.

"I don't think I am."

"You need to know."

"Perhaps I am then. I'm still broken apart about the whole situation..." I swallowed back. "I don't know how to pick myself back up. I hate starting over."

"There's nothing wrong with starting over. Everything in our life starts over, we just pay more attention to the things that involve our emotions."

I sat silently and thought about what he said. "Well enough about me, tell me something about you."

He smiled, "I really wouldn't know what to tell. I'm single, I work, I don't have kids..."

"Hold on back up. You don't have kids?"

He laughed, "out of the three things I said that's the one thing you got?"

"Hell yeah, it's damn near impossible to find a man your age without a baby mama."

"Nah no baby mama's; I know what it's like to be a kid in a single parent home, so if I'm not going to make a woman my wife, I'm damn sure not going to make her a mother."

"I respect that." I sipped my drink. "So, you haven't met anyone you wanted to marry?"

"Nope, I haven't met a woman that can keep me interested enough to commit to forever. I mean I was in a long term relationship, but it was a routine. We were just comfortable with each other and never built anything. I started to feel kind of void. We hit a dead end."

Manny and I talked a bit more and ate our breakfast then he dropped me off to work and told me he'd pick me up. I walked into the office energized and ready to work. I removed my jacket and placed it on the back of my chair then walked into my bosses' office to start my routine.

"You have a 9:30 meeting and right after that a 10:45 with Mr. Jones."

"Feeling better are we?" my boss asked.

"Yes I am." I smiled and headed back to my desk.

I sat down and smiled. I had experienced temporary peace with Manny and I liked it. I logged onto my computer then searched the internet for the dealership where I purchased my car, so I could get that handled the moment I was off from work. Today was going to be a good day.

~~*~*

I pulled up to my apartment in my brand new candy apple red Hyundai Sonata. I liked this color so much better. I grabbed my purse and pressed the alarm on my key pad to lock and secure my car. I skipped up the steps humming the last song I had just heard on the radio and opened my door. I clicked on the light and my heart stopped as I jumped back and Tavis was sitting on my sofa. "What the…!" I grabbed my chest.

He stood up with his hands out, "I'm sorry I didn't mean to scare you."

I caught my breath, "why are you here?"

"I thought we should talk."

"Damn near three months later?" I pushed past him and walked through the kitchen to get to my bedroom.

"I made a mistake." He said as I dropped my purse on the bed and removed my jacket. "I'm so sorry Eliza."

"Sorry for what? Abandoning me or standing me up?" I flopped down on the bed in disbelief that he was standing right in my face.

"Both," he moved over to me.

"Don't come near me Tavis I can't promise that it's safe."

He stood where he was, "I got scared…"

I swung my head around and gave him a look that could kill then stood up slowly, I took a deep breath and folded my arms across my chest, "two months, almost three and you come back here to tell me you're sorry and you got scared?" I walked toward him slowly and he backed up, "do you have *any* FUCKING idea what I went through?!" My anger started to rise and I prepared to release my fury, "I cried! I bargained with myself! I waited day in and day out for you to walk through those doors!" My voice cracked as my anger was expressed through tears, "I stood alone in front of OUR friends and family and told them it was over!"

Tavis stood still and I took a swing at him. "You feel better now?" I hit him again. "Come on hit me until you feel better."

I hit him until I couldn't anymore, then he wrapped his arms around me.

"What do you want from me?" I sobbed.

"I want you to forgive me," he dug into his pocket and pulled out the ring that I threw at his mother, "I want you to put this on and never take it off again, I'm so sorry," he said as she slid the ring back onto my finger.

I looked down at it and up at him, "you need to leave."

"What?"

"You need to leave!" I snatched away from him and pushed. "Get out!" I pushed him hard as he apologized and protested. I shoved him until he was out of my apartment. I slammed the door in his face and ran into my bedroom and fell across my bed. I didn't know what the stronger feeling in my body was, my anger or my stupidity for wanting to take him back. I lay in my bed fully dressed and crying until I dozed off.

~~*~*

A hard knock at my front door woke me up. I shot up fast and looked around my room. "Shit!" I said as hurried to look for my phone. *10:30am* was across the screen. The knocking came again. I jumped up out of bed and ran to the door. I swung it open. "Manny what are you doing here?"

"Madra sent me."

"She gave you my address?"

"Yeah."

"Why?"

"Your boss called her and said you didn't come in today and you hadn't called and wasn't answering your phone."

"Why didn't she come herself?"

"Her kids doctor's appointments now would you quit drilling me and call your boss?"

"Shit, shit, shit," I said as I scrolled through my phone. I walked away to explain to my boss why I wasn't at work. I lied and told him my mother was sick and I lost track of time taking care of her. He wasn't upset. I hung up and headed back to where Manny stood, "well close the door behind you." I said as I walked into my room and crawled back into bed. Manny walked in behind me. "That was your signal to leave." I said.

"I would have left, but you still have on the clothes you wore yesterday, so umm…"

"I was tired."

"You were tired or taking a trip back down memory lane?" he reached his hand beneath my pillow and pulled my ring from my finger. He was clearly observant.

I sat up.

"This wasn't on your finger yesterday." He said.

"What do you care?"

"I don't, but I can tell you this won't help you get over him." He tossed the ring on my mattress and I grabbed it and placed it back on my finger.

"Thanks for the advice," I laid back down and pulled my blanket back over my head and Manny

snatched the entire blanket from my body. "What are you doing?!"
"Get up."
"For what?"
"Because Madra sent me to check on you, now if you want me to call her and tell her your still in here crying over your ex I can."
"You are more annoying than she is!" I hopped out of bed and stomped to the bathroom to turn on the shower. Manny laughed as I slammed the door.

Emmanuel

I invited myself into Eliza's kitchen as I waited for her to come out of the bathroom. I opened her cabinets and all of her canned goods had the label faced forward and they were lined neatly in rows. I shook my head and closed the cabinet then walked into her living room where she had a CD rack. Her CD's were in alphabetical order by artist. This girl was too damn organized. I headed back into her bedroom. I opened her drawers and everything was folded neatly. I pushed everything around and messed it up. I walked over to her closet and opened the door and laughed when I noticed it was arranged by color. I pulled my phone from my pocket and snapped a picture of it. I had never seen anything like that in my life. I moved a few of the shirts out of place then shut the door.

My phone rang as I eased it back into my pocket, "hello."

"Hey is she okay?" Madra asked.
"Yeah she just overslept and didn't hear her phone."
"Where is she let me talk to her?"
"She's in the shower."
"Okay good. Would you get that girl out of the house please?"
"Already on it, this place is depressing." I looked around.
"What do you mean?"
"It's so damn clean and organized. I feel like I'm in a library and I should be whispering."
Madra laughed, "Yeah, she goes overboard with cleaning and organizing, but look thanks so much. I have to get back in this office."
"No biggie, talk to you later." I hung up and looked for more things to possibly destroy.

Eliza

I showered and realized I didn't bring any changing clothes into the bathroom. I wrapped a towel around myself and poked my head out to see if Manny was still in my room. He wasn't. I tiptoed out and saw him standing right by my desk. "Would you get out?" I dropped my free hand against my side.
He turned around and grinned, "My bad." He walked toward me to leave.
I closed the door behind him and walked over to find something to wear. When I opened the door I noticed a few things out of place. I grabbed a t-shirt and

slammed the door then walked over to my dresser to get a pair of jeans. I dressed then headed into the living room. "Okay I'm clean and dressed, happy?"

"I was happy with the towel," he smiled.

"Yeah yeah now get out and go give your report to my best friend." I pushed him toward the door and he pushed all his weight back on my hands making it harder for me.

"What's up with the organization?"

"Excuse me?"

"The CD's, the food cabinet, your closet…"

"You went through my things?" *That's why my clothes were messed up* I thought to myself.

"I was bored what else was I supposed to do?"

"Ugh!" I pushed him harder.

He spun around me, "Come spend the day with me."

"Don't want to, have a nice day."

"I'm not taking no for an answer, you need to get out of this house."

"I'll take a walk later."

"I was trying to avoid this." Manny turned and lifted me from the floor.

"Put me down!" I kicked, but he ignored me and grabbed my purse and keys. He locked my door with me over his shoulder and headed down the steps. He opened his truck and tossed me in.

"I need to get my driver's license from my car."

"For what? I'm driving today."

"I still need identification on me."

"What kind of woman doesn't have her license in her purse?"

"One that might leave her purse somewhere, I don't know, but I need it."

"Alright I'll get it, where is it?"

"The glove compartment."

Manny walked over to my car and opened the door. He got inside and started it up. He turned up his face and ejected the sad CD I had made for myself then he opened my glove compartment and retrieved my license. He locked the door then headed back over to me.

"You had to turn on my car to open my glove compartment?" I asked.

"No I just wanted to see what it sounded like."

"And my CD?" He held it up and broke it in half.

"Why did you do that?!"

"Listening to that will keep your mind right where it is, better listen to some rap or something." He dropped the broken CD to the ground then dangled my keys in front of me and I reached for them, but he placed them in his pocket. "If you try to get these out of my pocket I'm going to scream rape," he said and closed the door then walked over to his side. I couldn't help but laugh and shake my head.

Manny started the car, "Just think of me as your stand in best friend today." He winked then pulled off.

Optional, but sexy tattoos and own place

Eliza

We pulled up to his shop and he parked around back. Once we got inside he handed me a pair of clear glasses that looked kind of like goggles, "I am not wearing those."

"Yes, you are now put them on."

I rolled my eyes and put the ugly glasses on my face. "You are my employee for the day." He handed me a little scanner tool.

"What's this for?"

"This is how you write up the customers."

"Are you seriously about to put me to work?"

"Yep, might teach you how to work on a car or two if you're lucky."

I looked down at my finger nails. I was not getting my hands dirty. I walked over to the cash register to learn how to use it. "Where is your cashier today?"

"She called off."

"How long have you had your business?"

"About a year," He said as he changed his shirt right in front of me as if I wasn't standing there. I took a deep breath as I counted his eight pack. He turned as he pulled his shirt down and I caught a glimpse of the tattoos that covered his back then bit my lip. I traced the tribal markings that stretched from shoulder to shoulder and down his back in dark black ink. I needed a fan and a cool drink of water. I looked away so he wouldn't catch me as he pulled his shirt down and adjusted it. I had not had an orgasm in months and that night with porn was an epic fail. I shook my head at myself as I thought to myself that Manny was a man, a real man, he had the

Idris Alba stance with the Hill Harper swag and it was all topped off with the Denzel charm. It helped that he loved to get his hands dirty. I took a deep breath. "How long are we going to be here?" I asked.

"Just until the manager gets in, he usually comes at about one." He said then headed to help work on a car. I watched him as he carried tools and tires back and forth. Sweat dripped from his skin and I drooled. He was the epitome of sexy. *He must workout* I thought to myself.

I liked that fact that he got dirty with his men, he didn't just sit in his office all day pushing out orders.

"Ma'am, ma'am" an elderly black lady walked up to me and I snapped out of my lust trance.

"What can I do for you?"

She handed me her ticket and I checked her out then continued to gaze through the cut out that separated the shop from the inside office.

Manny showed me around the shop. He pulled down tires showing me the difference in good ones and bad ones then we walked over to where another mechanic worked to look under the hood.

"Let me look at this one for a minute." He said to his tech and grabbed a clipboard.

"What's wrong with this one?"

"It needs a tune up."

"Yeah because I know exactly what that is."

"You always this damn flip?" he asked.

"Most of the time," I said then looked under the hood like I knew what I was doing.

"Well smart ass that is the motor," he said pointing at a metal part. "Beneath it are three plugs that need to be changed. The other three are right here." He pointed at three wires in front of the motor. "Then you have the air filter, fuel filter, the oxygen sensor, distributor cap, rotor, and PCV valve that need to be changed." He licked his lips and looked over at me to see if I was paying attention.

I was definitely focused. I loved a man that loved his craft.

"Touch it." He said pointing at something dirty under the hood.

"Not."

"Why not, don't want to get your hands dirty?"

"That's exactly why."

Manny grabbed my hand and placed it on the motor and I popped his arm.

He laughed then explained what a tune-up was for, and then he showed me how to check and change my oil. Maybe Manny wasn't bad company after all.

"You ready to get out of here?"

"Yes."

"Cool, I'll meet you at the truck," he tossed me his keys and stepped into his private office.

Manny joined me in his truck moments later and we pulled off, "where are we going?"

"My place, I need to shower."

I swallowed back. I wasn't sure I wanted to be in his place, but I really had no other choice. We rode and listened to the music.

~~*~*

Manny lived in a beautiful studio apartment. It was filled with black art. I was impressed. "Did you decorate?"

"No my ex did."

Figures I thought to myself as I walked around looking at the beautiful art on his wall. I heard the shower run as he cut it on and I took a seat on his black leather sofa. I hated leather. It looked nice, but definitely was not comfortable. This was strictly for show.

Manny took fifteen minutes in the shower and another fifteen getting dressed. He carried his shoes into the living room and sat them by the sofa then walked over to his fridge "you thirsty?"

"No, I'm fine, but thanks." He pulled a sprite from his fridge and popped the can open guzzling it down. He then joined me on the sofa.

"Can I ask you something?"

"If I say no, you're just going to ask anyway."

"You're right," he smiled, "what is it that hurts so bad about losing a relationship?"

"You've never had your heart-broken?"

"Can't say that I have. I mean I've had my feelings hurt and been used, but never anything devastating."

"No wonder you're so optimistic." I shook my head, "what about your ex, did you love her?"

"Yeah, but that was all it was, we didn't see a future together so we split."

"So there was no spark, nothing that made you want to stay?"

"Nope."

"Wow and how old are you again?"

Manny laughed, "Not everyone experiences love early on in life and if they do it's puppy love, some people don't fall *in love* until their well in their thirties and forties."

"How would you even know the difference?" I looked over at Manny and he faced me, catching my eyes and making my heart race. He sat his drink on the floor and locked his fingers together, "I imagine that I'd feel it somewhere past my heart. It would be a soul-shaking experience. I'd…" he looked up, "I'd feel overprotective of my own love for her and I'd always be happy no matter what we go through. The feeling would be something beyond wanting or desire, it would feel like an excruciating need, right?" he shook his head to answer his own question as I lingered on his every word. "You've felt that before right?"

I swallowed and came back to reality, "can't say that I have."

"Then why were you getting married?"

"We had history and I loved him…"

"What exactly does history mean if most of it is bad memories?"

"It wasn't all bad…"

"But mostly right?"

I didn't say a word.

He stood up, "come on."

I stood and followed him back to his truck. "Where are we going now?"

"You'll see."

I hopped into the truck again blind to our destination. Memories of Tavis rolled around in my brain, opening old wounds and making the fresh ones deeper. *Why was I about to marry him?* He had stressed me out so much over the years. I guess I was just happy that he gave me a ring and wanted to make me his wife and not one of the trifling sluts I caught him with. I lived inside my thoughts until the truck came to a complete stop.

"A gym?" I asked.

"Boxing."

"Why'd you bring me here, I don't fight?"

"According to Madra you have a mean right hook."

I laughed to myself as I pictured Tavis' mom hitting the floor at the church. Manny opened the door and I stepped down and followed him into the boxing club.

"Randy!" he yelled as he walked through the doors.

An older black man stepped from the back and walked toward us. "Boy quit yelling in my gym," he smiled and faced me. "Who is this beautiful young lady?"

"This is Eliza."

"Nice to meet you Eliza, I'm Randy."

"Quit drooling all over her old man and get the lady some gloves."

"Don't get embarrassed boy," he joked and walked away in a boxing stance and swinging at the air. He returned with black gloves that fit my hands perfectly.

I was happy that I had on flats today as I walked behind Manny to a body bag. "What am I about to do?"

"Beat the shit out of this bag."

"Why?"

"It'll make you feel better, you have to release some of that frustration and anger."

"Who says I'm angry?"

"What was the first thought that came to mind when you found out about your boy stepping out on you?"

"Murder…"

"Okay your angry, now hit the bag."

I took a breath and swung. The bag barely moved and Manny laughed. "See I'm not angry enough."

"First off you're not even standing right."

"What's wrong with my stance?" I looked down at my legs with a puzzled expression.

Manny walked from behind the bag and stood behind me. I tensed up and he moved close, pushing up against me and sliding his hands down my arms to position my upper body. "Put your right foot forward." He said into my ear as his pelvis pushed on me. I could feel a bulge in his pants as he moved me. I thought to myself *if his package was that big when it's soft then my gawd!* I tried to focus as he stepped back then walked back behind the bag. "Now close your eyes and think about lover boy and get angry."

I let flashes of Tavis flood through my mind. I felt sadness then I felt fury. I opened my eyes and I hit the bag with all my might.

"There you go, hit it again."

I let loose on that bag as Emmanuel held it. I imagined it was Tavis' face and I just kept punching until I wore myself out.

Emmanuel

"Thank you." She said as I pulled up to her building. She looked relieved but I could tell that just the thought of walking back into her apartment depressed her. I didn't understand why I was doing all that I was doing for her like I had known her all my life and promised to protect her. Something about helping her feel better filled that void in me that gave me endless nights without sleep.

Her cell phone rang and she laughed after looking at the caller ID.

"Somebody you don't want to talk to?"

"Normally I'd say yes, but I was just thinking I was going to have to sleep alone again tonight and now one of my distractions is calling."

"You don't have to go inside and be alone you know or have a night cap with a dude who's company you don't really want."

"Hold up a second." She said answering her phone. I felt a twinge of jealousy, but I shook it off. I listened as she told her distraction that'd she'd call him back in a few then hung up.

"So, where would I go?" she asked me with sadness in her voice.

I had lost my mind as her sad eyes looked up at me like a puppy that needed to be stroked, "stay with me…"

She snickered, "you're a stranger and you live in a studio where would I sleep?"

"Girl you've been with me all day and I bought you food, so technically you owe me some booty, but since I'm a nice guy I'll let you slide." I joked and she laughed. Her smile was infectious and much more appealing than the frown she wore when *he* was on her mind. "But seriously, you can sleep in my bed and I'll take the couch."

"I don't know."

"You need a new environment. You don't have to stay long," I tried to convince her still not understanding why myself. I adjusted in my seat, "It only takes twenty-two days to start a habit, take twenty-two days for you then come back and see how you feel. What do you really have to lose?"

"Nothing I guess…"

"Truth or dare?"

"Huh?"

"Truth or dare?"

"Truth."

"Is he on your mind right now?"

She swallowed back hard then nodded her head.

"Go get your stuff Eliza. Think of it as a day that never ends."

She didn't protest. She eased out of my truck and I watched her as she headed up her steps switching that *thang* behind her side to side.

I waited as she sat her bags outside then I hopped out of my truck to retrieve them. This was interesting even to me.

Eliza

I placed all of my bags near Manny's bed. This felt too weird. I was really starting to wonder what was wrong with me. Here I was an independent woman with everything that I needed in the apartment of a man I barely knew.

"What do you want to do tonight?" he asked.
"Sleep."
"Hell no, out of the question."
"What am I supposed to do then?"
"Want to go out?"
"I don't go to clubs."
"What do you do then?"
"Stay home…"
"What? Why?"
"Because clubs are full of half-naked, young, desperate women, and the pitiful men that pursue them."
"Not all clubs are like that."
"I haven't been convinced in the years that I did go."
"Okay then we'll stay in tonight, but eventually within these next 22 days you're going to a club."
"Fine."
I sat down on the sofa and kicked my shoes off. Manny sat down in a single chair and stared at me.
"Why are you staring?" I looked around awkwardly.
"No reason," he continued to stare. "What's your full name?" he asked.
"Eliza Campbell, why, what's yours?"
"Emmanuel Levi."
"You have a very powerful name."
"Thank you, so Eliza Campbell what is it that you are looking for I mean if you were looking…"
"Is this the 21 questions game?"
"No, I'm just getting to know you. You're the one who called me a stranger earlier."
"I did, didn't I?" I smiled. "Fine," I got up and went over to my purse. I pulled out the list I created for

what I wanted in a man and handed it over to Emmanuel. He sat and unfolded the slip of paper then read it. "A man that does not exist..." I said as I sat back down.

He laughed, "You think this is hard to find?"

"Yeah, a man might have some of those qualities but usually he lacks the best ones."

He shook his head, "and women say men are all the same. If you got this man you wouldn't know what to do with him."

"Why do you say that?"

"Because women get a good thing and then make a list of what should be wrong with a man."

"That is not true!" I moved to the edge of the sofa.

"It's very true, y'all think too damn much."

"What do you know about women anyway, you've never even been in love?"

"I know love has no real standard. You love all or nothing about a person, good or bad, qualities on and off this list." He shook the paper in hand. "You know what this is?"

"What?"

"It's expectation. Expectations are bad. Have you ever heard the quote *if you expect nothing from anybody, you're never disappointed*?"

I shook my head *no* then sat silently thinking.

"Why do you think your ex cheated on you?" he asked.

"Because he's a dog that obviously can't commit."

Manny shook his head, "all men are dogs baby and they all can be tamed."

"Yeah, then what did I do wrong then Mr. KnowItAll."

"I don't know it all, I'm just a man and number one you're too damn perfect. Number two you forgave him one too many times, people only do what you allow them to. I'm not saying that second chances are bad, but usually the second time around they already know what they can get away with and they will test you."

"Okay I agree with second chances thing, but perfect, I am not."

"Yes the hell you are, you hold yourself up to this ridiculous standardand I'm sure you held lover boy up to the same one. Did you take him with you to get his eyebrows waxed?"

"What does appearance have to do with this?"

"Everything, do you ever just take a risk, let your hair down from the safety of that ponytail."

"I take it down to wash it."

"Exactly."

"Men don't like perfect women, maybe a gay dude, but a real man loves a flawed woman, flawed women are real and more like us. If you're perfect what you need us for?"

I smacked my lips, "Whatever."

"I'm serious, okay, truth or dare?"

"This again," I exhaled.

"Yep, now answer."

"Dare, see I took a risk."

"I dare you not to shave your legs for a week." He smiled.

"And if I don't accept?"

"Hmm then you have to cut your hair."

"That's just cruel!"

He shrugged his shoulders, "I don't play fair."
I sighed, "Fine…deal."
"I'm not done," he grinned. "You have to wear shorts too."
"This is torture and not going to happen…"
"I'm just trying to loosen you up."
I shook my head.
"I need to ask you one more thing…"
I looked Emmanuel in the eyes and waited for his question.
"What is it that you do for you?"
"I take care of myself."
"Something that doesn't involve money."
"I don't know. I guess I care more about the dreams of others and what they like to do and I kind of forget about my own."
"What are you good at?"
"You really want to know?"
"Yeah, humor me."
"Writing fiction."
"Bullshit."
"Really, I've been writing it since I was a little girl. I used to post teasers online for my friends, but once I discovered boys I stopped."
"Why don't you start again?"
"I can't…"
"Yes you can Eliza."
"I don't know what to write about anymore."
"You live in a story every day."
"I can't seem to get my words past my pain."
Emmanuel sighed, "the best time to do anything creative is when you're in pain."

"What are you trying to do save me from myself? I don't need to be saved, especially not by some man I just met."
"I'm not trying to save you. I'm nobody's superhero. No woman really needs to be saved. You can save your damn self. I'm just trying to be here, be supportive." Emmanuel stood, "I swear women don't know what the hell they want. Only you can save yourself Eliza, but sometimes it's easier when you have help." Emmanuel didn't push me anymore after that. "Get some sleep, it's going to be a long 22 days." He said and walked away.

I rolled my eyes then headed to shower. I packed a bag strictly for pajamas. I pulled out the first thing at the top and headed to the bathroom. I showered longer than I needed to. When I was done I headed to bed. Manny laid on the sofa reading with his lamp on.

"Eliza…" he said as I walked towards the bed.
"Yeah," I said stopping in my tracks.
"What is that you have on?"
"Boxers and a t-shirt."
"I know that, but whose boxers?"
I spoke in a low tone, "Tavis'."

Emmanuel took a deep breath and stood from the sofa, dropping his magazine. He walked over to me and stopped, "take them off."
"What? No, why?"
"How do you expect to move forward if you're sleeping in your past? You already stuck with the memories, don't keep the stuff attached to memories; take them off."

I stood staring at him.

"You're shirt is long, it's not like I can see your lady friend." He said with a grin on his face.

I rolled my eyes and pulled the boxers off. He snatched them from my hands as soon as they were off my body. He went over to his drawer and pulled out a pair of his boxers and tossed them at me.

"What else you have in my apartment that belongs to him."

I didn't answer.

"Don't make me go through your stuff." He put one hand on his hip.

I walked over to my pajama bag and pulled out his t-shirt, a pair of basketball shorts, and one more pair of boxers then handed it all to Manny. He tossed it all in the trash then brought the trash out to the dumpster.

"You can go jump in behind it if you want." He said sarcastically.

"Jackass." I said under my breath.

"What? I couldn't hear what you said."

"I said goodnight."

This man new me for a few hours and thought he had me all figured out.

Considerate

Eliza

"You know I'm going to kill you right." I reprimanded Madra as I sipped on my Arnold Palmer.

"What did I do?"

"Sending Emmanuel to my house."

"Who is Emmanuel?"

"Manny."

"Oh that's his full name, that is powerful."

"That's what I said, but anyways you know I'm staying with him right?"

"What? Did I miss something?"

"It's kind of a long story, but yeah I'll be at his place for twenty-two days and you'll never guess what happened."

"Y'all slept together!"

"No!"

"Oh, well what?"

"Tavis popped up."

"What! What did he have to say for himself? I better not see that mother…"

"Would you calm down and let me talk."

"I'm listening." She said reluctantly.

I sighed, "I hate that I love him so much I swear. I kicked him out, but the moment I did I wanted to let him right back in."

"You better not. I promise I'll disown you E, enough is enough."

"Tell my heart that."

"Put the bitch on the phone." She joked and we both laughed. "I don't even want to talk about Tavis, give me more juice on that fine ass Emmanuel."

"I'm about to call your husband."

"You wouldn't."

"Would," I laughed. "He is crazy. He told me I'm too perfect."

"I think I have to agree with him."

My mouth dropped, "Madra!"

"What? I'm just saying girl. I thought women who overdid the weave and make-up were insecure, sometimes I have to wonder if your perfect ass is insecure too."

"Why would you say that?"

"Because you try too hard to keep everything together E, it's okay to be a little messed up and vulnerable."

"I hate both of y'all."

"No you hate the truth. You own four pair of jeans and a few t-shirts. Hell I hate to shop with you because you're always looking for work clothes as if there is nothing else in the world to do, but work. Relax and let go girl. I'm married and I have more fun than you."

"Forget you my food just came, I'll talk to you later."

"Love you!"

"Whatever, love you too." We hung up and I fed my face and my thoughts.

I ran my hand over my ponytail. I liked my ponytail. I liked my suits too. I was a woman and liked to dress like one. I liked being neat and sophisticated. I poked out my lips. I thought about Emmanuel bringing up how neat my apartment was. I didn't consider that perfect. I just liked to be organized. How could organization be a problem? I was going to prove to Emmanuel and Madra that I could let loose.

Emmanuel

I carried that stupid list around in my pocket all day. It was burning a hole in my pocket like it was money. Women did some stupid shit. I wish I would catch one of my boys sitting around and making a list to find the perfect chick. Women did the most when it came to men always trying to figure out the inevitable, always comparing men and women as if we are so different. Always trying to force men to be something they never will be. There was a list of *always*, now that was a list she could create.

I had the right mind to make her a list of the things women should work on before making their impossible standard list that no man would live up to. Number one would be getting pissed off and expecting us to read their mind instead of just telling us what the hell was wrong. Second would be nagging, then insecurity and paranoia.

I stopped my own thoughts trying to figure out why I was so upset in the first place. It was just a stupid piece of paper that belonged to a woman that was not mine.

I headed back to my office and sat down at my desk. My cell phone rang. It was Ms. Perfect. "Hey, what's up?"

"You busy?"
"Nah just taking a break."
"I want to go to the club tonight."
"You do?"
"Yep, so it better be a nice one."
"No problem. See you when you get off."
"Umm are you ever going to let me go get my own car?"
"No for what, so you can back out of our agreement?"
She laughed, "No, so you can stop driving me around like I'm Ms. Daisy."
"If you're Ms. Daisy you need to ride in the back seat when I pick you up."
She laughed again, "Bye Emmanuel."
Although she was the way that she was, she had an infectious personality and something in me wanted to know every part of her.

~~*~*

"You like?" she said as she spun around. "And I didn't shave my legs." She smiled.
Eliza shocked me as she walked out of the bathroom in a little, strapless navy blue dress that hugged every curve she owned and grey heels. Her hair was still in a ponytail, but I didn't care since my attention was elsewhere. "You clean up nicely." I said.
"Oh bite me."
"Don't tempt me." I said as I walked to the front door and held it open. "Ladies first," I said as I watched Eliza walk past me. Her perfume welcomed itself into my nose and I was lost as I looked her up and down and

managed to keep control of myself. I had never had a woman in my apartment that I wasn't trying to sex before and I was starting to struggle with it before we were good into the twenty-two days. I shook it off.

We drove out to the club and I found it hard to make conversation as I drooled at her thick thighs. I let the music be our communication until we reached the club.

I found a decent parking spot then hopped out to help Eliza from my truck. I held my hand against her waist to make sure she was okay walking in her heels. I'd never let a woman fall and embarrass herself. We headed toward the club.

"Is that Paul and Madra waving at us?" she asked.

"Yeah I invited them, is that cool?"

"Yeah, that's fine," she smiled and walked over to her friend.

"Girl look at you!" Madra said as she circled Eliza.

Eliza blushed and we all headed into the club. I made sure I picked a nice grown and sexy place so Eliza could see that all clubs didn't carry the same definition of a good time. It was a mixed crowd and the music varied as well. I placed my hand on the small of her back and moved her toward the bar. "What do you want to drink?"

"Anything fruity." She responded.

"Hell no, I'm getting you a real drink, who are you trying to impress woman Jesus? He died for your sins already."

"I don't drink!" she yelled over the music.

"You're drinking tonight!"

The bartender walked over to us and I ordered two crown and cokes. I waited then tipped her and handed a cup to Eliza. She sniffed the glass then sipped it.

"This is gross!" her face was scrunched.

"Drink it!" I said as I placed my hand below her glass and pushed it upward to make her down it then I ordered her another one.

After about four of those Eliza was on her feet taking over the dance floor and posing for the camera each time that I positioned it to snap. Madra and Paul said they had never seen her have so much fun as they danced around her and jumped in on a few photos.

As the night came to an end the music slowed down. "Dance with me," Eliza said boldly as she grabbed my hand and pulled me to the dance floor. She was toasted. She laid her head in my chest and I rocked her side to side slowly as Lalah Hathaway's *forever, for always, for love* shook the floors of the club. I found myself glued to her body as she leaned against me. I had not slow danced with a woman since prom. I couldn't help myself as we danced. My hands began to explore her body, moving up and down as she swayed her hips. Eliza turned pushing her ass against me. I wrapped my arms around her and nestled my face into her neck, inhaling the perfume that still lingered. I twirled her back around and pulled her into me. She looked up and I looked down and for a moment it felt like she was mine and strangely I liked the idea.

Eliza was done after that song, barely able to stand. I lifted her from her feet and carried her from the club as Madra and Paul followed. "Y'all get home safe." I said as I headed off in the opposite direction.

"Take care of my friend!" Madra yelled.

I placed Eliza into the truck and she did not budge. I laughed and shook my head. She was beautiful even when she was messed up. I ran around to the other side and took us back to my place.

I carried her inside and laid her across my bed and removed her shoes. I walked over to my drawer and pulled out a t-shirt then walked back over to her and pulled it over her dress. I slid my hand beneath the t-shirt and unzipped her dress to remove it so she could sleep comfortably. I pulled the blanket over her body and lingered a moment as she slept. I pulled my phone from my pocket and snapped her picture. I kissed her forehead then headed for the sofa.

God-fearing and funny

Eliza

My head pounded as I sat up in bed and reached to shut off the alarm that beeped on the clock next to me. I looked down and noticed I was wearing a t-shirt. I grabbed both of my breasts then looked to the side of me where Emmanuel stood making coffee.

"Good morning." He said enthused.

"Morning," I replied in a raspy voice that scared me. "What happened last night?"

"You had fun. You don't remember anything?"

I shook my head *no*. Emmanuel walked toward me holding a coffee cup.

"Drink this you'll feel better."

"This is why I don't drink."

"From what I was told last night you should drink more often."

"Don't listen to a word Madra or Paul says."

"They said they've never seen you the way you were last night."

"Did I dance on the bar or something?"

"Almost." he laughed.

"Shut up." I stood from the bed. "I need to get dressed for work."

"Me too."

"Who put this shirt on me?"

"I did."

"Did you rape me?"

He laughed, "no."

"I'm shocked; most men would have taken advantage of me."

"There you go with that most men stuff again. Let's just separate these categories now, so we don't have to have this conversation again." He headed to pour himself a cup of coffee. "Real men have self control, fake men rape women, and lil boys and sociopaths slip mickies in their drinks. If I'm going to take advantage of a woman she's going to be fully aware so she can remember how good it was."

I tooted my lips, "Cocky ass."

"I'm not cocky, I just don't half step and I can give you references."

I shut the bathroom door on Emmanuel and he laughed loudly.

Emmanuel knocked on the door as I brushed my teeth. "What?"

"Truth or dare?"

"Truth."

"You brush your teeth naked."

"False, now get away from the damn door."

I could hear him laughing as he walked away. He was such a pest. I stepped out of the bathroom and he was fully dressed and cooking.

"You can cook?" I asked.

"Yeah, how do you think I survive here alone?"

"I don't know maybe you go and have it your way."

"Haha whatever, come get your breakfast."

I walked over and grabbed my food. He had turkey bacon, eggs, and cheese on toast. I chowed down like I had missed several meals. Drinking really made you hungry. I got dressed after eating then gathered my things and watched Emmanuel out of the corner of my eye, grinning at the fact that he had the opportunity to do as he wanted with me, but didn't hop at the opportunity. I respected him for that.

"You ready?" He asked as he tucked his wallet into his back pocket.

"Yeah." I responded and headed for the door. I stopped in my steps as I realized the day. "Can you bring me to bible study tonight?"

"Bible study?"

"Yeah."

"Can I come too?"

I gave him a look of confusion, "you want to come to bible study with me?"

"Yeah, something wrong with that?"

I smiled, and headed outside, "not at all."

It had taken me an entire year of begging and persuasion to get Tavis to come to bible study with me, then another three months to get him to a Sunday service. He never really paid attention, but somehow I convinced myself to be satisfied with his presence even if the lessons weren't filling his spirit the way that they did mine. With each passing minute I was learning the value of my relationship with Tavis wasn't what I thought it was. Maybe I was that woman that Emmanuel said I was, changing a man to the definition of what I thought was appropriate, trying to make him perfect.

~~*~*

Work was slow and steady as usual. I played on the internet and Madra teased me through a chat about my drunken night at the club. She swore up and down that something was going to happen with Manny and I, but I just did not see it or maybe I just didn't want to.

Mr. One and Five blew my phone up while I sat at work, but I didn't answer. I thought they'd all stop calling by now, but they didn't. Even Mr. Two called trying to apologize about his atheist beliefs. Some men would say anything if they thought they could get some. I didn't knock anyone for their beliefs, but on a romantic level we could never be.

Work was finally over and Manny was in front of my job at four on the dot. He had not been late once picking me up. We grabbed something to eat and chatted then we headed off to bible study.

Emmanuel and I sat in bible study as the pastor went on and on about forgiveness. It was definitely a lesson I needed because I was still struggling with forgiving Tavis. It was hard to let God handle my battle. I wanted revenge in the worse way, but it just wasn't me to take it. I'd just be bitter until the end.

My eyes traveled to Emmanuel often as he nodded his head in agreement with the pastor and praised so openly. I was impressed. I did not see him as a man of faith. He just kept on shocking me.

It started to rain as bible study went on. I prayed that it would be over once it was done, because I was not in the mood to wash my hair and it wasn't time. My prayers were answered as the sound of the rain lifted and bible study came to an end. We all held hands as we prayed and for some reason I felt nervous as Emmanuel held my hand. I listened to the prayer with my eyes opened as I looked down at the way our fingers were locked together.

I said my goodbyes to my church members then headed for the exit. Manny held the door, as usual. I gave

him a polite smile and stepped outside. "It feels nice out here."
"Doesn't it, let's take a walk." Manny suggested.
"Now?"
"Yeah, right now." Manny walked as if he knew where he was going. "Question time," he said.
"Oh boy. Go ahead."
"Before you created that retarded list, what kind of man did you want?"
"Hmm I don't know..."
"Yes you do."
"Well this may sound kind of retarded, but I'm obsessed with 19th century men."
"The goofy looking dudes in white wigs and capris pants?" He laughed.
I laughed along with him, "They're called knee breeches fool and that was in the 18th century. They moved up to tights and dress pants in the 19th century." I laughed. "I didn't dig the style, but the way they respected women was admirable."
"Women could still be respected now, but most of them don't respect themselves."
"I respect myself."
"One in a million, women have gotten so independent now that they are insulted by a man who opens doors. They either don't say thank you or tell you they have hands and can do it themselves."
I smiled, "I know, I can't even argue with that." I listened as our feet hit the pavement. "I'm still a sucker for that kind of thing though; the hand kissing, the standing when a woman enters or leaves a room...everything was so different back then, people

actually cared about morality, manners, marriage, and education."

"Oh, I know what you like, well stop right here." He placed his hand in my path and started unbuttoning his work shirt.

"What are you doing?" I laughed as he removed his top shirt and walked over to a little puddle of water that we were about to cross and placed his shirt over it. I shook my head.

"Don't want those sexy toes to get all wet."

"You are a clown you know that, now your shirt is ruined."

"That shirt has had worse things happen to it; you forget I'm beneath cars most of the day."

I nodded my head in agreement as I laughed and stepped on his shirt to continue walking.

"You said something about people caring about marriage," Manny said.

"Yeah…"

"Do you care about marriage?"

I stopped in my steps to think about it then I looked up at him, "Do you?"

"I do, I want what comes with it if it happens."

"And what's that?"

"Everything, the struggle, the trust, the honesty, the commitment, I want the works, so I never get bored."

"I used to want that. I'm not sure I'll ever be able to let someone in that deep again and accept a ring from them." I started to move forward again.

"We just left bible study woman, don't you know the tongue is powerful. You have to speak what you want into existence. Why would you want to shut yourself off from something so beautiful?"

"You know why…"

"So you don't think you'll ever love again is what your telling me?"

"Probably not."

"Love can't be controlled, it just happens."

I agreed.

"Who was your first love?" he asked.

I smiled, "Aiden Hensley…"

"Wrong."

"How am I wrong?"

Emmanuel grabbed my shoulder and stopped me then turned me around and lifted me swiftly up on his hip like a child that weight no more than ninety pounds. I wrapped my arms around his neck and my legs around his back so I wouldn't fall. I had no words.

"Who was the first man to hold you like this and look at you like you were the most beautiful thing in the world?"

My heart was still racing from him lifting me so quickly without warning, "My daddy…" I said as I looked into his eyes and he looked into mine.

"I bet you felt safe there."

I shook my head yes as I thought about how much I loved my father before he left. I was the child that liked to be carried and he would never put me down.

"He rocked you in his arms to put you to sleep, he rubbed your back, and he laid your head on his shoulder…" Emmanuel placed me back on my feet, but we never broke our stare."I imagine that's what the right kind of love should feel like. That should be the man you want to marry."

I wanted to kiss Emmanuel's lips at that moment. Strangely he felt like the man that I was supposed to love, but I dare not utter those words. I turned and started to walk slowly again. I needed to catch my breath.

Emmanuel cracked a few more jokes and asked a few more questions. I even asked a few of my own. He gained more and more of my respect and my belief that he was definitely not like most men. We found our way back to his truck and then back to his place. My mind was at ease and my heart was working against me, leaning in an unexpected direction.

~~*~*

I didn't say much once we got back to his place because I couldn't stop thinking about that moment we shared. Emmanuel was just supposed to be a friend, a twenty-two day getaway, but here I was making more of it than it needed to be.

Emmanuel seemed the same, unaffected, but that's how men were. They never showed change or much emotion unless they were really mad or really hurt.

I showered and changed into my pajamas so I could be rested for work in the morning.

"About time you got out of the bathroom."

"You should have knocked I was just wrapping up my hair."

He grabbed a black bag and headed to the bathroom. I followed him. "What are you doing?"

"About to line my hair."

"You don't go to a barber shop?"

"No, I went to barber school. It was my plan B if I didn't get my business."

"Let me do it." I said as he pulled out his clippers.

"So you can mess me up, hell no."

"Show me how to do it then. I always wanted to learn."

He looked at me with doubt then walked back out into the studio, "okay."

"Really?"

"Yeah," he said and moved a chair over to the counter. He plugged up the clippers and sat down.

"You aren't going to tell me what to do?"

"Nope, it's common sense, just do a straight line."

"What if I mess up?"

"Then you'll cut me up and I'll bleed to death, come on its just hair."

I took the clippers from his hands and turned them on. I stayed on the line he already had there. I didn't see why he needed to line his hair anyway. I was nervous as I went from left to right and the buzzing annoyed my ears. I stopped, "Okay my hand is shaking too much; I can't do it anymore."

"You have serious confidence and trust issues."

"And you figured this out from me using clippers?"

"Yeah, this is the simplest thing you can do." He stood and took the clippers from my hand. "Sit down."

"Are you going to cut my hair?"

"What? Girl no, sit down."

I sat down in the chair and Manny walked away. He pulled out a bandana and walked back over to me and tied it around my eyes.

"What are you doing?"

"Ever heard of the trust test?"

"No."

"Well, usually it's done with stairs. You get somebody you either don't trust or do and get them to blindfold you and guide you upstairs, while you walk backwards."

"That's insane."

"Only if you don't trust anybody."

"Are we about to go walk up steps?"

"No, I'm improvising, grip the chair."

I gripped the side of the chair and felt Manny walk behind me.

"I'm going to lean you back slowly okay."

I nodded my head yes.

"You have to trust me not to drop you and trust your own balance."

I took a deep breath and Manny leaned me back a little. I was okay for the first three seconds then I screamed and jumped up.

"Eliza sit back down."

I felt around for the chair and sat back down.

"Relax and trust me."

I told myself I could do this over and over again in my head. He leaned me back further and further. I couldn't feel my feet beneath me. I just knew he was going to drop me, but I had to show him I could trust.

"Take off the blindfold." He said.

I removed the bandana from my eyes and I looked up at Emmanuel as he looked down at me. There we were again, face to face. I wished he would just kiss me already.

"Scared?" he asked.

"No…" I whispered.

"You must trust me."

"Maybe." I said as I stared at his lips.

He lifted me up slowly and I regained my composure.

"I'm going to bed, I have to work tomorrow." I said as I walked over to the bed quickly.

He laughed, "Goodnight Eliza."

He knew exactly what he was doing.

Makes the first move, great kisser, great....

Eliza

I decided to do a little shopping after work. I called Emmanuel and told him that Madra would pick me up. She had her two bad ass children with us and it was hard for me to do all that I wanted to do. I pushed shirts and pants around on the racks looking for things that I liked. Madra tapped me hard on my shoulder.

"That's her." She whispered.
"Who?"
"The girl."
"What girl Madra?" I looked up now annoyed.
"The one I caught Tavis with."

I shifted my eyes quickly to the direction that Madra was looking in. "You're kidding."

"Nope, that's the bitch."

The woman was covered in tattoos, her nose and labret was pierced, and her weave was at least three different colors. She looked like a stripper as she walked in stilettos. My body was hot and I wanted to walk over and snatch the weave from her head. She looked over at us with her fake ass green contacts then rolled her eyes. I guessed she had noticed Madra. She placed the shirt she was examining back on the rack and walked off. I grabbed Madra and followed her. She headed for an exit door. I followed her to the parking lot. I didn't know what had come over me.

"Go get the car."
"We're leaving?"
"Yes we're about to follow this bitch."
"For what?"
"Get the car Madra."

I stood and watched as she hoped into Tavis' car. I was really pissed now. Madra hurried to where I was and I hopped in. We followed little miss fake eyes all the way home.

"That motherfucker," I said as my anger rose. "Take me home."

Madra sped off and I screamed to the top of my lungs then punched her dashboard. She dropped me off and I banged on Manny's door. He swung it open. "What is wrong with you?"

"Tavis is a lying piece of shit!"

"What happened?"

"I just saw that bitch driving his car, well my car."

"Huh? Would you calm down and quit talking in riddles."

I took a breath then placed my hand on my forehead to focus, "I was at the mall and Madra pointed out the girl she caught Tavis with, so we followed her outside then followed her home and she was driving his car."

"You said it was your car too."

"Well it is my car, I put down the down payment and then paid it out for him because he didn't have one and his credit was messed up. He claimed his ex took his car and that she lived in Texas still and he couldn't get to it. I put the car in my name and he promised to keep up with the insurance."

"So it's still your car?"

"Yes."

"Well let's go get it. If he wrecks that car, you're responsible for it."

"How would I get it?"

Emmanuel walked to go grab his cell phone. I got on mine and called my brother. I wanted Tavis' ass kicked.

"Hey you know the address?"

How I knew the address I didn't know. I had no idea I wasn't even paying that much attention. Anger masked so much. He gave the address to whoever was on the phone.

"Come on, my boy will meet us over there with the tow truck."

We rushed out of the house and headed to the location I had just left. My brother met us there too after I texted him the address. He hopped out of the car pissed at what I told him.

"Where that motherfucker at?" he screamed as he slammed the door.

Emmanuel's friend proceeded to lift the car and all the noise must have captured the attention of fake eyes. She swung the door open, "What the fuck y'all doing?" Nobody answered her so she yelled into the house, "Tavis they towing our car!"

Our, I thought. "Bitch this is MY car!" I yelled and my brother held me back.

Tavis rushed outside. "Put my fucking car down!"

"This ain't your car!" My brother Eli yelled.

"This is private property!" Fake eyes screamed from the door.

"Call the cops then bitch and I'll just tell them y'all stole my car!"

"This is Tavis' car!"

"Yeah, go read the registration then, probably can't read, bootleg looking bitch!"

"Man Eliza why are you doing this?" Tavis asked and moved to approach me, but my brother blocked his way.

"Your best bet is to step the fuck back and go inside."

"This is between me and Eliza, Eli."

"It stopped being between me and you a long time ago." I spat.

"It's all chained up where you want to bring it?" Emmanuel walked over to me and asked.

"Who the fuck is this nigga?" Tavis looked him up and down.

"The nigga that's taking your transportation and you are?" Emmanuel reached out his hand then pulled it back, "wait, that's right you're the duck ass nigga that got females taking care of your broke ass."

Tavis lifted his hand to swing at Emmanuel and my brother hooked him before he could. He just needed one reason to tear into him and that was it. He had come looking for a fight. Tavis' little girlfriend stood as my brother beat him to the ground and Emmanuel tried to pull him off. Once he finally broke up the fight he yelled for the tow truck driver to drop the car to his shop then he pushed my brother to his car.

"Get in my truck Eliza!" he yelled at me and I did as I was told before I was the next one swinging at somebody. My brother sped off and Emmanuel ran to his truck and jumped in and did the same thing. We headed back to his place.

"You think I did the right thing?" I asked.

"Hell yeah, I mean that dude was cute. I almost made the tow truck put the car back down for pretty boy."

I laughed, "Can you be serious for a second."

"Just trying to make you feel better…"

"Thank you."

We pulled up to his studio apartment and I went inside ready to just put the day behind me. I walked over to the bed and flopped down. "I need to wash my hair."

"Let me do it." Manny volunteered.

"Why, you wouldn't even know what you're doing."

"I am the only son of a single mother, you have no idea what I was forced to do growing up." he joked.

"You can wash it if you really want to."

I grabbed my shampoo and conditioner and headed to the bathroom to grab a towel. I met Manny in the kitchen. He had the water turned on.

"Make sure it's not too hot." He said.

I placed my hand beneath the water and the temperature was just right. "Let me take my shirt off, don't get all skirmish because I'm in my bra."

He smiled as I removed my shirt and the hair tie from my hair. I placed my head under the warm water and let it soak my roots. It felt so good. He removed the water and I could feel the cold shampoo trickle onto my head. His hands came next and they felt so good as he massaged my scalp. He moved from the front to the back and ended on the sides lathering the shampoo and making my head feel free and clean. He knew exactly what to do as he rinsed then shampooed my hair again and conditioned it. He rinsed my hair one last time then shut off the water. I squeezed the remainder of the water from my hair and he wrapped a towel around it. I stood and faced him and he swiveled the towel around on my head. I erupted in laughter then pulled the towel from my head so he could see my hair down.

"You should leave it like that." he said as he moved closer and ran is fingers through my damp hair. I looked up at him and he looked down at me. I swallowed back hard.

Emmanuel

I held my hand against Eliza's face with strands of her moist hair looping my fingers. I had to do it. I dare not ask permission for fear that she'd tell me no and I hated rejection. I leaned in and kissed her. I had no idea how I had restrained myself this long, but now here she was so close. I pushed my tongue into her mouth. Her lips were soft and her hands were softer as she reached up and placed her hands on each side of my face. I was going to take my time. I pushed her head back and looked her in her eyes; something about that woman had me in another place. "I want to see you naked." I said as I ran my hand down her back to unlatch her bra.

She stepped back before I could remove it and unsnapped it with one hand. Her beautiful "C" cups made my mouth water as I licked my lips at her wanting to taste her skin. She unbuttoned her pants and let them fall to the floor. She stepped out of them slowly then her panties followed suit.

I had a sly grin on my face and she stood there looking like she wanted to cover herself, but if only she knew how much I was appreciating what I saw.

"Completely naked," I said.

She looked at herself and back up at me with a confused look on her face. I walked over to her and grabbed her wrist pulling her hand up toward my face. It was time she took that ring off. I slid my hand up to her fingers, straightening them then pulling her ring finger into my mouth pulling off her ring with my teeth. She gasped. I dropped her hand and removed the ring from my mouth and placed it on the counter.

I didn't leave her standing free alone. I pulled my shirt over my head and showed her the body that I worked hard on. I pulled my wallet from my back pocket and sat it on the counter then dropped my jeans and boxers exposing my man. Her eyes widened which let me know she liked what she saw.

She turned and walked toward my bed and her backside moved up and down. *Damn* I thought. I bit my bottom lip and pulled the condom from my wallet. I stroked my dick as I walked behind her, ready to sex her down and make her soak up my sheets. I clicked the light switch on the wall; placing us in total darkness and making her lose her way as she stood frozen in place. She didn't know that studio like I knew it. I pulled the condom over my man and grabbed her from behind, squeezing her breast and kissing all over her neck and back. I pushed her down flat on her stomach and before she could protest I spread her legs and dipped my middle finger into her wetness to see how moist she was. I got a surprise myself as her walls clung to my finger. She was so tight and warm. "Mmm" I said as I removed my finger and leaned down to bite her right ass cheek. There was a pain that she could appreciate. I liked to tease women until they begged for it, but today was a different day with a different woman. I damn near lunged inside of her, anxious to hear her pleasure music.

    She moaned out loud as I entered her and stroked her one time, easing all of me into all of her. I kissed the back of her neck as I moved in and out of her slowly, making sure she could feel every inch of me. I needed to get deeper, do her so good that she had tears in her eyes. I pulled out and flipped her over, letting her settle on her back as I pushed in once again. I felt welcomed inside of her as she moaned my name and pulled me in deeper, "you like that?" I whispered into her ear and her body shivered as she responded.

    It was time to dance. I stroked her hard, trying to push her into my headboard as her body went up and down with every hard thrust. She beat into my back; I beat into her womanhood. I closed my eyes as her sweaty love box pulsated and sucked my love stick up like a vacuum. I wanted her to cum for me. I leaned up and lifted her leg to turn her on her side, holding my man in place inside of the deepest crevice on her body. I laid behind her and placed my hand over that happy button that every woman had to give her ultimate pleasure. Her moans were almost screams as I stroked her and played with her little kitty. I loved the way her body shuddered against mine as she pulled the sheets from my bed and took all of me.

    Her words were music to my ears as she screamed she was cumming and bit down on my pillow. I wasn't sure how much longer I could hold on. I wanted to look at her face. I slanted her body so that I could look her in her eyes as her bean jumped beneath my fingers and her juices leaked. There was nothing like watching the face of a woman pleased and at the point of climax with their mouths wide open and eyes closed. I splashed inside of the condom inside of her box. Eliza and I came at the same time and I slept without void.

Dancing

Eliza

The sun rose over our naked bodies as we laid in bed just staring at each other. Nothing before last night mattered in that moment as we both had nowhere to be and nothing to do.

"So tell me about your parents." Emmanuel said.

"Well there really isn't much to tell. They hate each other," I laughed. "The day I canceled my wedding was the first day I had seen them stand near one another and not try to kill each other."

"Why did they get a divorce?"

"My mother and father were complete opposites. My father was more old school and very strict, whereas my mother was a party girl and never really wanted to settle down. Hell she still parties." I laughed.

"My mom loves to party too, but she deserves it, she spent so much of her life on me."

"She did a good job." I smiled at him then looked down blushing.

"You're parents did a good job too."

"They didn't do anything, my dad didn't become part of my life until about three years ago and my mother, well I raised her. I'm still raising her."

"I still think you turned out alright."

"I'm damaged…"

"You shouldn't say that. You are exactly what you think of yourself and other people will see you the same way."

"Do you see me that way?"

"I see you as you, a beautiful girl who fell for the wrong guy. It's a popular story, now you just need to choose your ending."

"I don't even know where to start to end."

"Forgiveness helps, your pastor said it best: express yourself, be positive, be empathetic, don't agree, but accept, forgive yourself then move on."

This man was unbelievable. How could he exist in this world, knowing exactly what to say or not say? I smiled and moved closer to him.

"Dance with me?" he said.

"Now? We're naked."

"Yes, now." He reached for his phone and went to a music playlist. Lalah Hathaway streamed from the speaker. "You were drunk the first time we danced to this, so you owe me a do over."

I laughed as he stood from the bed and reached for me. I put my hand in his and allowed him to lead me. He rubbed his hands up and down my back. I rested on his chest as he rested on my wild hair. How could something feel this good? The cool air in the studio felt good against my skin as it mixed with the warmth of his firm body. I loved his strong hands on my back as we moved in a slow circle.

The song ended and he still held me. He was not mine. I couldn't get comfortable again. I stepped back, "I need to shower." He released me and watched my naked body walk to the bathroom.

I turned on the shower and pulled down a towel and sat in on top of the toilet. I waited for the water to warm up then I stepped in. Only minutes later Emmanuel stepped in behind me.

"I wasn't done with you." He said as he pulled me toward him and coalesced our lips, sliding his thick tongue into my mouth and twirling it around. I moaned as he held me close to him tightly. I felt his manhood get hard again as he moved back to give it room. He turned me around and now I couldn't tell the difference between the water running down my legs and my juices as he pushed into me from behind. His thickness stretched me and his length made my eyes roll to the back of my head as water ran over my head and down my back. He gripped my waist pulling me into him, pausing his stroke to hit me hard when I least expected it. I had never been one to have sex all day and night, but the way this man made my body feel, I was his for the taking. He burst inside of me as I exhausted against him.

I leaned up and he turned me around and just held me beneath the water as we caught our breath. He kissed my forehead and I closed my eyes. This is what people meant when they said to live in the moment. I decided not to over think the situation. It didn't matter that he wasn't mine. It just felt good. He could wash my back and I'd wash his.

I walked out of the bathroom with a towel wrapped around my body. He followed grabbing shorts and a t-shirt for himself. I walked over to my bag to grab my blow dryer. I had to do something with my hair. I dug around for my flatiron and carried it into the bathroom with me too.

"How long does it take you to do your hair?"

"Two to three hours. I'm going to dry it first and grease my scalp."

I stood in the mirror and dried my hair and brushed it. Emmanuel walked into the bathroom and grabbed my grease from the sink. "What are you doing?"

"Come here." He said as he walked away and flopped down on the sofa.

I followed him. He patted the spot in front of him and told me to sit down on the floor. I smiled grabbing a pillow from the bed and walked over to sit down between his legs. I laughed as he parted my hair straight down to grease my scalp. I closed my eyes as his finger ran down my scalp. He messaged my hair once he was done and I was somewhere between reality and a dream.

"All done." he said as he capped the grease and I came back to life.

I thanked him and went back into the bathroom to flatiron my hair. I decided to keep it down because I knew he wanted to see it that way. I ran my fingers through it as I finished making sure I liked the way that it fell. I walked into the kitchen to get a drink. I noticed my ring sitting on the counter. I grabbed it and looked at it. I had no reason to ever put it back on my finger. I walked over to my purse and dropped in inside. I noticed Emmanuel's phone on the nightstand and picked it up. I clicked the button on the side and the screen lit up revealing a picture of me sleeping as his lock screen photo. I smiled then sat it back down. I walked to let Emmanuel see my hair. I stood directly in front of the TV.

He just sat and stared at me.
"You like it?"
"Don't ever wear that ponytail again." He said as he stood to move closer to me. Before he could steal

another kiss my cell phone rang interrupting our temporary perfect world.

It was my sister's ringtone. I walked to answer, "Hello?"

"Eliza, Eli is in jail!"

"What?"

"Yeah he came to get me from work and the police pulled him over talking about assault, battery, and trespassing."

"Motherfucker!"

"What's wrong?" Emmanuel ran over to me.

"I'm on my way." I said into the phone and hung up to toss on some clothes. "Fuck!"

"What?"

"Tavis called the police on Eli."

"That bitch ass motherfucker." Emmanuel walked away to get dressed.

We rushed out of the house.

"Bring me to my car." I said as I walked outside and Manny followed.

"Why?"

"Because I don't need you tangled in this mess, just bring me to my car."

"I got tangled in it when I towed the car."

"Emmanuel can you chill with the hero shit for a minute and just do what I say, this is my family and my mess and I don't want you in it."

"Hero shit?"

"You know what I mean."

"No I don't. I've been trying to cheer you up and keep your mind of the dude that messed over you and that's how you come at me?"

"I never asked for your help!"

Emmanuel let out a sarcastic sound of laughter as he turned around to the direction of my apartment. We didn't say anything else to each other. He pulled up to my complex and drove through the gate then pulled up behind my car.

"I'll have superman drop your shit off tonight." He said and sped off.

I shook my head and rolled my eyes. I didn't have time for his pettiness. My brother was sitting in jail because of me. I hopped into my car and started it up. I pulled off and went straight to where Tavis was now laying his head.

~~*~*

I beat on the door hard, waiting for somebody to answer the door. Heat covered my skin. I could hear them talking and just ignoring the door. If somebody didn't answer I was going to be in jail next for breaking and entering. The door finally swung open. It was fake eyes. I pushed her out of my way. "Where is he?"

"Bitch don't just walk in my house!"

I ignored her and headed to the back of the dirty house. There were clothes, toys, and shoes everywhere. She obviously had kids. "Tavis!" I yelled through the roach motel they called home. "Tavis!"

"How the fuck did you get in here?" Tavis asked approaching me.

I slapped Tavis hard across the face and he grabbed my arms and pulled me. "Why the fuck did you get my brother locked up?" I asked angrily using more cuss words than I would on a regular day.

"Why the fuck did you take my car?"

"It's not your car!"

"I was paying the insurance on it!"

"Boy please, the insurance has been cancelled for three months; I checked! Let me go!" I struggled to get free from his grasp.

Tavis threw me down on the floor hard. "Bring me back my shit and I'll drop the charges."

I kicked him hard in the leg and he weakened almost hitting the floor. I dug in my purse for the pepper spray I carried around when I went places alone. I kicked him hard again and fake eyes ran up behind me ready to swing. I sprayed her and her contacts. She covered her face. I kicked Tavis hard again and he hit the floor. I spit in his face and stood up. "I did everything for you! The shirt on your back, mother fucker I have the receipt for that and you repay me by getting caught by my best friend a week before my birthday, then not even having the decency to tell your family the wedding was off and leaving it to me to embarrass myself!" I kicked him hard again, this time between the legs. Tears started to crowd my eyes and I let loose on Tavis. "You are worthless and this life your living now is exactly what you deserve! Invest in a bus pass motherfucker!" I yelled as I headed for the door and ran to my car so I could get to my brother.

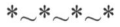

~~*~*

My father, sister, and brother stood outside of the jail house. I pulled over and ran across the street, not even bothering to add money to the meter. I ran up to my brother and hugged him. "I'm so sorry."

"It's okay sis, it was worth it. I should have broken his jaw."

My father stood shaking his head, "let's be glad that you didn't. You are 32 years old Eli."

"Daddy I'm not in the mood."

"You better get in the mood. I should not be bailing out my grown ass son."

My brother had a short fuse. He scowled at my father and turned to face him. "Maybe if you would have stuck around and showed your two daughters how men should treat them I wouldn't be correcting niggas."

"Eli calm down." I grabbed his arm

He snatched away and walked toward my car. "I'll catch a ride with Eliza!" he yelled back at my dad and sister.

I hugged them both then headed across the street. I unlocked the door and Eli and I hopped in.

"You okay?" I asked.

"Yeah I'm good. He could have left me in jail. I hate when he comes around trying to play daddy. Now he gon start acting like I owe him something."

Eli had grown up much differently than my sister and I. My mother came down hard on him after my father left us. He was only twelve at the time. He rebelled, living on the streets and selling drugs; when he was tired of doing that and tired of detention centers, he joined the military, which to me only made him worse. I was left to take care of my mother and my sister just did as she pleased. All of us were the splitting image of each other even though four years separated us each. I was still trying to figure out the mystery of us all having the same father when my parents hated each other most of our lives. I guess sex was the one thing they had in common.

"Where's your car?" I asked him.

"Mom went and got it, just drop me at her house."

"I can give her back the money for getting it from the pound."

"Sis don't insult me."

"Tavis will drop the charges if I give him back the car."

"Hell no, you better not give him nothing. I got friends who can handle my situation. I'll get community service at the most."

I didn't argue with him. There was no point in arguing with him. I dropped him off at my mother's house then headed back home. It had turned out to be a long day.

I pulled into my lot and Tavis' car was in the spot I usually parked in. I figured Emmanuel had it towed. I threw my head back on my seat as I thought about our mini-argument. I shouldn't have said what I said. I started my car up and headed back to his studio.

Emmanuel

I was too pissed to do anything so I cut off all the lights and got into bed. Women were so unappreciative. No matter what you did for them they found a way to shoot you down. I closed my eyes and waited to doze off.

My front door crept open and a feminine figure walked towards my bed. "Eliza?"

"Shhhh," she said and eased into the bed. She tugged at my boxers and grabbed my member. If this was her way of apologizing then she was forgiven. I braced myself as she pulled my man into her mouth and sucked him slowly. I groaned, letting her do her thing as she licked the shaft and stroked me at the same time. I closed my eyes and relaxed enjoying the wetness of her mouth. *Fuck.*

The light switched on and my eyes popped open.

"The door was unlocked..." Eliza's voice trailed off as she noticed the extra pair of legs hanging from my bed. I snatched the cover back. "Desiree what the fuck!" Eliza stormed out of my house and I jumped up from the bed and ran behind her. "E!"

"Leave me alone!"

"Eliza please, stop! It's not what you think!"

"I don't think anything, you're a single man and you can do what you want."

"Eliza just listen to me," I reached for her and she slammed my fingers in her car door. "Shit!" I beat on her window with my other hand and she backed out and sped off. I walked back inside and headed for my freezer to get some ice to put on my hand. I looked over at Desiree who was still lying in my bed. "You need to get the fuck out."

She laughed, "you weren't saying that when I was swallowing you a minute ago."

"Why are you even here?"

"I missed you."

"You couldn't call and say that?" I asked aggravated.

She laughed again.

"Why is this funny to you?" I turned my face up at her.

"Because not too long ago you was talking all this shit about how you wanted something more and blah blah, but here you are shacking up with somebody you don't know."

"You don't know who she is to me."

"The streets talk Mr. Levi. My girl told me she saw you at bible study with the chick so I did a little research of my own and sure enough there you were with her night after night in this studio."

"Get out Desiree."

"No, I want to know why you lied."

"I didn't lie to you."

"Who is she then? You can't be in love, it hasn't been that long and you've never been in love, you wouldn't even know what it feels like."

"And you would?"

"I've been in love before."

"It damn sure wasn't with me, so why are you here?"

"We were good together Manny, why'd you have to mess that up?"

I had never wanted to choke the shit out of woman so bad in my life. I leaned against my counter holding ice on my hand and listening to Desiree ramble on about our past. I spaced out as she talked. This was too much drama. I remembered why I had never fallen in love. I never gave myself the time to and every time I encountered drama I ran for the hills and dove into school and my career. It was time for me to get back to that.

I walked over to Desiree and grabbed her then patted her down. I found my key in her pocket. "I escorted her to the door. "Now Desiree you are a smart woman so I'm just going to say this once. Stay the fuck out of my life!" I slammed the door in her face and tossed my key to the side. I hurled my ice at the wall. "Shit!"

Eliza

I sped to Madra's house with tears in my eyes. I couldn't be alone. I hoped Paul wouldn't be angry with me for showing up without calling. I pulled up to her house and hopped out of my car, running to her front door and knocking on it hard. She answered quickly. I wrapped my arms around her and cried on her shoulder.
"Eliza what's going on? Manny just called Paul."
"I caught him with a chick's face in his lap."
"What?"
"Yeah, we argued earlier, Tavis locked Eli up, everything is just a mess."
"Come sit down." Madra walked me over to the sofa "Why didn't you call me and tell me all of this was going on?"
"I don't know. I was doing what Emmanuel told me to do. I was giving myself 22 days to change and heal."
"I'm so lost right now." She looked me in the eyes and held my hands as my tears fell non-stop. I just wanted my life back the way it was when I knew what

was going to happen day to day. I was going to be in church bright and early.

I sat and told Madra everything. She was shocked because she had no idea what was going on between Manny and I. It put me at ease to know he wasn't one of those men that gossiped with his boys. Even Paul was shocked as he eavesdropped on our conversation.

Paul walked into the living room and handed me a bottle of water. "Can I jump in for a minute?" he asked.

I nodded my head *yes*.

"Emmanuel might be in love with you."

"Yeah so in love he lets some slut suck his dick while he's mad at me."

"No just hear me out. I've never heard him like that."

"What do you mean?"

"When I talked to him he was very upset, damn near disturbed."

"Did he tell you who the girl was?" Madra asked.

"His ex…"

I rolled my eyes, "that really helps."

"No, she let herself in." he defended.

"Why did she have a key?" I asked.

"He forgot to take it back." Paul stated.

"That's no excuse." I said.

"…well," Madra turned to look at me. "Tavis still has a key to your apartment Eliza, put yourself in his shoes. Maybe he thought it was you."

"I never had a key."

"Well, still, he was upset, he wasn't thinking straight…"

I wiped my eyes and stood up, "I think I'm just going to go home and get some sleep."

"Okay sweetie, call us if you need anything."
They stood to see me out.
    I hugged them both then I went home to my own bed.

Loyal

Emmanuel

I had been living in a fairytale too damn long as I pulled up to my shop that was all taped off with lean notices on the door. I jumped out of my truck and ran to the doors of my shop that was chained up with locks I didn't own the keys to. My techs stood outside looking lost as I punched the door. I didn't give them an explanation. I hopped into my truck and sped off to the one place that always made me feel safe.

I was happy to see my mother's car in her driveway as I pulled up. I let myself in with my key then walked to her bedroom where she was watching TV.
"Boy what I told you about just walking in my house, what if I had a man up in here?"
"I'd just shut the door," I smiled.

I kicked off my shoes and got in the bed with my mom and pulled her arm around me.
"Uh uh what's going on?"
"Why something gotta be going on?"
"Boy you haven't laid in my bed since you were six years old."
"They locked up my shop."
"You knew that was going to happen, you've been getting notices for months, now cut the shit."

I hated that she knew me so well.
"What's her name?"
"What makes you think it's not Desiree?"
"It's not, so stop giving me the runaround."
I took a breath, "Shit man, I don't want to feel like this."

"Boy watch your mouth and what are you talking about?"

"I met this girl and she is amazing. I've met so many women, but this girl just...I can't even explain it."

"Then why are you sad?"

"She walked in on me and Desiree last night."

SMACK!

"Ouch what you do that for?" I rubbed my head and sat up.

"I raised you better than that."

"You didn't even let me explain."

"I don't need to; she should have bust your head open."

"Mama I wasn't cheating or nothing dang."

"Then what were you doing with her?"

"She came to my place and tricked me."

"Umm hmm okay you can lie back down, it's safe."

I laid back down beside my mother and she resumed comforting me.

"It sounds to me like you're in love baby."

"How?"

"Did it hurt you to see her hurt?"

"Yeah..."

"You might have found your girl baby. Now what are you going to do about it?"

"She doesn't want to talk to me and besides I don't have time for all that. I have to find a hustle so I can get my shop back."

"You can hustle and apologize at the same damn time, how does that song go?" She started trying to recall the beat and words of *Future's* song.

"Mama stop," I laughed and continued to lay under her until I could clear my head and figure things out.

Eliza

After church it felt like a weight had been lifted from my shoulders. I got into my car and drove to the Nissan dealership to request a key for Tavis' car. I brought all the information with me that they told me to have. I was putting that car on Craigslist the moment I got the key. It wasn't like I could drive two cars. I could get 25 G's easy for a brand new Nissan Altima. Twenty-five thousand probably didn't touch on how much money I spent on Tavis in five years, but it definitely made up for a good bit and since he gave me this ring back I was definitely going to look high and low for a receipt, which should at least get me an extra three thousand. I was about to take a much needed vacation so I could re-evaluate.

I gave Nissan all my info and they told me the key would be ready within twenty-four hours. I smiled and went on my way. I drove back to my apartment to lie down and enjoy my last few hours before I had to get back to work.

I walked into my apartment and tossed my keys and bag on the sofa. I walked to my kitchen and opened the fridge. It smelled horrible. It felt like I had not been home in forever when in reality it had only been less than a few weeks. Being with Emmanuel slowed time down. I didn't want to think about him.

I shut the fridge so I could put on some cleaning clothes to get whatever was bad in there out and maybe run to the store. I opened my room door and jumped back. "Get the fuck out of my bed!"

"Eliza calm down. I just came to talk."

"Tavis we have nothing to talk about."

"We have a lot to talk about."

"I'm calling the police." I stomped out to go to my purse and grab my phone.

"And tell them what? Your estranged fiancé came home and broke in with a key?"

I stopped in my tracks and turned around, "why are you here?"

Tavis got down on his knees in front of me, "to beg…to plead." He wrapped his arms around my legs. "I'm stupid and I messed up bad."

"Let me go Tavis."

"Not until you forgive me."

"Okay I forgive you."

"For real E, I need you to forgive me and take me back."

"I've learned how to translate your bullshit Tavis, sounds like give me back my car, I'm doing bad and the moment you think everything is okay I'll mess up again." I mocked him.

Tavis stood up. "Eliza I'm sorry. I don't know why I keep fucking up, but I promise I won't mess up no more."

"I know you won't because I'm not taking you back."

"E stop it, okay your hurt I get it. I know it's my fault and all this is from anger."

"I stopped being angry when I towed your car."

Tavis made a frustrated sound, "I don't care about the car. I just want us back. Don't you miss us?"

I didn't answer.

"Not even a little bit?" Tavis looked me in my eyes. "Kiss me." He leaned down and attempted to kiss me, but I turned my face. He lifted his hand and turned my face back toward him then stole what I wasn't willing to give.

I gave in and kissed him back, but I felt nothing. He stopped kissing me and he stood there and looked at me. "You really don't love me no more."

I stood silent.

"Did I hurt you that bad?"

"Worse, now get out and leave my key."

"Who is he?"

"Nobody."

"You're lying, because you've taken me back thousands of times, we've never had this problem."

I laughed. "Wow."

"What?"

"Do you hear yourself; you just called me stupid in so many words." I shook my head.

"How?" he stood dumbfounded.

"We've never had this problem? Me taking you back? Shit sounds pre-planned to me. It's like you know that I'll take you back so you go out do what you do then come running back here to me right?" I thought about what Emmanuel said about second chances and people knowing exactly what to get away with.

"E ,that's not what I meant."

"Stop calling me E like we're friends. We aren't friends, we aren't lovers, we aren't shit. Give me my key and go hitch-hike your ass back where you came from because this here is DONE!"

Tavis swallowed back hard. I had never talked to him like that before. He took a step back as if he were afraid. He pulled my key from his back pocket and placed it in my hand then headed for the door. When the door closed so did the pain that came with him.

I shut my eyes tight and took a deep breath. It was time for me to move on completely.

Passionate and Romantic

Eliza

I sat in the middle of my shower letting the water hit me as I cried uncontrollably. I let it all out. I missed Emmanuel so bad. He'd be doing something to make me laugh right now, but I was too stupid to even let him explain himself. We had not talked in days. I had suffocated myself with *Tamia's almost* on repeat trying to figure out how something so simple was so complex.

I hopped out of the shower after all of my tears were done. I grabbed a towel and wrapped it around my body then headed into the kitchen to read the newspaper. I had nothing but time to waste so I decided to read every section. I saved the comics for last.

I grabbed the Real Estate section to look at properties I'd never be able to afford alone unless I hit the lottery. The cheapest were always the ones repossessed by the bank. I looked at those first; they were more in my range. I let my eyes scan the section then I almost fell out of my chair as I laid my eyes on Emmanuel's property. I grabbed my cell phone and called Madra.

"Hello." Her baby cried in the background.

"Did you know Manny's business was shut down by the bank?"

"Yeah, it's been shut down for about a week now. It goes up for auction in two days."

"Why didn't you tell me?"

"I didn't think you cared."

"I have to go I'll call you later." I said then hung up. I walked into my room and got dressed. I grabbed my checkbook from my bag and wrote it out for $27, 000. I was now grateful that Tavis' car had sold so quickly. I silently thanked the old white couple that took it off my hands for their granddaughter's birthday. This check would empty my savings, but what Emmanuel had done for my heart was worth so much more. I was free of Tavis.

    I slipped my shoes on and headed out the door to Emmanuel's apartment. I pulled up and parked then took a deep breath as I thought about what I could say to him. I popped my glove compartment open and grabbed a blank envelope to place the check in. I held it to my chest and hopped out of my car and walked up to his door and knocked. The birds chirped as I waited.

    The door unlocked slowly and an older woman who resembled Emmanuel opened the door. "Yes can I help you?"

    "Hi, um is Emmanuel home?"

    "He's not here at the moment, but I can tell him you stopped by, what's your name?"

    "I'm Eliza."

    Her eyes widened, "my God you are gorgeous."

    I smiled awkwardly, "thank you."

    "Come in and have a seat."

    I walked in and did as she said. I never argued with my elders. If they say come in you go in. If they say have a drink you have a drink. I took a seat on the sofa and she sat beside me. "I'm Emmanuel's mother by-the way."

    "He looks just like you."

    "I wish I had made him by myself, his daddy was worthless."

    I laughed. "Do you know where he went?"

    "No he didn't say."

"Do you know what time he'll be back?"

"He didn't tell me that either. Men are mysterious with everything."

I laughed and looked down.

"So how long have you been dating my Manny?" she asked.

"Oh we…."

She laughed, "nevermind."

"Emmanuel is a wonderful man Ms. Levi."

"I'm glad you think so. Nice to know I did one thing right in my life." She placed her hand on top of mine. "Can I tell you something?"

"Yes ma'am."

"I'm really happy that you came by. He has been so upset lately and you just might be the person to cheer him up. He cares about you so much."

I wanted to blurt out "really," but instead I smiled. The front door swung open just as Ms. Levi was about to speak again. Emmanuel walked in and froze near the front door. I know that he had seen my car outside. There was an awkward silence.

"Let me get out of here, you two have some talking to do." Ms. Levi said as she patted my knee and stood to leave. She kissed Emmanuel on the cheek as she headed out and waved goodbye to me. Emmanuel shut the door behind her.

I stood up to greet him, "Hi."

"Hey." he said

I reached out the envelope that I was holding to him.

"What's that?"

"A thank you."

"For what?"

"For everything you did for me to keep me sane."

He reached for the envelope and opened it. He pulled out the check and damn near choked. "Eliza I can't take this."

"I'm not taking it back."

"Why are you giving me this?"

"You know why…"

"I won't accept it."

"You can rip it up, I'll just write another one. I'm not taking it back."

Emmanuel stood at a loss for words as he stared at the check.

"Well, that's all I came over for. I'll see you around." I headed for the door as Emmanuel stood in shock. I twisted the doorknob and opened it. Emmanuel placed his hand on my waist from behind and pushed the door shut slowly. I couldn't turn around as he breathed down my neck.

"What did I tell you about this ponytail?" he asked as he pulled my hair tie from my hair and tossed it to the floor. He turned me around slowly and pushed me up against the wall and stared into my eyes. "What did you do to me Eliza?"

I shook my head, "Nothing…"

Emmanuel placed his hand as the seam of my shirt never breaking his stare as he moved his hand upward against my skin. I swallowed hard. "Can I make love to you?"

"You have to love me in order for that to happen."

"What if I said that I did?" he spoke in a subtle voice.

"I wouldn't believe you." I returned his tone.

"Why?"

"It's too soon."

"Love does not have a time limit." his stare was intense. "It is foundations that have to be built, not love." He moved his hand up to my lips and ran his thumb across them. "Love just happens…every second and every minute." He lifted my face and did what he did best with those luscious lips of his. I closed my eyes and got lost in him as he pulled me away from the wall and led me to his bed.

He placed me in front of his bed and left me standing there as he walked over to his stereo and cut in on and shut the curtains shutting out all sunlight. Usher's *Can U Handle It* filled the room. He pulled off his shirt as he walked back towards me. He grabbed me and kissed me aggressively then tugged at my shirt to pull it over my head. I didn't put up a fight. I lifted my arms and let him undress me. I ran my hands across his chest as he licked from my shoulders up to my neck. I loved his mouth on me. I loved that he always knew what to do with his hands, even if he was on the receiving end of pleasure. His hands never lay idle. He removed my shoes and loosened my pants and let them hit the floor then laid me back on the bed, placing my thighs on his shoulders. He kissed my inner thigh and licked my panty line, then went in for the kill as he wrapped his mouth around my pearl and sucked on it for dear life, then teased it with the tip of his tongue. I lost my breath as he suffocated himself beneath my waist. I tried to push his head away, but he held onto me digging his fingers into my things to keep me in place.

He released me on his time and stood. I saw the print in his pants and leaned up to grab for his belt. He stopped me and grabbed my wrist, pushing me back on the bed. He pinned my wrist above my head and looked me up and down. "You are so beautiful." He said then loosened his belt and pulled it through the loops while still holding both of my wrists down with one of his hands.

    He wrapped the belt around my wrists and tightened it. There was no point in struggling, so I lay there as his lips invited themselves to every inch of my body starting at my neck, moving down to my nipples, and ending at my toes. I squirmed as he pulled each toe into his mouth. It wasn't something that happened often and I couldn't believe the way I reacted to this strange pleasure.

    He stood from the bed and undressed completely, stroking himself. I loved it when he did that. My lady was throbbing, waiting for him to come into her. He made me settle for two of his thick fingers as he pushed inside of me and watched my facial expressions. I closed my eyes and bended my knees. I wanted him now, right now. He heard my silent cry for him as he moved over my body and eased into me, loosening the belt from my wrists and taking my hand and placing it behind his head. My eyes remained closed, but he did not fancy that as he whispered, "look at me."

    I was obedient as he moved in and out and the track switched to Jaime Foxx's *storm*. The music was faint to me as I listened more to my own moans and Emmanuel's breathing.

    I refused to let him have all the glory as he sexed me into another dimension. I rolled him over onto his back and wrapped him between my thighs. I moved my hips up and down his manhood and he groaned beneath me squeezing my ass cheeks as I pushed into his chest. I leaned in to kiss him and he trapped me there locking his arms beneath mine, gripping my shoulders, and taking over again, this time stroking upward. I moaned his name into his ear. He licked my neck and sucked my earlobe. I bit down into his shoulders trying to hold on as he massaged my g-spot at full speed.

    I couldn't take it. I announced the arrival of my release and he begged me to wait for him. He pushed me up, sliding us to the edge of the bed, holding my chest to his chest. Our bodies were one once again as he pushed inside of me and we both exploded. He was just too good to be true.

~~*~*

    "Stop staring at me." I said with my eyes half-open.
    "Go to sleep and you wouldn't notice."
    "I'm not sleepy. I'm relaxing."
    Emmanuel turned to his side and ran his fingers up and down my shoulder. "Move in with me."
    "Why would I do that?"
    "Because I want you here."
    I rolled onto my side to face him, "I can't…."
    "Why not?"
    "It's still so soon and all that time I spent living with Tavis I…"
    "Don't you dare do that; don't compare me and him."
    "Who else would I compare you to?"
    "Nobody, I'm my own man Eliza, let me be that."
    "I'm trying…"

"Move in with me, take one risk. I dare you."

I lay there seriously contemplating his offer as he talked. I wanted a change in my life and this could possibly be it. I didn't really have much to lose.

He continued to convince me, "you can move anything you want into my studio. I'll even let you color coordinate my closet and shoes." I saw his white teeth as he smiled in the darkness.

"Why are you in such a rush?"

"Why aren't you? We get one life Eliza. We've found something special in each other and I want to explore it completely."

"What's your sign?" I asked.

"Pisces why?"

"Explains a lot…"

"Yeah I'm a dreamer so what."

"I'm a Taurus I live in the real world."

"Good then we can balance each other out." He licked his lips. "I won't stop until I change your mind."

I had lost my mind, "Okay…"

"Really?" he asked in an excited tone.

I nodded my head yes. Emmanuel pulled me into his arms, kissed my forehead and held me. I was getting a second chance at my twenty-two days plus some.

Loves trying new foods

Emmanuel

  I stomped my ass into that bank and slapped the check Eliza wrote out down on the desk. It was enough to cover my loan and pay off my taxes. My next stop was going to be the post office to give the IRS their cut. I'd be excited to check the mail again. I never thought the idea of seeing only regular bills would excite me so much.
  I drove off with a smile on my face as I thought about Eliza and how amazing she was. I didn't know too many women that would hand over 27 stacks that easily without at least getting herself a good pair of shoes out of the deal. I wanted to pay her back, but she refused any offer that I made.
  I rushed home so that I could call all of my techs back to work and maybe increase their pay once business picked back up, which I hoped happened soon. I had money left over after paying off my debts and decided I needed to spend it wisely. I was definitely going to look into some sort of paid advertising. It was the best investment I could get myself.
  I pulled up and parked in front of my studio then ran inside to start making calls to my employees. Eliza was still there.
  "No work today?" I asked as I walked through the door and she dressed.
  "Yeah, I just have a late day."
  "Why don't you just quit?"
  "Who's going to take care of me if I do?"
  "Me."
  "Excuse me."

"I don't mean you just staying here all day. You can work with me."

"Doing what?"

"Exactly what you do now; you can process payroll and anything else administrative that needs to be handled."

"First you want me to move in and now you want us working together?" she shook her head. "Sounds like a recipe for disaster."

I walked over to Eliza and grabbed both of her hands. "You just saved me from losing the business I invested everything in, let me invest in you. I may not have the money, but I have the heart."

She laughed and looked away.

"Are you going to do it?"

She rolled her eyes with a smile on her face, "fine."

I picked her up and swung her around. Everything in my life was starting to feel complete.

"At least let me quit the right way with a two weeks' notice."

"Do whatever you have to baby." I kissed her lips and let her finish dressing.

Eliza

I walked into the tall hotel with a smile on my face. I couldn't ever remember feeling this good. I couldn't wait to get to my desk and type up my resignation letter. I needed to call Madra too. I pressed my floor and smiled at everyone as they entered and exited the elevator.

I stepped off at my floor and hurried to my desk. I turned on my computer, typed in my username and password and waited for it to load.

"Eliza!" My boss yelled like we weren't in a professional setting. I became instantly irritated as I stood and headed for his door. He never waited for me to greet him.

"Do you have a minute before you start working?"

"Yeah sure."

"I need you to sign this." He handed me a paper and I instantly recognized the write up with its two carbon copies attached.

"You know I don't usually reprimand you, but your attendance has really gotten out of hand and that's not like you."

"So you wrote me up? You couldn't give me a verbal warning?"

"Think of it as motivation to do better."

I stood and ripped the paper in my hand. "I quit."

"What?"

"I quit." I pulled my badge and keys from around my neck and sat it on his desk then walked out to my chair and grabbed my purse so I could leave. Suddenly the idea of working for Manny was more appealing. I knew he wouldn't write me up; he'd just tie me up in the bedroom.

A sly grin crossed my lips as I dug for my cell phone and pressed the button back to the first floor so I could get back to my car. The only thing I was going to miss about my job was the free downtown parking. I waited until I was off of the elevator to call Madra. She picked up on the first ring.

"Dang were you expecting me?"

"No girl I was about to dial out, but what's new?"

"I just quit my job."

"What!"

"What about your bills Eliza! That was so irresponsible of you."

"Would you shut up and let me tell you the rest."

"Oh there's more?"

"Yes, you should know me better."

She laughed, "I'm listening."

"Well, I took the money from Tavis' car and helped Emmanuel with his business. He wants me to work with him."

"That's good! You'll kind of be your own boss!"

"Yeah and that's not all."

"Aw hell what else?"

"He wants me to move in."

The phone was silent. "You sure that's a good idea? I mean is that what you want?"

"I don't know what I'm sure about anymore. I just know that he makes me feel good, he makes me happy."

"E, I have to be real with you, living with someone is hard. Look what you just went through with Tavis. Emmanuel may seem like the answer now, but what about a year from now?"

"I guess I'm about to learn the hard way. I'm always so careful. I want to make some mistakes."

"Tavis was a mistake and a big one. Think about this girl."

"I have and this is what I want to do."

"Well I won't argue with you. You're my girl and I love you. You know I always got your back."

"Thanks Madra," I smiled. "Could you get me some more boxes?"

"You know I got you. I'll meet you at your place later to help you start packing okay."

"Okay," I said then hung up. I needed to call and cancel my electricity account and let my complex know I would me moving out and not renewing my lease, but before I could search for their number Manny called.

"Hey"

"Baby they are removing the locks to my building as we speak!"

"That's so good!"

"I want to take you somewhere special for dinner, so when you get off, go home and dress nice, I'll pick you up at six."

"Okay," I said without struggle or hesitation. It felt nice to be appreciated for once.

I called Madra back to let her know that I'd meet up with her tomorrow.

~~*~*

Emmanuel rushed ahead of me as usual to open the door so that I could walk through it. I smiled as I passed him then waited for a hostess to seat us. A tiny pale-skinned girl with a big smile and a bouncy ponytail walked over to us then escorted us to our table. I reached for my chair and Emmanuel placed his hand over mine to stop me from pulling it back. I looked up at him.

"Haven't learned your lesson about doors and chairs yet?" he asked with a smile that made me blush.

"What is this place?" I asked looking around as I sat down and Emmanuel pushed the seat beneath me.

"They serve African cuisine."

"And what's that?"

"Look at the menu, it's in English and African, you have to be open to whatever, because I love food."

I laughed and shook my head at myself as I thought about my list. He was crossing things off with ease without even knowing it. "I'm open and I love food too." I said as I scanned the menu.

I didn't know what to have a taste for since I had never tried African food so I trusted Emmanuel to order for me. I could tell that he ate their often, because he made it his business to know his favorite dishes in African. I was impressed yet again as I had been since this whole thing with us started.

"I have something for you." Emmanuel said in a sweet tone.

"What is it?"

"It's nothing too special, but I thought maybe I'd help you live your own dreams for a change. Wait right here."

"Okay," I said with a smile as Emmanuel stood from the table and headed out of the doors.

He returned with a gift basket.

My eyes were wide as he sat the basket in front of me and sat back down.

"I had a nice little amount left and just wanted to do something nice for you, because I knew you were going to spend that money on yourself. It's nothing major, but it's something I thought you'd appreciate." he smiled with excitement in his eyes as he waited for me to confirm or deny if I liked his gift.

My eyes watered as I pulled the plastic back from the basket and pulled out ink pens and sticky notes. I pulled out a composition notebook that he personalized by writing, *share your pain with me...please* on the front of it.

"You didn't have to do this." I said as my eyes watered. The little things mattered so much.

He placed his hand on my face, "Yes I did. I never want you to feel alone. If I'm not around to listen write it down. Do what you're good at if it makes you happy. I believe in whatever you believe in."

I placed my hand over his and kissed his palm, "Thank you."

He wiped away my tears with his thumbs and I placed my basket on the floor.

"I think I better go freshen up," I said and stood and he stood with me. I looked him in the eyes. "You respect women that much?" I asked acknowledging his gesture.

"I just always want to be admirable in your eyes."

I smiled as butterflies entered my stomach then I walked away. That man, that man.

Loves to read, lover of all things art

Eliza

Madra and I stood in my kitchen boxing up dishes as music played through my apartment. I bobbed my head and sung along to the words of Beyonce's *Best thing I never had.* I was feeling like a new woman and I had not even turned over my keys yet.

Madra almost made me talk myself out of my decision, but then I told myself that I deserved this. I needed a change. As I packed and walked from room to room all I had were memories of Tavis and me. The lovemaking on every surface of my apartment, the arguments, the broken lamps from arguments, him slamming me into walls and choking me because he accused me of the things he was doing himself, the constant tears, the lies told against these walls the movie nights on the couch with junk food and drinks. I wanted his name stripped from my vocabulary and his existence completely shattered.

"Ohhh girl can I have these glasses?"

"Take whatever you want." I said over the music.

"You sure?"

"Yep, I'm donating most of this stuff to Salvation Army anyway. All of it won't fit in Manny's place and I don't want to carry too many memories with me."

"You're really feeling Emmanuel." Madra stopped and placed her hand on her hip and smiled at me.

"He's a good guy." I smiled

"In other words he put something on that ass!" She laughed out loud.

"Madra!"

There were two quick knocks at the door then it eased open. Paul and Emmanuel entered with Popeye's bags and drinks.

"I like how y'all just walked in here and didn't wait for us to say come in," Madra snapped.

"My bad baby we wanted to sit these bags down." Paul said to Madra and pecked her lips.

"What did y'all get?" I asked.

"It's a mix of dark and white and spicy and mild." Emmanuel answered.

"Okay cool, I still have a few plates down, I'll grab them." I walked over to the cabinet and Emmanuel walked behind me reaching up as I reached up and pushing his pelvis against me.

"I got it, go sit down and relax for a minute." Emmanuel said.

I did what was suggested with a smile on my face.

We all sat around talking and eating up the chicken and biscuits. I ate up most of the fries as Emmanuel and I passed seductive looks across the table. Madra eyed us both, smiling and shaking her head each time that she caught us stealing glances.

"We're going to step outside." Paul said as he and Manny stood from their chairs and headed for the door.

"And do what?" Madra asked.

"Smoke a cigar." He responded and Madra shook her head.

"Come sit outside with us. Y'all have the rest of the month to pack this place up. Come get some fresh air." Paul suggested.

"The air is about to be contaminated with cigar smoke." Madra retorted.

"Woman come on now," Paul grabbed Madra's hand and pulled her from her seat. She laughed and followed him outside.

Emmanuel leaned against my counter, "After you." He smirked.

I stood and walked past him and he licked his lips at me and shook his head as he followed me out the door.

Emmanuel and I stood on the balcony as Madra and Paul sat on the steps. Madra was sitting between Paul's legs. It felt like we were in high school, chilling outside my mama's house because boys weren't allowed inside. Emmanuel reached down for the cigar that Paul was smoking then puffed it. He held it in front of my face and I just looked at it. "Let me guess; you don't smoke either?"

I shook my head no and he stood behind me, wrapping one arm around my waist.

"You need to learn how to live," he whispered into my ear and placed the cigar against my lips. I leaned and puffed it just barely and he laughed.

"No pull on it and hold the smoke, really inhale it." He held his hand against my stomach as I did what he said and coughed a little bit then fanned the smoke away. "Women," he said as he shook his head and handed the cigar back to Paul.

It was getting dark outside now, so Paul and Madra decided to go so the babysitter wouldn't tag on an extra fee. Emmanuel and I headed back inside. I locked the door and headed back into the kitchen to organize the boxes. Emmanuel walked up behind me and swung me around, placing his lips against mine before I could get a word out. I wrapped myself in his kiss as his tongue danced around in my mouth. He sucked on my bottom lip, then the top one and forced my mouth open and pulled out my tongue with his lips sucking on just that alone. His hands gripped my ass as he pushed me back against the counter.

I pulled back, "I have to finish packing."

"Later..." he breathed against my skin and his mouth latched onto my neck.

Emmanuel's hands moved all over my body, gripping my flesh. He pulled my shirt from my body and tossed it to the floor.

"We have to get back to your place," I breathed heavily.

"We can sleep here tonight," he said as he unbuttoned my pants and pulled them from my body.

"Manny..."

"Eliza, be quiet." He said firmly as he lifted me onto the counter and pulled my panties down. He pulled out that long thick stick that I had become addicted to and pushed it inside of me. There were no more words from my lips as I held myself up with my hand against the cabinet. His grunts and groans turned me on. I loved knowing that my lady was good to him. His eyes were closed as he moved in and out and held onto my hips. I cussed and my toes curled as my ass slid back and forth on my counter. Manny lifted me and fell back on the chair that was pulled from beneath the table. I straddled him and gripped the back of his neck with my hand to give him the ride of his life. I closed my eyes and moved my hips against him. I bit down on my bottom lip and rode him until he couldn't take it.

He lifted me again and carried me to my bed, ripping the remainder of his clothes off and snatching me up into the doggy style position. He was in complete control as my face pressed against my mattress and I felt the waves of my ass each time he slammed against me. I was not going to miss this place, but at least I'd leave it with a great memory.

~~*~*

"Do you ever go to sleep after sex?" Manny asked.
"No," I smiled.
"I'm about to start feeling insecure since I'm not knocking you out."
I laughed, "You are definitely knocking me out. You never see me attempt to walk do you?"
"Right, right," he smirked, "...tell me something."
"What?"
"If you could get the type of love you wanted, what would you choose?" he asked.
"Meaning?"
He cleared his throat, "there are so many ways a person can love, ya know, and there are different types of love."
"You're going to have to explain this one to me."
"Alright there's storage which is affection, phillia is friendship, romance is eros, and agape which is unconditional love."
"I've never heard of any of those, but I want them all."
"You need to pick up some books." he smiled.
"I'm going to have so much free time now I'm definitely going to have to do that."
"Now tell me your love story."

"Love story as in what?"

"The movie you'd want your love life to be like."

"Hmm," I adjusted my arms beneath my naked body, "I want my love story to be the greatest love story ever told…like *The Notebook* or *The Lake House*, no, *the Time Traveler's Wife*."

Manny shook his head.

"What?"

"And you said I'm a dreamer. I thought you would have said something like *Love Jones*, *Jason's Lyirc*, or *Disappearing Acts*. That's real love stories to me. Those characters had real problems. Love is not just glitz and glamour or make believe. It's trials and tribulations. It's withstanding. If you can't make it through the test how real is the love?"

"You have a point."

"I know I do. First you want men to act like those men in the 1800's with white hair and capris pants and now this."

"What's wrong with the men from the 1800's?"

"Girl we live in the south, your black ass would have been a slave falling in love with me in a wooden cabin, behind a mansion on a plantation." He laughed out loud.

I poked out my bottom lip then smiled.

"I can't argue with *The Notebook* too much, but the other two are questionable." he raised his brow in the darkness that my eyes had adjusted to.

"Well I'll take Darrius from *Love Jones* any day," I teased.

"Oh yeah? That's the kind of dudes you go for?" he cleared his throat once again and began mimicking *Lorenz Tate*, "say baby can I be yo' slave? I got to admit girl you're the shit girl and I'm digging you like a grave..."

    I giggled at his dead on impression and watched as he switched to a serious expression and his voice went back to normal. He took a deep breath and spoke.

*"...Once again I've wasted some of my best lines
on what turned out to be
nothing more than a good time.
As I openly revealed emotions you were evoking..."*

He took a breath.

*"...I manipulated real feelings into spoken words
Feeling my heart and mind had finally chosen
The girl who was most deserving of me
And eventually the gate to my emotions was opened
as feelings flowed from inside of me..."*

He took a breath.

*"...I allowed my poetry to confide for me
The beauty in you sharing your life with me
Now I find myself choking back the very tears
I most feared that were always nearby..."*

He took a breath.

*"...Crying the same type of tears
I was promised I would never cry
Facing an end I was promised would never come...*

*Yet now that it's all said and done
I realize never is an insincere time to promise..."*

He took a breath.

*"...Because it's not our wants
that keep the inevitable from coming
Now I'm left rereading the very lines
written just for you
The supposedly permanent boo
That turned a good half in two..."*

He took a breath.

*"...Temporarily...
Now I'm writing some of my best lines
about the inconvenient truth
Of how loving all of you
couldn't ensure the promise
you would love me too..."*

He took a breath.

*"...As your sincerity wasn't well-perceived by me
Because you turned out to be
everything you declared not to be..."*

He took a breath.

*A parody of your so-called truth
While the inconvenient truth is
I'm still writing some of my best lines
about you but without you..."*

I sat up in the bed beside him and looked down at him. "You wrote that?"
"Yeah, in college…"
"Who was she?"
"My high school sweetheart; we dated, until she didn't want to be in a relationship no more."
"So, you have been in love…"
"If I was I would have never let her leave. I recited that poem out loud everyday to keep me focused on school and not women or my own feelings."
"What's the title?"
"Write about you…" he looked down at me and sat silently staring.
"You think women and men love differently?"
"I know they do." He looked away. "We both love hard, but it's the end where we differ. Women get a broken heart and spend the rest of their life trying to find someone to fill that void. Men get a broken heart and we spend the rest of our lives trying to forget and avoid any woman who could make us feel that way again."
I leaned down and kissed Emmanuel on the lips then laid back down beside him. We laid in silence as he ran his fingers through my hair and massaged my scalp. I lay with my eyes clothes wondering how someone like him, who cared so much and had so much to offer could be alone this long. He was more than just some void filler for me. He was obviously the man that God had to be saving for me and in order for me to appreciate him I had to deal with trouble first, which is what Tavis was. Everything was clear.

~~*~*

Emmanuel left that next morning, leaving me in my apartment alone for the next few weeks. We slept on the phone night after night and I woke him up for work every morning, soon I would be joining him as his colleague. We went on lunch dates and dinner dates, laughing and talking about everything like we always did. His laughter was contagious. He was contagious period. I watched women look at him from the corner of their eye as he walked by, a few of our waitresses even tried him, but he only saw me. He treated me like I was his. I had no idea what we were and most days I really didn't care, because he was good to me. And good was a word I had forgotten the definition to long ago.
    We spent many isolated moments together in silence just staring at one another. I found peace in his eyes. A peace I had never experienced before. A peace I never had with Tavis. Being with Emmanuel brought about a lot of questions about the people in my past and the way they treated me. All of them seemed to be a waste of time.
    Sometimes I felt like the old me, who had no idea what heartache was. I thought it was impossible to feel happiness after shedding so many tears, but I was learning slowly and surely that you can feel whatever you want if you are open to it. Emmanuel wouldn't allow me to use Tavis' betrayal as a crutch. He called me on it each time that I brought it up. I admitted to him that sometimes I still needed more validation of why he did what he did. Emmanuel recited a *Mario Puzo* quote to me, *"what is past is past. Never go back. Not for excuses. Not for justification, not for happiness. You are what you*

are, the world is what it is." It only eased me temporarily as my past with Tavis fused with my future with him.

    I worried about seeing him every single day. Would I grow tired of him? Would he grow tired of me? It seemed like the perfect opportunity for change, but perhaps I was in over my head and enjoying what I was feeling a bit too much. All my life I had been careful. I never wanted to make a bad decision for my life because I saw what bad decisions did to other people. I could end up homeless or hungry. My mother wasn't the best woman in the world, but the one thing that she always preached was to have your own, because when it ever came down to it, nobody could take away from you what was yours.

    It was a hard lesson she learned as a single mother, dating man after man and constantly having to start over when they were done with her and her kids and we were left sleeping on the floors and sofas of family members who really didn't want us there, but on the strength of blood they felt obligated.

    I had a lot of time to reminisce while I was alone in my apartment with nothing to do. I felt a wave of emotions as the days went by. The hatred for my father leaving my mother to struggle with three kids while he went on living life like we never existed, the promiscuity of my mother, and the rebellion of my siblings. There was no wonder I was messed up.

    I sat and thought about all the different distractions that Madra attempted to place in my life and how each of them had their own turmoil of the heart. I was selfish and made everything about me as if no one in the world hurts. One of them could have been a great man, but there I was angry and bitter, ready to chew off the head of every man that crossed my path.

My final thoughts were about Tavis. I wondered why I loved him so much when all he was was a black cloud over my head. I used to watch my mother take care of men better than she took care of us and I always said to myself that I'd never be that stupid and there I was being that stupid when I was with him. I bought a man a car and he cheated on me before my birthday. I wanted to get over it, but something in me was still sour about the situation, even after I had said what I said and sent him on his way. It was almost impossible to run out of words. I gave him five years and I wanted five years to tell him exactly how I felt. I wanted to give him back five years of misery. I made him who he was and I wanted to destroy him.

On the final night in my apartment. I lay awake staring at the ceiling with a nervous feeling in my gut. I was really about to move in with Emmanuel. I couldn't admit out loud that I was scared to death. I took a deep breath then exhaled. My heart sped up in my chest. I sat up to calm myself. I was having some sort of anxiety attack. I eased out of bed and walked to the fridge to get some water. I leaned back against the counter and looked around at my now empty apartment. The only thing in there now was a bed that would be gone first thing in the morning when Salvation Army knocked on the door. I placed my hand over my chest and my heart was beating steadily again.

Rick Ross' The Boss feat Nicki Minaj echoed down my small hall-way from my bedroom. It was louder than it usually would be since there was no furniture. I sat my water on the counter and ran to answer it.

"Hey you." I answered.

"What took you so long to answer?" Emmanuel asked.

"I was in the kitchen?"

"Doing what? All your dishes are here." He laughed.

"Drinking water, I had an episode."

"What happened?"

"I was just thinking about us living together and got really dizzy."

"Dizzy? That doesn't exactly sound like a good thing…"

"I'm fine."

"You sure? You know I'd never pressure you into doing anything you don't want to do."

"I know that. It was just a mix of thoughts and emotions…"

I returned back to my bed connecting my phone to my charger and sliding my headset into my ear so that Emmanuel and I could have our nightly conversation until we both dozed off. His voice soothed my nervousness. I was making a good decision. Hopefully everything I had felt in the last few weeks would stay in this empty apartment.

Misery Loves Company

Eliza

"Madra why you keep calling me?" I answered my cell as I sat on the toilet seat slipping my foot into my heel.

"I was just checking on you since this is your first official day as a permanent resident at Manny's place AND your first day as his employee."

"The day just started." I stood and took one last look at myself in the mirror. I ran my hands down the black pencil skirt I wore and straightened out the collar on my blouse.

"Well you make sure you call me later and tell me how it went."

"Whatever nosy, bye, I have to go before we're late."

I stepped out of the bathroom and headed into the kitchen where Emmanuel stood reading the newspaper.

"Damn…" he said.

"What?"

"You look good."

I blushed, "thank you."

"You sure you want to wear that?"

"I'm comfortable like this."

"Okay baby, I'm not picking, let's get out of here."

Emmanuel and I took his truck to work. He parked behind the shop then we headed inside. He introduced me to the techs and his two cashiers, one of which gave me an ugly look and barely spoke when I shook her hand. I already knew what that meant.

He was still in the process of hiring a manager. I had no idea what my job title was exactly, but I was getting paid and I didn't really have a boss so that worked for me. Emmanuel and I walked into his office and shut the door.

"So what is it that you need me for?"

"Well I need you to keep the books balanced and for you to process payroll. I've put everything on my desk that you need."

"I'll be using your office?"

"Yeah, I'm ordering you your own desk, but for now you can sit at mine. I'm usually in the shop working with my techs anyway."

"So what do we need another desk for?"

"I use my desk sometimes."

"Uh huh."

Emmanuel stood from his chair and motioned for me to sit in it. He leaned down over my shoulder and showed me everything I needed to do.

"You smell good," he said in my ear.

"You're supposed to be training me Mr. Levi not sniffing me."

"I can't help it," he said as he stood up straight and swung me around in his chair. "I asked you if you were sure you wanted to wear that to work."

"Are you hitting on me Mr. Levi?" I smirked.

"I'm trying to restrain myself," he said as he placed his hand on my thigh and eased it up my skirt.

"This is sexual harassment you know?"

"Sue me." He said as his fingers reached my panty line and he leaned in to kiss me.

I pushed him back, "I have work to do Mr. Levi."

He eased back with all his might, placing each hand on the arms of his chair and looking me in the eyes, "you better watch yourself at lunch time." He stood and walked out of the office.

Once he shut the door I laughed and shook my head, "Whew!" I exhaled and swung around in the chair and got to work. I had a lot of catching up to do.

Emmanuel

I could barely concentrate on the car I was working on as I tried to calm myself down. Music blared through the shop and my techs joked with each other. I wasn't really feeling the work environment and the vibe. I stood to get a tool that I needed and one of my cashier's walked over to me with a frustrated look. I was not in the mood to deal with an unruly customer this early.

"Brandy you know you aren't supposed to come into this part of the shop."

"Yeah I know, but there's a woman looking for you."

"What woman?"

"She won't tell us her name. She threatened to come out here herself so I just came to get you."

I tossed my tool back into the box and grabbed a towel to wipe my hands on. I followed Brandy back inside. Desiree swung around with a grin on her face.

"Been awhile lover," she said as she approached me. She walked over to me and tried to wrap her arms around me and I pushed her back.

"What are you doing here?"

"I had some news I wanted to share with you."

"Why me? I'm sure we have nothing to discuss." I said folding my arms.

My office door swung open and Eliza came walking out.

"Can somebody…." She looked up and saw Desiree. "What's going on out here?" She stepped out from the office and looked back and forth between Desiree and me.

Desiree extended her hand to Eliza, "Desiree, you're Eliza right? I'm the ex and baby mother."

"Baby what?" I jumped in.

Desiree faced me, "you heard me; I'm pregnant. I thought you should know."

"It's not mine."

"I'm exactly three months, we were still fucking, so it's yours."

Eliza walked back into the office and grabbed her purse, she walked between Desiree and I quickly. I grabbed her arm. "Where are you going?"

"Call my apartment to see if it's still available. Looks like your place is about to be a little cramped."

"She's lying Eliza, look at her."

Eliza looked her up and down and then jerked away from me and headed for the exit.

"Eliza!" I ran outside behind her and Desiree walked slowly outside with an evil grin on her face.

"I knew it was mistake moving in with you."

"No it wasn't, I promise it wasn't." I followed behind her as she continued to walk.

This was not me. I had never been a man to run behind a woman. If they wanted to go they could go. There was too many fish in the sea. I felt pathetic walking behind her, but I also felt guilty and I hadn't even done anything.

"Eliza please stop," I grabbed her arm and stopped her in her tracks. I pulled my keys from my pocket and placed them in her hands. "Here take my truck, go home, and just wait for me, please."

"Why would I do that?"

"Because I want you to. Desiree is miserable and she wants me miserable with her. Just go to the house and don't leave, please?"

Eliza snatched my keys and started walking back toward the shop. I walked behind her. Desiree was still standing out front when I walked up. I walked past her and she followed me inside. I walked behind the counter and grabbed the keys to one of my customer's cars then turned and snatched Desiree by the arm dragging her out the door. I tossed her into the passenger side then hopped in on the driver's side. My techs and cashiers watched me as I drove off, all with confused looks.

"Where are we going?" Desiree asked amused.

"Don't say nothing to me." I said angrily as I drove.

I pulled up to a hospital and drug Desiree from the car. I had never been so rough with a woman, but she had pushed me. I drug her inside and pushed her to the counter.

"What is the procedure to get a pregnancy test done on a pregnant woman?" I asked the woman behind the desk.

The nurses eyes got big, "well we'd have to call your insurance company and see if we have a doctor here who does that procedure. It's very dangerous and could cause miscarriage."

"You want us to lose our baby?" Desiree said desperately.

I ignored her. "Ma'am I don't care if you have to call every hospital in this city. Find me a doctor."

The nurse asked for my insurance and identification.

"Okay, wait." Desiree grabbed me.

"You ready to tell the truth?" I gave her a look that could kill.

"Manny I'm sorry," she burst into tears. "I'm so lonely without you and you just moved on like we never were together. How could you just tell me I wasn't enough and leave me like that?"

"I was honest with you. I didn't want to stay somewhere I wasn't happy anymore. You wanted to be strung along? Cheated on?"

She didn't answer.

"You couldn't have been too lonely! You're three months pregnant. Were we not still together?"

"I made a mistake." She tried to hug me and I grabbed both of her wrist and held them in front of her face.

"I've never hit a woman in my life Desiree, but if you come near me or Eliza ever again, I'll forget the man my mama raised and knock your ass into labor. Don't come to my job, don't come to my crib." I pushed her back forcefully and walked out of the hospital with my blood pressure up as high as it could probably go. I hopped back into the car and sped to my studio.

When I pulled up Eliza was tossing bags into her trunk. I hopped out and ran over to her and grabbed the bags.

"Put them back Manny!"

"No!" I said carrying them back into the house. Eliza walked behind me tugging at them as if she could really get them from my grip.

"I'm leaving weather I have those bags or not."

"You're not going anywhere!" I raised my voice at Eliza for the first time.

"I'm a grown woman! I can leave if I want to!" She headed for the door and ran and slammed it before she could get out of it. I wrapped my arms around her tight. "I'm not letting you leave!" I squeezed her from behind locking her arms to her sides.

Eliza started to cry. I hated when women I cared about cried.

"Why does she keep popping up Manny? Are you fucking her?"

"No! I don't have anything to do with that girl." I released her and turned her around gripping her arms and looking her dead in her eyes.

"Just let me leave…" she said calming herself.

"Why?"

"Because you're just eventually going to do what Tavis did. One day I'll be just like Desiree."

I let her go and bald up my fist tight squeezing it then punching a wall. "I'm so fucking tired of you comparing me to that dude! What is it Eliza? You have commitment issues now?"

"No I just want to go."

"And all you needed was an excuse right?"

She stood silent looking afraid, but her obvious fear didn't calm me. I walked over to my nightstand and opened the drawer where I had tossed her list weeks ago. I pulled it out and walked over to her.

"Here you want this back?!" I balled it up and tossed it at her. "You want to keep trying to find some shit that doesn't exist?"

She stood shaking, "if you had it all this time then you would know it clearly states no ex drama!"

"Fuck that list Eliza!" I paced around her, "I'm better than that stupid list you wasted your time writing, why can't you see that? I'm something you failed to write down!" I looked for something to hit or knock over. "I'm a man of substance. I'm willing to sacrifice for you." I hit myself in the chest. "I'd invest all of myself in you, take chances and risk loving you even if you don't love me back!" A tear fell down my cheek as my anger grew to rage. "See us for what we could be, see me for me." I scorned her.

"All I see is that you're like everybody else."

I walked over to her and grabbed her face. I forced her to look at me. Look me in the eyes, "Am I? Can you honestly say I'm just like everybody else?"

She stared at me.

"Come on say it. I need to hear you say it."

"Will you let me leave after I say it?" she asked in a whisper.

"No…"

A tear fell from her eye and the words never escaped her lips.

I was calm now. I wrapped my arms around her waist. "You want me to sleep on the sofa tonight? I will, but you're not leaving." I reached for her arms and placed them around me forcing her to hug me. I had no understanding of why I needed this woman. I should be running for the hills.

Eliza pulled away from me and went to lie across my bed. I joined her. We laid fully dressed until she dozed off. I left her there and headed back to the shop to return the car I borrowed and to make sure everything was in order then I went right back to my studio. I didn't want to give her enough time to think about going anywhere.

She was still lying in the bed when I walked back in. "You awake?" I asked.

"Yeah…"

I shut the door behind me and rejoined her in the bed, wrapping my arms around her. "I'm sorry I overreacted."

"I'm not upset with you. You had every right to be mad, you were caught off guard." She said.

She rolled over, now lying on her opposite side, facing me. She placed her hand on my face and just looked into my eyes not saying a word. She made me feel weak and I was far from a weak man. Women had no idea the kind of power they had over a man weather his heart was involved or not.

I saw so many things in Eliza and the possibilities made me crazy. I just needed her to see what I saw. I hated that Tavis character and I didn't even know dude like that.

"Truth or dare?" I asked as she stared at me.

"Dare…" she whispered.

"I dare you to love me…

Hurricane season with Mr. Intellectual

Eliza

"Are y'all sure y'all want to stay there alone?"

"Madra we'll be fine."

"I just don't feel comfortable with y'all staying in that studio when this storm is a category three and then y'all are on the first floor."

"It doesn't flood in this area, if anything all we have to worry about is wind damage. Emmanuel has a little generator we can plug our phones up to and whatever else we might need."

"I guess that makes me feel a little better. You know I'm going to call you every hour once this storm gets bad."

"And you know I'm going to ignore you every hour right?"

Madra laughed, "This isn't funny E, you remember what happened with Katrina."

"Of course I remember I was sitting on a damn roof, but that was so long ago. I'm over it, I'm not running."

She sighed, "I guess there really is no changing your mind, well, y'all be safe okay. I'll call you when we reach our destination. Love you."

"Love you too."

We hung up.

I sat the phone down and joined Emmanuel as he prepared the studio for the storm. We unplugged everything and taped the windows.

"We could have evacuated if you wanted." He said as he pulled out candles and flashlights.

"We'll be fine. Don't start acting like Madra."

He smiled and set the candles up around the house. I walked over to the television and turned the news on. The meteorologist gave updates on the storm that was said to touch down the next morning. Hurricanes scared everybody, well, almost everybody because they didn't bother me much. There were natural disasters everywhere, from earthquakes to volcano eruptions. I couldn't see myself dealing with any other one than this one. I sat Indian Style on the sofa and Emmanuel joined me. He grabbed the remote and changed the channel.

"I was watching that." I protested.
"It's going to be on all night."
I pouted as he channel surfed.
"Hey go back that was Obama." I said as he continued to flip.
"I'm not watching that." He said.
"Why not?"
"I don't care about politics."
His words rubbed me the wrong way, "you don't vote?"
"Locally yes, but for the president, nah."
"Well, why not?" I said trying to give him a chance to explain himself before I was completely turned off.
"I honestly just don't believe one man should have all that power. I'm not saying Obama isn't a good dude, I just don't believe one person can fix a mess.
"One person created it."
"Yeah, because America let him. We have to fix problems locally first before we start trying to conquer the whole damn world. People in other countries are better off if you ask me."

"Explain…"

"Think about it, they get free health care and education in other countries then they come here and don't even pay taxes. You don't see a problem here yet?"

I wanted to argue with him, but I couldn't because he had stated a fact.

"I stopped caring about elections after Katrina, how do you call people in your own country refugees. There were people who didn't even know a disaster had happened right under their noses, but will sit and cry and send all their money overseas to feed children that aren't thinking about them."

I sat thinking about how hard of a time I had after the storm. I was hassled just to get my own social security card because I didn't have two forms of ID. They escorted me out of the building that day after I tossed everything on the representative's desk at her. I had lost everything in a storm, how was I supposed to provide anything?

"Do you plan on voting next election?" I asked.

"Probably not, I don't keep up with politics when it comes to presidency, so I'd rather not vote at all than to make an ignorant decision…"

"I respect that." I had to agree to disagree. I never really argued when it came to politics, because people were mostly firm in their beliefs, so it wasn't a deal breaker for me. I voted and that was all that mattered to me. I moved closer to him and waited as he found something for us to watch.

~~*~*

The storm hit at about ten in the morning. The rain came down hard and the wind shook the windows of the apartment. We still had power so we started to cook up all the meat in the fridge that could go bad. I seasoned the ground meat while Emmanuel seasoned the chicken to fry it.

"I don't think you've cooked since you've been here, do you know how?" he asked.

I laughed, "Is that a trick question?"

"Not really."

"Yes I can cook. I used to cook for my sister and brother all the time when we were younger. If I didn't we'd never eat. My brother believed cooking was a girl's job, so he hustled the money to buy the food and I cooked it."

"Your brother is a survivor."

"He most certainly is. I love him so much. He was the only man I ever really had in my life."

"So was he going to give you away at your wedding?"

"Actually yes."

"How did your dad feel about that?"

"He didn't have the right to feel anything…"

"I guess I understand that."

"You're always prying in my life, why don't you ever say much about yourself or your family?"

"There isn't much to say, I didn't know my father, still don't and my mother did all she could to make sure I had everything I wanted and needed."

"So you're a mama's boy."

"I'm definitely not a mama's boy." He smiled

"Did you ever want siblings?"

"I did at first but being around other kids at school changed my mind about that quickly. They got on my nerves enough."

"Siblings are not that bad."

"I'll take your word for it." He said dropping chicken into a bag of flour and shaking it up.

"Do you have any grandparents?" I asked prying more.

"My grandmother is on life support because my mom won't let her go and I never knew my grandfather, seems the men in my family have a history of vanishing, what about you?"

"They all died, two from cancer, one from a heart attack, and one from a stroke."

"Damn that sucks."

"They lived long lives."

Emmanuel washed his hand then walked up behind me and placed his hands in the bowl where I mixed the ground meat. "Let me help you with that."

"You just wanted to push up on me."

"Guilty." he said as he kissed my cheek.

It took us two hours to cook up everything in the fridge. We tried to eat as much as we could, before storing the rest in the fridge. The weather outside grew worse as lightning and thunder roared, making my heart skip a few beats. I stayed close to Emmanuel.

The lights stayed on until nine that night. We both looked around in the darkness and listened to the rain.

"Sit still I'll get a flashlight," he said and I could hear his feet moving." I heard a drawer open then a light flashed on. "Are you tired yet?" he asked.

"No." I responded.

"What do you want to do?"

"When I was little my siblings and I would play games during the storm."

"I have some cards."

Emmanuel retrieved the cards and the candles he pulled out earlier so that we could preserve the battery of the flashlight. We set up on the floor right in front of the television. I sat Indian Style and he sat with his legs stretched. He shuffled and dealt the cards for a game of Pitty Pat.

"You know I don't know anyone outside of Louisiana who knows how to play this game?" I joked.

"I wonder why that is."

"I don't know."

It was getting hot in the apartment fast with no electricity. That was what I hated most about hurricanes. We played several hands of Pitty Pat and moved onto Tunk. He had never played battleship so I taught him that and he taught me Jim Rummy. My clothes started to stick to me in the heat so I sat my hand down and removed my shirt. He stopped what he was doing to look at me then he dropped his hand and pushed me back onto the floor.

"It was your turn," I said looking up at him.

"I quit," he replied and pushed his lips against mine. This would surely pass some time. He leaned up again, "do you love me yet?" he asked.

I nodded my head yes and he kissed me deeply again. He leaned back on his knees, removing the wife beater he had been walking around in. I sat up and ran my hand down his sweaty chest. He grabbed my hand and placed my fingers into his mouth, sucking them, then standing to remove what was left of his clothes. I watched. He kneeled back down and pulled my clothes from my body. It seemed I never undressed myself. I liked it when he did it. He always took his time and he always looked me in the eyes. He laid me back down on the floor and invited himself into me. I closed my eyes. Suddenly the lightning and thunder didn't seem so shocking to my heart as Emmanuel thrust upon me. Our skin was wet with sweat, but it didn't stop him from licking my sweaty skin as he held his hand beneath my neck. We slid across the carpet. I knew I'd feel the burn later, but for now all I wanted to feel was him.

    I thought we'd never stop as the candles melted down and we lay beside each other exhausted. "Cold shower?" he asked.

    "Sure." I said, leaning up.

    Emmanuel stood then lifted me from the floor wrapping my legs around his back.

    "My legs work." I said with my arms around his neck.

    "I know." He said in a satisfied tone.

    He carried me into the bathroom and cut on the water. He stood still and held me up, pulling the shower curtain back and turning on the water. He held me tight in his arms and I knew what he was about to do.

    "You better not! Let me down!" I screamed and laughed.

    He smiled and stepped into the shower. The cold water hit my back and I screamed as he let me slide down and get my grip against the bath mat. "Ahhhh!" I screamed and laughed some more waiting for the temperature not to bother my skin anymore.

    He wrapped his arms around me and kissed my forehead and we both shivered under the cold water. I washed his back and he washed mine.

We dried each other after our shower and headed back out into the heat. My skin was cooled off from the water, but I was sure it was a matter of time before I started to sweat again.

The heat made me restless. Emmanuel slipped into pajama pants and I tossed on one of his t-shirts. He flipped through apps on his phone while I sat at the edge of the bed fanning myself with one of his magazines. Isley Brother's for the love of you filled the studio from his phone and he walked over to me.

"What are you doing?" I asked.

"Come on girl, you know you want to dance with me. It's not like we're going to sleep."

"What do you know about that kind of music anyway?" I asked teasingly.

"Let me show you." He reached his hand out to me and pulled me from the bed.

I left the magazine behind and Emmanuel and I stepped around each other until his battery died.

~~Secure and confident~~

Emmanuel

I had taken on a difficult task loving a damaged woman. Some days she was hot and others she was cold. Her mood would change for no reason at all and she'd space out into another world. I knew where her mind would go, but I didn't say it out loud to keep myself from getting into my own feelings.

The skies had cleared and everything was back to normal in the city after the storm. We were back to our routine. There were no more pop ups from my ex at home or at work, but there was a new issue with a tech I had just hired. I didn't like the way that he looked at Eliza or the way he flirted. I wasn't an insecure dude, but there were certain lines that I wanted respected. It was no secret who Eliza belonged to even if I never said the official words, it was understood. We were adults; there was no need for us to say oh that's my girlfriend or boyfriend.

I would watch him every day as he found a new excuse each day to make small talk with what was mine. I had never been the jealous type. I always knew where I stood with a woman, but this was different. I had let myself slip into a place deeper than I could explain. I wanted to bring physical pain to this dude.

He had only been working there a month and a half so he was still on probation and could get his ass kicked to the unemployment office at any moment.

I stood behind the counter watching him as he giggled like a bitch with Eliza. He was only twenty-three. He couldn't do half of what I could do for Eliza, but I also knew how women were when it came to younger men. I used to be that young man running game on older chicks because I knew it was easy to make them feel young again and make them open their wallets. All women seemed to go through that phase where they wanted to feel young again and still feel desired. I always caught them at that beginning stage. They were the perfect women for a broke college kid. They'd cook for you and let you knock some dust off that experienced box.

 My jaws clenched as I let my imagination get the best of me. I slammed the register shut after counting it down and they both stopped to look at me. I cracked a smile. "You ready to get out of here baby?" I asked Eliza.

 "Yeah just let me get my purse."

 Eliza headed into the office to grab her purse then we were out of the door. I let all the techs walk out first then I set the alarm and locked the doors. Eliza and I hopped into my truck and pulled off.

 "You might as well take off all that jewelry." I said to Eliza.

 "Why?"

 "Because you'll lose it on the rides at the fair."

 "I still can't believe I let you talk me into going to a damn kiddy fair." She said as she removed her chain.

 "Fairs are not just for children."

 "If you say so; I'm just going for the funnel cake."

 We had an hour to just ride and talk until we got to the fair. Each day I learned something new about Eliza and the feelings I had for her grew stronger.

 "I have an idea." I said to Eliza as she stared out of the window.

 "What about?" she turned to look at me.

"I think I want to let everybody wear their costumes to work next week for Halloween."

"That's a nice idea."

"You want to dress up with me?" he asked.

"Do I have a choice?"

"Not really."

She laughed and shook her head. "What did you have in mind?"

"I want to be Robin Hood; you can be my Maid Marian." I smiled.

"That is so cheesy."

"It was the most descent one I could think of for work."

"So you're going to wear tights?"

"Hell no!" I laughed out loud.

"Just thought I'd ask." She giggled.

We pulled up to the fair and Eliza reached for my hand. It was the first time she had shown any type of public affection. I just assumed she wasn't into it since she always pulled away when I reached for her hand or tried to kiss her in public. Eliza was changing and it made me feel good to know that it was because of me.

We paid the entrance fee and got wristbands for unlimited rides. I had never seen a woman so happy. She resisted when I asked her to come to this fair and now her eyes lit up like a child as she drug me from ride to ride and every rip off game they had set up. She clung to me on every ride screaming in my ear. I had never seen her smile so wide or laugh so loudly. She bumped me constantly on bumper cars, kept her eyes closed in the haunted house, and didn't resist my kiss at the top of the Ferris wheel. We shared funnel cake, a turkey leg, and lemonade. I couldn't remember the last time I enjoyed someone's company that much.

Loves to travel

Eliza

Halloween

 I felt ridiculous in a costume. I had not dressed up for Halloween since middle school. Emmanuel was in full on character jumping in and out of the office, calling me fair maiden and holding his hands on his waist with his chest out. All I could do was shake my head and laugh. I hated Halloween, but I didn't want to kill Manny's spirit. I just sucked it up. I could snatch this costume off the instant the work day was over.
 I sat going through payroll for the week and I saw that the tech that Manny had just hired not too long ago had not clocked in that day. He was still on probation and couldn't miss any days or he would be automatically terminated. I hated that rule and I hated to see people lose their job, especially with the holidays so close. I stood from the desk and poked my head out to look for Manny, "Emmanuel can you step in here for a minute?" I asked when I spotted him.
 "Yeah sure," he said and stopped what he was doing.
 I closed the door behind him once he stepped in. "Did Kyle call in or something today?"
 "No, I fired him."
 "What? Why?"
 "Because…"
 "Because what?"
 "Look it doesn't matter just take him out of the system."

"When did you plan on telling me you fired the boy?"

"It wasn't that important."

"Emmanuel the holidays are coming up."

"I know that."

"Well what did you fire him for?"

"Do we have to have this conversation now?"

"Yes we do."

He sighed, "I didn't like the way he looked at you and flirted with you, so when he forgot to put oil in a customer's car last week I fired him."

"You took his job because you were jealous?"

"That and he could have blown that's woman's gasket out. Eliza don't do this right now. Shit if you wore jeans around here and not those damn office clothes and heels, I wouldn't have to worry about techs smiling in your damn face all the time. This is a damn car shop not a corporate office."

"I work behind a desk!"

He rolled his eyes.

"You might as well get rid of everybody who works here then, they all look, shit I don't say nothing when Brandy pushes up on you."

"You want me to fire her?"

"No!" I threw my arms up. "Just get out." I shook my head and returned back to the desk.

Emmanuel walked out of the office with a stressed expression. This was one of the reasons I hated Halloween. I felt that evil lurked, bringing about confrontations and mass confusion. I was ready to go home.

~~*~*

Emmanuel and I had not spoken two more words to each other for the rest of the day. Even after we got home I watched television and he read his business magazines.

I crawled into the bed once I was tired of watching television and Emmanuel shut off the light and wrapped his arms around me like we weren't angry with each other. I inched over and he moved with me.

"Get off of me."

"Nope, if you sleep in my bed, I'm holding you."

"Well I'll sleep on the sofa." I jumped out of bed and went to lie down on the sofa.

Emmanuel eased out of bed and hopped on the sofa behind me. "You sleep on my sofa, I'm holding you."

"I'll get on the floor then." He gripped me tight as I attempted to move.

"I have all night to move around. You're not sleeping without me."

I wanted to be angry, but I couldn't. I smiled in the darkness and let him hold me as we dozed off on the sofa.

2:00 AM

My cell phone rang over and over again. I thought I was dreaming until I heard Emmanuel in my ear. "Baby answer your phone, whoever it is wants to talk bad."

I eased from the sofa, eyes half shut and stumbling to answer my phone. "Hello." I finally got to it. There was loud crying in the background and the voice on the line was barely speaking. I rubbed my eyes and held the phone away from my ear to look at the ID. It was my sister. "Ella I can't understand a word your saying, slow down, what's the matter?"

"Eli" she snorted

"Eli what? Where is Eli?"

"He" she sniffed "he-he"

"ELLA WHAT IS IT?"

"He was killed!" she screamed and sobbed into the phone. I stood frozen with the phone glued to my ears as my body tingled in the worse way. My stomach twisted up in knots and the light switched on. Emmanuel walked over to me.

"Baby?" he said to half-deaf ears.

I just looked up at him and then reached him my phone. He put it to his ear and I walked over to the sofa and plopped down, staring at the black screen on the television. I felt pain all over, but it would not reflect in my eyes. I wouldn't believe it. I couldn't believe it. Emmanuel ran over to me quickly kneeling down in front of me.

"Eliza, look at me."

I didn't look at him. I just sat there.

"Come on I'll take you to the hospital."

I shook my head no.

"You don't want to go?"

"He's not dead…"

"Eliza…"

I laid back down on the sofa. "Can you turn off the light?"

Emmanuel sat and stared at me for a moment then he walked and turned off the light and laid back down with me. I closed my eyes and went back to sleep. It was all just a bad dream that would be over in the morning.

Emmanuel

    Eliza walked around like a zombie for days. She didn't speak and she didn't cry. She barely ate and we sat up each night until four in the morning. She refused to deal with what happened. She recorded the news report on DVR and watched it over and over. The story was that her brother had gotten into an argument with somebody on Bourbon Street and the dude pulled out a gun and shot him three times in the chest. Nobody could identify the shooter because he was wearing a mask. It seemed Halloween was the perfect time for murder.
    Eliza sat far away from her family at the funeral and she refused to watch him be placed in the ground. I forced her to stay home and grieve, but she didn't shed one tear. I was getting worried. I had never dealt with a loss like that before and had no idea how to comfort her when she needed me most. I just asked her daily what she needed. She only kissed me and didn't answer.
    I knew today would be no different as I dressed for work. I stood waiting for Eliza to come out of the bathroom. She walked out fully dressed. I looked at her confused. "Where are you going?"
    "To work," She spoke for the first time in weeks.
    "You're talking." I walked behind her, examining her expression and movements.
    She cleared her throat, "yeah."

"Are you sure you want to go to work?"
"I'm positive. I can't sit in here another day."
"Baby but you haven't…"
She looked at me, "don't do that."
"Eliza he was your brother, you can hurt and shed tears. It's okay."
"Emmanuel," she faced me and placed her hand on the counter, "I just want to have a nice normal day."
I surrendered, "Okay, whatever you want." I stood there watching her as she pulled a coffee mug down then reached for the coffee pot, something wasn't right. She stood and poured the hot coffee into the mug until it ran over burning her hand.
"Shit!" she said dropping the coffee pot and the mug on the floor. They both shattered instantly and she jumped back. I grabbed a dish towel and kneeled down to clean it. She squatted and grabbed a piece of glass, cutting her hand.
"Ouch!" she fell back and leaned against the cabinet and then it happened. She broke. Her pain had been triggered physically and she could no longer sit in denial. "Shit, shit, shit!" she screamed and cried uncontrollably. I grabbed a napkin and pressed it against her bleeding hand and then wrapped my arms around her. She let her head fall into my chest as she released all the pain she held in. I couldn't stand to see her like this.
I stood and picked her up from the kitchen floor and carried her to the bed. I let her soak my shirt as her painful cry cut me. Her body jerked, she screamed questions that I couldn't answer, and she gagged on her tears.
I removed her clothes then grabbed a bag and tossed a few of her things into it. I did the same for

myself. I was about to share a coping world with Eliza. I pulled out a t-shirt and some sweatpants and walked over to dress her.

"What…are…you…doing?" she spoke through tears.

"We're going to take a ride."

"Where?"

"Don't worry about that."

I dressed Eliza then made a call to the shop. I let them know I'd be out for a few days and I told my best tech he'd be in charge while I was away.

"Come on get up."

"I don't want to go anywhere."

"I'll drag you kicking and screaming Eliza."

Eliza stood from the bed and pushed her feet into her slippers. I grabbed her arm as she walked past me, "I'm going to take care of you," I said looking her in her eyes then releasing her. She walked slowly to the door. I left the mess in the kitchen to clean another day. I had a more serious matter at hand that needed my immediate attention.

I helped Eliza into my truck and tossed our bags in the back then we were on our way. Her cell phone rang as I drove up our block. "Eliza answer you phone."

"I don't want to."

"Baby people are worried about you."

"I just…I don't have much to say to anyone right now."

"I understand."

Eliza

We drove for seventeen hours, stopping in little towns to get gas and eat. We even pulled over and slept on the side of the rode for a few hours since Emmanuel insisted on driving and not telling me exactly where we were going. I had no idea what he was up to, but whatever it was was working as I rode with the window down just leaving all my problems miles behind.

Eli was the one problem I could not leave behind. I couldn't stop thinking about the disturbing phone call about his death. I always knew that him being a hothead would get him into trouble, but I never guessed it would get him into his grave. It was hard to accept that I was living in a world where fist-fighting was not the way to settle a score anymore. Who shoots you over an argument? I couldn't piece it together in my mind.

"We're here?" Emmanuel announced.

"Where is here?" I asked.

"Downtown Maryland."

I looked around at the buildings. The structure was so different from home. I felt a bit of warmth in my heart in this strange place. I had not paid attention to a single sign. *Were we really in Maryland?* I thought. This was a long way from home for me, being one of those people from New Orleans who loved the city so much I vowed to never leave it. I had always said I wanted to travel, but I always found an excuse not to. I was scared of planes, I refused to ride a bus, and driving alone was just not an option when the thought of eighteen-wheelers running me off the road came to mind.

I smiled for the first time in weeks when we pulled up to our hotel. Emmanuel valeted the car and we went inside. He didn't have a reservation, but they did have one room available. It was a suite.

"Can you afford that?" I asked.

"Let me handle this okay."

I didn't argue.

We didn't have much luggage, so Emmanuel carried all of our bags to our room. I had never stayed in a suite before. My eyes widened as we walked into the room. I removed my shoes the moment I crossed the threshold, curling my toes into the rich carpet. I walked over to the wide window that showed off the skyline and probably the entire city. I ran my hand along everything in the room from the hardwood dresser to the heavy comforter. Emmanuel sat our bags down beside the door and walked over to the bar that sat on the opposite side of the room.

"Want a drink?" he asked.

"Yes." I said and he looked up at me shocked.

He poured us both a drink. He tossed his back and it was gone in one swallow. I sat on the end of the bed and sipped mine turning up my face at the bitter taste. I heard the water in the tub shut on. I just sat there looking around the luxurious room.

Emmanuel walked from the bathroom and over to me. He took my glass from my hand and sat it on the dresser beside the bed then reached for my hand.

"Is that water for me?" I asked looking up at him.

"Both of us." He said pulling me to my feet.

I stepped into the bathroom. The lights were bright and the tub was huge. Emmanuel walked over to me and pulled my shirt over my head then unsnapped my bra and dropped it to the floor. I covered myself as if he was seeing me for the first time. I felt lost and vulnerable after he saw me break down. I never wanted him to see that side of me.

He shut off the water and removed the rest of my clothing then told me to get in. I tested the water with my foot then eased in as my body agreed with the temperature. I sat down in the water and allowed it to take over my body as Manny undressed to join me. He sat behind me and I rested my head on his chest.

"How you feeling?" he asked.

"Empty, helpless..."

"It's okay to feel that way you know."

"Is it?"

He wrapped his wet arms around me and just held me against him. "Why do you always have to hold it together?"

"I don't know. I've always been the strong one in my immediate family. I'm the one everyone can depend on."

"You don't have to be that way with me okay." He exhaled. "While we're here I'm going to take care of you. Anything you want me to do I'll do it."

I could hear him, but at the same time his voice was a whisper to me. Emmanuel had come into my life and done everything no one else could and it still wouldn't register in my brain that he was real. I knew that at the very moment that I surrendered to complete happiness I would wake up from this amazing dream and I'd be back in my apartment with Tavis lying next to me dreaming of his next lie. I was so messed up, but Emmanuel loved me still.

We soaked a bit longer before he washed my entire body and I sat emotionless in the water before him. He rinsed me then dried me and carried me to the bed.

Emmanuel did exactly what he said he would. He took care of me. I sat in the middle of the bed in the hotel robe as he brushed my hair for me. It felt good. I finally believed that he was that one exception to the "most men" category.

"Eliza…"
"Yeah…"
"When was the last time you prayed?" he asked.
"I'm not sure…"
"You want to pray now?"
"Now…with you?"
"Yes."

Emmanuel sat the brush down and sat in front of me on the bed. He grabbed my hands and pushed them together into prayer hands and he held his hands over mine. He closed his eyes, so I closed mine too. His voice sent vibrations through me. I had never prayed with a man in my life unless you counted my pastor in a room full of people.

"Father..." he paused. "God we are coming to you tonight because Eliza needs you. I am asking that you heal her broken heart and not just for the recent struggle, but for everything that she has been through. I ask that you continue to give *me* strength so that I may be here for her no matter what. I understand that you have a plan God and we both will try to be obedient and follow whatever that plan may be. We have not been perfect God, but we know that you love us anyway. I pray that Eliza can sleep without trouble tonight and Thank you for simply being who you are. In Jesus name we pray. Amen."

"Amen."

I slept peacefully that night.

~~*~*

If I was insane I would have dropped everything to stay right where we were. I loved Maryland. The grass was so much greener, no pun intended. I smiled when I watched the city get smaller in our rearview. I made a note to myself to visit again one day, but at that moment I had to get back to my life.

We pulled up to Emmanuel's mother's house. She greeted us with a smile and a kiss on the cheek the moment we walked through the door. I guessed that Emmanuel told her what happened to my brother because the hug that she gave me lingered longer than just a friendly hello. I smelled baked chicken in the air as she embraced me. My stomach growled reminding me that I had not been eating like normal.

"You hungry?" she asked.

"Yes ma'am."

"Then come and eat then." She said, placing her hand in mine as if she had known me her whole life. She walked me into the kitchen and it felt nice to be loved by someone's mother who saw me as good and knew it for sure.

She instructed me to sit down at the table and I did as I was told sitting my purse down near my feet. Emmanuel joined us, smiling in my direction. He leaned over the table and whispered. "She's never liked anyone I dated."

I cracked a smile and felt warmth in my heart because it was probably the first time that anyone's mother had not given me a hard time. She welcomed me with open arms the first time that she met me.

Emmanuel's mother fixed us some food then placed it on the table in front of us. I closed my eyes and blessed my food then dug in.

I felt a vibration against my foot. I knew it was a text because it only happened once. I leaned down to pull my phone from my bag. The name on my screen made my heart stop.

Tavis: Hey, heard about your brother. I'm really sorry. I know we had our differences, but I wouldn't wish that on anyone.

I could see Emmanuel watching me from the corner of my eye so I kept the same expression and continued to eat. He never asked who it was.

We sat with his mom for a few more hours then we left. I was looking forward to being back home once we got close to the studio, but we drove right past it.

"Where are we going?"

"I don't think I should tell you…"

"Why?"

"You might get mad at me."

"Well don't bring me."

"I have to. It's for your own good."

I sat in the passenger seat silent and upset that he wouldn't tell me where he was bringing me.

After about twenty more minutes of riding we came to a stop and I read the name on the board in front of the entrance.

"Why would you bring me here?" I asked angrily as we sat in front of the cemetery.

"Eliza you need to tell him goodbye the right way."

"I said goodbye."

"You sat at the back of the church and then went home. Your family is still blowing you up."

"I'm not going."

"Baby…I'm right here with you. I promise you'll feel so much better."

Emmanuel got out of the truck and walked over to my side to open my door and help me out. He walked with me over to my brother's plot. I stood frozen as I read his name on his headstone. His body was beneath the very dirt I stood on. Emmanuel stepped back and I fell to my knees. It was real. He was gone. I let the rest of my body fall. I was face down on the grass. The tears came before I could think about them. I beat on the ground. "WHY DID YOU LEAVE ME?" I screamed."WHAT AM I SUPPOSED TO DO WITHOUT YOU?" I continued to beat into the dirt and sob.

Emmanuel lifted me from the ground once my pain became too much for him. I was covered in dirt and tears, but just like he said I felt better. Seeing his name made me accept that he was gone. I had to deal with it.

~~*~*

"It's about damn time you answered the phone. Are you okay?" Madra asked.

"I feel a lot better." I said sitting in the middle of the bed and recovering from my cemetery breakdown.

"Are you sure?"

"Yeah I'm sure. I'm just ready to get back into my routine."

"Well, before you do that, do you think you could have a little fun and come to a card party tonight?"

"I think I just might do that."

"Good, you and Emmanuel can bring paper plates, napkins, and utensils."

"Does Emmanuel know already?"

"Yeah, Paul told him. The original plan was to just drag you here against your will."

"I've been forced to do a lot against my will the past couple of months. I don't think a card party would have killed me." I smiled.

"I'm just happy to hear your voice. I was worried."

"Don't be Emmanuel has been wonderful."

"Well you and Mr. Wonderful better get here before seven."

"We'll be there." I laughed then we said our goodbye's until later. I hung up my cell and stretched. I had slept all day, while Emmanuel ran errands.

The front door opened, "Hey sleepy head."

"Hey."

"You talked to Madra?"

"We just got off the phone a minute ago."

"Well why aren't you up getting dressed?"

"I'm getting up."

I hopped out of bed and got dressed. It would be good to get around some good people and have a few drinks and a few laughs. I had isolated myself long enough. I needed to call my mom and dad when I got a chance, because they had called the most. I just still wasn't ready.

I dressed and Emmanuel and I headed to the store to get our items for the party. We pulled up to the dollar store and went in.

"I'm going look for cards." Emmanuel said.

"I'm sure they have cards. It's a card party."

"I don't trust people. They can rig the deck." He said then headed off.

"Whatever, I'm going find the plates and stuff."

I walked off into the opposite direction. I walked down to the last isle and turned to my left. I stopped in my tracks when I saw Tavis stocking shelves. I tried to turn around so he wouldn't see me, but I didn't move fast enough. He stopped what he was doing and walked over to me.

"I texted you, did you get it?" he asked urgently.

"Yeah I've just been real busy…"

"Busy ignoring me?"

"It's not like that."

"It's cool. I understand. I just wanted you to know I was sorry for your loss…"

"Well thanks…"

"You can call me if you ever need to talk."

"That's probably not a good idea."

"Why not?"

Emmanuel yelled out my name just as I was about to answer Tavis' question. He turned at the other end of the isle and saw Tavis talking to me. He was calm as he walked in our direction. He bumped Tavis out of the way.

"You got the plates?"

"They're right there." I pointed at the plates on the shelf.

He grabbed a pack and looked Tavis up and down then grabbed my arm and pushed me toward the register. I was saying a silent prayer in my mind as Tavis walked to the front of the store watching our every move. I hoped that we could leave in one peace. Tavis was the double standard guy. He could do whatever he wanted with whomever he wanted, but the thought of me with someone else killed him. I was sure he recognized Emmanuel's face from the day we went to tow his car.

We checked out and got into Emmanuel's truck.

"Shoot!"

"What?" Emmanuel asked.

"We were supposed to get napkins and forks too."

"I'll go back in and get them."

"No, let's go somewhere else."

"I'm not worried about your ex Eliza."

He wasn't, but I was and the moment he said that Tavis was out the door and walking full speed in our direction. It would be easy for him to attack Emmanuel since there was only one car parked on his side and it had one empty space between them.

"You the motherfucker that towed my car!" Tavis yelled and headed for Emmanuel.

Emmanuel turned to step out of the truck, but before he could get all the way out Tavis had ran up to him.

"Tavis no!" I screamed.

Before I could stop it Tavis slammed the door on Emmanuel's leg. He slammed it so hard I heard the bone in Emmanuel's leg crack. I screamed and Emmanuel fell down in agony. I jumped out of the truck and ran to the other side as Tavis kicked Emmanuel over and over. I tried to pull him away and he pushed me back into another parked car. I ran into the store and grabbed his manager. The manager ran outside with me and grabbed Tavis. A few people had gathered in the lot watching. Emmanuel cussed at Tavis, yelling threats on his life as police sirens came up the street. I tended to Emmanuel until the police pulled me away for questioning. Tavis was arrested and placed in the back of the squad car. His manager had him surrender his tag and keys before he was cuffed. I didn't feel any remorse. He was going where her belonged.

    I followed behind the ambulance with tears in my eyes. Emmanuel didn't deserve this. Had I not brought him into my drama in the first place we'd be at the card party right now. It seemed that bad things had been happening for two weeks, first with his ex, then my brother, and now this. I felt like a bad omen for his life. I needed to leave.

    Once he was at the hospital, they drugged him up and put a cast on his leg. I gave the nurse at the station his mother's number for when it was time for him to be discharged then I left to go pack my things. I couldn't do this anymore. I refused to let him keep trying to fix me while it was hurting him in the process.

Emmanuel

"Where'd Eliza go?" I asked my mom once I was aware of my surroundings again.

"I don't know. She wasn't here when I got here."

"Did she call you?"
"No a nurse did."
"Where's my phone?"
My mother stood and walked to retrieve my phone. She handed it to me as a nurse walked in with a wheelchair. I scrolled to Eliza's name and hit talk. The phone didn't even ring it just went to voicemail. I called again. It did the same thing. I felt confused for a moment. *Where could she be? Why would she leave me here alone?*

The nurse helped me into the wheelchair. My mother had crutches in her hand as she followed us out of the door. I looked up and down the halls of the hospital. Eliza had to be there somewhere. I looked down at my leg and a feeling of anger ripped through me. I had never broken a bone in my life. I better not catch Tavis' ass anywhere when they released his ass. Everything I did to make myself an educated and civilized man was for damn sure going to go out the window. He could have at least fought me man to man, but instead he did some bitch ass shit like that. *Where the fuck was Eliza!*

I called her number again.

You have reached 504... I listened until I got the beep. "Eliza, where are you? Call me back please." I hung up.

My mother and the nurse helped me into my mom's car. I pulled the door shut behind myself and my mother placed the crutches on the back seat. She closed the door then hopped in on the driver's side. My mother looked over at me. "You want to tell me what's going on?"

"Not right now mama, just get me home." I sat staring out of the window.

My mother didn't pester me like she usually would. She let me sit inside my own mind.
We pulled up to my apartment and my truck was parked outside but Eliza's car was gone. I was really confused now. My mom walked around to help me out and help me balance myself on my crutches. She grabbed all the papers that the nurse gave to her then she followed me to my door. I turned to face her. "I don't have my keys."
My mother pulled out her key and unlocked my door. We went inside and it was an instant vibe change. Something wasn't right. I called Eliza again– voicemail. Something told me to check my drawers so I did. I pulled the top one open and it was empty. I checked another one– empty. Eliza had taken all of her things. I sat down on my bed and looked around.
"What's wrong?" my mom asked.
"She's gone…"
"Eliza?"
"I don't understand…" I said out loud to myself.
"She'll come back baby."
"Mama EVERYTHING is gone…"
My mother stood there thinking of something to say. I had a million things to say, but it all involved cuss words, so I just kept it in my brain. I felt stupid. I opened up my heart, soul, and home to this woman and she left me. Her ex attacked me and she fucking left me.
"You want some time to yourself?" my mom asked.
I just nodded my head yes. I had a ball of anger stuck in my throat. My mom walked over and kissed me on the cheek then she was out of the door.

I scrolled through my phone and called Madra. The phone rang four times before she answered. "You and E better have a damn good excuse why y'all didn't make it to the party?"

"Have you talked to Eliza since earlier?"

"No, is something wrong?"

"She's not answering the phone for me."

"Well, why not?"

"That's what I'd like to know. We ran into her ex at the dollar store earlier and something went down. Long story short, he slammed my leg in a door and broke it and now Eliza is nowhere to be found."

"Emmanuel stop playing with me."

"I'm not joking Madra. You can come see my leg for yourself. I've been in the hospital for hours."

Madra took a deep breath, "Maybe she just needs some time."

"You don't take all your things if you need some time."

"Damn…"

"Yeah…" we sat on the phone silently, "if you talk to her can you just tell her to call please. Tell her it's not her fault and I'm not upset. I just want her to come back."

"I'll tell her Manny. I'm so sorry."

"Thanks." I said then hung up.

Eliza

My mother had not seen me since my brother's funeral and even then I had not said two words to her. I knocked on her door with my bags beside my feet. I could hear her walking slowly to answer the door. She pulled the chain back and it eased open. Her eyes were bloodshot red and her hair looked like it had not been combed in days. I broke into tears the moment I looked into her eyes. She swung the door open and pulled me into her arms and held me, patting my back as I sobbed. I pulled back and wiped my eyes. I grabbed my bags and walked inside without a word. I carried my things to the room that I shared with my sister growing up. It used to have two twin beds, but now it only had one full sized one; that was big enough for me. I placed my bags at the foot of the bed and kicked my shoes off then laid across the bed. I laid in silence.

My mother pushed the door open and poked her head in, "you hungry?"

"No ma'am."

She nodded her head and turned to leave then she stopped. "You want to talk about it?"

I shook my head no.

"Hiding isn't the answer."

"Who says I'm hiding?"

"You're my child. I know better."

I turned over on my back and looked at my mother, "did you talk to him that day?"

She shook her head yes.

"What did you say to him?" I asked sitting up in the bed.

"What do you mean?"

"What did you say to him? I know you said something to him. There are only a few people that could have made him so mad that he'd go and get himself killed and you are number one on that list." I raised my voice.

"You better calm your ass your down little girl. I'm your mother!"

"Lucky me…" I said then laid back down and turned on my side.

My mother moved quickly to the bed, snatching me up by my arm. Tears ran down her face. "All of you are so damn ungrateful! You, your sister! Eli had to remind me every day how much of a shitty mother I was, but what about me? Do you think it was easy feeding three kids with one minimum wage paying job? You had a roof over your head, you ate every single night!" She threw her hand up for her own confirmation. "No, you didn't get everything you wanted, but I gave you what you needed and I'm sorry if that wasn't good enough for you! It was my struggle, yes you all were there and you all may have felt pain, but I took the big blows. There is nothing sadder than knowing you can't do everything you needed to do as a mother for your kids, but I did my best. I was young and alone but I never made excuses!" My mother released me and stood from the bed. Her face was soaked and so was mine.

I choked out the words, "I'm sorry."

She wiped her eyes, "it's okay, you're hurting; we all are. We are all looking for someone to blame. None of us want to face the truth of how your brother was."

I bit my lip and nodded my head in agreement. My mother headed for the door again.

"Mama can I ask you something?"

"It's may I and yes you may, she said returning back to the bed and sitting down beside me."

"Why didn't you ever tell me what love was supposed to be like?"

She smiled and looked up at the ceiling, "I couldn't teach you something I didn't even know." She placed her hand on my thigh, "You know your father was the only man I was ever in love with?" she smiled and shook her head. "I made so many mistakes and before I could realize it, it was too late to fix them." She laughed. "That man was good to me and I spent years trying to replace him."

"I thought daddy left you."

"He did. I cheated on him. He gave me a choice when he found out too. Told me it was him or my boyfriend and I chose my boyfriend. Your daddy was crushed and I couldn't blame him. It wasn't even a week later that me and my boyfriend broke up."

"Why did you cheat on him?"

"I was young, felt tied down, and wasn't ready for what your father was ready for."

We sat silent for a moment. My mother had never talked to me like that before. It was then that I realized I never really knew much about her. I had always only looked at her as a provider and not a person with her own life.

"Mama I met a man."

"Is he good to you?"

"Yes."

"Then what are you doing here?"

"I'm scared that I'll never be able to love him the way he loves me and now we have all this drama with his ex and mine...."

My mother shook her head, "baby all relationships have drama. There will always be somebody that doesn't want to see you happy, but the way you beat them is by remaining happy and on the days you two aren't doing so good, still be happy and keep it to yourself. When you can withstand anything that comes your way in a relationship, you have found true love."

"Tavis hurt me so bad though and you remember all that drama with him."

"Tavis didn't get enough love from his mama. I felt the same way about Jarrod. You can't let your past dictate your future. You'll be miserable just like he's going to be for the rest of his life."

"Thank you mama," I grabbed her putting my arms around her and squeezing her tight.

"Anytime, now you stay as long as you like and get your head together, but don't let that man look for you and wait too long, you'll lose him and you'll regret it." My mama stood and left me to rest. I saw her in a new light and she gave me something to think about.

I went back out to my car to get the gift basket that Emmanuel had given to me. It was time I put that notebook to use.

Thirty days and thirty nights

Eliza

I had no idea that depression could take on so many different forms. It was one thing to be depressed because of something someone else had done to you, but it was another thing to be depressed when something was your own fault. From what I knew Emmanuel didn't see what happened as a big deal, but I did. He was temporarily paralyzed because of my stupid ex.

Okay maybe paralyzed was a bit extreme, but he may as well be since there wasn't much that he could do on his own. I thought about calling him every single day that I hid at my mother's house, but for some reason, leaving him alone just seemed like the better option.

I had convinced myself that I needed to take heed to all the bad signs right now, because I hadn't done it in the past with Jarrod or Tavis. I let one bad thing after the other happen and I just stayed and took it all. I wasn't going to let that be the case this time.

It was so hard.

Every night I laid in bed thinking about how wonderful Emmanuel was. I thought about stupid things like him taking out the trash without being asked or told or him pumping my gas for me. Men like him just didn't exist anymore. I didn't want to ruin him. It was women like me who ruined men like him.

I was cursed, possibly doomed to be alone forever because everything that I touched turned to shit. I was right back down memory lane again with the stupid men of my past. Why couldn't all love be like puppy love?

I thought about my very first boyfriend, when things were much simpler. His name was Aiden Hensley.

He was the first boy that I had ever kissed and laid in the same bed with. We used to play video games and he would sneak into my house in the middle of the night and sit up talking to me until it was time for school the next day. He never tried too hard and I never caught him in a lie. I just knew we'd be together forever. That dream was short lived, but my feelings lived on.

After he and his family moved away I kept all his things in hopes that he and I would one day be together again. I still remembered the day he left like it was yesterday. I held my hand as I high as it could go waving at him in the tan car that drove off. The moment he was out of my sight I collapsed to the ground and sat there until the sun went down. I knew I'd never feel that kind of love again.

I laughed at the memory. I laughed because I did exactly what Emmanuel said women do after heartache. I kept trying to fill the void that my first love left behind and in doing so I accepted anything. I needed to pray, God would tell me what to do.

Emmanuel

The sun had set and rose thirty times and each day I showered with a plastic bag over my leg then I sat in the same spot with depressing music playing on my phone. I didn't visit my family on Thanksgiving and I loved to eat. My mother froze me a bowl of gumbo so I was good.

I felt soft just sitting and listening to *Tank's I can't make you love me* and drinking beer in the dark. I sang along to the song off key and really feeling each word. There was a knock at the door.

"Who is it?"

"Paul, open up!"

I grabbed my crutches from beside my bed and hopped to open the door. Paul walked in and looked around.

"Where is the light switch?" he asked.

"Why?" I said hopping back to my bed.

"Two dudes, in a studio, in the dark? That's suspect my boy I need some light."

I laughed, "Behind you."

Paul switched on the light and walked over to where I lay. "How's that leg doing?"

"It's alright, itches like crazy and I want to scratch it, but I can't. I don't even have any wire hangers to stick down there."

Paul laughed, "I'm going to invite myself to a beer, cool?"

"Yeah man, go ahead." I said as I adjusted myself in the bed. "Hey, have you heard from Eliza?"

"Nah man I haven't."

"Are you lying to me? I know Madra tells your ass everything."

"Not everything. She and Eliza have some kind of twisted bond I'll never understand. I can't get words out of her about Eliza."

I shook my head.

"I can't believe you're still around here moping about that girl man it's been a whole month. If she hasn't called or texted after all this time, she probably won't."

I exhaled, "I don't want to believe that. Had her ex not pulled this stunt, we'd be laid up right now."

"You gotta shake it off man." Paul said then sipped his beer. "You want to hit the strip club with me tonight?"

I tooted my lips and looked at Paul like he had lost his mind, "do you not see my leg?"

He laughed, "Oh yeah I forgot that fast." He continued to laugh.

"It ain't that funny jackass."

"You're a better man than me. My kids would be visiting me behind glass right now had a nigga broke my leg."

"You think I didn't want to handle that shit myself? He pulled a bitch move for real."

"He's still in jail huh?"

"From what I heard, he'll be there awhile too. I have a cop that comes to get his car fixed at my shop and he told me he had priors and didn't even get bail."

"I'd hate to be him. An assault and battery charge ain't no joke."

"Good, I hope his ass rots in there." I said and finished off my beer. "What are you doing here anyway?"

"I just needed a break from the Madra and the kids and I needed to check on my boy."

"I appreciate it."

"Anytime my dude."

"Can you do me a favor though?"

"What is it?" Paul asked skeptical.

"Would you give Madra something for Eliza?"

"What makes you think she'll give it to her?"

"That's what you're for. If you're putting it down right, then she'll do it if you talk her into it."

"Man I puts it down."

"Uh huh…"

"What is it?"

"None of you business," I reached into the night stand beside me and pulled out a brown envelope. "Just give it to her."

"You lucky you my boy." Paul said.

"Whatever, go turn on the TV and find a game or something." I laughed and Paul headed over to the television.

Paul stayed over a few more hours and for a second Eliza wasn't on my mind, while I laughed off my pain with my homie. I really hoped he gave her that envelope and that she received it. If she didn't respond I'd take that as my closure.

Eliza

Madra and I crossed the city limits from Baton Rouge and back into New Orleans. It was nice to finally get out of the house. My mother and I had talked more everyday and gotten closer than we ever had. I thought about Manny a lot, but I still could not face him after what Tavis had done to him. Madra had relayed his message, but it didn't convince me that it wasn't my fault. It was totally my fault.

"I hope you know you're letting me borrow those pink shoes you bought today." Madra joked.

"No I'm not."

"Oh yes you are! Consider it a trade for gas; making me drive all the way to BR so you won't run into Manny anywhere."

"Shut up."
"You know it's the truth."
"Whatever."
"How long are you going to ignore him E?"
"I'm not ignoring him."
"What do you call it then?"
"Clearing my head."
"It's been a month," Madra said and rolled her eyes, "He's a good one E, you're going to lose him."
"He deserves better than me anyway." I said with my head down.
"Uh uh don't talk like that. I'll make you walk home from here. You deserve that man E."
I sat silent.
"Tavis has your head so messed up that you don't even know your worth anymore?"
I looked over at Madra, "he has everything messed up…"
Madra shook her head, "If I give you something will you take it?"
"That depends, what is it?"
"I don't know what it is exactly, but it's from Emmanuel."
"Who told him where I was?" I panicked.
"Nobody heifer calm down. He gave it to Paul and Paul gave it to me, so will you take it?"
I nodded my head yes.
"Reach into that pocket behind yourseat, it's in a brown envelope."
I pulled out the envelope and then tucked it into my purse.
"You aren't going to open it?"

"Yeah, when I get inside, you're always in my business." I laughed.

"You tell it to me." Madra laughed with me as she continued to my mother's place to drop me off.

~~*~*

I placed all my bags in the chair in my room and sat down on the bed. I pulled the envelope from my purse and took a deep breath and opened it. A letter and a CD fell out. I placed the CD to the side and unfolded the letter:

Eliza,

I can't say that I've written many of these in my lifetime because I haven't, but it seems to be the only way that I'll be able to say anything to you. I'm predicting right now before you even read further that this letter will do one of two things: one, it'll make you hate me for the truth or two, show you exactly what you mean to me. Well, here goes...I've sat here day in and day out trying to figure you out, but I've come to the conclusion that you don't want to be figured out and you damn sure don't need to be. Brace yourself for this next line. You have no idea what love is. I say this because you kept a man in your life that did his best to make sure you were a broken woman. You forgave him over and over again, but me a man who truly loves you has to be tossed to the side. You know your problem Eliza? You want everything to be perfect, you want a man to give you the lie, but I have news for you, real men don't do that. I have been exactly who I said I am since the day that you met me in your best friend's yard sipping beer and eating barbeque. I never fed you corny lines about how the most beautiful curve on your body was your smile and although it is, it wasn't the first thing I noticed about you. In all honestly I took one look at your ~~ass~~ backside and said to myself damn, now that is a woman. I'm a man and I don't deny that for a second, because I believe that we see what we like at first then see what we love later. I knew exactly what I was getting myself into when I learned your story, but I still took a chance on you. Don't ask me why, because for that I have no real explanation, maybe a few theories, but nothing more. What I can tell you though is that ever since I saw the things about you that I love, it's been real hard for me to go a single day without you. I'd surely like to know if it's been easy for you to be without me. I'm going to take a wild guess and say that it's been easy for you. I know that it's been easy because you are bitter. Bitterness will eat you alive and make you hate the things that are good for you. It can convince the mind that nothing is right and before you know it years have passed and you're living in regret of something you should have done or could have done. Can I tell you a secret just between you and me? You don't owe him anything Eliza. You did everything you could. You were good enough. He wasn't. Now all you have to do is forgive him and forgive yourself. He did not get the best part of you. I did. I know that part of you well, I've kissed her, held her, seen her, cry, and I've made love to that girl.

      I've been trying to figure out what it is that you need from me to make you feel secure. I think that maybe you need to understand that there are things that I can do for you that you will never be able to do for yourself. Do something for me Eliza. Wrap your arms around yourself right now. I'm sure your embrace ends just behind your shoulders. Well, my arms can go a little further than that and I would hold you much tighter. I'll always be able to wash your back like I've been doing since you moved into my place. If you get sick I can do all the things you won't have the strength to do like cook for you or just hand you the remote to watch one of those ridiculous reality shows until you get better. I'll always be there to help you make a decision and to push you into the things that you fear you can't do. I'll always be able to make you laugh and smile even when you don't want to. I could sit here all day telling you things that I can do for you. I think now I'll hit just a little below the belt if it will get you to at least consider the possibilities of us and keep in mind that I've never been a persistent man. Eliza, you are a woman of God and if you know the bible then you know the verse that says "two are better than one, because they have a good return for their work; If one falls down his friend can help him up. But pity the man who falls and has no one to help him up." I never want to be the man that has nobody. I want to be the man who has you. I have never asked you for anything and that's because I'm hell bent on showing you that not every man will take from you, but I'm about to ask you for something right now. Would you hold on to me Eliza? Even if it's just with your fingertips hold on to me. I'd be happy just to feel the brush of your skin because to me it would say that you're trying and I'm not sitting here alone feeling like a damn fool. I know that running from all that has happened seems to be the solution to you and it seems hassle free, but it's not. Anything worth having

is worth fighting for, broken leg and all I'd go to war for you.
  I made a CD for you. Remember when I first met you and you had that depressing CD in your car? Well, I figured you needed a new one to show how much you've grown as a woman since you've been with me. It has twelve tracks on it, twelve because you are a woman of God and it is a relevant number in the bible. There were 12 sons of Israel, 12 Apostles, 12 gates of pearls, 12 angels at the gates... it is a number of perfection and that's exactly what you are to me. I hope you like it and I have one more thing to say. I'm sorry. If I've been selfish wanting more from you than you have to give then I'm sorry.

Love,
Emmanuel

  P.S. Once you've been IN love, just LOVING someone will never be enough. I'm in love with you Eliza Campbell. (You better not show anybody this letter I have a rep to maintain lol).

  I laughed with tears in my eyes then walked over to the CD player in my old room, hoping that it still worked. He wrote "Promise not to break this one" on the cover and I smiled. I popped the CD in then plopped back down on my bed and dropped my face into my hands as *Bobby V* started with *turn the page*. Each song hit me hard: 2. *Mary J-Just Fine* 3. *Chrisette Michele-Goodbye Game*, 4. *Joss Stone-Bruised but not broken*,

5.*Chrisette Michelle- I'm okay*, 6. *Estelle-Thank you*, 7. *Beyonce-Me, myself, and I*, 8.*Alicia Keys- Lesson Learned,* 9.*Mary J- Enough crying* 10. *Jazmin Sullivan- Ten seconds*, 11. *Beyonce- Lost yo mind*, 12. *Tamia-me*
After the last track played I packed my bags. There was nothing left to think about.

~~*~*

I left my bags in the car and walked up to Emmanuel's door. My heart was pounding in my chest and I could barely breathe. I was nervous to see him. I heard something inside fall over and he cussed, yelling "coming" to the door.

I stepped back when I heard the door unlock. Emmanuel froze when he swung the door open.

I took a deep breath and a single tear fell from my eye as I had lost all the words I had prepared to say. We stood just staring at one another. I could see the pain my absence caused.

I finally spoke up, "truth or dare?" I asked him with my voice cracking.

"Truth," he said.

"You miss me and you love me."

"Not true…"

I hung my head and sadness took over my body because I felt I was too late. My mama told me not to make him wait. "I started a story…" I spoke with my head down. "…and I finished it." I lifted my head so I could meet his eyes. "It probably won't mean much to anyone else, but it means a lot to me. It's about a really great man who loves this difficult woman with these ridiculous standards…" I rambled and a tear fell down my cheek. "I brought it for you to read, but you don't have to if you don't want to, I'll understand…"

"I'd like to read it."

I took a breath and headed back to my car, pulling the notebook he gave me from my passenger seat then bringing it over to Manny. He flipped through the first few pages then looked up at me.

"About that truth or dare earlier…" he licked his lips. "I would have said truth, but you didn't make the right statement."

"What did I say wrong?"

He motioned for me to come close until our chest touched then he whispered in my ear, "I miss you and I'm *in* love with you."

I wrapped my arms around him and kissed him like it would be the last time. He was my greatest love story ever told. "I'm in love with you too."

Second Chances

Eliza

Emmanuel and I got back on track like nothing had ever happened. It was taking his leg longer than expected to heal, but Tavis was getting exactly what he deserved. I'm sure he'd think twice before attacking anyone else. Thanks to the witnesses that were testifying against him, he looked like a maniac and they didn't even grant him bail pending his trial. I wished him well.

I sat in my office stressed out while I listened to this customer ramble. I just wanted to get back to pretending to work, so I could finish the book I was working on.

"Yes ma'am, we'll cover the cost of anything that may have been damaged while the car was in our possession." I said rolling my eyes as I held the phone. This lady was still complaining after being offered two free oil changes and half-off a brake job.

Emmanuel poked his head into the office and I muted the line, "you still on the phone with that same woman?" he asked.

I looked over at the clock, "damn near thirty minutes." I shook my head.

"When you're done can you print the tire warranty for the Chevy Cruz outside and put the papers into the glove compartment?"

"Yeah, I'll do it now."

I took the phone off mute and rushed the lady off the line. I printed the papers that Emmanuel asked for then headed outside to place them into the car.

"Brandy where are the keys to the Chevy Cruz?"

"Oh they just pulled that one into the bay area, it's on a lift, so the doors are probably unlocked."

"Ok, thanks," I said.

"Eliza." A voice called out to me and I turned quickly.

"Hey Madra, what are you doing here?"

"You forgot our plans for lunch today?"

I hit myself in the head, "shoot it slipped my mind, just let me put these papers in this car and I'll get my purse so we can go."

"Alright I'll be right here."

I walked out to the shop. I spotted the gold Cruz on a lift at the very end of the garage and headed over to put the papers inside. Emmanuel usually never asked me to put papers into a car until he was completely finished with it. I walked around to the passenger side and sat down to open the glove compartment. The moment I took a seat the car started to lift. "Hey, I'm in here! Hey!" The car continued to go up so I pulled the one leg I had dangling out into the car. "This isn't funny! Let me down!" I wanted to pull the door shut, but I was afraid I'd fall out.

Everyone started to gather around. "Will y'all let me down?"

"Can't..." one of the techs said.

"Why not?"

"Bosses orders."

I'm going to killEmmanuel I thought to myself. Madra and Emmanuel walked out at the same time and looked up at me.

"It's not April fools, so I'm really not understanding this joke." I spat in their direction.

Emmanuel dug into his pocket and pulled out a little black box. He opened it and flipped it open then held it up in my direction. I threw my hands up over my mouth.

He cleared his throat as he leaned on a crutch. I could tell he was nervous. "I would have gotten down on one knee, but with my broken leg and all I figured I'd be a bit more creative, which kind of works out since what we've had together hasn't exactly been traditional." He laughed to himself, "Eliza I want you to be my wife, the mother of my kids if you see that for yourself and us. I know you've been through a lot, we both have, but I need you to know that you can trust me with your heart. I won't leave you at the alter and you'll never sleep without me." A tear fell from Emmanuel's eye and he had to take a deep breath. "I'm not just proposing to you, but your family too because I want to be a part of it, so Mr. and Ms. Campbell may I have your permission to marry your daughter?"

I looked around for my parents as tears streamed down my face, "are they here?" I asked.

Madra hell up her cell phone, "they're on speaker."

My mother started to sob loudly. I could tell she had been holding them in. "You have my permission son." I heard my father say.

"Marry that boy today!" my mother said and everyone laughed.

Emmanuel held the ring up higher, "Eliza?"

I nodded my head, "yes!"

Everyone clapped and the lift lowered. I jumped out of the Cruz and into Emmanuel's arms. I had never been so happy.

"Now you can never leave me again." He said as he kissed me once more.

~~*~*

We laid in bed after our eventful day just staring at each other.

"Emmanuel?"

"Yeah?"

"I don't want a big wedding."

"That's fine with me."

"I just want something small and intimate."

"I got you covered," he hopped out of bed and grabbed the laptop he had purchased a few days ago.

"What are you doing?" I asked. "Come sit back down before you fall hopping around without your crutch."

He hopped back into bed then logged on and pulled up the internet. He Googled wedding ceremony samples.

I laughed and shook my head.

"Hold my hand." He ordered.

I placed my hand in his.

"Dearly beloved…nah, we can skip all that," he scrolled down, "okay here we go," he turned to face me, "Eliza, it is my duty to be a considerate, tender, faithful, loving husband: to support, guide and cherish you in prosperity and trouble; to thoughtfully and carefully enlarge the place you hold in my life; to constantly show you the tokens of my affection, to shelter you from danger, and to cherish for you a manly and unalterable affection, it being the command of God's Word, that I love my wife, even as Christ loved the Church and gave

His own life for her. I, Emmanuel Levi, take you Eliza Campbell, to be my wife, to have and to hold from this day forward, for better or for worse, for richer, for poorer, in sickness and in health, to love and to cherish; from this day forward until death do us part…"

"Is it my turn?"

Emmanuel shook his head no, "Just say I do," he whispered.

"I do." I said and wiped the tears of joy that fell from my face. This was what happiness felt like. It was his first time loving someone and it was my first time being loved by someone.

Standard List

~~God-fearing~~	~~Family Oriented~~
~~Opens Doors~~	~~Tall~~
~~Courteous~~	~~Parents have to like me~~
~~Nice job~~	~~Nice car~~
~~Own place~~	~~No kids~~
~~No ex drama~~	~~Dresses well~~
~~Loves all things art~~	~~Knows how to dance~~
~~Loves movies~~	~~Enjoys food and trying~~
~~new ones~~	~~Educated~~
~~Intellectual~~	~~Honest~~
~~Faithful~~	~~Funny~~
~~Romantic~~	~~Passionate~~
~~Great kisser~~	~~Loves to travel~~

~~Makes the first move~~   ~~Loyal~~

~~Communicates well~~   ~~Never been married~~

~~Secure and confident~~   ~~Good~~ ~~Great in bed~~

~~Tattoos (optional but sexy)~~   ~~Considerate~~

~~Keeps up with politics~~   ~~Doesn't flirt~~

~~Loves to read~~

~Fin~

About the Author

Christiana Harrell is a 26 year old Author from New Orleans, La. She has six other published works and still resides in New Orleans.

Made in the USA
Charleston, SC
25 February 2013

Curious About the Internet?

Ned Snell

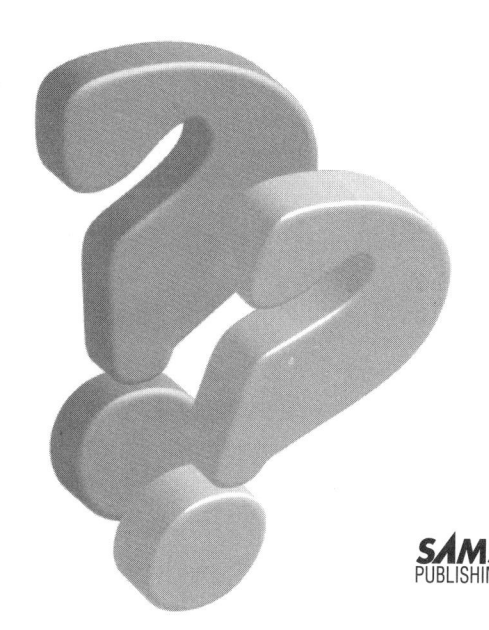

SAMS PUBLISHING 201 West 103rd Street,
Indianapolis, Indiana 46290

For Nancy and José, for their love and patience.

Copyright ©1995 by Sams Publishing

FIRST EDITION

All rights reserved. No part of this book shall be reproduced, stored in a retrieval system, or transmitted by any means, electronic, mechanical, photocopying, recording, or otherwise, without written permission from the publisher. No patent liability is assumed with respect to the use of the information contained herein. Although every precaution has been taken in the preparation of this book, the publisher and author assume no responsibility for errors or omissions. Neither is any liability assumed for damages resulting from the use of the information contained herein. For information, address Sams Publishing, 201 W. 103rd St., Indianapolis, IN 46290.

International Standard Book Number: 0-672-30459-7

Library of Congress Catalog Card Number: 93-87658

98 97 96 95   4 3 2 1

Interpretation of the printing code: the rightmost double-digit number is the year of the book's printing; the rightmost single-digit, the number of the book's printing. For example, a printing code of 95-1 shows that the first printing of the book occurred in 1995.

Composed in Goudy and MCPdigital by Macmillan Computer Publishing

Printed in the United States of America

Trademarks

All terms mentioned in this book that are known to be trademarks or service marks have been appropriately capitalized. Sams Publishing cannot attest to the accuracy of this information. Use of a term in this book should not be regarded as affecting the validity of any trademark or service mark.

Publisher
Richard K. Swadley

Acquisitions Manager
Greg Wiegand

Managing Editor
Cindy Morrow

Acquisitions Editor
Mark Taber

Development Editor
Mark Taber

Production Editor
Fran Hatton

Editor
Deborah Frisby

Editorial Coordinator
Bill Whitmer

Editorial Assistants
Carol Ackerman
Sharon Cox
Lynette Quinn

Technical Reviewer
Jill Ellsworth

Marketing Manager
Gregg Bushyeager

Cover Designer
Dan Armstrong

Book Designer
Alyssa Yesh

Director of Production and Manufacturing
Jeff Valler

Imprint Manager
Juli Cook

Manufacturing Coordinator
Paul Gilchrist

Production Analysts
Angela D. Bannan
Dennis Clay Hager
Mary Beth Wakefield

Graphics Image Specialists
Clint Lahnen
Tim Montgomery
Dennis Sheehan
Jeff Yesh

Page Layout
Katy Bodenmiller
Elaine Brush
Mary Ann Cosby
Beth Lewis
Scott Tullis
Dennis Wesner
Donna Winter

Proofreading
Don Brown
Mona Brown
DiMonique Ford
Kimberly K. Hannel
Donna Harbin
Brian-Kent Proffit
Kris Simmons
S A Springer

Indexer
Christopher Cleveland

Overview

	Introduction	xi
1	What Is the Internet?	1
2	Who Uses the Internet, and for What?	33
3	How Has the Internet Made the World a Better Place?	59
4	Why Do Some People Worry About the Internet?	81
5	Can I Use the Internet (and Should I)?	101
6	How Do People Communicate on the Internet?	125
7	How Do People Pick Up Information on the Internet?	145
8	What Fun Do People Have on the Internet?	173
9	Where Is the Internet Headed?	187
10	Still Curious? Where to Find More Information	213
	Glossary	229
	Index	237

Contents

Introduction xi

1 **What Is the Internet?**   1

   It's a Network 7
   It's a Loose Organization 8
   It's a Coffee House 11
   It's a Mailbox 15
   It's a Business Tool 18
   It's a Library 21
   It's a Software Shop 25
   It's a Newspaper 27
   It's a Living Thing 29
   So Now You Know… 31

2 **Who Uses the Internet, and for What?**   33

   Scientists Use It to Solve 35
   Educators Use It to Educate 41
   Professionals Use It to Consult 43
   Businesspeople Use It to Compete 47
   Governments Use It to Disseminate 51
   Activists Use It to Activate 53
   Miscellaneous People Use It to Do
      Miscellaneous Stuff 54
   So Now You Know… 57

3 **How Does the Internet Make the World
   a Better Place?**   59

   It Supports Scientific Discovery 62
   It Saves Trees (Maybe) 63
   It Exposes the Truth 64
   It Gives Away Free Stuff 66

It Creates New Business Opportunities 67
It Accommodates the Disabled 69
It Brings People and Nations Together 70
It Plays Cupid 72
It Prevents Pointless Walks to the Coke Machine .. 73
It Makes People Laugh 75
It Turns People On 77
So Now You Know … 79

4 Why Do Some People Worry About the Internet? 81

It Separates and Isolates People 83
It Distributes Unreliable, Unchecked
   Information 84
It Spreads Hate 86
It Creates Job Insecurity 87
It Threatens National Security 88
It Enables Piracy and Sabotage 89
It Invades Privacy 90
It Enables Fraud 94
It Carries Unrestricted Pornography 96
It Empowers the Few and Excludes the Many 97
So Now You Know … 99

5 What Does It Take to Use the Internet? 101

It Takes a Need for Information or Services 102
It Takes a Properly Equipped Computer 108
It Takes a Communications Hookup 110
It Takes Software Tools for Navigating
   the Internet 114
   Eudora 118
   NewsReader! 118
   Mosaic 119
   Archie 120
   WinGopher 121
   QVT WinNet 122

Contents   vii

It Takes Basic Computer and
Communications Skills 122
It Takes Knowing
Where to Look 123
It Takes Practice 124
So Now You Know… 124

6 **How Do People Communicate on the Internet?**   **125**

They Exchange E-mail 126
They Have One-to-One Conversations 134
They Chat in Groups 135
They Subscribe to Mailing Lists 137
They Post and Read Messages in Newsgroups 139
They Find Each Other Through
Directory Services 142
So Now You Know … 144

7 **How Do People Pick Up Information
from the Internet?**   **145**

They Use Other People's Computers
as Their Own 146
They Locate and Copy Files 156
They Burrow with Gopher 162
They Search with Veronica 164
They Browse the World Wide Web 165
So Now You Know… 171

8 **What Fun Do People Have on the Internet?**   **173**

They Play Interactive Games 174
They Play E-mail Games 176
They Try to Win the Internet Hunt 177
They Read the Funnies 178
They Listen to the Radio 179
They Play Pretend in MUDs 182

They Create Their Own WWW Home Pages 185
So Now You Know… 185

9 Where Is the Internet Headed? 187

The Internet Is Headed Down the Highway 188
The Internet Is Headed into Business 199
The Internet Is Headed into the Classroom 204
The Internet Is Headed into Your TV 206
The Internet Is Headed into Oblivion (Maybe) 209
So Now You Know… 211

10 What If I'm Still Curious? 213

Contact an Internet Organization 214
Consult an Online Service 215
Read a Magazine 216
Hop Online 218
Read a Book 221
So Now You Know… 227

Glossary 229

Index 237

Acknowledgments

For their invaluable assistance, I'm grateful to…

My good friend and editor Mark Taber, who deserves more of the credit for this book than I will admit past this page.

Fran Hatton and Deborah Frisby for putting the shine on this thing.

…and all the good people at Sams.

About the Author

A native of Massachusetts, Ned Snell successfully ignored computers and networks through all of high school and college. While failing as an actor in New York, he marched through a variety of day jobs—test-prep course writer, second grade schoolteacher, telemarketer, and VCR tape-changer at Bloomingdale's. In 1986, he took a proofreading job at a large software company and soon discovered a knack for making plain sense of technology.

He went on to senior writing and editing positions at several software companies, then switched sides and jumped to computer journalism. Snell has served as an award-winning writer and editor for several major computer industry publications, covering the breadth of computer topics from mainframe and PC computers, to networks, to software.

Today, he continues his acting career but lives pretty well anyway, thanks to his writing. He lives in Indianapolis with his wife Nancy and son José. Snell is also the author of *Souping Up Windows*, published by Sams.

Introduction

What's All This Fuss About the Internet?

Time. U.S. News & World Report. Newsweek. Harpers. The New York Times. The Wall Street Journal. Entertainment Weekly.

These and many more in the print and broadcast media have lately devoted an increasing amount of space and time to the Internet, that vast, confusing computer community floating out in what journals call "cyberspace." While alternately hyping the Internet and spinning Orwellian warnings about it, members of the media usually mention the fact that at least 20 million people—maybe 25 million, depending on whom you ask—use the Internet. To better inform their readers, journals also interpret those figures, pointing out that 20 million is "a lot" and 25 million is "even more."

So it is. In fact, that's more than the populations of 7 of the 12 nations in the European Community, and more than the population in 49 of the 50 U.S. states. Still... maybe I'm not cyber-hip, but it seems to me that 5.5 *billion* minus 20 (or 25) million leaves an impressive number of people who are on the planet but off the Internet. Not all of the Internet have-nots read *Time*, of course. The fact remains, however, that many people have heard about the Internet, know it's important, and know that it's growing like a fungus, but don't know much beyond that. They represent a potential customer base of more than 5 billion buyers for this book. (But if only half of those people buy it, I'll be satisfied.)

Many have heard Al Gore—in his 1988 presidential campaign and as U.S. Vice President since 1993—wax lyrical about the "Information Superhighway" that will bring everyone a gift bag of currently ill-defined, nonspecific treasures (but treasures nonetheless), and many know that the Internet is somehow related to the Superhighway scheme. But again, their understanding ends there. (Not Al's fault...historically, vice presidents have trouble holding anyone's attention long enough to explain anything complicated. That's why vice presidents find themselves in charge of stuff like the Information Superhighway and the space program, projects that make better progress when no one is paying attention—something a vice president's involvement ensures.)

By now, discussion about the Internet has spiraled up to a rare and peculiar example of cross-miscommunication. Everybody's talking about the Internet, but nobody's saying anything. If it's important and growing and valuable, some folks might want to know what it's all about—whether they plan to actually use it or not. Many people read about politics without running for office or without even voting. I know people who've read books about India but never traveled east of Philadelphia. Every discussion of the Internet longer than an article in *Time* is, however, written in a language that can be decoded by only the kind of people who already know all about the Internet.

Here we discover an unpleasant gap in our book publishing infrastructure. Astronomer Carl Sagan (*Cosmos*) and historian Daniel J. Boorstin (*The Discoverers*) write books solely to satisfy our curiosity. Neither author provides any information of immediate, practical use to the average reader. When Sagan says Mars is always at least 35 million miles from Cleveland, he's not helping you plan your trip. When Boorstin tells you Christopher Columbus went to his grave convinced that Cuba was, in fact, China, you probably can't use that information to get a raise.

I think I'm relatively safe in writing that, with the exceptions of Carl and Daniel, most modern writers attempt to tell you how to *do* something—assuming, as they do, that you really *want* to do something. They don't care if you're busy or really tired.

At this writing, neither Carl nor Daniel has written a book about the Internet. That means the existing books about the Internet have the annoying habit of attempting to teach every reader how to use the Internet, step by grueling step. If, however, the Internet is really so big and important, if it's really a first step toward the Superhighway that's headed into every home, shouldn't there be a way to learn more about it—in the abstract—without tripping over instructions?

I think so, and because Carl and Dan were dragging their feet, I decided to give it a shot. Welcome aboard.

Who Is This Book for?

I wrote this book so that everyone—even those who've never touched a computer—could become well informed about what the Internet is, what it means, and where it's going. I think you'll find that the Internet is exciting, useful and even fun—but I've deliberately tried not to "sell" you on the Internet. I'll show you what it's about. You can decide whether you like it or not.

This book does not attempt to teach you how to use the Internet or, for that matter, how to use a computer or network. I do not expect you to know the least thing about computers or the Internet to get started. This book simply provides an overview of the world of the Internet; the subject is the Internet, not the machines that provide access to it. If you do have computer experience, you'll still find this book valuable.

Also, this book does not assume that you are planning to become an Internet user. It assumes only that you are curious. (No commitment, no strings, honest!) If you think you may ultimately become an Internet user, it does provide a quick, painless way to get grounded before moving on to the specifics of Internet operation. If you're undecided about whether or not to join the Internet crowd, you'll make a decision by the time you reach Chapter 9.

That reminds me—a word must be said about the Glossary at the back of this book. You don't need it. Nobody needs it. There are no technical terms of any kind in this book. OK... you'll see a few, but I hardly ever use them, and when I do, I explain them very simply. And I left out completely the hundreds of terms you would find in any other Internet book.

The truth is that I was afraid I might run out of material before I wrote 200 pages, so I put a glossary in my outline and my editor made me write it. If you read this book front to back though, trust me, you can forget about the glossary. (If you jump around a lot, you might jump past the place where a term is explained, and then you'd need the glossary; but that's not my fault.)

How Is This Book Organized?

This book asks 10 big questions. Nine of them lead to the nine most important aspects of the Internet, and one (Chapter 10) leads to other resources for the deeply curious. Within each chapter, everything you'll see is an answer to the question posed in that chapter's title.

Feel free to read the questions and answers in order or out of order. You may find it most rewarding to read them in order, or at least to read Chapters 1 and 2 to get initiated before going on to subsequent chapters.

In Chapter 10, you'll find information about other Internet resources for further study or entertainment. At the back of the book, you'll find the complete glossary, a detailed index, and a form you can use to order more advanced books about the Internet.

1

What Is the Internet?

Read this chapter to satisfy your general curiosity about what the Internet is and what it can be used for. The answers include these:

- It's a network.
- It's a loose organization.
- It's a coffee house.
- It's a mailbox.
- It's a business tool.
- It's a library.
- It's a software shop.
- It's a newspaper.
- It's a living thing.

2 Curious About the Internet?

For starters, though, here's the basic answer: The Internet is a loose organization of thousands of computers all over the world that can communicate with one another to exchange messages and share information. The Internet offers roughly 20 million people—from nearly every country and from many different walks of life—a way to correspond with one another, do research, learn stuff, and fool around. Physicians use it to heal, journalists use it to report, activists use it to activate, and everyday folks use it to do everyday things.

The computers that constitute the Internet come in just about every size, shape, and type in use. They're spread all over the world—in every continent, including Antarctica. According to the Internet Society, a volunteer organization, the number of computers on the Internet is almost doubling every year. A million new computers got hooked into the Internet in the first half of 1994 alone!

Table 1.1 shows the number of Internet-connected computers in different types of U.S. organizations and in other countries. Note that the table shows the number of computers, not the number of users. Many of the computers on the Internet are large types that may each support dozens, hundreds, or even thousands of users.

Table 1.1. The breadth of the Internet, July 1994.

Country/Type of Organization	Host Computers	Percent of Total
U.S.-educational (higher)	856,234	27
U.S.-commercial	774,735	24
U.S.-government	169,248	5
U.S.-defense	130,176	4

What Is the Internet?

Country/Type of Organization	Host Computers	Percent of Total
U.S.-non-profit organization	66,459	2
U.S.-network operator	30,993	1
U.S.-local	16,556	1
Total U.S.	2,044,401	63
United Kingdom	155,706	5
Germany	149,193	5
Canada	127,516	4
Australia	127,514	4
Japan	72,409	2
France	71,899	2
Netherlands	59,729	2
Sweden	53,294	2
Finland	49,598	2
Switzerland	47,401	1
Norway	38,759	1
Italy	23,616	1
Spain	21,147	1
Austria	20,130	1
South Africa	15,595	<1
New Zealand	14,830	<1
Korea	12,109	<1
Denmark	12,107	<1

continues

Table 1.1. continued

Country/Type of Organization	Host Computers	Percent of Total
Belgium	12,107	<1
Taiwan	10,314	<1
Hong Kong	9,141	<1
Italy	8,464	<1
Poland	7,392	<1
Brazil	5,896	<1
Czech Rep	5,639	<1
Hungary	5,390	<1
Mexico	5,164	<1
Portugal	4,518	<1
Singapore	4,014	<1
Chile	3,703	<1
Ireland	3,308	<1
Iceland	3,268	<1
Russian Fed. (SU)	3,145	<1
Greece	2,958	<1
Czech&Slovak (CS)	1,869	<1
Malaysia	1,322	<1
Turkey	1,204	<1
Thailand	1,197	<1
Slovakia	868	<1
Croatia	838	<1

What Is the Internet?

Country/Type of Organization	Host Computers	Percent of Total
Estonia	659	<1
Slovenia	574	<1
Costa Rica	544	<1
Romania	453	<1
Luxembourg	420	<1
Venezuela	399	<1
Ukraine	339	<1
China	325	<1
Russian Fed. (RU)	322	<1
India	316	<1
International organizations	315	<1
Kuwait	297	<1
Ecuador	256	<1
Argentina	248	<1
Latvia	180	<1
Colombia	144	<1
Uruguay	101	<1
Bulgaria	79	<1
Peru	75	<1
Philippines	65	<1
Indonesia	54	<1
Lithuania	53	<1

continues

Table 1.1. continued

Country/Type of Organization	Host Computers	Percent of Total
Egypt	52	<1
Tunesia	46	<1
Peru	42	<1
Cyprus	38	<1
Liechtenstein	27	<1
Panama	24	<1
Nicaragua	23	<1
Macau	12	<1
Algeria	7	<1
Fiji	5	<1
Iran	4	<1
Antarctica	4	<1
Moldova	2	<1
Saudi Arabia	1	<1
Total International:	1,180,77	37

Source: The Internet Society

Most of the computers on the Internet don't exist simply to be part of the Internet. They're actually the computers used every day by governments and their agencies, universities, research organizations, corporations, libraries, and individuals. Because each computer is on the Internet, however, its users can take advantage of some of the information that's

What Is the Internet? 7

stored on many of the other computers. Each computer's users can also exchange messages with the users of the other computers.

It's a Network

The computers on the Internet can talk to one another because they are *networked;* they are connected in some way so that they can exchange information with one another electronically. On the Internet, the connections take many different forms. Some computers are directly connected to others with wire or fiber-optic cables. Some are connected through local and long-distance telephone lines, and some even use wireless satellite communications—the same types used today for some long-distance phone services and cellular phones—to communicate with other computers on the Internet.

Curious About the Word?

\,in|ter-'net\

A *network* is made up of two or more computers that are connected so that they can exchange messages and share information.

An *internetwork* is two or more networks that are connected so that they can exchange messages and share information.

The Internet is the world's largest internetwork. It includes computers hooked together in networks, those networks hooked together in internetworks, and those internetworks hooked together in still bigger internetworks. There are at least 18,000 networks within the Internet today.

A simple network

A simple internetwork

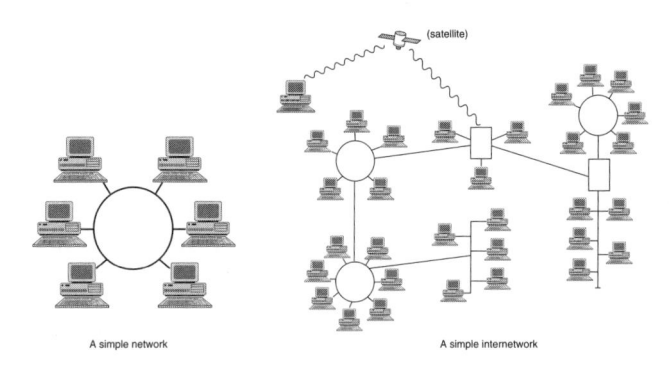

Figure 1.1. Networks and internetworks.

Because the Internet is an internetwork, each computer is not necessarily directly connected to every other computer (see Figure 1.1). In other words, any computer on the Internet can talk to any other, but the message may have to travel through several other computers on its way there.

Think of it like air travel. From Indianapolis, you can fly anywhere in the world. For some destinations, however, you can't get a non-stop flight. You have to fly to Chicago or Cincinnati first, then from there to your destination. Information makes its way around the Internet similarly.

It's a Loose Organization

Although most people talk about the Internet as if it were some giant company or club, it really isn't. No single entity or organization controls it. The computers on it are controlled by their owners—MIT controls its computers, the Library of Congress controls its, the University of Pisa controls its, and so on.

What Is the Internet? 9

> **Did You Know...**
>
> Many discrete organizations on the Internet have their own rules for which types of activities are allowed on their computers and which aren't. These rules are called Acceptable Use Policies, and usually they're not very carefully enforced. There isn't a single set of Acceptable Use Policies that covers the whole Internet.

Nobody controls the Internet—people simply join up and participate. It's like a neighborhood where people communicate because they're able to, but they haven't established a formal organization with rights, rules, and leaders.

Just as each computer on the Internet is under its owner's control, some networks that make up a large part of the Internet are controlled by their owners. For example, the Internet today arose, in part, from a project called *NFSnet*, a network of researchers and universities created by the National Science Foundation and therefore funded by Uncle Sam. The NFSnet and other federally funded networks that are part of the Internet set their own Acceptable Use Policies. But again, although government and industry control pieces of the Internet, nobody controls the whole, nor is anybody likely to do so soon.

> **Really Curious?**
>
> The Internet as a whole is unlikely to be brought under any single point of control—if such a thing were even possible, considering the number and variety of different people and organizations who use it. Because of the lack of central control, different

> resources on the Internet require different steps and skills—which is what makes using the Internet difficult.
>
> People are working on better software to make the Internet (or parts of the Internet, anyway) appear as one smooth system to its users. (You'll learn more about that in later chapters.)
>
> Also, efforts are underway to smooth out the wrinkles between the many networks run by federal agencies and to hook them together with the entire academic and research community, forming one, high-speed network. This early step in the creation of the Information Superhighway will effectively put much of the policymaking power for a big slice of the Internet under U.S. government control. For more about this issue, see Chapter 9.

Looseness is the Internet's blessing, but also its curse. Because it's been so open and so free, it has evolved on its own into a giant resource that probably never could have come about if the U.S. government, IBM, Kraft Foods, or Walt Disney Productions were holding the reins. Unfortunately, because nobody's in charge, the Internet is inconsistent and sometimes difficult to use. As people use it to access different computers and services, they find that not everything operates the same way on the Internet. There are some general rules that people follow—a sort of traditional Internet etiquette. These rules are very general and are loosely followed, at that.

The Internet is, in effect, a democratic, egalitarian, and consensus-driven thing. It doesn't work as efficiently as a top-down, totalitarian machine—but who wants that?

Did You Know...

Although no single group really controls the Internet, there are groups that influence it.

Two volunteer groups—a council called the Internet Architecture Board and a technical advisory team called the Internet Engineering Task Force—work together to enforce minor rules to keep the whole thing working, such as deciding which kinds of communications languages should be supported by the network. Although the Internet includes many different types of computers and networks, it can't work unless everybody observes a few basic rules in their underlying communications technologies. These volunteer groups develop those rules to keep the Internet running smoothly.

People who want to use the Internet, but can't access it through computers at their company or school, often have to pay a commercial dial-in service for access to the Internet. (Dial-in and other types of Internet connections are explained in Chapter 5.) The Internet itself is free and open to all (although lately some fee-based services have appeared on the Internet), but some people have to pay a service provider to open the door. You'll learn more about that in Chapter 5.

It's a Coffee House

Well, maybe it's not a coffee house. Maybe it's a tavern, a barber shop, or a city park. The point is that several of the most important Internet resources enable users to exchange information in an open, public way. These resources provide a forum where users can write and post messages for other users and where they can read messages posted by others. In that sense, these resources play the open-air-exchange-site role played by a coffee house or other public meeting place. The coffee-house-type of resources actually come in several different types, each of which is used differently. (You'll learn more about the specific types—such as newsgroups, mailing lists, and bulletin boards—later in this chapter and in Chapters 6 and 7.)

Each coffee-house-type resource typically handles a specific topic or area of interest. Some are for professional specialists, some are for hobbyists, some are for fans, some are for the generally curious. Because these resources are divided by subject, users can easily find messages related to their interests and can post messages where the messages will be read by people who share the user's interests. For example, a user interested in the Central Intelligence Agency can read messages about the CIA in the resource that covers it. He or she can also respond to or comment on those messages or write messages for other CIA buffs to see.

There are hundreds of these resources, but the following list may give you a feel for the range of topics.

>   Ceramics
>
>   Computers
>
>   Disabilities
>
>   Film and TV
>
>   Folk Music
>
>   The Grateful Dead
>
>   *Star Trek*

What Is the Internet? 13

The Simpsons

Holistic Medicine

Nutrition

Law

Beer

SCUBA Diving

Erotica

Sign Language

Mystery Fiction

Astrology

Pet Birds

Middle Eastern Politics

Architecture

Employment

Religion

Biomechanics

AIDS

Gun Control

Hockey

Even though they're divided by subject, the coffee-house resources can become overcrowded; they can pile up hundreds of messages, which makes keeping up with them or finding any particular message difficult. Often, people who use these resources have access to a special computer program that helps them find messages on a particular topic. They can instruct the program to sort through the messages and show only the messages that match a very specific interest. This helps people find what they're looking for quickly, without having to wade through an overwhelming pile of messages. Users can also browse through messages, looking for something of interest.

Really Curious?

There are different types of Internet resources that fill the coffee-house role, and each type is used a little differently—that's just one of the inconsistencies that bug Internet users.

Fortunately, though, many such resources fall into one of two major types: newsgroups and mailing lists.

Newsgroups (sometimes called *Usenet newsgroups* or *Network News*) are more sophisticated (and more difficult to use) in the ways they enable their users to work with messages. There are newsgroups available for a huge range of topics—the professional, the personal, and the plain weird.

Mailing lists (also known as *discussion lists*) are simpler and usually based around professional topics. Mailing lists send all messages related to a particular topic directly to the user by electronic mail (see "It's a Mailbox" later in this chapter). Subscribers to a mailing list can also send in their own messages, which are then sent out to everyone else on the list.

What Is the Internet? 15

Many of the rest of the Internet resources that serve the coffee-house role are grouped under the name *bulletin boards*. Although they all share a category name, each bulletin board works a little differently. You'll learn more about them in Chapter 7.

You can learn more about newsgroups and mailing lists in Chapter 7.

These resources offer Internet users a way to get the answers to questions when they don't know whom to ask. Home beer brewers, for example, can post questions about brewing techniques on an Internet resource for home brewers. Other brewers will read the message, and those with an answer or a tip will post replies. There are more serious applications, of course. Scientists and scholars use this capability to exchange news and information about important topics, from fusion to fat cells.

It's a Mailbox

Without question, the most-used Internet facility is electronic mail, also known as e-mail.

Curious About the Word?

Electronic mail, or *e-mail*, is the practice of writing messages—memos, letters, and so forth—on a computer, then transmitting them to another computer so that the addressee can read them on a computer screen. E-mail skips the whole process of printing messages on paper and hand-carrying them to the addressee—which saves paper, time, and energy.

> Traditionally, all you could include in an e-mail message was words, and that's still true today for most Internet e-mailing. With the increased use of graphical computing environments such as Windows and the Macintosh, however, people are beginning to include pictures (and sometimes even video clips or sound) in e-mail messages.

Everyone who uses the Internet has a unique Internet name, called—quite accurately—an *address*. Like any address, an Internet address is made up of several words or partial words, and it typically includes the person's name and location. Increasingly, people are listing their Internet addresses on their business cards and stationery. (You can see a sample Internet address in Chapter 5.)

No two Internet users have the same address, so to send a message to an Internet user, anywhere in the world, all the sender has to know is the address of the recipient. The sender types up a message in his or her favorite word processing or e-mail software program, hops onto the Internet, types in the address, and sends the message on its way.

In theory, the message should arrive at the recipient's computer almost instantly—after all, it's traveling through wire at nearly the speed of light. Remember, though, that there isn't always a straight line between any two computers on the Internet. The message may have to pass through a gaggle of networks and computers before it reaches its destination, and it could get held up, temporarily, anywhere along the way. In a little while though, the message is delivered to the addressee's computer.

What Is the Internet?   17

> ### Really Curious?
>
> To send an e-mail message, the sender must know the address of the recipient. It would be great if there was one big directory of all the addresses on the Internet—but there isn't. There are, however, tools that help people find one another on the Internet.
>
> For more about e-mail and how it's used, see Chapter 6.

The great thing about e-mail is the way in which it enables users to work with the messages. They can instantly send a reply to a message they've received. They can forward a message to someone else (perhaps a person who can answer a question the message asks). They can even print the message. Senders also have e-mail options. They can send the same message to several recipients at once or post the message for anyone to send.

Senders can also send messages to people who aren't on the Internet by routing messages through commercial e-mail services such as CompuServe or MCI Mail. They can even send to people who don't have computers by routing the e-mail message to the recipient's fax machine!

> ### Did You Know...
>
> Using e-mail on the Internet, people have...
>
> - Romanced one another.
> - Smuggled news bulletins out of countries in crisis.
> - Taken college courses.

- Ordered pizza.
- Complained to manufacturers.
- Sent letters to the editors of magazines and newspapers.
- Submitted articles and manuscripts for publication.
- Advertised products (controversially—see Chapter 4).
- Bought stuff.

It's a Business Tool

Or is it? This is one of the big debates raging across (and beyond) the Internet. No doubt, given the increasingly global business climate and the great extent to which big companies rely on computers, the Internet looks like a great vehicle for national and international business communication. It is certainly cheaper and more flexible than building a private, global computer network from scratch.

There are, however, reasons why business use of the Internet has been heavily restricted through the years. Much of what is now the Internet began as an experimental research network for the defense department, evolved into a project of the federally funded National Science Foundation (NSF), and is now evolving into a new federally sponsored network of government agencies and academia, dubbed NREN. (See Chapter 9.)

What that boils down to is that the U.S. government has sunk a lot of money into the domestic parts of the Internet, and is sinking still more. Taxpayers are generally agreeable about money spent "in support of research or education," which is what the NREN portion of the Internet is chartered to do (after all, that stuff makes our kids smarter and cures diseases). But ugly arguments sometimes ensue when the likes of Wal-Mart and PepsiCo are permitted to use a tax-subsidized network for the benefit of their own bottom line.

Beyond that political issue is a philosophical one. Although it's always had business users of a sort (after all, many of the principal users of the Internet in its formative years were defense contractors), some users have come to think of the Internet as a big co-op, the world's largest community garden and pitch-in lunch. They believe that the lack of central control of the Internet and the exclusion of mercenary corporate interests is what kept the network healthy, growing, and—for lack of a better word—pure. They want the Internet preserved as a forum for scientific and social inquiry and global exchange—a vehicle for the public good, not private profit.

There are still more problems in doing business on the Internet, including the fact that the precise laws and policies regarding copyrights, monetary transactions, international currency conversion, taxes and exchange, privacy, and security have yet to be ironed out to everyone's satisfaction.

Thus, the rule for the parts of the Internet subsidized by government has long been "no commercial traffic," as described by the NSF's Acceptable Use Policy for its NSFnet, which by itself comprises a big chunk of the Internet. Many smaller government and academic networks have similar policies, and even beyond these networks there has been a traditional discouragement of commercial activity. Business users, like anyone else, have always been welcome to use the Internet for research. But when they begin to use it to send their purchase orders from sales offices to headquarters, or as an e-mail system for the overseas marketing staff, or as a junk-mail delivery system, Internet purists cry foul.

Yet, the commercialization of the Internet has been growing rapidly for the last several years. The policies restricting business activity have been little enforced, despite the grumbling of some purists. In 1991, some of the government restrictions on commercial use were lifted. That opened the door for a dozen networking companies to set up their own major sections of the Internet to support commercial traffic while working around the NFSnet and its no-business policy. The "anything goes" commercial networks set up by this group are called the Commercial Internet eXchange (CIX). CIX supports a wide range of business activities, with more to come.

A few examples? In addition to the obvious examples of on-screen advertising and e-mail, businesses already use the Internet to

- Sell real estate, books, concert tickets, handmade dolls, and flowers.
- Provide credit reports, legal services, consulting services, and customer support.
- Publish newspapers, newsletters, and magazines that can be read on the computer screen and are paid for by reader subscriptions, advertising, or both.

Most Internet watchers agree that commercial use of the Internet will continue to expand, and will do so far more rapidly than will the research uses. Already, more than half of all Internet users are in commercial enterprises. As you may have noticed in Table 1.1, the number of U.S. business computers on the Internet is second only to the number in educational institutions, and it is expected to exceed the number of educational computers within a few years.

> **Really Curious?**
>
> For more on the controversy regarding business use of the Internet, see Chapter 4. For more on where business use is headed, see Chapter 9. For a detailed examination of the Internet's business uses, consult "The Internet Business Guide" in Chapter 10.

It's a Library

Well, in fact, it's several libraries—at least 500 of them—all over the world.

Among the earliest and most avid users of the Internet were colleges and universities. Many have their whole computer network tied into the Internet—including the computerized card catalog for the university library.

These schools use the Internet to operate interlibrary loan programs. When a student or professor requests a book that's not in the stacks, the library can locate the book at a branch campus, another university, or even at a public library or private research collection, and can have it sent from there. Of course, the university pays for that privilege by making its own collection available to all the other libraries it borrows from.

All this interlibrary networking leaves many public, private, government, and academic catalogs accessible to any Internet user. Curious readers can plumb the collections of the great universities to find exactly the material they're looking for. The choices include public and private libraries, and specialized libraries for medicine, law, and other subject areas.

There are hundreds of libraries on the Internet, including many public libraries. Here's a sampling:

> The U.S. Library of Congress
> The Environmental Protection Agency Library
> The U.S. Food & Drug Administration Library
> The Law Library at Columbia University
> Yale University
> Harvard University
> University of Massachusetts
> University of Minnesota
> Dartmouth College
> Cleveland Public Library System
> Detroit Public Library System
> New York Public Library System
> Seattle Public Library System

Now, of course, whether or not an Internet user can actually borrow anything is another story. Different libraries enforce different policies about who can borrow and who can't. Some libraries do allow people to order a title right over the Internet, to be delivered by mail. For those that don't, Internet users can usually go to their own local university or public library and ask a librarian to make the request. (Libraries are pretty friendly about loaning to other libraries; they stick together that way.)

No matter how they finally get their hands on the book, the value of the Internet is that it lets users *find* the book—almost no matter where it's stacked. To help, there are bibliographic indexing services on the Internet that list where materials on certain subjects can be found.

What Is the Internet?

In the information age, there is, however, another kind of library. The text of reports, papers, and even whole books can be (and usually is) stored in computer files. Here is where the library resources on the Internet shine. There are literally millions of files of information out on the Internet that savvy users can locate and then copy—right over the Internet—from the distant computer to their own, where they can read the information on their computer screens or print it on a printer.

Next to e-mail, this may be the most often used and most valuable resource on the Internet. It allows researchers (or the merely curious) to acquire the latest and most detailed information about every topic imaginable. In fact, much of the information available this way may not be published in any book—the Internet offers people access to information that's unavailable to them in any other way.

Did You Know...

As more and more computers today acquire multimedia capabilities—the capability to show pictures and play video and sound clips from computer files—more stuff has appeared on the Internet to serve those machines. Although most of the computer files on the Internet contain just words (which users can read by opening the files in their word processing programs), a growing group holds pictures, video, and sound.

You can, in fact, find entire books in computer files on the Internet, in many different places. Perhaps the best known source is Project Gutenberg, a volunteer project to transfer important reference works and works of literature to computer files and make them widely available. Already through Project Gutenberg, people can copy from the Internet the following:

- Anything from Shakespeare
- *Roget's Thesaurus*
- *Moby Dick*
- *The Book of Mormon*
- *The CIA World Fact Book*

Much more is available now, and still more is on the way. There are other electronic book providers on the Internet, such as the Online Book Initiative (OBI).

Of course, the same Internet power that enables users to retrieve *Paradise Lost* also enables them to copy beer recipes from the American Homebrewer's Association's computer. To each his own.

Really Curious?

You'll find more about looking up books and files on the Internet in Chapter 7.

Also, if you think you may want to try your hand at Internet research, you'll find good beginner's instructions in two books from Sams Publishing, *Teach Yourself the Internet* and *Navigating the Internet*. These books are described in Chapter 10 of this book.

It's a Software Shop

If computer files containing books can be copied across the Internet, so can files containing anything else—including, of course, computer software.

> **Curious About the Word?**
>
> \,in*ter-'net\
>
> *Software* most commonly describes a computer program—a word processor, a personal finance program, a game, and so on. Keep in mind, though, that there are other types of software. Most importantly, there are software files that contain images, video, music, or other types of information that can be viewed or played through a computer program that knows how to work with them. This other type of software is available on the Internet, just as programs are.
>
> You can learn more about the general types of computer files in Chapter 7.

People find software several different ways on the Internet. When they find it, they can copy it to their computers and use it there, just as if they'd bought it at a software store. People often post on the Internet software they've written—much as they would post a message for others to read. That software can be copied and used by others. Some software companies also make their products available on the Internet to paying customers.

Curious About the Word?

\,in**ter**-'net\

Software available through the Internet comes in three basic types.

Freeware software is absolutely free of charge and available to all.

Shareware is offered on a "try before you buy" plan. Users can copy the software and try it out for free, but they are instructed to send a nominal fee (usually $10 to $50) to the programmer if they intend to use the software regularly.

Commercial software is like the packaged software sold in stores (but without the box) and is offered by the same commercial software companies. Commercial software requires payment up front; typically, the user must supply a credit card number before copying the software files.

There's software available on the Internet for almost any type of computer and for almost any purpose—business programs, personal programs, games, and so on. Among the most popular programs found on the Internet are tools that help people use the Internet more easily or effectively. Often available as freeware, programs such as Mosaic help people use the inconsistent, difficult-to-navigate Internet as if it were a much smoother system.

What Is the Internet?   27

> **Really Curious?**
>
> To learn more about the tools that make using the Internet easier, see Chapter 5.
>
> To learn more about how people actually copy software from the Internet, see Chapter 7.
>
> To learn more about software on the Internet with no purpose other than a good time, see Chapter 8.

It's a Newspaper

Just as the coffee-house-type resources on the Internet can keep users informed about the Grateful Dead, Michael Bolton, or *Star Trek*, they can also serve up hard news about specific topics.

There are resources that keep Internet users abreast of the latest events in every country from Afghanistan to Zaire. Sometimes, these services are the best (or only) way to get current and complete information about a particular region. It's often told that, during the Soviet coup attempt in 1991, a small electronic mail company in Russia was about the only way to get news into and out of the region. Through e-mail, that company served news through the Internet to the likes of CNN and the Associated Press and, of course, to others on the Internet.

Internet users can tap into resources that supply up-to-date news and discussion on every imaginable topic. In addition to the various country- and region-specific resources, there are others that supply news about environmental events, sports, global and U.S. politics, party politics (separate groups for Democrats, Republicans, Libertarians, and the like), civil rights, the economy, and much more.

In addition to what the coffee-house resources offer, there are actual newspapers, magazines, and newsletters that users can access through the Internet and read through their computer screens. Some are scholarly or scientific journals, but a growing number are general interest, consumer publications. Some were created just for the Internet, but some are special electronic versions of publications that are also available in print, like the magazine shown in Figure 1.2.

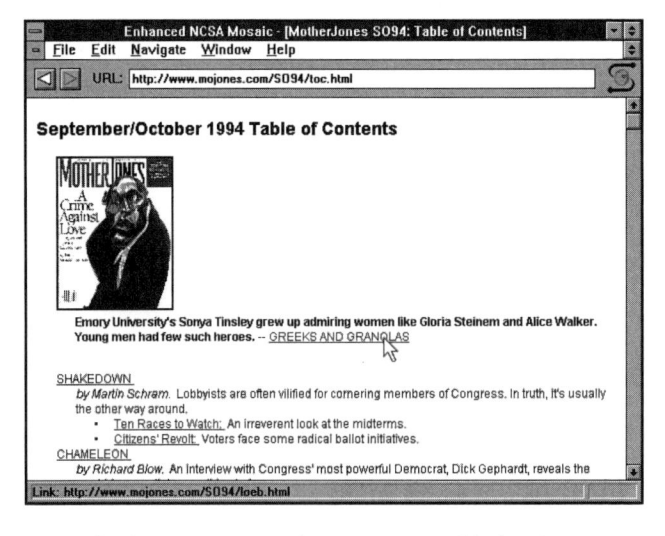

Figure 1.2. Veteran counterculture magazine *Mother Jones*, now available on the Internet.

Finally, there are even general-purpose national and world news services on the Internet. Among others, Cable News Network (CNN) publishes the text of the stories it broadcasts as CNN Headline News (see Figure 1.3). These are updated several times a day.

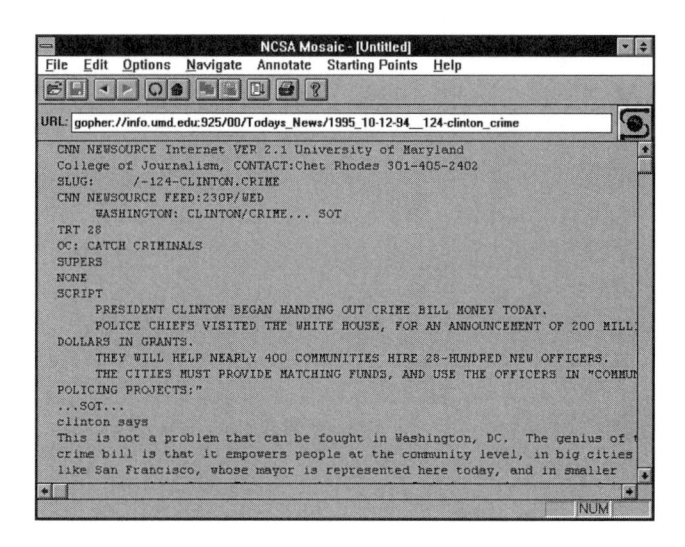

Figure 1.3. CNN Headline News on the Internet.

Using these resources, Internet users can acquire more timely, more detailed news about their areas of interest than they could ever find in the national broadcast or print media. Perhaps more importantly, in many cases they can respond to the news, add to it, or ask questions about it. It's that kind of power and immediacy that's getting people hooked on the Internet.

It's a Living Thing

To appreciate where the Internet is going, you have to understand where it's been. The Internet that exists today began in 1969 as an experiment of an agency of the U.S. Department of Defense. The agency hooked various defense department computers, defense contractors, and universities doing defense research into a classified network that accomplished two things. First, it enabled users to share expensive computing resources, which saved money, and second, it gave the defense department a network upon which to test various methods for keeping military networks operational in times of war.

Throughout the 1970s and early 1980s, that network grew, and portions of it were declassified. During the same period, other, separate networks were established to hook together university researchers and scientists.

In 1986, the National Science Foundation established its network, NFSnet, to allow researchers across the country to share access to a few expensive supercomputers (the fastest and most powerful type of computer for scientific applications). Quickly thereafter, the various, separate research networks began hooking to NFSnet, and therefore, in effect, to each other. In 1990, the original defense department network was retired, its work having been taken over by NFSnet. Eventually, the resulting internetwork got hooked into the various internetworks abroad, and *Voila!* The global Internet we know today had congealed from a lot of separate parts.

So, although you may hear much praise for the value and potential of the Internet, you must remember that the whole thing is an unplanned, disorganized, rattletrap contraption—an information-age afterthought, a mutant strain, a casserole made from leftovers. It has no real purpose or mission, except perhaps the somewhat fuzzy goal of enabling communication. It's really more a patchwork of links between lots of separate networks and organizations that—despite their participation in the Internet—still have their own way of doing things and don't feel particularly pressured to conform what anybody else on the Internet is doing. "Wanna use our computer?" they say. "Fine, go ahead. Just do it our way."

What Is the Internet? 31

As the Internet has grown like crazy, that hasn't changed. As of this writing, estimates say that the Internet picks up 1,000 new users a day, and it is nearly doubling the number of users every year. Nobody really knows for sure; in fact, nobody even knows exactly how many people are on the Internet. Recent guesses say about 20 million and counting.

The Internet is a living thing, growing its own way, at its own pace, perhaps according to a divine design, but not according to any earthly plan. Anything that big, involving that many people, and behaving that unpredictably is very threatening to some folks. In the coming years, you'll hear increasing concern over the global economic, political, and cultural implications of the Internet.

> **Really Curious?**
>
> For more on the implications of the growing Internet, see Chapters 3 and 4.

So Now You Know...

The Internet is a network, or more accurately, an internetwork, a vast collection of different types of computers all over the world that can share messages and information with one another.

Each computer on the network is controlled by its owner, and large parts of the network are overseen by the U.S. government or its agencies. The Internet as a whole, however, is under the direct authority of no one—which makes the Internet open and free, but also complex and inconsistent.

Curious About the Internet?

Using the Internet, people are able to perform a range of activities for work, pleasure or even simple curiosity. These include

- Posting and reading public messages to exchange news and information about certain topics or areas of interest.
- Sending messages to, and receiving messages from, other Internet users through electronic mail (e-mail).
- Conducting research by reading or copying information stored on other computers.
- Receiving news updates about specific events or topics.
- Finding books and other resources stored in libraries all over the world.
- Reading newspapers, newsletters, and magazines.
- Copying computer software.

You also know that the Internet can be used for academic or government research, personal pleasure, or business—and that the latter two uses are newer and evolving quickly. In fact, it is the business and personal aspects that will have the major role in shaping the Internet into the 21st century.

2

Who Uses the Internet, and for What?

Read this chapter to satisfy your curiosity about who's out there on the Internet and what those folks accomplish on it. The answers include:

- Scientists use it to solve.
- Educators use it to educate.
- Professionals use it to consult.
- Businesses use it to compete.
- Governments use it to disseminate.
- Activists use it to activate.

For each of these groups, this chapter offers a description of how the Internet serves them and which Internet resources each typically uses.

First, though, take note: these groups overlap. There are scientists and professionals in business, activists who are scientists, government workers who study business, and so on. That's OK because few resources on the Internet are restricted to one type of user (though indeed, some are). Just because a resource is especially useful to ornithologists doesn't necessarily mean it can't be used by birdwatchers, bird-seed companies or, for that matter, birds—as long as they can get an Internet account. Just keep in mind who the primary users of certain resources are while also remembering that most resources can be applied in many different ways.

That brings up the other, fluffier answer to the question this chapter asks: Everybody uses the Internet for everything. Unfortunately, that provides little structure to hang a book chapter on. But it's really the way people need to begin thinking about the Internet.

So one final group needs to be added to the list of who uses the Internet and what for. Near the end of the chapter, you'll discover that:

- Miscellaneous folks use the Internet for miscellaneous reasons.

It's a squishy category, but as you'll see, there's much about the Internet that defies pigeonholes.

Who Uses the Internet, and for What?

> **Really Curious?**
>
> Throughout this chapter, you'll see general references to the Internet resources used by various groups of people. When these people use a resource, they need to know more than just the name of the resource. They need to know how to access it. Unfortunately for beginning Internet users, different kinds of resources are accessed in different ways.
>
> You'll learn more about the different types of resources and how they're accessed in Chapters 6 and 7.
>
> For listings of popular Internet resources and specific instructions for accessing them, check out *Teach Yourself the Internet* or *Navigating the Internet*, which are described in Chapter 10, "Still Curious?".

Scientists Use It to Solve

As the original Internet surfers, scientists may benefit more from the Internet than anyone else. The great (as well as the mediocre) scientists of this world usually hole up in universities and other institutional think-tanks, nearly all of which have Internet connections.

If there's one thing scientists hate, it's duplication of effort. In embarking upon a scientific investigation, they try to start out with what others have already learned from previous studies and experiments. Then they move forward from that work, building on it and adding to the body of scientific knowledge about a subject.

Historically, scientists have published findings in journals for exactly that reason—so other scientists could build on that work instead of reinventing the wheel. But information in journals can be hard to locate and incomplete (it's often summarized to fit), and it falls out of date quickly. The Internet provides an intermediate solution to that problem by giving scientists a way to publish journals right on the Internet. Because they don't have to be printed and mailed, the journals can be kept more current than printed journals. Beyond the electronic journals, scientists can get even more complete and up-to-date information by simply accessing one another's work directly. What, the querying scientist may ask, have the folks at MIT learned about nuclear fusion in the time *since* they last published their findings?

The Internet offers scientists a way to gain access to each other's work, including the latest research results and papers about them. (Obviously, scientists keep some stuff secret, in which case it's stored in the computer in a way that keeps it off-limits to the general Internet public.) And they can also exchange e-mail messages to ask and answer questions and get up-to-the-minute information.

Really Curious?

Internet users most often exchange information though e-mail messages or public postings. But when necessary, users can have an actual "live" interactive discussion through the Internet. Through a facility called *Talk*, two users can establish a connection with one another so each can see everything the other types, as it's being typed. Talk splits the screen in half so that each user's typing appears on only one side. Both can type merrily away—discussing, arguing, even interrupting each other. Scientists no doubt use the Talk facility for heated discussions on weighty issues, as do many others.

For more on Talk, see Chapter 6.

Using the Internet, scientists can do their work better and more efficiently by picking the brains of the best minds in their fields and by avoiding duplication of work somebody else already did (unless, of course, they *want* to duplicate the work to prove their colleagues wrong!).

Specifically, scientists use the Internet to

- Query and collaborate with their colleagues all over the world (through e-mail or posted messages) on matters of scientific importance. For example, geneticists from various institutions are collaborating on a project to map all of the 100,000 or more human genes. Each institution is taking a part of the job, but they're all sharing information and consolidating their findings through the Internet. (For more, see Chapter 3.)

- Run special scientific programs that are not available on their own computers. For example, the National Center for Atmospheric Research (NCAR) offers a service that allows Internet users (sometimes for a fee) to use the sophisticated atmospheric modeling programs on NCAR's computers for their own research.

- Tap libraries and databases at other universities, research institutions, or government agencies to consult stored files of scientific papers, studies, reports, and abstract data from experiments and studies.

Curious About the Word?

\ , in‐ter‐'net \

Data is simply another word for information.

A *database* is a store of information from which one can extract specific pieces of information. A phone book is a database; it's a big pile of information that's set up so that your brain (a pretty good computer) can locate and extract specific pieces of information: telephone numbers.

Computerized databases such as those on the Internet enable researchers to use their computers to locate and extract specific pieces of information quickly, or to locate entire computer files of information that can be copied across the Internet into the researcher's computer for local use.

There are Internet resources available for every conceivable scientific discipline. Among many more, there are those listed in Table 2.1.

Table 2.1. A sampling of Internet resources for scientists (and the scientifically curious).

Field	A Few Resources
Astronomy	MIT's Astronomical Databases; NASA's databases.
Biology	The electronic newsletter *Biotech Briefs*; the TAXACOM service that offers journal files and taxonomic resources.

Who Uses the Internet, and for What?

Field	A Few Resources
Botany	Databases and other resources at the Australian National Botanic Gardens and the Missouri Botanical Garden.
Chemistry	University of Minnesota's Periodic Table; Washington University's molecular graphics software.
Computer Science	The Free Software Foundation's files of free software; the documentation for a Cray supercomputer; a database of university computer ethics policies.
Forestry	An annotated bibliography of the Forestry Library at the University of Minnesota; a database of tree care from the University of Delaware.
Geography	The CIA World Map; a service at University of Michigan that supplies latitude, longitude, elevation, and other information for any location.
Meteorology	Weather maps from several sources; climatology data from the University of Minnesota.
Oceanography	The information resources of the Oceanic Information Center and for the Bedford Institute of Oceanography.

40   Curious About the Internet?

Did You Know...

What do scientists see when they use these resources? Well, that depends on the resource at hand. Many, many resources on the Internet offer just text—words and numbers. Scientists can read what's there or copy it to their computers and read it later.

But science does not live by words alone. A growing number of resources show scientists pictures or video, and even play sound. A resource from NASA's Lunar and Planetary Institute shows detailed images of the planets. A medical service from the University of Minnesota shows full-color pictures of patients with specific illnesses to help physicians learn how to diagnose them.

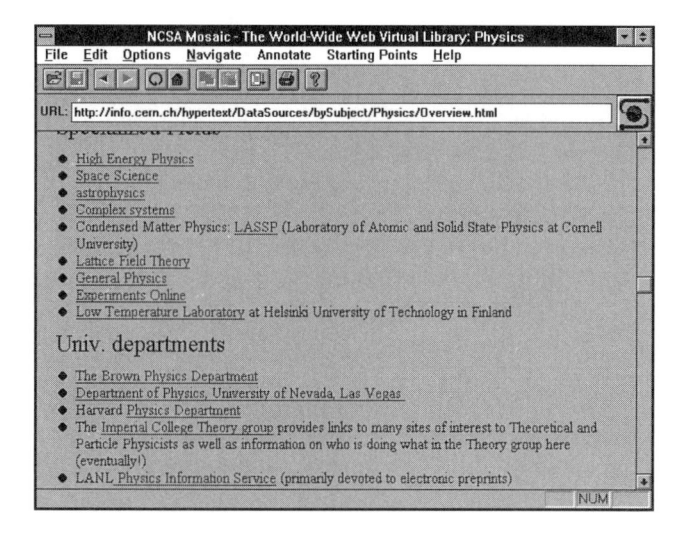

Figure 2.1. A screen showing an index of resources about Physics.

Figure 2.1 offers a glimpse of what scientists see when consulting a physics resource through a special slice of the Internet called the World Wide Web, being viewed here with a program called Mosaic (both of which you'll learn more about in Chapter 7).

Scientists are not limited to scientific communication. All kinds of information comes into play in science, and the Internet gives scientists access to it through the many resources that aren't designed for scientists, but are certainly available to them. Any of the resources described in this chapter for educators, businesspeople, professionals, and others could be valuable in one or more lines of scientific inquiry.

Educators Use It to Educate

Teachers have a huge variety of potential information sources on the Internet.

Among those specific to education is the Federal Information Exchange, which details federal programs for education, scholarships, fellowships, and more. Teachers also use a service run by the U.S. Department of Education to keep them informed about department projects. Another Internet resource called Learning Link, run in part by the Public Broadcasting System, supplies information and activities to support grade K-12 teachers, such as conferences with other teachers around the country. A resource called AskERIC supplies information about teaching methods and technologies. Teachers tap AskERIC to consult the vast body of educational literature compiled by the Educational Resources Information Center (ERIC).

Teachers also benefit from Internet resources designed to actually teach their students. Provided their schools are equipped with computers and Internet connections, teachers can get their students involved in fun, educational projects such as

- Academy One, which involves students in interactive science projects, such as space shuttle simulations.

- KidLink, which supplies interaction and projects between U.S. students ages 10-15 and other students from around the world, to nurture the students' global awareness.

- The JASON Project (see Figure 2.2), an Internet version of an ongoing initiative to get kids more involved in science.

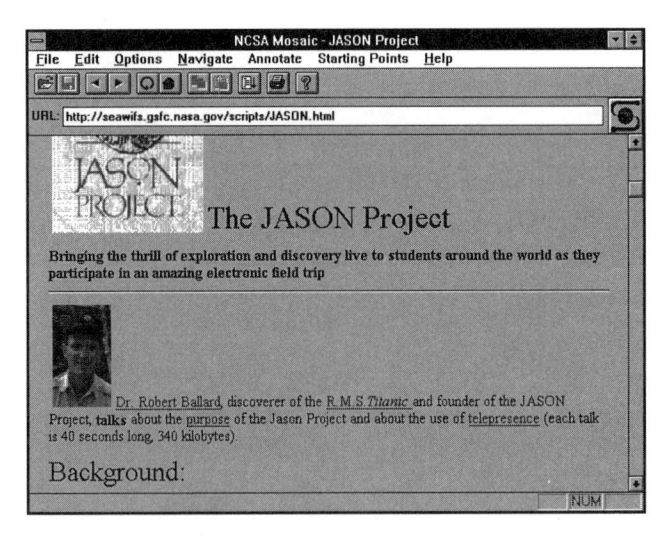

Figure 2.2. The JASON project, an Internet field trip for students.

University professors, of course, also make use of the vast array of Internet services covering subjects of academic and cultural interest: social issues, linguistics, politics and culture in other countries, music, art—the works. They also use it to communicate with colleagues and to publish (and co-publish) scholarly articles. When all else fails, there are even Internet resources that help professors locate new jobs.

Professionals Use It to Consult

It's impossible to list here the Internet services available to help various professionals do their jobs better. Perhaps it's enough to say I can't think of a profession for which there are no services on the Internet. And I can think of many for which there are rich service choices.

Professionals who use the Internet have the ability to stay up to date about developments in their fields, and to network with their colleagues the world over via e-mail and posted messages.

For a taste of what's possible, consider the following.

- *Lawyers* consult the catalog of Columbia University's Law Library, or the library of Washington and Lee University, which includes the text of federal and state laws. Other services list major employers of lawyers and the details of recent U.S. Supreme Court decisions. There are also several legal journals published on the Internet (see Figure 2.3).

Figure 2.3. A law journal published on the Internet.

- *Doctors* access the National Institute of Health's National Library of Medicine for clinical practice guidelines and treatment recommendations. They tap the U.S. Food and Drug Administration's bulletin board service, which covers FDA actions, including announcements of recent drug approvals. The Alcoholism Research Database offers doctors the latest and most complete medical literature about substance abuse, while a database called MEDLINE supplies indexed article citations from thousands of medical journals. Doctors can also tap into a database that covers whatever's up at the World Health Organization. There are even medical textbooks on the Internet (see Chapter 7).

- *Journalists* tap into the University of Ontario Graduate School of Journalism's Journalism Periodicals Index, a database of citations from the Index to Journalism

Periodicals. They can also consult *The CIA World Fact Book* and *The Reader's Guide to Periodical Literature*, and keep up on the government through the information services it provides (see "Governments Use It to Disseminate," later in this chapter). Journalists also get news about events in other countries from Internet resources that publish news and through e-mail from their international colleagues. Many journalists can even send their stories from the field to their editors through the Internet.

- *Writers* use the Internet to do research and to submit their work and communicate with editors. They can send stories to electronic publications on the Internet, but increasingly, they can use the Internet to submit stories to regular print publications, as well. Among the print publishers and publications accepting submissions through the Internet are Macmillan Computer Publishing, *Interior Design, Fortune,* and the *Wichita Eagle & Beacon.*

- *Researchers*, by definition, may have use for anything and everything on the Internet. But of specific interest are the libraries and bibliography services. The University of Minnesota offers a comprehensive list of libraries accessible through a special Internet service it created, Gopher (see Chapter 8). Another resource is the Research Libraries Information Network, a guide to accessing most major U.S. research libraries. A researcher favorite is a service run by the Colorado Association of Research Libraries (CARL). The CARL service (see Figure 2.4) catalogs nearly every academic and public library in Colorado and tosses in a variety of other research tools.

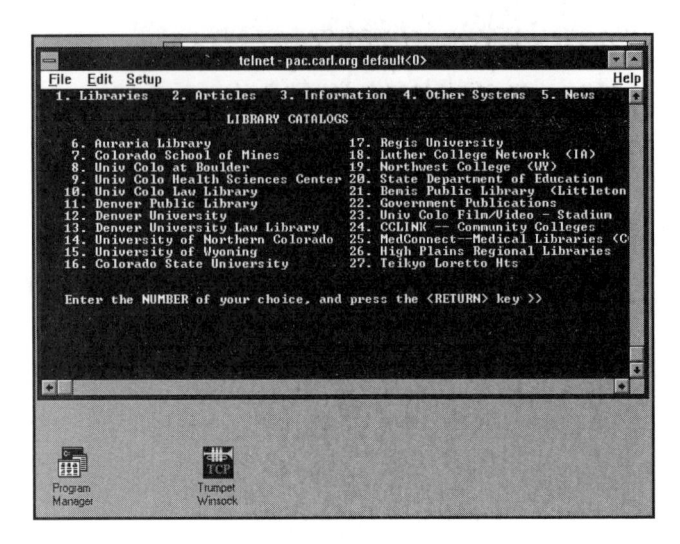

Figure 2.4. CARL, a service offering access to Colorado academic libraries.

- *Pilots* use a service called DUAT to develop flight plans and get weather forecasts.

- *Farmers*—yes, farmers—harvest a bushel of agricultural information services. For example, the Advanced Technology Information Network supplies news about weather, market conditions, jobs, and other agri-info. The U.S. Department of Agriculture puts some of its information on the Internet, such as results of USDA research and daily reports on farm commodities activity.

The Internet offers resources for many more professionals—musicians, writers, genealogists, and more. For each of these, and for each of the above professionals, there are resources that cover information and issues related to the field and offer professionals an open exchange of ideas with their colleagues.

Businesspeople Use It to Compete

The use of the Internet for business is a subject of some controversy (see Chapter 4), but no one can deny that the Internet is a useful business tool today, and will only grow in importance over the next several years. In a time when businesses increasingly

- Do business internationally and globally.
- Require rapid communication.
- Require up-to-the-minute information.
- Form inter-company collaborations for certain projects.
- Seek new markets, new groups of potential customers, wherever they may be.

The traditional rules about what business can and can't do on the Internet are still evolving at this writing. Businesses can do four things on the Internet without getting into any trouble:

1. Look stuff up. They're as welcome as anybody else to look at the public information on the Internet.

2. Make their own information available to others. If a company wants to set up its own service that Internet users can access to get information about the company's products, that's fine. (What's important is that the Internet users must deliberately go to the company's service; the company may not reach out and fish for customers.)

3. Use e-mail for inter-company and intra-company communications. This capability is becoming especially popular among telecommuters, workers who do

their jobs on computer at home and communicate with the office by computer, phone, and fax.

4. Post brief, non-intrusive public announcements in subject-specific Internet resources whose users may have a specific interest in the company or its products.

Companies are not supposed to send out unsolicited advertisements via e-mail. Actually, because the Internet isn't controlled by any organization, there's nothing to stop companies from breaching etiquette and advertising through e-mail, other than the wrath of Internet users who have been known to punish advertisers by burying them in e-mail or overloading their fax machines.

Nevertheless, the use of the Internet for advertising is growing dramatically (see Chapter 1). The Internet is also becoming a popular place to sell products and services. Companies set up "electronic malls" or "storefronts," Internet resources in which users can read product descriptions and place orders. Because these uses of the Internet are evolving quickly and are still somewhat experimental, many businesses will wait for the technology and other aspects of Internet business to mature before taking the plunge.

In the meantime, there's plenty of business to be done right now.

Business Research: Business thrives on all kinds of general information. Demographic and statistical information is essential for planning sales and marketing strategies. There are resources that supply listings of (and access to) major business libraries and to

Who Uses the Internet, and for What? 49

pending business-related legislation. And of course, any of the general-purpose information on the Internet may be of use to some businesses. In particular, marketers may gain insight into potential customer bases by scouting out the message activity in Internet resources covering certain topics.

Financial research: The type of information big business likes best is information about big business, and there's plenty. The Internet offers several ways to get current stock quotes and stock histories, Securities & Exchange Commission filings, mutual fund performance data, U.S. Department of Commerce reports, and financial/business newsletters (see Figure 2.5).

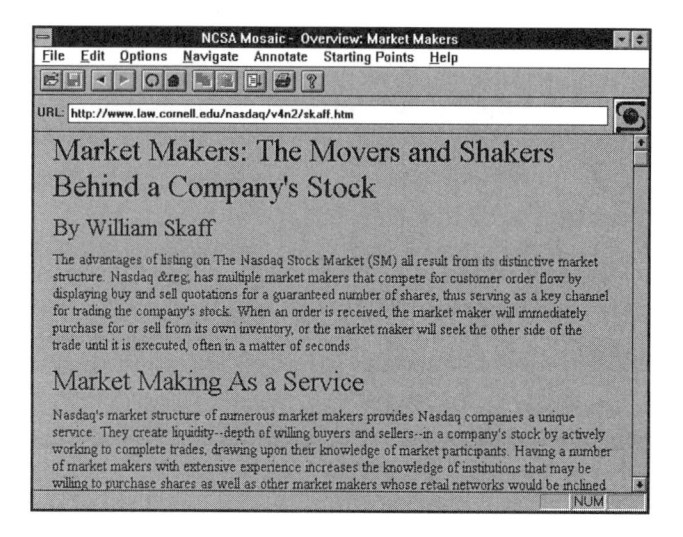

Figure 2.5. *The Financial Journal,* a joint publication of Cornell University and NASDAQ.

Legal Research: As mentioned earlier in this chapter, the Internet offers a range of resources of special interest to lawyers, including several law libraries and databases of laws and court decisions. These are as available to corporate lawyers as to any other type.

E-mail: Most large companies have their own, private e-mail networks for intercompany communication. But businesses today form lots of partnerships—big and small, temporary and permanent. Cooperative development deals, subcontracting and outsourcing—when a company contracts another company to provide some basic operational service, such as secretarial work or data processing—are on the rise, and they demand rapid, efficient *intra*-company communications, which the Internet provides.

Really Curious?

Some describe the trend toward cooperative business ventures as the beginnings of the *Virtual Corporation*, a new business model in which temporary companies are formed from alliances among two or more companies for a specific project, then disbanded when the project is complete. Business gurus say the Virtual Corporation may represent the model for doing business for the rest of the decade.

The Internet's capability to link up different companies, no matter where they are, makes it an important vehicle for the Virtual Corporation. For more, see Chapter 10.

Who Uses the Internet, and for What?

Governments Use It to Disseminate

As you may already have noticed, there's a ton of government information on the Internet. The government is in the business of creating unspeakable mounds of information, most of which it is required to make available to citizens. Every time an Internet user gets a dose of government data from the Internet, it represents a book Uncle Sam doesn't have to print. The goverment will continue to print material for those who want it, but it hopes to reduce the amount of printing by encouraging people to acquire government information through the Internet.

Internet users have access to the complete text of the federal budget, to thousands (yes, thousands) of reports and updates about goings-on at NASA, to complete reports from the National Science Foundation, to publications from the Social Security Administration and the Federal Communications Commission, to the rules enforced by the Occupational Safety & Health Administration...you get the idea.

Really Curious?

Congressional studies have determined that the government could save plenty—in printing costs, mailing, handling and storage, etc.—by offering more via computer and less on paper. So you can bet that, over the next several years, you'll hear about a steady increase in the Internet availability of government data.

That's great for Internet users, but maybe not so great for non-computer-using citizens (or computer users without Internet access), who have just as much right to that information as their networked neighbors. Some worry that the government's emphasis on computerizing its communications will create a new technological elite, and leave others ignorant of government goings-on. For more about the controversy, see Chapter 4.

There are over 100 separate Internet resources that supply government information. Fortunately, there's also a resource called FedWorld—run by the National Technical Information Service—that helps users find and access many of them. Another popular starting point is the White House, whose service sends Internet users, upon request, the complete text of White House publications via e-mail. Curious citizens can analyze presidential speeches, studies, reports, plans, and proposed legislation. They can also send e-mail to the president and vice president, who I'm sure read it all.

Did You Know...

The U.S. government isn't alone on the Internet. The Canadian government is developing a single resource from which Internet users can get government documents and exchange e-mail with officials. Other resources supply information from governments the world over—sometimes supplied by the government itself, sometimes by third parties who, in effect, smuggle news and information out of isolated countries.

A number of U.S. Representatives—though certainly not all—participate in the Constituent Electronic Mail System, a pilot project that enables Internet users to exchange e-mail with their representatives and some House committees. The project plans to get the whole House signed up, but that may take a while. In the meantime, at least two other Internet services offer names, addresses, phone and fax numbers for Senators and House members, so Internet users can find out how to complain to Congress the old-fashioned way.

Activists Use It to Activate

Tons of detailed information about the government...open, unfettered information exchange worldwide...e-mail access to government officials, committees, and corporations... posted messages that can be read by thousands of interested people...

Yup. The Internet is political/social/environmental activist's dream.

That's not news to the activists, who have used the Internet for many years to distribute information and ideas, and to accumulate information to be used in the fight. Hundreds of resources center around various causes—gay rights, the environment, gun control, the death penalty, world hunger, and more. Activists exchange information through these ready-made, grass-roots services; use e-mail to lobby government officials (see "Governments Use It to Disseminate," earlier in this chapter); and use the whole range of Internet resources to locate information in support of their causes.

Environmentalists make use of the Environmental Protection Agency's library catalog, or the Environmental Activism Server, which serves up detailed information on environmental initiatives. Those concerned about overpopulation can tap into a resource detailing the proceedings of the 1994 Cairo population conference (see Figure 2.6). And human rights workers can examine the thousands of documents in Diana, a human rights database jointly run by the University of Cincinnati and Yale Law School.

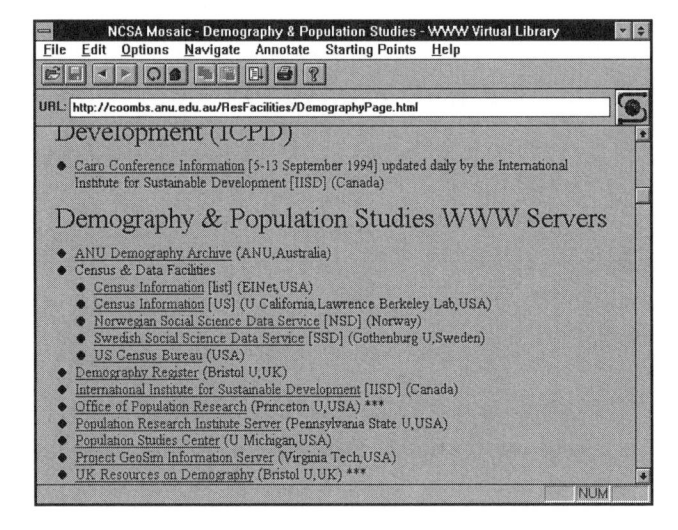

Figure 2.6. A service showing population information discussed at the 1994 population summit in Cairo.

Miscellaneous People Use It to Do Miscellaneous Stuff

Well, let's face it. Around 25 million people use the Internet, and they can't all be scientists, teachers, professionals, businesspeople, governments, or activists. And for that matter, even if a user does fit one of these categories, he or

Who Uses the Internet, and for What?   55

she may well use the Internet for purposes that don't relate directly to their job.

Awareness of the Internet has expanded dramatically over the last couple of years. During that time, the Internet has adopted a huge constituency outside its formative brethren of scientists and researchers. Consider the reasons for this expansion.

- Special software tools have evolved to make using the Internet much easier for network-neophytes—and even computer neophytes. (See Chapter 5.)

- Commercial online services such as Prodigy and CompuServe—which are not nearly as rich as the Internet but are more consumer-oriented and easier to use—have helped everyday folk catch on to the joys of computer-based communication and information retrieval. Having gotten their feet wet through such services, some get greedy for more—and they find it on the Internet.

- The Internet's gotten a lot of mainstream press coverage. Every rag from *Time* to *Entertainment Weekly*—plus local newspapers everywhere—has told readers about the wonders of the Internet and how to climb onboard.

- Local access providers have begun courting everyday consumers with affordable Internet connection plans (see Chapter 5).

As the number and variety of users on the Internet has expanded, so has the range of services catering to every job, hobby, whim, and...curiosity.

A sample? Don't mind if I do! Here's a quick slice of general-interest Internet resources, just to give you a feeling for how eclectic (and, in some cases, weird) it's getting out there. But I can't really tell you *who* the users of each of these services are because they don't fall into neat little categories. Just call them curious.

Table 2.2. The wonderful world of everybody's Internet.

Service	Description
Cyber Sleaze	Nasty gossip about the music industry.
Barney Haters	For non-fans of the big purple dinosaur.
Nasty Jokes	'Nough said.
Elvis Sightings	A scholarly exchange of reports of the whereabouts of the world's best traveled dead pop icon.
Chinese Politics	News and discussion about goings on over there.
Conspiracy Theories	An exchange of either a) paranoia, or b) "The terrible, hidden truth that's been suppressed for decades!" Your pick.
Rocky Horror	A discussion of the *Rocky Horror Picture Show* and its offspring.
Yellow Silk	A journal of erotica.
Song Lyrics	A database of the words to hundreds of songs.

Service	Description
Hang Gliding	Tips on gliding and ballooning.
Sri Lanka	A resource about a lesser-known country.
Diabetes	Information and advice for diabetics, their families, and the curious.
Comics	An exchange of comments and questions about comics, plus a way to find trading partners.
Poetry	In several different resources, from the sublime to the ridiculous.
Antique Autos	More than you could possibly want to know about old cars.
Video	In several different resources, covering every type and subject on video.
African-American Culture	A sociological exchange/debate/information source.

So Now You Know...

People in science, various other professions, commercial enterprise, and activism exploit the resources on the Internet to stay informed, do research, make announcements, and exchange messages with colleagues, partners, and opponents. You also know that the U.S. government uses the Internet as an electronic publishing house, making staggering amounts of detailed government data available to the politically curious.

Perhaps most importantly, you know that the Internet is too big, open, and varied to be boiled down into any reasonable set of categories. Professional interests overlap, and a growing number of Internet services have no clear professional purpose—other than to satisfy the curiosity of Internet users who, while thus engaged, also seem to have no professional purpose. Even those who have Internet access for professional reasons have been known to fool around on it when nobody's looking.

Like a town square, the Internet has evolved into a public meeting place. Business and politics happen there, and they reign the square in. But in the square itself, people interact as they please, and enjoy discussing subjects of infinite number and variety.

3

How Does the Internet Make the World a Better Place?

Read this chapter to satisfy your curiosity about good things the Internet fosters. The answers include these:

- It supports scientific discovery.
- It saves trees (maybe).
- It exposes the truth.
- It gives away free stuff.
- It creates new business opportunities.
- It accommodates the disabled.
- It brings people and nations together.
- It plays Cupid.

- It prevents pointless walks to the Coke machine.
- It makes people laugh.
- It turns people on.

As someone who's curious about the Internet, you're going to notice a lot of discussion about it in the media and perhaps among your friends and acquaintances. Two extremes will frame the discussions you encounter:

1. The Internet is the best thing since sliced bread.
2. The Internet is Big Brother waiting to happen, a sinister conspiracy that destroys our privacy, steals our freedoms, and reduces us all to electronic ink.

As with most debates, the truth lies somewhere in-between. To help you develop your own perspective on the debate, this chapter and the next present a sort of point-counterpoint. Here, you'll get a wholly partisan look at what's good about the Internet. In Chapter 4, you'll get a tough dose of unalloyed Internet paranoia. My hope is that by examining the two extremes separately, you'll equip yourself to find your own middle ground on this complex—and ongoing—controversy.

Now, I have to point out that this chapter is only about half as long as Chapter 4, which would tend to create the impression that I think the "cons" of the Internet outweigh the "pros." Well, I'm not telling what I think — I don't want to influence your judgment. But I will explain that Chapter 4 is longer because it is the *only* chapter that really covers the potential downside of the Internet. The chapter you're reading, on the other hand, has help. By showing you all the wonderful things people can do on the Internet, Chapters 1, 2, 5, 6, 7, and 8 are all pro-Internet, in effect.

How Does the Internet Make the World a Better Place?

With that in mind, here we go. I will now put on my "I ♥ the Internet" hat, and take inspiration from the Internet's biggest booster, the Vice President.

Did You Know...

"The Global Information Infrastructure offers instant communication to the great human family.

"It can provide us the information we need to dramatically improve the quality of our lives. By linking clinics and hospitals together, it will ensure that doctors treating patients have access to the best possible information on diseases and treatments. By providing early warning on natural disasters like volcanic eruptions, tsunamis, or typhoons, it can save the lives of thousands of people.

"By linking villages and towns, it can help people organize and work together to solve local and regional problems ranging from improving water supplies to preventing deforestation...

"Let us build a global community in which the people of neighboring countries view each other not as potential enemies, but as potential partners, as members of the same family in the vast, increasingly connected human family."

U.S. Vice President Al Gore in a speech to promote the Global Information Infrastructure presented at a conference of the International Telecommunications Union, March 1994.

It Supports Scientific Discovery

As discussed in Chapter 2, the Internet helps scientists and researchers do their jobs more effectively by giving them access to exhaustive, up-to-date information compiled by other scientists and researchers.

The Internet also gives scientists access to equipment that they do not have at their own institutions. For example, an observatory in New Mexico has a telescope that scientists in other countries can actually aim and look through (by looking at computer graphics sent to their computers) by way of the Internet.

Also made possible by the Internet are parallel, or collaborative, research projects. Teams of scientists located all over the country or over the world can work individually on portions of a larger research project, using the Internet to share and consolidate their findings. Major projects that would exceed the resources (staff, equipment, and computing power) of the largest institutions in the world can be undertaken this way, with each partipating institution performing the part that it is best equipped to handle.

A good example of parallel research is the Humane Genome Project (see Figure 3.1). Funded in part by the Federal Government and involving the world's best genetics labs, the project is a massive 15-year plan to identify all 100,000 or more human genes, possibly unlocking the secrets to preventing many birth defects and genetically influenced diseases, such as cancer. Fifteen years is a long time, but scientists have commented that such a project conducted by a single research lab could take a century. That's another 85 years of preventable human suffering.

How Does the Internet Make the World a Better Place?

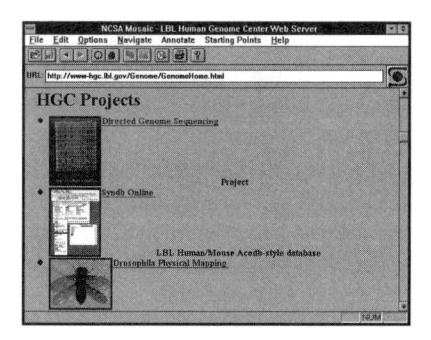

Figure 3.1. An Internet resource for learning about the Human Genome project.

Other cooperative initiatives that use the Internet are the initiatives for curing AIDS and other infectious diseases, developing alternative fuels, predicting earthquakes and volcanic eruptions, and saving species from extinction—and all that's just the beginning.

It Saves Trees (Maybe)

In theory, every message exchanged by computer saves the paper that would otherwise have been used, plus the energy used and the pollution produced to make the paper. Ditto books and lengthy research materials available electronically over the Internet.

The only catch is, nobody really knows if it's working that way. For one thing, people have a funny habit of printing stuff that they could just as easily read on a computer screen. For another, the manufacture of computers, the generating of the electricity required by the computers and the network, and the radiation produced by computers and power lines may also be sources of pollution. So it's difficult to say for sure whether the Internet helps make the world a greener place. It is known that the amount of paper used worldwide has continued to rise every year, even as use of computers and the Internet expands.

But then again, nobody's proved that the Internet *doesn't* save trees. So if you want to see the Internet as an environmentally progressive development, be my guest. Nobody can prove you wrong, at least not yet.

It Exposes the Truth

There's a stubborn freedom-of-information tenet to Internet culture. Many Internet users believe (correctly, if you ask me and Thomas Jefferson) that secrets are anathema to freedom and democracy. These folks sometimes make themselves into investigative reporters who keep an eye out for important, unreported information and then spill the truth out onto the Internet. In particular, they're opposed to gag orders that prevent the media from reporting about certain stories. When the print and broadcast media's hands are tied, the Internet community kicks into high gear.

A good example involved the trials of Karla Homolka and her husband Paul Bernardo in Ontario, as reported in *The Nation*. In her trial, Homolka pled guilty to two gruesome murders, and while she was at it, she said Bernardo—who was scheduled to be tried later—made her do it. To prevent potential jurors for Bernardo's trial from learning too much about the case, the Canadian court forbade the media from reporting the details of Homolka's trial.

Offended that their government would dare to censor coverage of a public court proceeding, Internet users in Toronto created an Internet resource to which they posted daily updates about the trial, which were read the world over.

How Does the Internet Make the World a Better Place?

The Canadian Government went to great lengths to stop the Internet users. The police left threatening messages on the bulletin board (the *mounted* police, no less; presumably they use the Internet from saddle-mounted PCs), and the resource had to be renamed after all the Canadian universities switched off local access to it under pressure from the government. (The universities couldn't prevent Internet access to it, though, because to do so, they would have had to sever the university from the Internet entirely.) Ultimately, the Internet users were able to continue funneling information while successfully eluding the Canadian police.

> **Did You Know...**
>
> "There's a Dutch relief worker, Wam Kat, who has been broadcasting an electronic diary from Zagreb for more than a year and a half on the Internet, sharing his observations of life in Croatia.
>
> "After reading Kat's Croatian Diary, people around the world began to send money for relief efforts. The result: 25 houses have been rebuilt in a town destroyed by war."
>
> U.S. Vice President Al Gore

Another example is the smuggling of information out of Russia during the 1991 coup attempt. From the beginning of the fighting, the pro-coup KGB blacked out the print and broadcast media, preventing any news from circulating around the country or reaching the Western media, and also preventing any international news from reaching the Soviet people.

A small Russian e-mail company collected news from the banned newspapers and radio stations, local reports from its subscribers and even communiqués from Boris Yeltsin himself, and published it all on the Internet through a link in Finland. The Western media, including CNN and the Associated Press, culled the news from the Internet and spread it to the world beyond. The company also collected world news from the Internet and distributed it to Soviet citizens through its e-mail subscribers.

If the truth shall make you free, the Internet can indeed be a carrier for freedom.

It Gives Away Free Stuff

As you'll learn in Chapter 5, using the Internet is free, but not really.

Be that as it may, there's stuff users can get from the Internet that they don't have to pay for. So although the Internet isn't really free, the stuff really is. A few favorites are in Table 3.1.

Table 3.1. Free stuff on the Internet.

Stuff	Sources
Books (in electronic form, of course)	The Online Book Project and Project Gutenberg.
Software	Software companies that provide customer service on the Internet, the Free Software Foundation, hundreds of Internet resources that have software for copying, including files of sound and video clips.

How Does the Internet Make the World a Better Place?

Stuff	*Sources*
Advice	Newsgroups, e-mail.
Fine art	The WebLouvre, a facility that provides full-color computer files of masterworks. A growing number of museums and galleries also offer a peek at their holdings through the Internet.
Rare/historical photographs	The Smithsonian Institution, several universities.
General reference information	CIA *World Fact Book*, *Concise Oxford Dictionary*, *Oxford Dictionary of Familiar Quotations*, *Encyclopaedia Britannica*, *Roget's Thesaurus*.
Periodicals	Electronic Newsstand, which offers on-screen access to the text of *The New Yorker*, *The New Republic*, *Foreign Affairs*, *National Review*, *Eating Well*, and others. Also available are veteran progressive mag *Mother Jones*, a technology magazine called *Wired*, and many more.

It Creates New Business Opportunities

Business use of the Internet is controversial. Still, there's no doubt people are making money on, through, and around the Internet.

For example, a company called the Internet Shopping Network makes its database of information about the computers and software it sells available on the Internet. Customers can get their answers without costing the Shopping Network a printed catalog or live sales associate. Customers can also place orders through the Internet. The company uses the savings to underprice its competitors. There will be a steady growth in the number of such services, and they'll be joined by new ventures such as electronic banking, magazine subscriptions and classified advertising (see Figure 3.2). Visionary entrepreneurs will use the resources and community of the Internet to open new markets, design new products, and stimulate the economy.

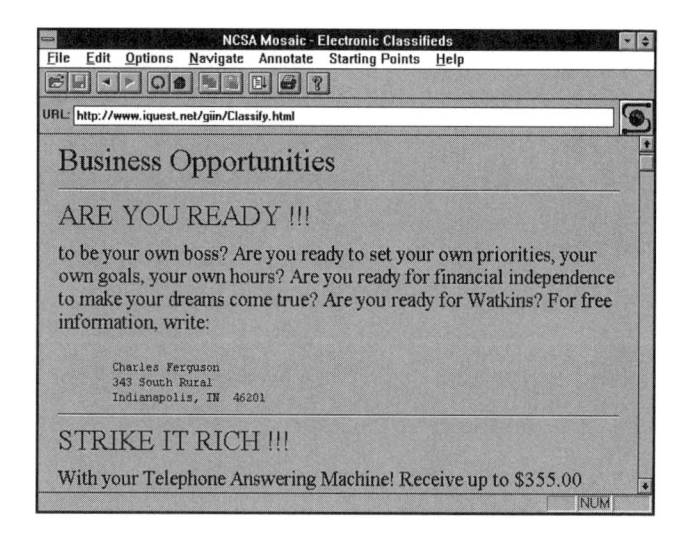

Figure 3.2. Classified advertising, a recent arrival on the Internet.

An emerging new business model, called the Virtual Corporation (VC), may depend heavily on the Internet. In the VC, the large company staffed with permanent workers is replaced by a small team of executives who manage an ever-changing field of freelancers who are hired and let go as needed. The VC can respond more rapidly to changing business needs than can a traditional corporation, and it can operate more efficiently by only paying workers when there's a specific project for which they're required.

Advocates say the VC will make businesses more competitive, and will also bring about a huge upswing in self-employment, which many people find more satisfying than traditional employment. The Internet will help make the the VC possible by making it easy for managers to find, hire, and communicate with the best freelancers, wherever they may be located.

It Accommodates the Disabled

People with certain disabilities can find traditional written communication difficult. For example, the blind can't read written paper mail, and those with motor impairments sometimes have trouble with letters and envelopes.

There are dozens of products that enable the disabled to use computers: Braille keyboards and finger-readers for the blind, and mouth sticks and other gadgets for the motor-impaired. For both the blind and the motor-impaired, there are voice-response systems that enable the computer to respond to voice commands and also enable it to speak words that appear on the computer screen. These tools empower disabled people to do anything that can be done with a computer. (Of course, typewritten communication by computer has obvious benefits for the deaf and hearing impaired— with no special accessories required.)

> **Really Curious?**
>
> Telecommuting, the practice wherein employees do their jobs at home with computers, can be an especially attractive option to people whose disabilities make getting around difficult or impossible. To learn more about telecommuting, see Chapter 9.

Given appropriate accommodations, most disabled people can use a computer—and thus the Internet. The Internet offers them a way to communicate with the world, perhaps even more easily than they do in person. There are also many Internet resources that serve the specific needs and interests of disabled people and enable them to exchange advice and ideas.

> **Did You Know...**
>
> Visually impaired people can get e-mail over the telephone. International Discount Communications in New Jersey receives Internet e-mail for its clients and converts the messages to spoken words. The company's computer then calls the recipient on the phone and plays the message aloud, or saves it in voice-mail for the recipient to hear later.

It Brings People and Nations Together

Through e-mail and other resources, the Internet provides an easy way for 30 million people, from everywhere in the world, to discover each other and to communicate on equal terms across a place with no borders, boundaries, or class

How Does the Internet Make the World a Better Place?

distinctions (language, though, remains a barrier). Other potential cultural divisions—such as race and religion—can be left out of the Internet discussion, or made an important part of them, at the user's discretion.

Because they are built around a specific topic, Internet newsgroups and mailing lists (see Chapter 7) make a natural meeting place for people with common interests to come together. There are also Internet resources dedicated to the idea that the Internet's ability to bring people together can make a better world. For example, PeaceNet is a cooperative project that distributes information and facilitates interaction among peace advocates worldwide (see Figure 3.3).

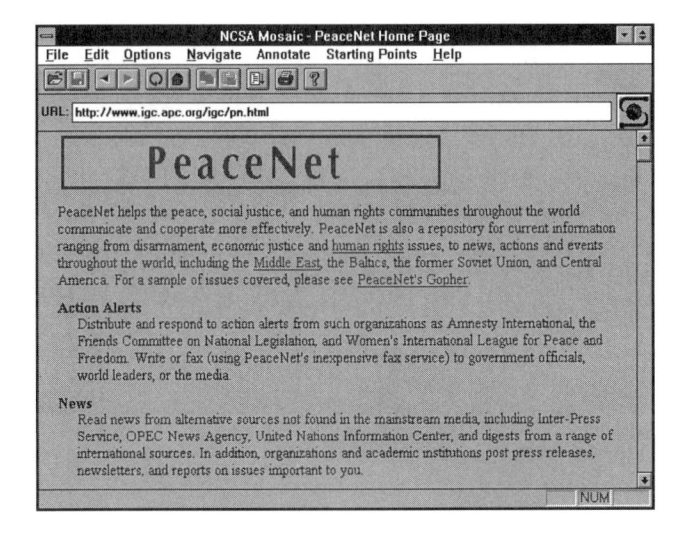

Figure 3.3. PeaceNet.

Some also promote the idea of Virtual Communities, subsets of Internet users who form their own little collective network with its own rules, membership requirements, and security.

That sounds like a step backward from the "everybody's welcome" spirit of the whole Internet, and it can be. But don't forget that the Virtual Communities are founded from people who discovered one another—and their commonalties—on the Internet.

> ### Did You Know...
>
> "A person on the Internet sees the world in a different light. He or she views the world as decidedly decentralized, every far-flung member a producer as well as a consumer, all parts of it equidistant from all others, no matter how large it gets, and every participant responsible for manufacturing truth out of a noisy cacophony of ideas, opinions and facts. There is no central meaning, no official canon, no manufactured consent rippling through the wires from which one can borrow a viewpoint. Instead, every idea has a backer, and every backer has an idea, while contradiction, paradox, irony, and multifaceted truth rise up in a flood."
>
> From Kevin Kelly, *Out of Control: The Rise of Neo-Biological Civilization* (Addison-Wesley).

It Plays Cupid

Let's see, ways to meet potential life-mates…bars…adult education classes…singles retreats…community theatre… the produce aisle. Telephone party lines. The Internet.

Yes, people meet and fall in love on the Internet, though I've heard it's rare. They can meet anywhere on the Internet, but a few resources are specifically set aside for posting "personals" to help people find one another. I suppose it's a pretty big step when the relationship moves past the personals and to the e-mail stage.

It Prevents Pointless Walks to the Coke Machine

This may seem like a very small way to make the world a better place, but not if you've recently had the misfortune to walk all the way to the Coke machine for nothing. People have started riots for less.

Having both access to computers and *way* too much time on their hands, enterprising folks at several universities have connected their cola machines to the school computer system so they could make sure the machine wasn't empty before trudging down the hall. (Refer to "It Separates and Isolates People" in Chapter 4.) Because these university computers are on the Internet, other Internet users around the world can find out whether there's enough Coke at Columbia or U. Wisconsin. While the early, groundbreaking work in this field was done on Coke machines, visionaries have also hooked a hot tub and a coffee maker to the Internet, as shown in Figure 3.4. (And you wondered why tuition was so high?)

74 Curious About the Internet?

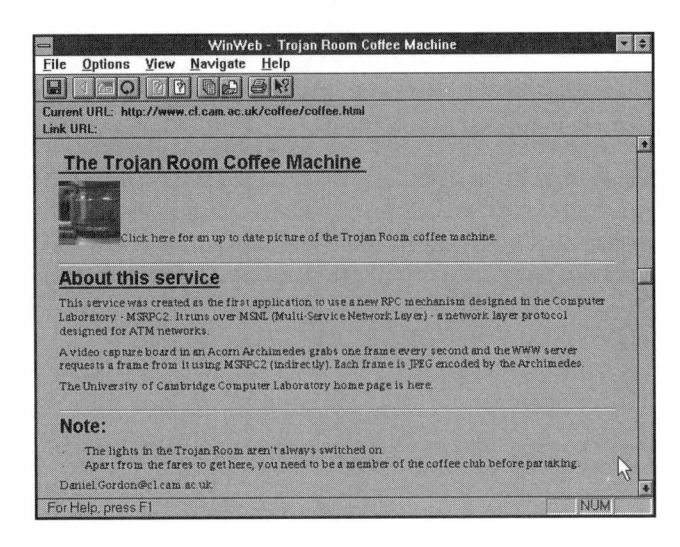

Figure 3.4. A program that monitors the coffee pot at the University of Cambridge, accessed through the Internet.

What Internet users get out of that I'm not sure. Maybe two colleges competing for a research grant can monitor each other's caffeine and sugar consumption, to be sure to keep the playing field level.

Really Curious?

Although hooking devices like vending machines and coffee pots to the Internet is an entertaining experiment today, it actually foreshadows tomorrow. Plans for the "Information Superhighway" include the development of electronic devices—including a new generation of TV sets, VCRs, telephones and more—that will be connected to high-speed, two-way communications lines. The lines will deliver information and programming to the devices, and you'll be able to use the devices to communicate with service providers.

For more, see Chapter 9.

It Makes People Laugh

Did you hear the one about the Internet user who took a job on a fishing boat because he liked the net work? ("Net work!" Get it?)

Plenty of yuks can be had on the Internet. As in any conversation, Internet messages are often punctuated with jokes. Because the messages are written rather than spoken, however, the users have time to try to be clever and to polish their material before sending it out. This results in more bad jokes than good, but it's the thought that counts.

Several newsgroups (see Chapter 7) are dedicated to humor. Internet users can visit these when they need a quick shot of silliness, but unfortunately, these newsgroups are not reliable sources of humor for most people's tastes. For reasons I do not know, the majority of jokes in these resources are of the *Beavis & Butthead* level. By that I don't mean the sly, satirical humor sometimes served up by the *Beavis & Butthead* show. I mean the kind of jokes Beavis and Butthead themselves would snicker at— adolescent, tasteless, crude, sick, dumb. Worse yet, many are also sexist or racist. Efforts have been made to clean up these resources by putting them under the supervision of a moderator, but they've not improved much.

Did You Know...

I had originally intended to offer a few genuine jokes from Internet newsgroups in this section. However, after several attempts over several weeks, I was unable to find anything that was both funny and fit to print.

The better humor on the Internet is found elsewhere: in the everyday exchanges between Internet users and in the odd resource that serves up humor with a little smarts. For example, I came across "Hamlet was a College Student" in a recent edition of *Gonzo*, an electronic publication of Georgetown University and heir to the subversive style of Gonzo journalist Hunter S. Thompson. The article uses accurate, verbatim quotes from Shakespeare's *Hamlet* to support its thesis (see Figure 3.5).

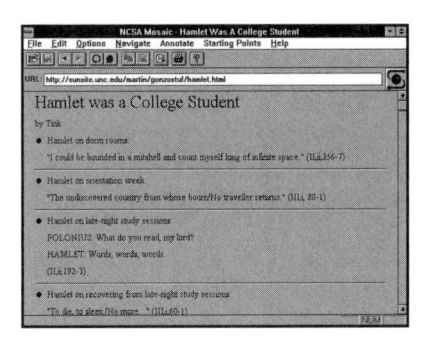

Figure 3.5. "Hamlet was a College Student," an article in *Gonzo*.

When injecting humor into their correspondence and other Internet message writing, Internet users are not unaware that written jokes lack the benefits of inflection and timing that often make spoken jokes funny. Over time, they've adopted an elaborate code of little typed symbols, called *smileys*, to expand the expressive range of written communication. Among the symbols used in the smiley language are those shown in the following list. To see the little faces of the smileys, you have to tilt your head to the left.

:-)	A basic smile, denoting happiness or sarcasm
:)	Also a smile
;-)	Wink
:-D	Laughing
:-}	Grin
:-P	Plbbbt!
:-(	Sad face
8-)	Wide-eyed
B-)	Wearing glasses
:-X	Close mouthed

The first five smileys are often typed adjacent to jokes, just so the reader can tell they're jokes even if they fail to be funny. (If Jay Leno's monologue was on the Internet, he'd have to use lots of them.)

It Turns People On

This is one of those issues that's good or bad (the bad perspective is covered in Chapter 4) depending on your own, private value system.

If you're among those who believe that looking at nudie pictures or reading erotic poetry and fiction is a positive—or simply harmless—pastime and promoter of a healthy libido, the Internet makes your world a better place. Through resources dedicated to the sexy side of life, users can read or copy erotic writing. They can also copy full-color, detailed, anatomically correct, photo-realistic graphics files of naked people and sexual acts. The pictures can be displayed on a computer screen (see Chapter 7), or even printed on a printer capable of handling high-resolution graphics.

Given the traditional demographics of both the Internet and pornography, the overwhelming majority of this type of material caters to the tastes of heterosexual men. But all genders, tastes, and preferences are served somewhere on the Internet.

Did You Know...

All jokes aside, there have been cases of pedophiles using public computer networks to cruise for victims. The pedophiles use network communications facilities such as e-mail to converse with young people and, after gaining their trust, arrange a meeting. Fortunately, undercover cops use the same networks to trap the abusers, sometimes by posing as potential victims and then arresting the pedophiles at the arranged meeting. Two such cases—one in San Jose and another in Chelmsford, Massachusetts—have made the press, but there have been others.

The well-known cases took place not on the Internet but on local computer bulletin board systems, where most or all of the potential victims lived near the criminal. Because it's so large and spread out, the Internet makes a poor tool for this purpose, and I'm not aware of any such case involving the Internet. That doesn't mean it hasn't happened, however, or can't happen.

So Now You Know...

The world is made better in part by the Internet and the people who use it. There are the big reasons, such as the free exchange of news and information and the support of science, and the little reasons, like laughs and love.

In any case, 20 million people can't be wrong. There's a lure to the depth of resources available on the Internet. And once people get hooked on knowing, they don't give up easily.

4

Why Do Some People Worry About the Internet?

Read this chapter to satisfy your curiosity about the reasons many people voice concern about the Internet and its long-term implications. The answers include these:

- It separates and isolates people.
- It distributes unreliable, unchecked information.
- It spreads hate.
- It creates job insecurity.
- It threatens national security.
- It enables piracy and sabotage.
- It invades privacy.

- It enables fraud.
- It carries unrestricted pornography.
- It empowers the few and excludes the many.

Can some of these fears be written off as mere technophobia or as the natural apprehension that accompanies the arrival of anything that's big, pervasive, and difficult to understand (like MTV)? Perhaps. Still, like any new technology from firemaking to genetic engineering, the Internet has plenty potential to be misused, abused, or applied to unsavory purposes. Only by extrapolating the worst-case scenarios can people ensure that the Internet will evolve in a way that minimizes the risks.

We will now put on our "I Want to 💣 the Internet" hats...

Curious About the Word?

Hacker refers generally to computer experts with the skills necessary to break into other computers. Although high-profile cases of hackers who used their skills to steal and spy have made the name a derogatory one, not all hackers are malicious. Lately, another term, *cracker*, is often used to describe computer break-in experts, malicious and otherwise. Still another word, *cyberpunk*, has been used to describe members of a growing culture of hackers who aren't out to steal, but rather to create minor (occasionally major) mischief and practice rebellious civil disobedience by breaking into computers through networks. To keep things simple in this chapter, I'll stick with the broadest term, *hacker*.

Keep in mind, though, that when I say hackers sometimes perpetrate a particular offense, the suggestion is not that all—or even most—hackers ever would do such a thing. Rather, the suggestion is that a person would have to have a hacker's skills to pull off the offense.

It Separates and Isolates People

This particular argument is as old as the telephone. People who inhabit an electronic neighborhood of Internet companions can experience human interaction without ever leaving their desks. This, sociologists have said, may ultimately isolate them, making them uncomfortable with face-to-face interaction. The Internet isn't the only culprit in that development—the phone, home video, telecommuting, and other homey trends are "cocooning" us in ways that divide us and make us unable to communicate with one another, the theory goes.

Despite the fact that it can interconnect people with infinitely varied backgrounds and interests, the Internet can also foster a certain narrow field of contact because people can restrict their communications to only those who share their interests. Those who limit their activities to hanging around narrowly focused newsgroups and other Internet resources need never interact with people whose interests are different.

Even the development of "virtual communities"—which aim to create balanced groups of like-minded people who communicate on a network—ultimately isolates those people from the rest of the Internet and its assortment of personalities and points of view. The resulting electronic provincialism may not be good for fostering tolerance and understanding among people of differing backgrounds.

Did You Know...

"Somewhere we have gotten hold of the idea that the more all-embracing we can make our communications networks, the closer we will be to that connection that we long for deep down. For change us as they will, our technologies have not yet eradicated that flame of a desire—not merely to be in touch, but to be, at least figuratively, embraced, known and valued not abstractly but in presence. We seem to believe that our instruments can get there, but they can't."

From Sven Birkerts, *The Gutenberg Elegies: The Fate of Reading in an Electronic Age* (Faber & Faber, 1994), quoted in *Harper's Magazine*, May 1994 (p. 17).

It Distributes Unreliable, Unchecked Information

As a news medium, the Internet is faster than newspapers or most television, and it benefits from the news noses of about 30 million potential reporters. On the other hand, few of the reporters are trained journalists, and the accuracy of their work does not bear the scrutiny and checks that good journalism demands.

Why Do Some People Worry About the Internet?

Like any largely unedited intercourse, the Internet can be a terrific medium for unsubstantiated rumors, gossip, libel, misunderstandings, misinformation, disinformation, and flat-out lies. Internet users have the ability to broadcast (and embellish) errors to millions in minutes. Fortunately, Internet users who discover errors are often just as quick to set the record straight.

At this writing, some legal questions regarding libel on the Internet are still being worked out. Precedent was set, in a case several years ago involving a libelous message sent through the CompuServe network, that networks cannot be held liable for the information they carry. That's good—it keeps networks from feeling an obligation to restrict freedom of speech over their wires.

It also means that individuals bear the liability for their words on the Internet. Today, if somebody sends a damaging statement about you on the Internet, you can sue. In Australia recently, an anthropologist successfully sued another anthropologist who posted a libelous message. In an American case that's still pending as of this writing, the publisher of an electronic newsletter on the Internet is being sued because his newsletter accused a direct-mail company on the Internet of fraud. Whether he wins or loses, he'll face a big legal bill.

Ultimately, the only guardians of truth on the Internet are the little-used libel laws (and something can be false and still not be libel), the sharp eyes of honest Internet users, and the moderators who gently oversee the traffic on some bulletin boards. In a conversational community of millions, that leaves a lot of room for bad information to go a long way.

It Spreads Hate

The Internet is a free-speech environment. That sounds great, until one notices that it also allows those who would spread bigotry and hate to expound upon their world view and to exchange ideas for making the world a worse place, all with relative anonymity.

There are Internet bulletin boards populated by neo-nazis, racists, gay-bashers, anti-Semites, and others of the kind. In the summer of 1994, *U.S. News & World Report* revealed that the Simon Wiesenthal Center had just completed a three-year study of computer hatemongering and had submitted an enormous dossier to the Federal Communications Commission, along with the suggestion that the FCC should look into whether it has the power to get the haters off the network.

But the FCC has no such power, and constitutionalists say there's not really any solution permitted by the First Amendment. So, just as in other communities, the Internet is going to have to continue policing itself. Some users actually visit the hatemongering bulletin boards to rebut—with documentation ready—factual errors used in support of hate (such as the persistent suggestion that the Holocaust never happened).

Other users do the only thing they can: They ignore it.

Did You Know...

A problem related to hate on the Internet is that the Internet is an inherently sexist culture. Nobody knows the precise demographics of the Internet, but it's clear that male users far outnumber females. Critics of Internet culture have observed that the male-dominated exchanges on the Internet often have the effect of drowning out or "shouting down" the voices and opinions of women users.

An article in *The Nation* ("Free Speech on the Internet," June 13, 1994) quotes Ellen Broidy, history bibliographer at University of California-Irvine's library. Broidy says that even in feminist-oriented resources, "two or three men will get on and dominate the conversation, either by being provocative, or by flooding the system with comments on everything. It's like talk radio, only worse." Cindy Tittle Moore, a moderator of a feminist Internet resource, told *The Nation*, "It should be mandatory for every male on the [Internet] to seriously pretend being female for two weeks to see the difference."

The fast growth in the number of Internet users is probably helping to balance the gender mix. As in other previously male-dominated environments, however, women on the Internet will probably have to endure belittling and bullying from some men even after the men no longer outnumber them.

It Creates Job Insecurity

As described in Chapter 3, the virtual corporation (VC) is a new, emerging business model in which the large company staffed with permanent workers is replaced by a small team of executives who manage an ever-changing field of freelancers who are hired and let go as needed. The Internet is an important part of enabling the VC because it provides a way for VCs to locate, hire, and communicate with freelancers wherever they may be.

Although many people are attracted by the growth in self-employment that VCs promise, VCs do away with the idea of secure, long-term jobs for most people, condemning them to a life of constant job-hunting.

As writer Bob Kuttner pointed out in a syndicated column about VC:

> *Every vocational virtue cannot be reduced to entrepreneurship. Creativity, diligence, self-improvement and teamwork often require a more stable work environment.... Yes, more people are self-employed today. But for every well-paid independent contractor who is a computer technician or financial consultant, there are dozens working at crummy 'temp' jobs who would rather have actual careers.*

(Column, "The Pitfalls of a Virtual Corporation," *The Boston Globe*, July 30, 1993)

By providing the workspace into which the VC may move, the Internet may well take part in shifting many of us into new work roles we'd rather not have.

It Threatens National Security

In his book *The Cuckoo's Egg*, author Cliff Stoll tells the true story of how, while manager of a computer system at Lawrence Berkeley Lab, he used computers to discover, locate, and catch a spy in Germany who was breaking into U.S. military computers and trying to steal secrets. True, Stoll used the Internet to catch the guy. On the other hand, it was the Internet that enabled the guy to break into the computers in the first place.

Other high-profile cases of computer espionage and mischievous corruption of sensitive information cast doubt upon the wisdom of having the world's computers—especially those storing government and military information—hooked into one big, uncontrolled network.

Given modern computer security systems, governments can keep some information on a computer inaccessible to Internet users while making other information available. Computers carrying highly classified information can simply be kept off the Internet, period—no wires in, no wires out, no problem. Other security measures include building a "firewall." A company or other organization that has its own computer network can make one computer on the network directly accessible to the Internet. That computer acts as a firewall, inhibiting access to the other computers on the network by enforcing strict security policies requiring passwords or other special procedures.

The fact is, however, that most computers today are connected to other computers, and most are equipped to allow users to dial in through the telephone lines from other computers. Even if a computer isn't on the Internet, it may be connected to a computer that is. A skilled hacker can break into a computer by going through several others on the way. This has the added attraction of helping to cover the hacker's tracks.

The principal means used today to make computers secure isn't keeping them off networks, but rather requiring users to know secret passwords to use them. And as hackers have proved time and again, passwords are usually easy to break.

It Enables Piracy and Sabotage

You've probably read about hackers who break into computers either to steal information or simply to scramble the works. You've probably also heard about computer viruses, nasty little programs that sneak their way into computers and destroy data at a predetermined time or in response to some selected event.

Obviously, by making it easier for people to connect to other computers, the Internet creates opportunity for computer crooks and also provides a nice growth culture for computer viruses. A lot of work has gone into improving computer security systems and filtering out viruses when information moves between computers. But none of it is foolproof, and the mischief continues.

There are also new variants of computer mischief. In July of 1994, *Time* magazine reported that someone had cracked into a restricted computer at Lawrence Berkeley Lab and stored thousands of dollars' worth of stolen software, and then made it available to others through the Internet. Ironically, Lawrence Berkeley is the same facility where Cliff Stoll, years earlier, had raised awareness of the importance of computer security by tracking down that German spy.

It Invades Privacy

OK, it's supposed to work like this: Messages people post on the Internet are assumed to be public and can be read and copied by anyone. So Internet users don't put anything too private in those messages. E-mail, on the other hand, is carefully addressed to a specific person and is intended to be read only by that person—as private and confidential as a letter dropped in a mailbox. So e-mail can be used to exchange state secrets, confessions, love letters, and financial statements.

Or can it? First of all, like any other mail, e-mail is the property of its *recipient*, not the sender. A person can do whatever he or she likes with e-mail received, including forwarding it to others (who then may do whatever *they* want with it) and even posting it somewhere for anybody to see. Even with e-mail, Internet users must be careful about who they send to and what they say.

Herein lies the question of whether e-mail really is private. Ask yourself: If hackers can use the Internet to break into government computers and steal secrets, how hard can it be for somebody to read somebody else's e-mail? The answer: Not very. Hackers can break into computers and read the e-mail received by those computers, or they may do something called *data harvesting*, in which e-mail or other information is intercepted and copied on its way across the network, *between* computers.

Hackers aren't the only snoopers. System administrators, also known as system operators or "sysops" for short, are the people employed to keep a particular computer system or network running. To do that effectively, they need the power to override any security restrictions built into the system. In effect, system administrators on most computer systems (including those that use the Internet) can look at any file—including e-mail files—stored on computers they control.

Like others in positions of authority, system administrators are supposed to exercise their power responsibly, but there's little to stop an unscrupulous system administrator from peeking at others' e-mail. People who use PCs and a commercial Internet access provider to dial-in to the Internet (see Chapter 5) often aren't aware that their access provider's computer is run by a system administrator who has the power to read their e-mail.

> **Did You Know...**
>
> There are Internet privacy worries other than e-mail. There's information about you and me stored on computers all over the place—the government, the department stores, the direct marketers, the credit-card companies, and so on. Many of these computers can be accessed through the Internet.
>
> Now, rest assured, all the organizations that have information about us have taken normal precautions to safeguard it from snoops. But if people really wanted to get to it, they might succeed. Having those computers on the Internet only multiplies the potential exposure of your privacy and mine.

While hackers have the power to invade e-mail, they're not the big problem. Under current law, reading somebody else's e-mail is a crime (a federal crime, no less) *if* the e-mail is sent across a public e-mail system. But if it's sent over a *private* e-mail system, such as the internal e-mail systems used in many businesses, then it isn't protected. That allows companies (or the government, for that matter) to surreptitiously read employee's e-mail—including e-mail they've received. Estimates say 20 to 30 percent of companies do just that.

The problem is that being a network of networks, the Internet is kind of a hybrid of a public and private e-mail system. Because the laws protecting e-mail are relatively new, nobody's decided yet whether the Internet really is public or private. That leaves open the strong possibility that anybody's e-mail is subject to legal intrusion. There have been a number of big instances of e-mail snooping.

Why Do Some People Worry About the Internet?

The mayor of Colorado Springs, Colorado, secretly read the City Council's e-mail. The U.S. Secret Service monitored e-mail and other computer communications in an effort to snare unscrupulous hackers.

The good news is that e-mail is safe from *casual* snooping; a person has to know what he or she is doing, and do it on purpose, to read someone else's e-mail. And there's so much e-mail traffic—most of it boring—that there's little danger of someone randomly invading e-mail in the hopes of finding something interesting.

The bad news is that because people have become so dependent on e-mail lately, anything less than complete privacy has big implications for the future of freedom of speech and privacy rights. Because the Internet is fast becoming the major e-mail network to the world, it is the battleground over which these issues will be decided.

Did You Know...

There are high-level initiatives underway to improve computer (and Internet) security, the most important of which is the Clipper project, a system designed by the U.S. government for translating e-mail messages and phone calls into code so they can't be snooped on a network.

Unfortunately, Clipper is the subject of controversy. The government wants the system to be secure from everyone but the government, who says it wants to be able to eavesdrop on messages that will help convict drug traffickers and terrorists. The government hasn't asked for unrestricted power to eavesdrop. The "key" to the code is to be held in escrow by two government agencies, who will surrender it to law enforcement officials only upon court order.

Many in the Internet community, however, want the system to be safe from everyone—*including* the government—who they charge with wanting a way into the system just so that the Internal Revenue Service can keep an eye on all the money that will change hands on the Internet as it becomes more commercial.

It Enables Fraud

As business use of the Internet expands, the logical next step is to allow Internet users to order products through the Internet and to pay for them by giving their credit-card numbers. Users are already paying for goods and services this way, and the credit-card traffic is expected to increase as more commercial resources debut on the Internet.

Credit-card commerce has always experienced a high fraud rate, especially since people began giving their credit-card numbers over the phone to telemarketers. But given the dangers of computer break-ins and data harvesting (see the earlier section, "It Invades Privacy"), allowing people to expose their credit cards to the Internet seems like an invitation to fraud. Just as hackers and unscrupulous system administrators have the power to read others' e-mail, they could easily steal credit-card numbers, use them to make purchases, and then cover up their tracks before the credit-card owner knows what's happening.

Beyond such flat-out theft lies the possibility of more prankish fraud, such as using someone else's name, address,

Why Do Some People Worry About the Internet? 95

and credit-card number to make bogus orders—like ordering 1,000 copies of *Das Kapital* to be sent to, and billed to, the Republican Party. Unlike straight credit-card theft, this time the merchandise is shipped to the credit-card owner, so he or she can return it and get the money back. But this person can't recover his or her time and trouble, and the seller may have to eat the shipping costs. Pranks can be a serious and costly problem, too.

The Internet leaves open doors to other types of fraud, as well. Commercialization of the Internet will lead to an increase in fee-based resources. Crooks could work around the billing system so that when they use the resource, the bill goes to someone else. On other fee-based systems in the past, crooks have done this so subtly that many times the user stuck with the inflated bill never detected the fraud.

Did You Know...

CommerceNet, a consortium of California companies formed to facilitate commercial use of the Internet, is developing a new version of the popular Internet access software Mosaic (see Chapter 7) that might help. The software would employ a new type of *encryption* (a system for putting information in code so it can't be read by anyone but its intended reader) that would supposedly prevent fraud by putting business communications such as credit-card charges in code, and by making absolutely certain that the purchase comes from the person whose name is on the order through the use of an "electronic signature."

CommerceNet hopes this will make the Internet safe enough not just for shopping, but also for electronic banking. One day, Internet users will be able to transfer money straight from their checking accounts to the merchants. (See Chapter 9).

The possibility of fraud is often cited by those who believe the commercialization of the Internet will proceed very slowly. Many companies will shy away from the Internet for doing any real sales until it becomes much more secure. And many users will shy away from using commercial resources until they have confidence that their credit-card numbers won't end up buying lingerie in Paris for some hacker's girlfriend.

It Carries Unrestricted Pornography

In Chapter 3, you learned that the curious can get sexually explicit writing and pictures through the Internet. Whether that's a problem or not is up to you. Like nearly all pornography, nobody forces it on anybody. You have to go looking for it to get it. But some people are offended by the very idea that it exists, and others have considerable concern that their curious, computer-literate children may find the stuff.

The Internet is unlikely to be censored any time soon, so the only solution for grownups who worry about the pornography is: Don't go looking for it and you won't find it. For those concerned about their kids, the options are:

a) Keep your kids off the Internet.

b) Supervise your kids.

c) Teach your kids well, then trust them.

The U.S. government, however, likes to appear to support wholesomeness—a quality that is definitely not inclusive of dirty pictures and erotic writing. So when the *Los Angeles Times* discovered a cache of hard-core porn on a computer at Lawrence Livermore National Laboratory—a U.S. weapons lab connected to the Internet—some officials began musing about trying to regulate the Internet.

But the Internet got a bad rap—it was later determined that the porn had been put there from within the lab (presumably by a lab employee), not across the Internet. So there.

It Empowers the Few and Excludes the Many

Here may be the most far-reaching sociological Internet debate. Chapter 3 pointed out that the Internet brings together people from many different countries, cultures, and backgrounds, and that such cross-cultural interplay may be good for global understanding and harmony.

Then again, the Internet may also divide people. Consider the basic similarities among Internet users. They all

- Can read and write.
- Have access to a computer.
- Have the education to use that computer and the Internet successfully.
- Have the money to pay for an Internet connection, or have the support of an organization that has the money.

To many in the American middle class, these criteria look pretty basic and not too far out of reach. But the fact is that the majority of American citizens—and the great majority of world citizens—cannot meet all four criteria. They are therefore shut out of this global meeting place, this window on the world that we call the Internet.

The privileged group that meets all four criteria can get more information far more quickly than everybody else. That gives them a tremendous advantage in today's world. They can locate a job before it even appears in a newspaper. They can stay abreast of world events that others may not even hear about. These "haves" will tend to be better-educated and wealthier than the "have-nots" in the first place, and their access to the information on the Internet may tend to widen both the educational and economic distinctions.

As described in Chapter 3, Internet users break "gag orders" and report about events on which the mainstream news media is obligated to keep silent. In those cases, Internet users become privy to information that nobody else is allowed to see. Critics argue that this distinction in information access is inherently undemocratic, and makes non-Internet users into second-class citizens.

Really Curious?

The solution is to get the Internet to everybody—and that's one of the goals of the National Information Infrastructure initiative spearheaded by U.S. Vice President Al Gore. Of course, merely providing universal access to the Internet doesn't fully address the problem. Experts say that as many as 20 percent of U.S. adults are functionally illiterate. If the schism described here is to be avoided, inequities in education and in other areas must be addressed, as well.

For more on the National Information Infrastructure project, see Chapter 9.

So Now You Know...

There are many reasons why people worry about what the Internet may bring about, and where it is headed.

The most important, immediate worries center around the security and reliability of information and computers on the Internet. Is the valuable information in government and business safe when their computers are on the Internet? Some think not.

There are also concerns about how the Internet is affecting our culture. Some fear it separates us more than it connects us. Others say it will foster changes to the way business is done that will turn us into a world of freelancers, and make job security a thing of the past.

As I hope you've seen, most of the worries can be resolved, or at least minimized. And the benefits of the Internet, described in Chapter 3 and throughout this book, make it worth a try.

5

What Does It Take to Use the Internet?

Read this chapter to satisfy your curiosity about exactly what's involved in using the Internet. The answers include the following:

- It takes a need for information or services.
- It takes a properly equipped computer.
- It takes a communications hookup.
- It takes software tools for navigating the Internet.
- It takes basic computer and communications skills.
- It takes knowing where to look.
- It takes practice.

As you know, this book is not called *Wanna Learn How to Use the Internet?*. True to its title, this book makes no effort to provide a "hands-on" guide to using the Internet, but rather it offers a concise guide to what the Internet is and why it's important, all to satisfy the curiosity of people who may go on to become users and of people who may not.

We've come to a point, though, where both future users and future non-users can benefit from a quick rundown of the general equipment, skills, and services using the Internet demands. If you're giving any thought to joining the Internet fold, this chapter should give you enough information to determine whether ramping onto the Internet is right for you. You may find it's all easier than you imagined. Then again, you may find that between you and the Internet there are financial, educational, or practical hurdles that aren't worth jumping.

It Takes a Need for Information or Services

As the Introduction pointed out, the Internet is now undergoing an image transformation similar to the one that redefined computers in the 1980s. (There's more about the Internet's evolution in Chapter 9.)

Before the pioneering personal computer work of Apple Computer, IBM, and others, computers were tools for business and science—period. In the public mind, computers had no purpose beyond that, and they required too much money and technical skill to be practical for other applications. PCs changed all that by redefining (in a transformation that's still underway) the computer as a consumer product—something anyone can use to speed and simplify everyday tasks, something that should be in every home for

What Does It Take to Use the Internet? 103

education and for play, something equivalent to a large, expensive toaster. Much of the mainstream press coverage has supported a similar transformation of the Internet from a complex tool of science into a consumer playland of online shopping, e-mail pen pals, and free software.

Curious About the Word?

\, in*ter-'net\

Online describes the condition of something while on a network. While one is in the act of using the Internet (or any computer network), one is online. When not using the network, one is *offline*. Both words are so new that you'll sometimes see them hyphenated, *on-line* and *off-line*.

Lately, the word *online* has been used as an adjective to describe resources available on a network like the Internet or CompuServe—themselves known as *online services*. *Online shopping* is a way to read about and order goods through a network. *Online newsletters* (also called *electronic newsletters*) can be accessed over a network and read right from the computer screen.

For any consumer product, there's a marketing campaign aimed at making everyone feel unable to live without it—and the Internet's no different. Through the next few years, you'll be sent this message repeatedly: *Get online. Don't miss out. Everybody has it but you. People who use it have more sex than people who don't. Hurry.*

So before you begin to learn how to get set up for the Internet, ask yourself The Big Question, the one marketing people really hate: *Do I need it?*

In the first four chapters of this book, have you seen anything that specifically makes the Internet an attractive tool for your profession or a terrific toy for your play? Is there a bulletin board that offers information or discussions about your job or hobby? Are there people with whom you'd like to exchange e-mail, and are *they* on the Internet? The answer is important, because using the Internet may require a significant amount of money (for computer hardware or an Internet connection), time, and trouble, as you'll discover in this chapter. If you don't really have anything to gain, don't let yourself be sold.

Really Curious?

Chapters 1 through 4 provide a good overview of the types of resources available on the Internet. Even so, a book this short can only generalize about the whole range of available resources. If you think that the Internet may offer some resources of special interest to you, try to find out whether such resources exist—and just how valuable they are—before taking the Internet plunge.

Unfortunately, the best way to find out what the Internet offers is to get online and consult some of the resource directories available there. Perhaps you have a friend who is already on the Internet and who can spend an hour online hunting down resources while you peer over his or her shoulder. Your local public or university library may also help you in this way.

Also, companies that sell Internet connections (see "It Takes a Communications Hookup") may be willing to track down some resources for you in

What Does It Take to Use the Internet?

order to entice you to sign up. Some of these companies also offer free trial periods; if you already own the equipment required to use the Internet (see "It Takes a Properly Equipped Computer"), you can try it out long enough to find out whether it's for you. If not, you can cancel your connection before the free trial runs out, and you've spent nothing but time.

Failing that, there are "offline" ways to find out what the Internet offers you specifically. For example, you can contact your professional organizations and associations; they may know about Internet resources used by others in your field. You can also consult a book such as *Navigating the Internet* or *Your Internet Consultant*, both described in Chapter 10.

While you're musing, you should be aware that much of what the Internet offers is available *without* the Internet. For example, if all you want is e-mail, commercial providers such as MCI Mail enable you to exchange messages with Internet users, as do the e-mail facilities offered by online services such as CompuServe, America Online, and Prodigy.

The online services also offer a variety of special-interest bulletin boards and news services, and they offer what they call "gateways" to the Internet, which allow users some ability to use the Internet from within the online service. Capitalizing on the publicity surrounding the Internet, each service is trying to position itself as the best and easiest way to get to the Internet.

For example, America Online—a relative newcomer to online services whose selling point is ease-of-use—offers easy access to some selected Internet resources and to newsgroups (see Chapter 6), with a promise to add more services soon. That's not the whole Internet by a longshot, but it's a start, and it's made simpler by America Online's easy-to-use menus. CompuServe announced in September of 1994 that it will incrementally roll out access to various Internet resources throughout 1995, with full Internet access scheduled to be available from within CompuServe by the end of that year. The service is also working on ways to make using Internet resources easier to use when accessed through CompuServe.

> **Really Curious?**
>
> The precise terms and limitations of the gateways between the Internet and the online information services are changing rapidly at this writing. If you want to evaluate an online service's Internet access, contact the service for more information.
>
> You can find contact information for America Online, CompuServe, and Prodigy in Chapter 10.

Note that Internet users can reach CompuServe through the Internet, as well, through a facility called Telnet (see Chapter 7). When they do, they have to supply billing information before entering CompuServe so they can be charged like regular CompuServe subscribers. Internet users can send e-mail to CompuServe subscribers, as well. In that case, CompuServe has no way to bill the Internet user, so it charges a special fee to the CompuServe user who receives the message. CompuServe is even adding its own page to the World Wide Web, a growing part of the Internet (see Chapter 7). At this writing, CompuServe is still working out

What Does It Take to Use the Internet?

how it will bill the Internet users who will access its World Wide Web page.

Because they are self-contained and professionally managed, online information services are much easier to use than the Internet, and they may or may not be cheaper, depending on what your options are for getting your own Internet connection (see "It Takes a Communications Hookup"). For many, they make a good set of training wheels before riding off to the Internet.

Did You Know...

Remember that many of the resources on the Internet weren't created for the Internet alone. They were created for the use of some organization and then made available to others through the Internet.

Because of that, some resources available on the Internet are also available *without* the Internet or any other network. For example, you can reach the White House's information system through the Internet, but you can also contact it directly through telephone lines from a properly equipped computer. You leave the Internet out of the process entirely. Ditto for many university libraries and other resources.

Before you acquire an Internet connection to use one or more specific resources, investigate whether those resources are available without the Internet. They may be easier to get to, and cheaper, without the Internet's help.

It Takes a Properly Equipped Computer

Those whose companies or schools supply them with Internet access don't have to think about this one—they use whatever is offered. Typically, they have a PC or computer terminal connected through a small network to a main computer called a *host*. The host is what is actually connected to the Internet. What the user can do on the Internet is limited to what the host is set up to do.

For these users, the best resource about the Internet is their own organization's system administrator, who can fill them in on the specifics of the organization's Internet connection and its capabilities. (Such users could benefit greatly, however, by reading the remainder of this book before talking to the system administrator. The administrator will seem to make much more sense and will also seem less impatient when talking to an informed user.)

Those thinking of setting up their own Internet connection need to know which kind of computer to use and what else they'll need to get connected. In theory, all that's required is any personal computer equipped with a modem, but it's not quite that simple.

Curious About the Word?

A *modem* is a device that allows a computer to communicate with another computer over the telephone lines. Both computers must be equipped with modems in order to communicate.

A modem can be built into the computer (an *internal modem*), or it can be a small box that is plugged into the computer through a cable (an *external modem*). In either case, the telephone line from the wall plugs into the modem, just as it would

What Does It Take to Use the Internet? 109

> otherwise be plugged into a telephone. (There are also wireless modems that use the same cellular networks used by car phones to communicate with other computers.)
>
> Modems come in different speeds. Slower modems make using the Internet more difficult because the user may wait an annoying length of time for the slow modem to send commands and messages to the Internet; the user may then wait some more for the Internet's response. Also, copying computer files from the Internet to a user's PC may take hours with a slow modem.
>
> When the two computers communicating have modems of different speeds, they converse at the speed of the slower modem.

Nearly any computer equipped with a modem and communications software (which controls the modem) can access and use the Internet. Many of the more exciting and recent developments on the Internet, however, can be exploited only by certain types of computers, and relatively powerful ones, at that.

As you'll see later in this chapter, most Internet resources show only text—words and numbers—on the user's screen; they don't display any pictures. Older, slower computers and modems can handle such basic text activities pretty well. But the addition of pictures (and video, and sound) makes far greater demands on both the computer and the modem. The computer files that store pictures and sound are very large, so they can take some time to travel through a modem to a user's computer, and they require a lot of processing power once they get there.

That's why the Internet software tools for exploiting these emerging features require powerful computers and fast modems and may only work on well-equipped, recent models of IBM-compatible PCs, Macintoshes, and UNIX workstations, all with very fast modems. The fast modems are required so that users aren't left waiting every time the Internet tries to show them a picture. The powerful computer hardware is required to display graphics and play sound, two activities that demand a lot of horsepower.

Users typically equip their computers with a *graphical user interface* (GUI), a computer program that makes using the computer easier and also makes displaying pictures simpler. All Macintoshes come equipped with a GUI, while IBM-compatible PCs and UNIX workstations can be equipped with optional GUIs (Microsoft Windows on the PCs, and Motif on the UNIX computers). While a graphical user interface is the preferred solution, computers lacking a GUI can also use pictures on the Internet through programs that first copy the pictures to the user's computer, then show them through special display software.

It Takes a Communications Hookup

Once again, those who have access to the Internet from a terminal in a company or college needn't think about an Internet connection—the organization has taken care of that for them.

Others need to acquire a line into the Internet. It's been pointed out that the Internet is free—and that's basically true. But for technical reasons having to do with the capacities of internetworks, the number of lines into the Internet are limited. That problem is alleviated when groups of people share a connection. Instead of all connecting to the Internet individually, they all connect to a large computer, and *that* computer is connected to the Internet.

Did You Know...

There are three basic types of Internet connections:

Permanent—The computer is connected to the Internet through a communications line leased from a telephone company or other communications carrier. This allows the computer to communicate with the Internet at all times. Large businesses, universities, and other heavy Internet users have permanent connections.

Dial-in—The computer uses a modem to communicate through telephone lines with another computer that has a permanent Internet connection. Dial-in connections are used by people who need the Internet occasionally, not all the time. These dial-in connections come in two types. *Direct* dial-in connections, also sometimes called *IP links*, enable the user to work as if he or she had a "personal" permanent connection, and to use whatever software tools he or she chooses (see "It Takes Software Tools for Navigating the Internet" in this chapter). The cheaper option, a dial-in *terminal* connection (sometimes called a *shell* or *command-line account*), usually limits the user to the capabilities of the computer he or she dials into, which may or may not provide a full suite of tools to work with. Dial-in terminal connections work well for most text-only Internet resources but may not support other

Internet resources. (For more on dial-up accounts, see the section "They Hop Online" in Chapter 10.)

Mail—This is a special link to the Internet that allows the user to send and receive e-mail but use no other Internet resource. When online services such as CompuServe allow users to exchange Internet e-mail, they are providing a mail connection. Users can also subscribe to dial-in connections that limit them to e-mail but may be less expensive than full-blown dial-in connections.

The folks that own and operate the computers that supply dial-in services charge a fee for each connection. They have to pay to keep their own computer running, and they have to pay for their permanent line to the Internet. (They don't actually have to pay for the Internet, but they have to pay a communications carrier a monthly fee for the use of the wires to connect to the Internet.) Those costs—plus a reasonable profit—justify the fee many Internet users pay to use the free Internet.

The fees vary by supplier; typically, an individual user pays from 75 cents to a dollar or more per minute, with a monthly minimum of $5 to $50. Some suppliers sweeten the deal by throwing in a package of software tools, or supplying free access to some non-free Internet resources, such as ClariNet, a fee-based news and information service. Typically, any software supplied by the access providers is available as freeware or shareware on the Internet anyway—but the dial-in supplier can save users the trouble of finding, copying, and configuring the stuff themselves, which really is a big help.

What Does It Take to Use the Internet?

> **Did You Know...**
>
> As mentioned earlier in this chapter, online information services such as America Online and CompuServe offer access to some Internet resources. Charges vary by provider, and all tack on an extra charge for Internet use.
>
> Connection shoppers will have to examine carefully the cost and completeness of each service's Internet offerings to determine whether an online service represents a better value than a dial-in connection from their local Internet dial-in suppliers.

Not all individual users have to pay, however. Some universities or other institutions with permanent connections allow a limited number of users who aren't part of the organization to tag along. Around the country there are also "Free-Nets," Internet connections supplied free (or for a very modest fee) as a community service by local governments, libraries, or other institutions. Only a scattering of Free-Nets exist today, including several in Ohio, a few in Illinois and others in the U.S., Canada, and abroad; but more will appear soon.

> **Really Curious?**
>
> You can find a list of Free-Nets and information about locating still more Free-Nets in *Navigating the Internet*, described in Chapter 10.

Usually, a Free-Net's capabilities are fairly limited. Most work like dial-in terminal connections and may not support the full range of Internet resources.

> **Did You Know...**
>
> Recently, the public library system in Maryland began offering low-cost Internet access through a program subsidized by Maryland and the Federal government. Maryland residents can get a mail connection for about $35 per year or more complete Internet access for a higher fee that's still far less than what commercial suppliers charge.

It Takes Software Tools for Navigating the Internet

For users to take full advantage of the resources on the Internet, they need access to various tools and facilities. These tools are computer programs that the user must be able to run, either on the user's own computer, on the access provider's computer, or on another computer the user can access through the Internet. For example:

- E-mail requires a software tool for composing, addressing, sending, receiving, and reading mail.

- Newsgroups require a program called a newsreader that locates selected newsgroups, searches through them for selected messages, and displays the messages. Newsreaders also provide features for writing and posting messages to newsgroups.

- A special family of Internet resources called the World Wide Web (WWW) requires a tool called a browser to locate resources on the WWW and to take advantage of its special searching and multimedia features.

What Does It Take to Use the Internet?   115

- Copying computer files (which may contain text information, such as reports, or software programs) from the Internet to a user's computer usually requires a tool called an FTP program.
- Interactive online discussions require a Talk program.

People who use computer terminals or dial-in terminal (command line) connections are typically limited to the tools located on the host computer to which they're attached, or to tools available on another computer they can access. For example, to use Talk (see Chapter 6), these users must be able to access a Talk program on the host computer they use. Users who have direct dial-in connections can take advantage of Internet software they can run on their own computers; they can run a Talk program of their own, in many cases. Depending on the tool involved, the user's own software can provide the tool, or can expand and improve the functions of a tool program that's running on another Internet computer.

Internet software tools do more than simply provide access to resources. They can make finding specific resources simpler by providing search features or indexes of resources. They can also feature handy menus or icons that make using some resources simpler. By evolving into more capable, easier-to-use versions, these tools are a big part of what's inviting more and more people to give the Internet a try.

Curious About the Word?

\, in*ter-*'net\

A *menu* is an on-screen list of choices, from which the user makes a selection. Most Internet software tools provide menus so that users don't have to remember commands to get things done. Many

Internet resources themselves also present menus from which users choose items in order to use specific features of the resource.

An *icon* is a little picture on the screen of software tools that are used with a computer mouse. The user moves the mouse pointer to the picture and then clicks the mouse button to start the action represented by the icon. For example, to print something, the user might click on an icon that looks like a little printer.

All software for the Macintosh and IBM-type computers equipped with the popular Microsoft Windows program offer both menus and icons in order to be easy to use and to learn.

There is a growing number of commercially available Internet software tools for users' computers. For now, however, most users prefer the freeware and shareware programs that can be copied directly from the Internet. (Of course, users must have enough Internet software at least to get onto the Internet and copy this stuff in the first place. Internet access providers typically supply a set of basic freeware or shareware programs when a user signs up.) Like all programs, these are periodically updated and improved. Internet users can copy the updates as soon as they're available.

The next several pages show examples of some popular Internet software tools for IBM-compatible PCs that have Microsoft Windows. In some cases, these tools are used to expand upon an Internet facility that's actually running on another computer. For example, the Archie program shown

What Does It Take to Use the Internet? 117

isn't required to use Archie (see Chapter 7)—anybody can use Archie by using the Internet to access a computer called an *Archie server*. The software tool shown simply makes using Archie easier, and adds an FTP tool so that a user can search for a file and then copy it without having to switch to another tool. Similarly, a user needn't have WinGopher on his or her computer to use Gopher menus, but WinGopher makes using Gopher menus easier.

In other cases, the software tool on the user's computer supplies a function unavailable any other way. For example, users can browse the World Wide Web without having a special browsing tool like Mosaic on their own computers. But taking full advantage of the WWW's special facilities (see Chapter 7) really does require Mosaic or another graphical browser on the user's computer.

Curious About the Word?

Software available through the Internet comes in three basic types:

Freeware software is absolutely free of charge and available to all.

Shareware is offered on a try-before-you-buy plan. Users can copy the software and try it out for free, but are instructed to send a nominal fee (usually $10 to $50) to the programmer if they intend to use the software regularly.

Commercial software is like the packaged software sold in stores (but without the box), and is offered by the same commercial software companies. Commercial software requires payment up front; typically, the user must supply a credit card number before copying the software files. In other cases, the software is "locked" and won't function until the user enters a code number that the software vendor gives him once payment is received.

Eudora

Eudora is an e-mail program available as shareware and in a more full-featured commercial version. It enables users to check whether there's mail waiting for them, read their mail, automatically reply to a message they've received, forward a message to another user, and compose and send new e-mail messages. Eudora features menus and icons to make the program both convenient and easy to learn.

For more on e-mail, see Chapter 6.

NewsReader!

NewsReader! (see Figure 5.1) is a shareware program for locating newsgroups, searching through and reading messages in newsgroups, and composing and posting messages on newsgroups. It can locate newsgroups on a specific topic; for example, the user can type cooking, and the program will display the names of newsgroups having the word *cooking* in their names. The user can then go to one of the cooking newsgroups simply by clicking a mouse button.

While the user is in a newsgroup, NewsReader! helps the user find messages related to a particular subject or to rearrange the messages to make finding information easier.

For more on newsgroups, see Chapter 6.

What Does It Take to Use the Internet? 119

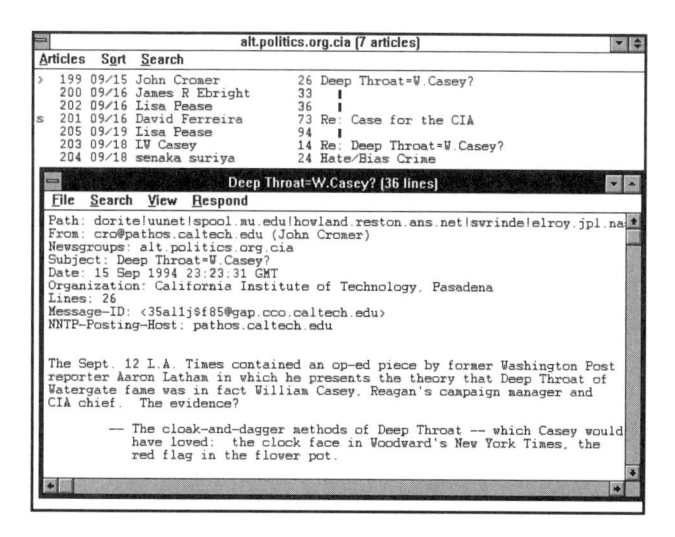

Figure 5.1. NewsReader!, a program for locating newsgroups, reading messages there, and posting new messages.

Mosaic

Mosaic (Figure 5.2) is a popular freeware browsing tool for the World Wide Web (WWW). It enables users to easily enjoy the special "hypermedia" searching capabilities of WWW resources and to play the multimedia resources available on the WWW. Mosaic is available not only for PCs with Windows, but also for Macintoshes and UNIX workstations. (Mosaic requires a special type of Internet connection; see Chapter 10.)

Curious About the Word?

Hypermedia is a new method of presenting information; it enables users to jump quickly from one presentation to a related one by choosing a keyword within the first presentation.

Multimedia is the ability to present many different kinds of information—text, pictures, video, and sound—on a computer. Mosaic allows Internet users to access and play multimedia resources from the WWW.

Hypermedia and multimedia are the great benefits the Internet gains through the WWW. You'll learn more about hypermedia and multimedia in Chapter 7.

For more on the World Wide Web, see Chapter 7.

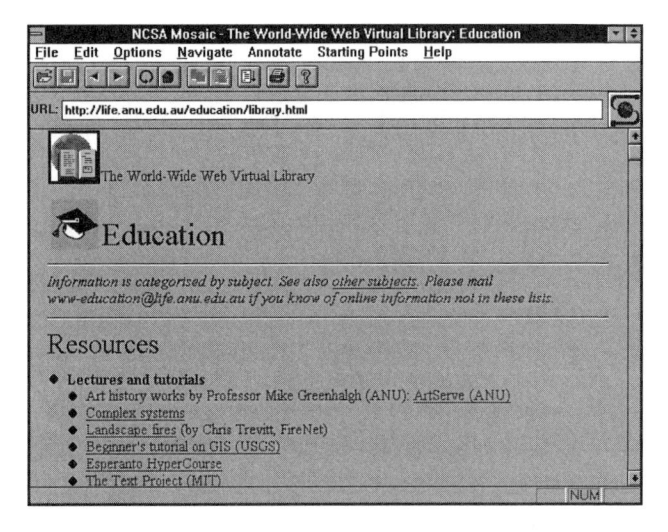

Figure 5.2. Mosaic, a tool for traveling through the World Wide Web and experiencing the multimedia resources found there.

Archie

Archie runs on large computers on the Internet, not on the user's computer. There are programs that make using those

What Does It Take to Use the Internet? 121

Archie programs on the Internet easier. For example, there's an FTP tool, so that when a user finds a file with Archie, he or she can quickly and conveniently copy the file to his or her computer. Without a tool like that, users have to find and copy files in two steps: 1) Use Archie to find the file, and 2) Use FTP to copy it.

For more on Archie and FTP, see Chapter 7.

WinGopher

WinGopher (see Figure 5.3) makes it easier to use Gophers—menus that make finding and using some resources on the Internet easier. The WinGopher software helps users search or browse through these menus, picking items as they go, to locate a particular resource, and to then access that resource.

For more on Gophers, see Chapter 7.

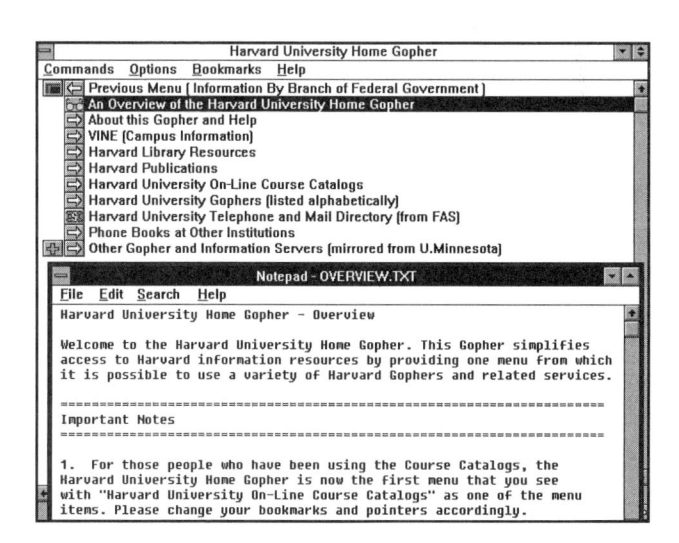

Figure 5.3. WinGopher, a program that makes using Gophers easier.

QVT WinNet

QVT WinNet (see Figure 5.4) is an example of a multipurpose Internet access tool. It supports basic access to other computer systems on the Internet through Telnet (see Chapter 7). It supports copying files from other computers, and it gives you the ability to read your e-mail and look at what's on newsgroups (but not to send e-mail or newsgroup messages). Each tool is started separately by clicking the mouse pointer on a rectangular button. So even though WinNet combines tools, the tools remain essentially separate.

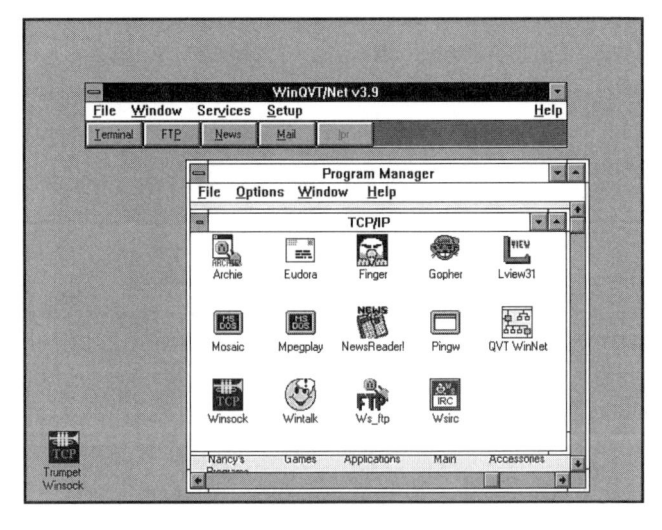

Figure 5.4. QVT WinNet, a program for accessing several types of Internet resources from a single tool.

It Takes Basic Computer and Communications Skills

Although Internet tools are improving to make using the Internet easier, there's no getting around the fact that users need basic competence with their own computers to use the Internet effectively. Productive Interneting means copying files, starting and exiting programs, using menus and icons, printing, typing and editing text, and more. Users may need to know how to perform decompression (also called *unzipping* and *unpacking*) of files that are sent over the Internet in a compressed state for quicker transmission.

Users also need to know how to "log on" or "sign on" to the Internet—a procedure that varies by computer and Internet connection, but that usually requires typing a unique username and secret password.

Internet users needn't be computer scientists, but computer novices who want to enter the world of the Internet need to become competent with their computers first, before branching out onto the Internet.

It Takes Knowing Where to Look

Despite the assistance available through tools, the Internet remains a varied, largely disorganized place in which finding specific resources can be tricky and time-consuming. To be productive, users must develop their Internet research skills.

They must become familiar with the many special indexes and search tools such as Archie, Gopher, and WebCrawler, a tool for searching the World Wide Web (see Chapter 7). These tools can streamline the search for resources by allowing the user to type a subject name or other "search term" and extract a list of resources to try. They must keep careful notes about how to locate resources they use often, so they can quickly return to those resources later without repeating the search. (To make revisiting a snap, some software tools keep records of resources the user has visited and how he or she got there.)

> **Really Curious?**
>
> In Chapter 7, you'll discover more about locating resources.
>
> For detailed, hands-on instructions for tracking down Internet resources, consult *Navigating the Internet* and *Teach Yourself the Internet*.

It Takes Practice

After what you have read to this point, the Internet may sound as much fun as a tax audit. There's just so much out there, it can be a little overwhelming.

After breaking in, however, most Internet users quickly settle down to a few tools and resources they use regularly. Then they don't have to worry about the ten trillion things on the Internet. They have to keep track of only the four or five things they do, which isn't very tough.

So Now You Know...

Using the Internet demands appropriate computer equipment, an Internet connection, software tools (or access to tools through another computer), and basic skills. It may also require money.

Most of all, it requires that you have a need for what the Internet offers. If the need is there, none of the other requirements is too difficult to manage. If the need is not there, most of the other requirements represent a waste of time, money, and effort. You're better off walking to the library.

6

How Do People Communicate on the Internet?

Read this chapter to satisfy your curiosity about exactly how people reach out and touch one another on the Internet. The answers include the following:

- They exchange e-mail.
- They have one-to-one conversations.
- They chat in groups.
- They subscribe to mailing lists.
- They post and read messages in newsgroups.
- They find each other through directory services.

For some, these activities represent all they ever use the Internet for. They don't seek piles of research data; they seek specific answers to specific questions, face-to-face (well, almost). E-mail and its relatives described in this chapter are the links through which the citizens of the online world relate.

As you'll see, though, basic e-mail can serve as a formidable research tool. Beyond the fact that it gives you a way to query experts around the word, e-mail can supply a steady stream of news and letters—automatically—about almost any topic.

They Exchange E-mail

Why do people use e-mail? Well…

- *It's cheap.* It costs nothing beyond what the user is paying for Internet access, if anything. Users save not only postage, but also paper and envelope costs. It's typically cheaper than faxing, too—saving the cost of fax paper and long-distance telephone charges. Long messages cost the same as short ones, and sending a letter to Switzerland costs the same as sending one across town.

- *It's fast.* Most e-mail messages are delivered within a few minutes or even seconds. Some messages can take a few hours, and in *very* unusual cases, days. E-mail nevertheless remains the overwhelming odds-on favorite in a race against carried paper mail.

- *It's convenient.* People who have access to computers do most of their writing on the computer anyway. With e-mail, they write on the computer and then send the message on its way with a few keystrokes—no paper, no postage, no problems. If they lack e-mail, they must print the letter, address and seal the

How Do People Communicate on the Internet?

envelope, affix postage, walk to the nearest mailbox, and say a short prayer to ensure delivery.

Really Curious?

For most practical purposes, e-mail is completely private and confidential. Unfortunately, it is not *absolutely* private and confidential. Illegal snoopers can secretly read other people's e-mail, and worse, some people are allowed to spy on e-mail *legally*. See Chapter 4 for more about privacy on the Internet.

The speed, economy, and convenience of e-mail is achieved by simply copying a computer file containing a message from one computer to another through the network. Boiled down, it works like this (refer to Figure 6.1):

1. The sender uses his or her e-mail software as a simple word processing program to write, edit, and proofread the message. The e-mail program creates a computer file containing the message. (Some people use their favorite word processing program to compose the message and then use the e-mail software to send the file created by the word processor.)

2. The sender types the Internet address of the recipient in the e-mail program and instructs the program to send the message. (The sender can type multiple addresses to automatically send the same message to several—or many—people at once.) The program adds a "header" to the message, a blurb at the top telling the Internet addresses of both the sender and the recipient, the date and time the message was sent, and a subject, if the sender typed one.

3. Using the recipient's e-mail address as a guide, the e-mail software copies the file containing the message across the network to the recipient's computer, where the message is stored (see Figure 6.1). Actually, the journey from one computer to another is the most complicated part of the process, possibly involving the participation of several other computers and numerous network components. Users don't have to concern themselves with this part, however; the Internet does it all, and amazingly, it almost always works.

4. The next time the recipient instructs his or her e-mail program to "check the mail," the program shows a list of unread messages stored on his or her computer. The list usually includes the Internet address of the sender and the subject of the message, so the recipient knows who the message is from and what it's about before deciding whether or not to read it right away. The recipient can then instruct the e-mail software to show him or her any of the messages listed.

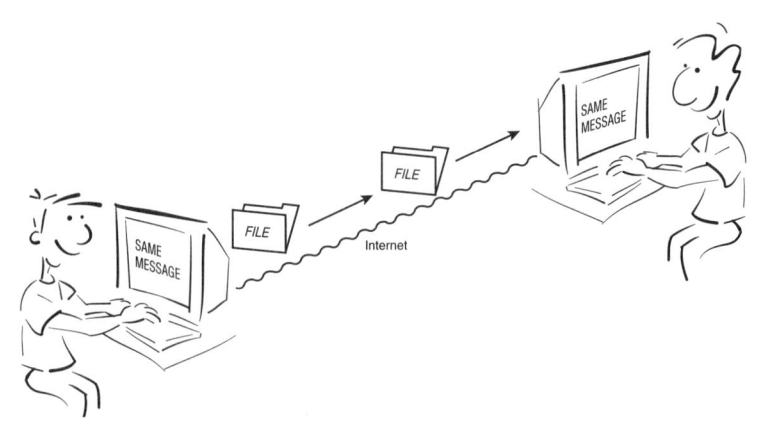

Figure 6.1. How e-mail works: sender types message and recipient's e-mail address; Internet carries message to recipient's computer; recipient reads message on his or her computer screen.

How Do People Communicate on the Internet?

Among the more handy features of e-mail are "forward" and "reply." The recipient can choose the forward feature in the e-mail program, type a new address, and automatically forward the message to another Internet user. If the recipient chooses the reply feature, he or she can type a reply message immediately, without needing to type the Internet address of the sender—the e-mail software automatically delivers the reply to the sender of the original message.

> **Really Curious?**
>
> To see what an e-mail program looks like to some Internet users, see Chapter 5.

The most intimidating aspect of e-mail may be the Internet addresses themselves. They look complicated, but they aren't really. Whether or not you plan to use the Internet, you'll see Internet addresses on people's business cards, in advertising, and even in paper mail and faxes you may receive. So it helps to understand what the addresses are about.

Like any address, an Internet address includes an individual's (or organization's) name and location information. Unlike postal addresses, the "name" is a made-up name for Internet use, and the location information is a series of abbreviations that identify a specific computer, on a specific network, on the Internet. For example, look at my Internet address in Figure 6.2.

nsnell@iquest.net

Figure 6.2. An Internet e-mail address, decoded as: Internet name "at" computer name network.

Did You Know...

The type of Internet address shown in Figure 6.2, made up of words, is used for the convenience of people, believe it or not. Internet addresses are actually formed from numbers. When someone types an address in words, the Internet looks up those words in a table that tells it the actual number address. This happens behind the scenes, however, so Internet users needn't think about it—the word addresses do the job.

The first part of the address shown in Figure 6.2 is my name on the Internet, nsnell. I could have made up any name I wanted—I'm especially fond of sparky and athol. But nsnell is easier for me to remember, and it can make finding me easier for others who want to send me e-mail. I don't have to be the only nsnell on the Internet; I do have to be the only nsnell at the place described by the rest of my address. The whole address, taken together, must be the only one of its kind so that any e-mail sent to that address from anywhere on the Internet can go only to one place.

The @ symbol means "at," and the rest of the address describes the computer or network I use. The first word is a name for the computer itself, and the remaining words indicate a "domain," which is the Internet's fancy way of describing the location or network of the computer. Figure 6.2 tells you I use a computer called iquest in the .net domain. (Using .net for the domain also indicates that the computer is part of an Internet-connected network.)

How Do People Communicate on the Internet? 131

Really Curious?

To send e-mail, all an Internet user has to know is the recipient's Internet address. But suppose the sender doesn't know the address? There are ways to look up addresses on the Internet. See "They Find Each Other Through Directory Services" later in this chapter.

I, like a growing number of people, use a dial-in Internet connection (see Chapter 5). My PC isn't actually connected to the Internet—my PC uses a modem to connect to another computer downtown, and *that* computer is connected to the Internet. So in my address, the computer and domain name describe the computer network downtown, run by my commercial Internet access provider. The e-mail I receive is also stored on that computer until I read it, at which time I can copy it to my PC.

Because the Internet includes so many different types of networks, there are some variations on the basic address format. Also, some addresses can be shorter or longer—three, four, five, or more words separated by periods may be necessary to describe the computers in complex environments with many users. The typical order, however, remains: `name@computer.location`.

Did You Know...

Some parts of an Internet address you can decipher on sight. At or near the end of an address, you may see any of several standard three-letter abbreviations that indicate the following:

`.edu`—A university or other *edu.cational* institution

.com—A *com.mercial* Internet user

.gov—A *gov.ernment* user

.mil—A *mil.itary* user

.org—An *org.anization*, often a non-profit type

.net—A *net.work*

Also, some addresses describe not just the computer, but also the geographical location of the computer. For example, the letters

.sf.ca.us

at the end of an address tell you that the user is in San Francisco, California, in the United States.

Here's one last important point about e-mail. Through the years, e-mail users have developed their own set of customs (OK, *rules*) about composing and sending messages. Most of these have been designed to keep e-mail communication efficient and to prevent wasting network resources, computer storage space, and the reader's time. (They're also designed, like many Internet customs, to separate the veterans from the novices, condescendingly dubbed "newbies." The Internet is open to all, but like any community, it has a few who'd just as soon close the borders.)

E-mail etiquette—part of what some call "netiquette," the complete code of Internet conduct—demands that messages be brief and to-the-point, without being cryptic and choppy, of course. Senders are encouraged to type accurate, meaningful subject lines in the e-mail programs so that readers know what the message is about before they choose to read it. Using CAPITAL LETTERS to add emphasis is gauche

How Do People Communicate on the Internet?

and uncivilized, but using smileys (also called *emoticons*; refer to Chapter 3) to add emotional notes is acceptable, if done with restraint.

Although everyone appreciates courteous communication, Internet users don't like to waste messages on pleasantries. For example, when someone answers someone else's questions by e-mail, he or she doesn't expect—and usually doesn't want—a thank-you e-mail back, which simply clutters the computer with messages that have nothing new to say. E-mail users try to save their *thank you*'s for the next message in which they have something more substantial to say.

Really Curious?

Internet users can send e-mail to folks who aren't on the Internet.

They can send to folks who use online information services such as CompuServe, Prodigy, or America Online. They do so simply by building an e-mail address out of the name (or other identification) the recipient uses on the online service and a computer/domain name for the service itself. For example, my identification number on CompuServe is 72727,3260. If I weren't on the Internet, Internet folks could still send me e-mail by using the address `72727.3260@compuserve.com`. Online service users can also send e-mail to the Internet, using a similar adaptation of the addressing scheme, which differs service to service.

Internet users can also send an e-mail message through the Internet and have it print out on any fax machine in the world—including those of non-Internet users. Several Internet services make this possible; there's a free service that can't fax absolutely everywhere, and other services that can fax anywhere but charge a modest fee.

For specific instructions on sending e-mail to online information systems and faxing, see *Navigating the Internet* and *Your Internet Consultant*, both described in Chapter 10.

They Have One-to-One Conversations

E-mail is the principal Internet communications tool. Sometimes, however, people want the immediacy of an interactive discussion in which messages are traded back and forth instantly, as in a conversation.

On the Internet, the principle one-to-one conversation tool is called Talk. Talk sets up a two-way conversation between two Internet users, who, for sake of example, I'll call Sparky and Athol. To begin, Sparky fires up an Internet software tool (see Chapter 5) that supports Talk and then types Athol's Internet address. The Talk program sends a message to Athol's screen (if he is currently working on the Internet), telling him that Sparky wants to talk with him and telling him how to respond if he, indeed, wants to talk with Sparky. The required response is typically nothing more than the word `talk`, followed by Sparky's Internet address, which already appears on-screen in the message.

When Athol responds, both Athol's screen and Sparky's are split in some way. On graphical, "windowing" computers like PCs running Microsoft Windows or the Macintosh, the screen splits into two separate windows. On more basic computers, a simple line appears across the middle of the screen horizontally, splitting it into top and bottom halves.

In either case, once the screen is split, everything Sparky types appears in one half, and everything Athol types appears in the other. This happens instantly; Athol can actually see each letter appear on his screen as Sparky presses each key on his keyboard. Even when one talker presses the Backspace key to erase a mistake, the other can see it happen. Athol and Sparky can now babble away at each other until one of them breaks the connection.

Did You Know...

Talk works across continents and oceans, and is widely used. Unfortunately, Talk requires special software at both ends of the conversation. Many computers on the Internet have the required software, but not all do. So some Internet users can't Talk; rather, they must exchange messages the old-fashioned way—by e-mail.

They Chat in Groups

Internet Relay Chat (IRC), the other method for Internet conversation, is less common than Talk because someone must set up the Chat before others can join in. Chat sessions allow many users to join in the same free-form conversation, usually centered (loosely) around a discussion topic.

Like Talk, Chat isn't available from every computer on the Internet because computers need special software to join in. Many can, however, and those that can't may be able to go through computers called "public IRC servers" that will give them access to Chat sessions.

Users enter a series of commands to find computers currently running Chat sessions. They then get a list of Chat sessions underway; the sessions are called *channels* (after the CB channels chatted on by truckers and radio buffs) and are labeled by topic. When users see a topic that interests them, they type a command to join and then type another command to choose a nickname. All of their contributions to the discussion will be labeled with the nickname in the session.

Nicknames allow people in the session to keep track of who's who and to chat with anonymity—which is sometimes a good idea, given the level to which the conversation can sink in Chat groups. Chat sessions are notoriously trivial, and sometimes degenerate into petty squabbles or sexually suggestive banter—much more boring than it sounds. Chats can be fun and informative, but also they're too often frequented by people who really ought to get back to work or get out more often.

Really Curious?

There is another way people interact instantly on the Internet: MUDs. A sort of experiment in virtual reality, MUDs are elaborate role-playing games wherein multiple people (*mudders*—did you guess?) simultaneously interact within an environment described through on-screen messages—a kind of electronic Dungeons & Dragons, with at least 500 variations on the Internet.

For more about MUDs, see Chapter 8.

How Do People Communicate on the Internet?

They Subscribe to Mailing Lists

Internet mailing lists (sometimes also called *discussion lists*) are exactly that: lists of people who have signed up to receive e-mail related to a given topic.

Earlier in this chapter, you learned that a person can forward to another user e-mail that he or she receives. A mailing list is a special Internet address that automatically forwards every e-mail message it receives to everybody on the list. People with something to contribute or a question to ask send e-mail to the mailing list, and within a few hours, everyone on the list receives a copy of that message.

Users sign up for mailing lists simply by sending an e-mail message to the list's Internet address, asking to join. Many mailing lists are run completely by computer; even the job of signing up new users is run by computer. These lists, sometimes called *listserv lists* or simply *listservs* to distinguish them from other mailing lists, require joiners to phrase the request in a special word order so that the computer recognizes it as a request to join.

Here's a very small sampling of what's offered, mailing lists catering to the interests of…

Kite enthusiasts
Romania buffs
Hemingway fans
Buddhists
Chemists
Beekeepers
Mathematicians
Drag racers
Baseball fans
Photographers
Accordion players

...and much more. There are also many foreign-language mailing lists wherein users from all over the world can exchange news and information in the language they know, love, or study.

Did You Know...

Sometimes mailing lists and newsgroups are *unmoderated*; that is, nobody's running the show and every message is posted or sent out to subscribers, whether it's worthwhile (and decent) or not.

Other mailing lists and newsgroups, however, are moderated by a person who reads messages before they get sent out to the list or posted to the newsgroup. Messages he or she judges irrelevant or in bad taste don't make it through to the subscribers.

Some Internet users decry moderation as an infringement of free speech on the Internet. Many who have experienced unmoderated mailing lists and newsgroups, however, value moderation as a necessary hedge against free crap.

For example, I have visited both unmoderated and moderated newsgroups dedicated to humor. There are so many messages on the unmoderated newsgroups, and so many of them are stupid, sick, or simply unfunny, that most readers would, I think, quickly give up and quit reading. The moderated humor newsgroups had far fewer messages, and a generally higher caliber of humor.

Even the humor on the moderated newsgroups is unprintable, though—which may give you an idea how bad the *un*moderated humor newsgroups are.

They Post and Read Messages in Newsgroups

There's a danger in mailing lists: They can get too big and too active, burying users in daily e-mail. That's why some people prefer newsgroups, a different way of obtaining the same kinds of information supplied by mailing list.

Really Curious?

Many people use newsgroups through an Internet software tool called a newsreader. In Chapter 5, you can see what a newsgroup message looks like when viewed with a newsreader.

Like mailing lists, newsgroups center around a particular topic. They don't, however, send out e-mail to members. Instead, the newsgroup member must go to the newsgroup to read new messages, search for messages on a given topic, or post new messages (although new messages can be posted through e-mail *or* right at the newsgroup). Typically, users go to the newsgroup at regular intervals, browse through the new messages and read the messages that interest them, post a new contribution, and maybe reply to a query that appears in a message.

The advantage to this more passive approach is that a user who gets too busy or goes away for a few days doesn't have to deal with hundreds of messages piling up in his or her e-mail box, as might be the case with a mailing list. The user can ignore the newsgroup when necessary and then get caught up when he or she has the time. The mailing list, however, provides its own advantage. When something important happens, mailing list users find out quickly. Newsgroup users stay in the dark until they go looking for news.

Did You Know...

Newsgroup names use their own little category system to help indicate what they're about. The general category the newsgroup covers is indicated first, followed by a period. After the period comes one word or more, each of which makes the newsgroup more specific. For example, the newsgroup called

```
sci.physics.research
```

falls under the broad category of science, in which there are many other newsgroups; then under a subcategory of physics, of which there are several; then under research, of which there is only one.

A few popular newsgroup categories are

sci.—Science

comp.—Computers

news.—Information about Usenet and its newsgroups

soc.—Social issues

rec.—Sports, hobbies, fandom, and other recreational activities

How Do People Communicate on the Internet? 141

> `alt.`—"Alternative" information and points of view from outside the mainstream. This is where users find the wild stuff, like the newsgroup for people who hate Barney the dinosaur or reviews of new counterculture tomes.
>
> `misc.`—"Potpourri," as they say on *Jeopardy*.
>
> `clari.`—News collected and supplied by ClariNet communications, including popular syndicated columnists like Dave Barry. (ClariNet newsgroups are among the rare Internet resource users have to pay for.)

You may see newsgroups, as a set, referred to by other names, such as *Usenet news* or *network news*. That's because the newsgroups are managed by a subset of Internet computers called, collectively, Usenet. The various Usenet sites handle the job of managing and administering the newsgroups and of keeping them all updated. Thousands of individual newsgroups exist, some serious (`soc.rights.human`), others practical (`misc.jobs.offered`), and still others just for fun (`rec.arts.startrek.info`).

One great advantage of newsgroups is that the Usenet sites maintain directories containing lists of newsgroup names. With a newsreader or any software program that can search through files of text, users can quickly search the lists for a newsgroup whose name contains a certain word, and in doing so they can find newsgroups related to a particular topic. For example, one might type `spain` and find the names of all the newsgroups with `spain` in their name. Using a newsreader, users can jump right into any newsgroup they find in the search, sign up, and see what's happening.

> **Did You Know...**
>
> Sometimes, when a newsgroup and a mailing list share the same topic, they are linked by a *gateway*. The gateway automatically posts all the mailing list messages on the newsgroup or automatically sends out every new newsgroup posting as an e-mail message to the mailing list. This helps make sure that all the news and other communication about a given subject gets to everyone who has declared an interest.
>
> It also means users don't subscribe to both the mailing list and the newsgroup when a gateway exists. Doing so would result in somewhat heavy *déjà vu*.

They Find Each Other Through Directory Services

Because of Usenet's directory, newsgroups are easy to find; and when it comes to the Internet, "easy to find" is not an often-used phrase.

In particular, people have trouble finding one another's e-mail addresses so they can easily send a message or initiate a Talk session. Unfortunately, there is no all-powerful, all-encompassing White Pages in which a user can look up another user's Internet address.

Not to state the obvious...OK, I'll state the obvious...for getting the Internet address of someone he or she already knows *or* the address of someone at a known place of employment, an Internet user's best bet is to pick up the telephone, call the person, and ask. It contradicts some of

How Do People Communicate on the Internet?

the wonders of Internet use, but if the user writes the number down, he or she won't have to call again.

Users can also get addresses from e-mail they receive and from newsgroup messages, both of which show the Internet address of the sender in the header blurb at the top of the message.

There are, however, Internet facilities that can help. Many Internet computers have on them the software to support two special commands: `whois` and `finger`.

The `whois` command, the more powerful of the two, allows users to find contact information about another Internet user by name. Doing so involves using the Internet to access another computer (see Chapter 7) and running the `whois` program there. Nearly 100 computers are available for this purpose, and their records about users vary—so `whois` is far from foolproof and far from complete. For those who are running out of options, however, it's a start.

The exact way a user operates `whois` varies according to the computer running the `whois` program. But typically, the user accesses the computer and types `whois` and the name of the person. If that computer has information about that user, it will display the information. Sometimes the display includes not only the desired user's Internet address, but also his or her work mailing address and telephone number. The `whois` command can also supply information about a specific computer or network on the Internet.

The `finger` command is less powerful, because the user has to know the Internet name of the computer used by the person being sought. To put it another way, if the user knows the part of the address following the @ symbol, `finger` can help him or her find the first part to complete the address. That's not much help, but it's something.

Failing all else, users sometimes leave a message in a newsgroup called `soc.net.people`, requesting information on the Internet whereabouts of a particular user. They don't often get a complete answer, but they sometimes get close enough to then use `whois` or `finger` to find the rest.

So Now You Know...

The Internet opens a world of interpersonal communication, and it supplies this communication in several different forms:

- E-mail, the sending of letter-like messages to other Internet users, to users of other information systems, and even to fax machines

- Talk, an interactive, one-to-one conversation between two users

- Chat, an interactive conversation among multiple users, typically centered around a discussion topic

- Mailing lists, the automatic sending of e-mail messages on a given topic to a list of users who have asked to be kept informed

- Newsgroups, open forums about a given subject, in which users post messages that can be read and responded to by anyone else

You also know that communicating on the Internet depends heavily on knowing the Internet addresses of others. The Internet does not, alas, supply an easy way to track down any individual user. There are, however, several directory services that help Internet users find one another.

7

How Do People Pick Up Information from the Internet?

Read this chapter to satisfy your curiosity about how people locate, retrieve, and use information that's available on the Internet. The answers include these:

- They use other people's computers as their own.
- They locate and copy files.
- They burrow with Gopher.
- They search with Veronica.
- They browse the World Wide Web.

I should point out from the beginning that any of the communications techniques described in Chapter 6 can also serve as research tools. People learn a lot from mailing lists and newsgroups—and when they don't see the answers, they can post their own questions and receive a dozen or more answers within hours.

When a user can scare up the Internet address of an expert (something that's getting easier as more folks list their Internet addresses in books and at the ends of articles in magazines and journals), he or she can e-mail a polite question. If the expert is not an especially busy expert, he or she may respond. Those lucky enough to establish an e-mail rapport with knowledgeable people may even dare to take the relationship a step further, initiating a Talk session to make those discoveries that come only through conversation.

So although the techniques in this chapter overlap those in Chapter 6, here you'll mostly see how users extract information straight from the other computers on the Internet, usually without having to enlist the assistance of another person.

They Use Other People's Computers as Their Own

Newsgroups and mailing lists (described in Chapter 6) are two Internet resources that make finding and supplying information easy because they all work basically the same way; that is, if a user knows how to find information and post information in one newsgroup, he or she knows how to use them all. Ditto mailing lists, for the most part. Newsgroups achieve this consistency because they all conform to the Usenet format. Mailing lists are consistent because they all rely on the same e-mail-based approach.

Unfortunately, many other Internet resources are not consistent in the way they look and in how they're used.

How Do People Pick Up Information from the Internet?

Out on the Internet are thousands of computer systems that are managed not for the benefit of the whole Internet community but for the use of a smaller group—a university faculty, a research staff, a federal agency. Each system has its own way of doing things: a different way of organizing information on the screen, a different set of commands, a different set of rules for who can do what. These systems are set up in whatever way best suits their primary users, and Internet visitors are expected to learn, when in Rome, to speak the local language.

To access most of these computer systems, Internet folk use a facility called Telnet. Telnet enables an Internet user to drop in on another computer system and use it as if he or she were one of the computer's primary users. (The procedure is sometimes also described as *remote login*.) Within some limitations that you'll learn about later, Internet users can look through a college's library catalog as if they were students at that college. Likewise, they can consult the resources of a think tank as if they were one of the researchers, and poke around in the computer systems of government agencies, public libraries, and businesses.

Did You Know...

The word *Telnet* is also used as a verb to describe the action of using Telnet to access another computer, as in "I just *telnetted* to the FDA Library to learn about recent drug approvals."

You may also hear references to "Telnet sites." These are simply the places where the computers that run Telnet-accessible resources are located.

But here's the catch: When an Internet user telnets into Harvard's campus information system, that user sees on his or her screen exactly what students and faculty at Harvard see— the same lists of options, the same information. If a user telnets to Dartmouth's system, that user sees what the students and faculty at Dartmouth see. The problem is that the systems of the two universities aren't used in exactly the same way (see Figure 7.1). Before the Internet user can use any given resource through Telnet productively, he or she may have to feel around a little to figure out how things are done there.

Learning to use e-mail, newsgroups, and mailing lists is a snap, as you may have discovered while reading earlier chapters. More than anything else, it is the inconsistency among the many Telnet systems that leads people to see the Internet as a complicated system usable only by computer virtuosos.

Fortunately, any computer user with a little experience can quickly come up to speed of most Telnet systems. As Figure 7.1 suggests, nearly all Telnet systems can be operated through menus.

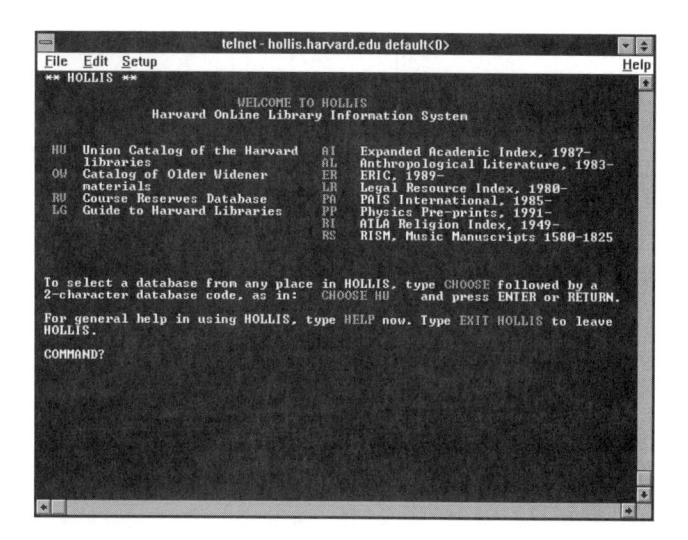

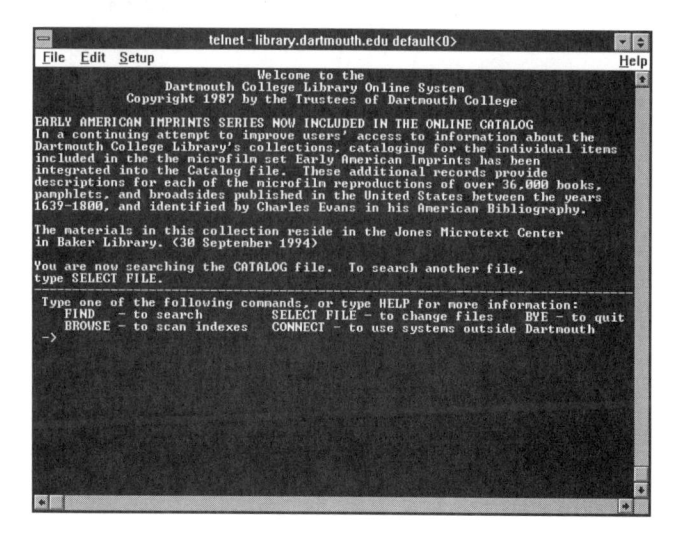

How Do People Pick Up Information from the Internet? 149

Figure 7.1. Two different university information systems on the Internet, reached through Telnet.

Curious About the Word?

A *menu* is a list of choices displayed on the screen. Menus are particularly important in using Telnet systems and in using Gopher and World Wide Web resources, both described later in this chapter.

To use a menu-based (often called *menu-driven*) Telnet system, users read each list of choices presented on the screen and pick what they want. Each menu item has a number next to it (see Figure 7.1); picking an item typically requires nothing more than typing the number of the desired menu item, then pressing the Enter or Return key. On a small but growing number of systems, the user may use a computer mouse to move an on-screen pointer to an item and click the mouse button to select it.

Typically, a user moves through several menus to get something done. The user will pick one choice from a broad *main menu* (also called the *opening menu* or *top menu*, it's the menu that appears as soon as the user arrives at the system). This will bring up a more specific menu of choices related to the chosen item. The next selection may bring up an even more specific list. Eventually, after passing through several menus, the user arrives at the information he or she seeks.

Often the wording of menu choices can be a little cryptic, so users sometimes take the wrong route and hit a dead end. It's usually easy, however, to "back out" through the menus to the starting point, from which the user can start over by trying a different menu item. A little trial and error almost always gets users where they want to go.

How Do People Pick Up Information from the Internet?

Telnet resources vary not just in their menuing systems, but in other ways. In particular, they may require a procedure called "logging on" or "signing on"—supplying a username and password in order to use the system. The username/password routine exists to enable the computer to keep track of its users and to control access to sensitive information or features.

For example, a professor at a university may be allowed to look at grade reports, but students may not be. In a business, the chief accountant and other executive officers are typically allowed to see financial data that most employees are forbidden to see. Because each user of a computer system signs on with a unique username, the computer knows who's who and can restrict a user from seeing what that person is not supposed to see. The secret passwords ensure that people can't use the system dishonestly by signing on with someone else's username.

Did You Know...

In the movie *Clear and Present Danger*, CIA agent Jack Ryan (the character played by Harrison Ford) secretly orders a CIA hacker to find the username and secret password of another CIA agent whom Ryan suspects of treachery. The hacker succeeds, enabling Ryan to read incriminating memos stored in computer files by the dirty CIA guy. All of that is technically accurate and possible, including the fact that the CIA probably knows how to look at anybody's files. (I'm feeling a little paranoid.)

What's *not* accurate in the movie is that when the bad guy discovers Ryan snooping, the bad guy erases the memos from the computer *while Ryan is looking at them* on his computer screen. Computer networks don't let you erase files that are in use—not even the CIA's network...not even Harrison Ford's network.

Not being the primary users of most computers accessed through Telnet, Internet users have no username or password for each individual computer system. So the Telnet computer systems have two ways of letting Internet users get on board:

- The first time the user telnets to the system, the system displays on-screen questions that ask the user to fill in some personal information and sometimes to choose a username and password to be used from that time on.

- The Telnet system has a special username—usually something like guest, visitor, or new—that can be used by visiting Internet folk. Most such systems display a message as soon as a new user telnets to them, listing what the guest username is and how a visiting user should go about signing on.

In either case, the computer systems typically give Internet users the most restrictive security setting, allowing them access only to the most public information available on the system and keeping them out of private information and services that may share the same computer.

Did You Know...

Internet users trying to hunt down a Telnet site for a particular purpose can use Hytelnet, a directory service that provides menu access to lists of Telnet sites, along with other helpful information about using Telnet.

Users of Telnet are vexed in yet one more way: terminal types. Again, because the various computer systems were designed primarily for their local users and not for everybody on the Internet, their methods for displaying information on-screen may be specifically tailored to a particular type of computer terminal or workstation. On other types of terminals, the displayed words may come out garbled.

Internet users get around this problem with *terminal emulation* software that teaches their computers to mimic the terminal the Telnet system wants. Even so, this is one more inconsistency that makes using the Internet trickier than using a commercial online service such as CompuServe or America Online, where everything looks and acts the same.

Many Telnet sites try to help users with this problem. And why shouldn't they? They've gone to the trouble of making themselves available to Internet users; they might as well smooth the path a little. The help available comes in several forms:

- "Help" may appear as a choice on one or many menus, as may other words (perhaps "About this Service") that offer users a way to get information about using the system (see Figure 7.2).

- A Help command may be available. When the system displays a menu, sometimes the user can enter a Help command (by typing `help` or sometimes just `?`) instead of the number of a menu item. Doing so usually displays a menu of choices that lead to screenfuls of information about the system.

- Computer files containing general information about the system—even entire user's manuals—can often be copied from the system. Users can copy the files, read them on the screen or print them out, and then return to the system with the know-how to use it. In addition to manuals, users may find Frequently Asked Questions (FAQ) files, described later in this chapter.

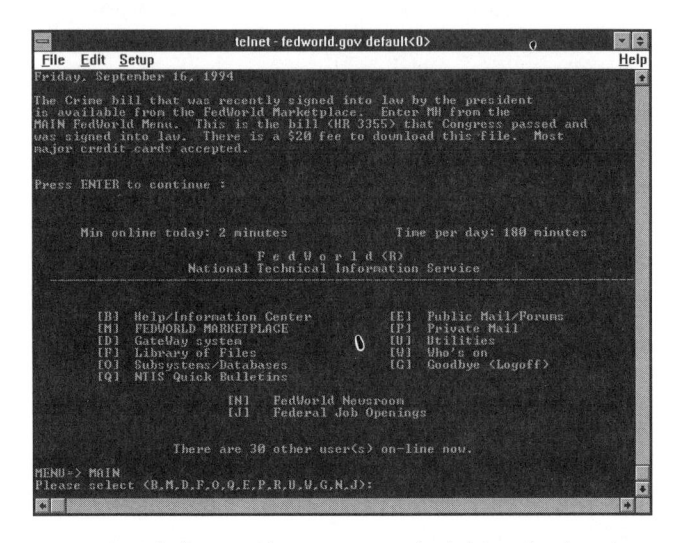

Figure 7.2. A help item (the top item in the left-hand column) on a menu in FedWorld, a database of Federal government information. To get help, the user presses B.

Most systems accessible through Telnet are overseen by one or more system operators, or *sysops*. Many systems display the name and e-mail address of the sysop when the user signs on, or they offer menu items that lead the user to a facility for communicating with the sysop. Sysops are busy people, and they're paid to assist the primary users, so they usually don't like answering zillions of questions from Internet people—especially when the answers are available through help items or other methods that don't involve the

How Do People Pick Up Information from the Internet?

sysop. When all else fails, however, Internet users can approach the sysop and almost always get the answers they need.

> **Did You Know...**
>
> How bugged can sysops become when users ask dumb questions that they should have looked up on their own? Among the many common abbreviations used by Internet folk to keep their messages brief is this one: RTFM.
>
> It stands for "Read the fine manual!" (That's the polite version.)

Systems available through Telnet include:

The Agriculture and Nutrition database at the University of Pennsylvania.

The Earthquake information system at Washington University.

CARL, a database of Colorado library catalogs, book reviews, articles, and more (see Chapter 2).

A thought-for-the-day service from Temple University.

Chess games and the oriental strategy game, Go (see Chapter 8).

NASA's National Space Science Data Center.

A history database at the University of Kansas.

The Concise Oxford Dictionary at Rutgers University.

A database of information about alcoholism and substance abuse at Dartmouth.

The Library of Congress catalog, through the University of Minnesota.

A bulletin board at the American Philosophical Association.

Many university information systems and their libraries.

> **Really Curious?**
>
> Much of the good stuff on the Internet is accessible only through Telnet. Increasingly, however, users can get to the resources and services on other Internet computers through special facilities that hide the differences and make the various computers seem as though they all work the same way, or nearly so.
>
> For more, see "They Burrow with Gopher" and "They Browse the World Wide Web" later in this chapter.

They Locate and Copy Files

Computer files are available all over the Internet, and they contain everything that can be stored in a computer file:

- Reports, books, and other texts
- Software programs (shareware and freeware)
- Photographs, drawings, and other pictures
- Video and sound clips

How Do People Pick Up Information from the Internet?

> **Did You Know...**
>
> The bigger a computer file is, the longer it takes to copy over the Internet and the more space it takes up on the computer that stores it. To alleviate that problem, many large files on the Internet are *compressed*; that is, they have been processed by a special program that makes them smaller without losing any of the information they contain. Users can copy compressed files in a fraction of the time the same file would require uncompressed.
>
> The file can't be used in its compressed state, however. After copying, the user must *decompress* the file to return it to its original, bigger form. To decompress a file, a user needs a software program capable of undoing the particular compression method applied.
>
> Fortunately, most files are compressed with one of just two or three popular compression methods. If a user has the tools to handle these, he or she will never find a compressed file that can't be set free.

There are four basic ways Internet users copy files from other computers on the Internet to their own:

- They can save newsgroup messages that have files attached to them. Users can post any type of file on a newsgroup by posting a message and using an option in their newsreader software that attaches a computer file to the message, sending it out on the Internet along with the message. Other newsgroup users then read the message, which usually describes the file attached to it.

If they want to have a copy of the file for their own use, they choose a Save option in their newsreader software to copy the file to their computer.

- They can send and receive e-mail messages that have files attached to them. This works in roughly the same way as the newsgroup method, except that the file is attached to an e-mail message sent directly to the user.

- They can Telnet to systems offering menu items that allow them to copy (*download*) files made available to the public.

Curious About the Word?

Downloading and *uploading* both describe the act of copying a file from one computer to another, through a network. When the recipient of the file initiates and controls the copying process, the activity is called downloading. When the sender is in control, it's uploading. Therefore, when a user employs FTP to copy a file from the Internet to his or her computer, the user *downloads* the file.

You'll see the term *download* used generically to describe copying files from the Internet or another online service to a user's computer.

- They can use a facility called FTP (File Transfer Protocol) to access other computers and copy files stored there.

This last option—FTP—offers the greatest breadth of information. A large subset of computers on the Internet are known as FTP sites. Many of these are also Telnet sites.

How Do People Pick Up Information from the Internet?

What the user sees when accessing these sites, however, depends on how he or she goes in: If the user goes in through Telnet, he or she sees menus for using the information services available there. If the user go in with FTP, he or she sees lists of files available for copying. As with Telnet, users are usually required to sign on to the computer with a username and password. The exception is "anonymous" FTP sites; these are set up to allow anybody to copy files without identification. (Actually, the process isn't completely anonymous. The computer at the FTP site still knows who the user is, thanks to behind-the-scenes communications between the user's computer and the FTP site. The advantage of the anonymous FTP site is that users don't have to remember passwords to get files.)

Did You Know...

Among the most popular files copied on the Internet are Frequently Asked Questions (FAQ) files, simple text files containing the answers to questions typically asked by new users of the newsgroup, FTP site, or other resource where the particular FAQ file is located.

FAQ files have two main goals. First, they bring new users up to speed quickly so they can use the resource productively. Second, they prevent new users from annoying the other users or the sysop with the same dumb questions asked repeatedly. Upon venturing into a place they've never visited before, savvy Internet users like to find, copy, and read the FAQ file, if one exists. It makes them productive more quickly and also saves them embarrassment.

Typically, the lists of files at an FTP site are organized in groups called *directories* (see Figure 7.3). Directories can contain lists of other directories, each of which can contain a list of still more directories. So it can take some effort to plow through the lists and directories to locate a particular file.

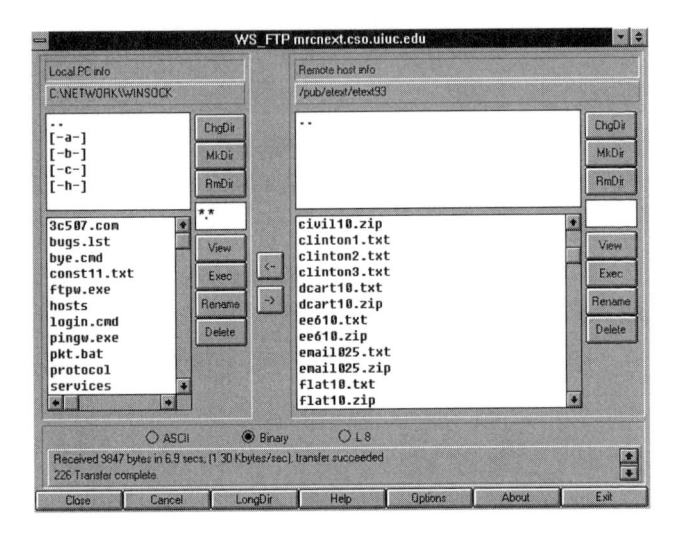

Figure 7.3. A list of files available for copying, as seen by an Internet user through FTP.

Did You Know...

A file is not a file is not a file. Different types of computers use different types of computer files, and because many different types of computers are on the Internet, not all files available for copying will be useful on any particular computer.

As a rule, text files are OK. There are only minor differences among the ways different computers store text files. Also, FTP automatically makes minor adjustments to text files to correct for those differences. Thus a user can use FTP to copy a text file from anywhere on the Internet (say, a nice book from Project Gutenberg) and be reasonably certain that he or she will be able to read it (or print it).

Other types of files—especially those containing software programs—will be useful only on the computers for which they were created. For example, a software program written for a Macintosh won't run on a PC, so there's not much point in a PC user copying it. Also, certain types of files can be used only with certain software. For example, the photographs and video clips available on the Internet require a program capable of displaying those types of files. Such programs are sometimes called *viewers* and are part of the Internet user's software tools arsenal.

Sometimes the names of the directories and files will help a user find what he's looking for, but more often, they're cryptic. Many FTP users don't go fishing—they use FTP only when they know exactly what they're looking for and where to find it.

There is a facility that makes finding and copying files through FTP easier. Affectionately named Archie, the facility finds files available through FTP that match a name (or part of a name) supplied by the user.

When a user has at least a vague idea of what the desired file is called, he or she accesses a computer called an Archie server. The user's access provider may have an Archie server; if not, any user can Telnet to any of several Archie servers. The user then types all or part of the filename and puts the Archie server to work. (The user can, in fact, tailor the search in several ways to make the search more accurate.) Archie searches a group of lists containing the names of files at various FTP sites, and if successful, it shows the user where to get the desired file. The user can then use FTP to access the FTP site and copy the file.

> **Really Curious?**
>
> To see a picture of an Internet software tool that makes using Archie easier, see Chapter 5.

There are, in addition to Archie, other Internet facilities that make copying files easier. They take care of the FTP steps behind the scenes and offer the user an easy-to-follow set of menus. These facilities include Gopher (described below) and the World Wide Web (described later in this chapter).

They Burrow with Gopher

Menus make using an Internet resource easier—after the user makes his way to the resource. The challenges of finding a resource, getting onto it, and figuring out the peculiarities of its menu and command system conspire against all but the bravest Internet users. But what if there were a system that allowed a user to find a resource, get to it, use it, and even copy files, all from a fairly consistent, easy-to-use set of menus? That's the idea behind Gopher, which along with Mosaic has made the Internet much easier to use and in doing so has opened up the Internet to a new group of users.

How Do People Pick Up Information from the Internet?

Named for the mascot at University of Minnesota where it was developed, Gopher is a system of menus that allows users to "browse" for information simply by moving through the menus (see Figure 7.4). The beauty is that Gopher's activities are spread across a wide range of Internet sites and resources, but it insulates the user from the tasks of choosing an Internet site, using Telnet or FTP to get to it, signing on, and more. All that stuff is done behind the scenes—or eliminated altogether.

Instead, the user picks through menus of subjects, sites, regions, or other ways of breaking down the possibilities—in effect, the user "burrows" for information (hence the other explanation for Gopher's name). Even upon arriving at a specific resource, the user sees the same style of menus, which work the same way. All the resources that participate in *Gopherspace* (the catch-all term describing the sum of all the resources accessible through Gopher menus) have agreed to play by the same rules to keep things simple.

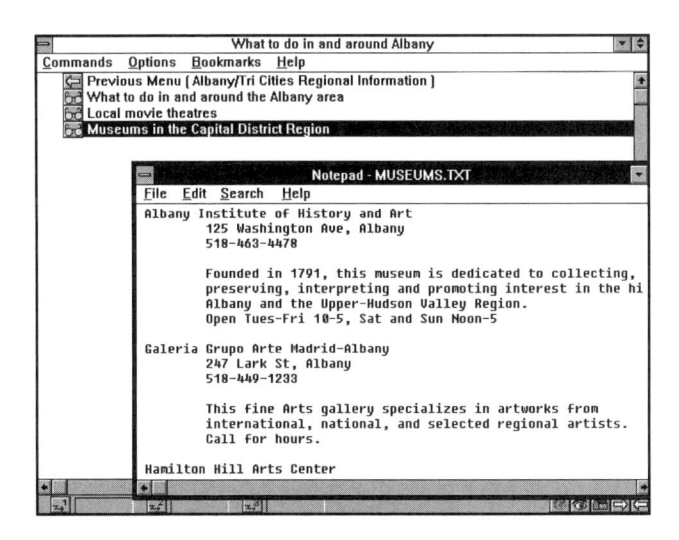

Figure 7.4. A Gopher menu, seen through a Gopher software tool.

While moving around the menus within Gopherspace, a user may jump from one Internet resource to another without even knowing it. Gopher makes the collection of resources that support it (which today include a strong collection of universities and other sites, but by no means all of the Internet) seem like part of one big, consistent, smooth service where everything works the same way.

Gopher is available to all Internet users, but it really shines for those who have software tools designed to take special advantage of it, tools like the one shown in Figure 7.4. A PC program that uses the Microsoft Windows environment, WinGopher allows the user to burrow through Gopherspace by clicking the mouse on items of interest.

At the end of a browsing session, a user may find himself at a menu of computer files. If he or she wants to copy one, the user simply picks it from the menu; just as Gopher shields the user from the details of Telnet, so too it hides the FTP activity required to copy the file.

They Search with Veronica

Browsing is a great way to find stuff, but if you've ever tried to find one book in a big library by browsing alone, you know that it's not an efficient approach.

To solve this problem, Gopher has a companion tool, Veronica. Just as Archie helps users find files, Veronica enables the user to type a "search term" to find Gopher menus and items on a particular subject. There are several ways to search with Veronica, but typically the user types one word or more for the search term. Veronica searches Gopherspace, finds all the matching menu items, and creates and displays a new menu listing the items that match. The user can then choose any item from that menu.

How Do People Pick Up Information from the Internet?

> **Did You Know...**
>
> The name Veronica is an acronym for *Very Easy Rodent-Oriented Net-wide Index to Computerized Archives*; the *Rodent* is our friend Gopher. The obvious relationship between Veronica and the file-searching tool Archie is said to be a coincidence, but I can't help wondering how many different names and terms the programmers had to experiment with before they happened to "coincidentally" come up with one from the same comic book. (Did they try "Betty" first? Or did they have a preference for Veronica from the start?)

They Browse the World Wide Web

Gopherspace is made up of Internet computers that are set up to play by the Gopher's rules so that users can access resources easily. Gopherspace includes only a small subset of the whole Internet, but when the superset is as large as the Internet, a small subset can be pretty big. There are hundreds of Gopher sites offering millions of documents, files, and other resources, and more sites and resources join Gopherspace regularly.

Another subset of the Internet is called the World Wide Web (also known as the WWW, or the Web). The sites on the WWW have also agreed to arrange their resources on menus and to make information "browseable" by subject or by site; but the folks on the WWW take browsing a step further.

When a user looks at menus, documents, or other screenfuls of information on the WWW, the user sees various words highlighted in some way so that they stand out from the rest. The actual way the words are highlighted varies a little by resource and depends on what type of software is used to access the WWW—a number may appear next to the word or the word may be displayed in bold or in a different color. However they're shown, the highlighted words are called *keywords* (see Figure 7.5). Keywords are doorways to information.

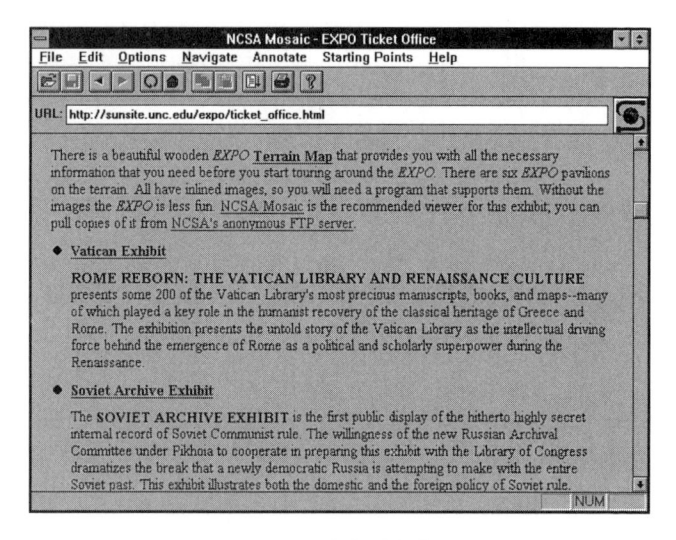

Figure 7.5. A WWW menu, with highlighted keywords that lead to related information.

A user chooses a keyword in much the same way that he or she might choose a menu item. When the user does so, a new screen appears with related information and perhaps still more keywords to choose from. Users find out what they need to know by reading what's on each screen, then drilling down to more specific, related information through the keywords. Users can also easily "back out" one step at a time through the screens they've read, to choose a different keyword and start down a different path. It's much like using menus, but far more powerful and flexible because it allows users to jump spontaneously from idea to idea. Every document can double as a menu to more documents.

Originally called *hypertext*, the keyword approach has recently been renamed *hypermedia* because the WWW is evolving into a source of multimedia information—including text, pictures, sound, and even video.

To take advantage of hypermedia, the user needs an Internet software tool that can deal with multimedia information. That's where WWW browsers come in. Several are available, including a program called Cello from Cornell University and Lynx from the University of Kansas, which is currently the most-used WWW browser. A newer freeware program called Mosaic, however, has been getting the lion's share of the attention lately. Perhaps second only to Gopher, Mosaic has encouraged the press and everybody else to rethink the Internet and consider its potential as a resource within the reach of novices. Mosaic isn't perfect—it has technical limitations that restrict it to users who have a particular type of Internet connection. (Users with the wrong connection for Mosaic can use other WWW browsers.) But it's catching on like wildfire among those who *can* use it.

Really Curious?

What makes the WWW special is its hypertext/hypermedia features, and that's why people use it. But the WWW is hooked into the rest of the Internet in a way that allows users to treat it like a window to the whole thing. From the WWW, users can reach Gophers, Telnet sites, FTP files, news-groups and more.

The WWW also functions as a doorway to the sites that make up a subset of the Internet called WAIS (Wide Area Information Servers). The computers in WAIS allow users to search for information not just by what's in the document name, but by what's actually *in* the document. Users can type a few words and select one or more WAIS computers; WAIS will then find all the documents on those computers that contain those words anywhere within their text.

The other resources weren't built as part of the WWW, so they don't feature hypertext or hypermedia—and of course, users can always get to them directly without going through the WWW. Still, the WWW presents easy-to-use menus that take a user most or all of the way to a resource, which makes it a handy, all-purpose Internet starting point.

You can learn more about using the WWW to reach WAIS and other Internet resources in *Navigating the Internet*, described in Chapter 10 of this book.

Created by the National Center for Supercomputing Applications at the University of Illinois at Champaign-Urbana, Mosaic provides a graphical window to the WWW through which users can "point and click" with a mouse to choose keywords. Because it can display graphics on the screen (it's available for several graphical computing environments, including PCs with Windows and the Macintosh), Mosaic can show on the screen little pictures (*icons*) that serve as keywords for accessing multimedia information.

When a user selects an icon that leads to a multimedia item, Mosaic determines which type of software is necessary to play that item, then starts up the required program. For example, if the user selects an icon that leads to a sound clip, Mosaic starts another program that is capable of playing sound clips. When the user has finished listening to the clip, Mosaic exits the sound program and returns the user to the WWW screen. If an icon leads to a picture, Mosaic starts a viewer program to display it.

Really Curious?

Just as Internet users can search FTP sites with Archie and search Gopherspace with Veronica, they can use any of several new tools—including Lycos, WebCrawler, and WWWWorm—to search the WWW for whatever information they desire.

Figures 7.6 and 7.7 illustrate the power of hypermedia through Mosaic. The resource shown is a multimedia medical textbook created by the University of Iowa. The user opens the textbook, reads each screen, and uses keywords to jump to related information at will. When an illustration is available to help the reader understand a concept, an icon appears on the screen, as shown in Figure 7.6.

When the user moves the mouse pointer to an icon and clicks the mouse button, Mosaic starts a viewer to show the full illustration, as shown in Figure 7.7. (Notice that the icon in Figure 7.6 is a miniature version of the full illustration shown in Figure 7.7.) When the user finishes looking at the illustration, Mosaic closes the viewer and returns to the screen shown in Figure 7.6.

170 Curious About the Internet?

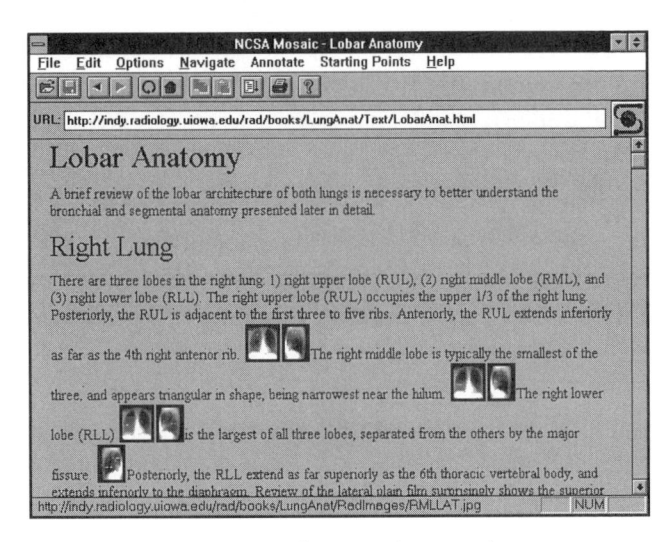

Figure 7.6. A Mosaic screen featuring hypermedia icons.

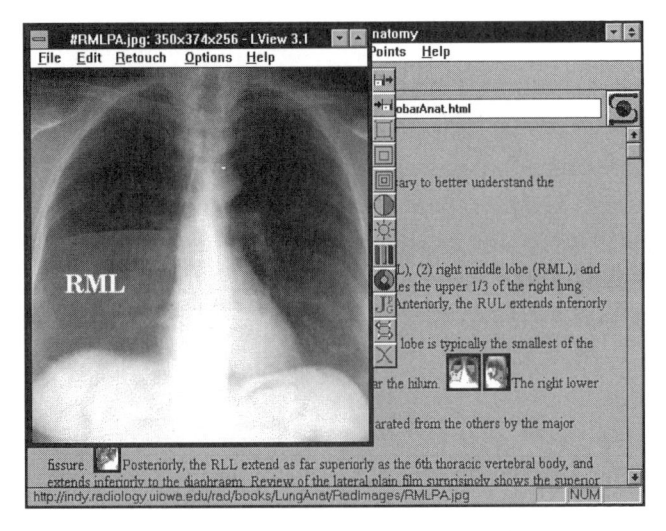

Figure 7.7. The picture displayed after the user selects an icon, shown through a viewing program automatically started by Mosaic.

How Do People Pick Up Information from the Internet?

> **Did You Know...**
>
> Mosaic can tap into other Internet resources through the window of the WWW. Mosaic can be used to browse through Gopher menus, do searches with Veronica, find and copy files with Archie, and more. A growing number of people make Mosaic their all-purpose Internet tool.

So Now You Know...

Internet users rely on a range of tools and techniques for digging up information—some are easy, some aren't. Among the research tools and facilities making the Internet both easier and more powerful are

- Gopher, a system of easy-to-use menus.
- Veronica, a tool for searching through Gopher menus.
- Archie, a tool for locating and copying specific files.
- Mosaic, a tool for finding and displaying the hypermedia resources on the World Wide Web.

Other Internet research facilities—such as Telnet and FTP—can require more skill and patience. Most folks, however, find the effort rewarding, given the great depth and breadth of resources the Internet provides.

8

What Fun Do People Have on the Internet?

Read this chapter to satisfy your curiosity about how people fool around on the Internet. The answers include these:

- They play interactive games.
- They play e-mail games.
- They try to win the Internet Hunt.
- They read the funnies.
- They play pretend in MUDs.
- They create their own WWW home pages.

Of course, because most folks are fun-seekers by nature, any of the Internet resources discussed in other chapters may be a source of amusement or hilarity. In particular, newsgroups and e-mail (see Chapter 6) provide a link through which jibes and jokes can be exchanged. For example, there are several trivia newsgroups in which some users pose trivial questions and others try to answer. This newsgroup thus is also a game.

Although I've pointed out several times that the Internet's appeal is expanding to all walks of life, the fact remains that few people use the Internet for fun alone—a fact that sets it apart from commercial services like Prodigy and America Online, which have many recreation-only users. When you are evaluating the level of fun on the Internet, expect no more than you'd find in any workplace where fun is permitted—encouraged, even—but stops before interfering with work.

As in most workplaces, the fun to be had on the Internet revolves around socialization. In many cases, it isn't so much the activity that's fun, but rather the fact that the participants know they're playing with interesting, new people from all over the world. Cool.

They Play Interactive Games

Several different multiplayer games on the Internet can be played "live" between opponents who may sit thousands of miles apart. Typically, each player needs special software to play the game; in some cases, a player can get around this limitation by first accessing another computer that has the special software and then connecting to the game from there.

Players use Telnet or Gopher (see Chapter 7) to access the Internet site where a game is being played. They can then ask to play, in which case they'll be matched with other players who have also requested a game. People can also join as "observers" who watch games being played by others.

Traditional board games make good computer games because a computer screen effectively simulates the confined playing space of a game board. That's why much of the play on the Internet is in such games, including old favorites such as

- Backgammon
- Chess
- Chinese chess
- Othello (also called Reversi)
- Bridge

The computers running the games often provide some type of Talk or Chat facility (see Chapter 6) so that players can trade comments, tips, or questions and answers—and, of course, find out about each other. That's especially exciting in the backgammon, chess, and bridge games, which are joined by some of the world's finest players.

But why should the Internet be limited to traditional games? It has several of its own, each designed to make better play out of the fact that the playing space is the Internet and not a folding card table in the basement. For example, there's a strategy game called Go. A two-player game, it's sometimes played in international tournaments featuring players from all over the world.

Another Internet game, Netrek, is a space battle for up to 16 players. Two teams of players try to take over each other's planets by slugging it out with fleets of spaceships. What's special about Netrek is that it shows good-looking pictures of the action on the screen. Most Internet games try to represent the game with simple letter characters, which is harder on the eyes but easier on computer and network horsepower.

They Play E-mail Games

Besides the interactive games, the Internet has others played through the simple act of exchanging e-mail—much as people have played long-distance chess matches through paper mail for hundreds of years. These "play-by-mail" games lack the interactivity and spontaneity of the other games, but because e-mail is their only requirement, they're open to all users of the Internet, regardless of what hardware and software they may have. However, note that some play-by-mail games are "commercial"—that is, players must pay a fee to the folks who run the game.

There are many more, but here are some examples of popular play-by-mail games, culled from the play-by-mail FAQ (frequently asked questions) file,

Adventurer's Guild (AG): a commercial fantasy arena combat game.

Arena: a free fantasy arena combat game.

Atlantis: a free strategic fantasy game.

Duelmasters (DM): a commercial fantasy arena combat game.

Galaxy: a free game set in space.

Legends: a commercial Dungeons & Dragons-type simulation in which 200 players wander around a large map trying to become more powerful.

Middle Earth (ME-PBM): a commercial strategic simulation of J.R.R. Tolkien's fantasy universe.

What Fun Do People Have on the Internet? 177

For programmers only, there's a nasty little game called King of the Hill, an Internet version of an old programmer's game called Code War. Using a special programming language, players write destructive little programs and send them by e-mail to a computer where they're run along with other players' destructive little programs. The winner is the one whose destructive little program is able to stop all the other destructive little programs and keep running. King of the Hill is like a demolition derby, with programs instead of cars.

> **Did You Know...**
>
> As discussed in Chapter 7, Internet users can copy computer files from the Internet to their own computers. Among the types of files available are software programs, and among those are games. The free game software many people copy from the Internet and play on their computers is a major source of fun. The fun part isn't exactly *on* the Internet, but it certainly is *from* the Internet.

They Try to Win the Internet Hunt

The Internet Hunt is a test of users' Internet research skills. Every month, a new list of questions comes out, challenging players to answer them. The only rule is that players can't answer the questions from an encyclopedia, public library, or personal knowledge. They must apply their Internet research skills (like those described in Chapter 7) to find out where on the Internet the answers can be found. The questions from a recent Hunt appear in Figure 8.1.

Rick Gates, the creator of the Hunt, ensures that the information required to answer any Hunt question can be found somewhere on the Internet—on a bulletin board, through a Gopher menu, in a newsgroup, in a file that can be copied…somewhere. The game helps players learn more about the Internet and sharpen their online research skills.

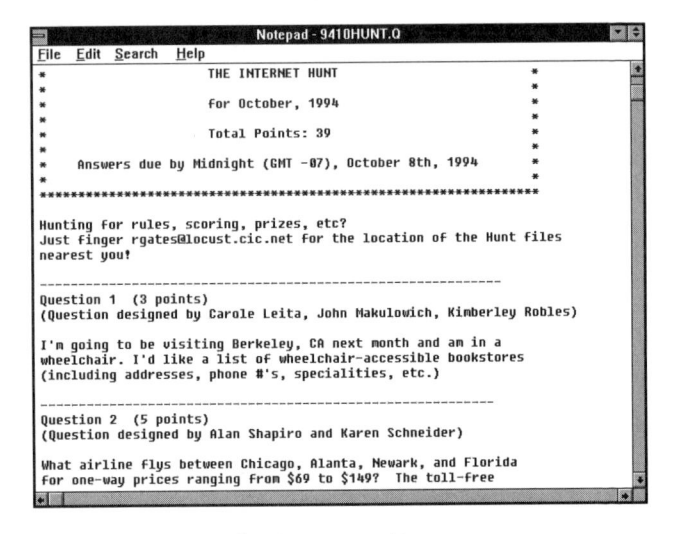

```
                         Notepad - 9410HUNT.Q
 File  Edit  Search  Help
 *                       THE INTERNET HUNT                        *
 *                                                                *
 *                       For October, 1994                        *
 *                                                                *
 *                       Total Points: 39                         *
 *                                                                *
 *       Answers due by Midnight (GMT -07), October 8th, 1994     *
 *                                                                *
 ******************************************************************

 Hunting for rules, scoring, prizes, etc?
 Just finger rgates@locust.cic.net for the location of the Hunt files
 nearest you!

 ----------------------------------------------------------------
 Question 1  (3 points)
 (Question designed by Carole Leita, John Makulowich, Kimberley Robles)

 I'm going to be visiting Berkeley, CA next month and am in a
 wheelchair. I'd like a list of wheelchair-accessible bookstores
 (including addresses, phone #'s, specialities, etc.)

 ----------------------------------------------------------------
 Question 2  (5 points)
 (Question designed by Alan Shapiro and Karen Schneider)

 What airline flys between Chicago, Alanta, Newark, and Florida
 for one-way prices ranging from $69 to $149? The toll-free
```

Figure 8.1. Questions for the Internet Hunt.

They Read the Funnies

Through newsgroups and other resources, a variety of cartoon drawings are available on the Internet. Particularly noteworthy is Dr. Fun, a daily strip Internet users can see on the World Wide Web by using a graphical browsing tool like Mosaic (see Chapter 7). The ClariNet service, an extra-charge set of newsgroups that feature news and syndicated columns, has also introduced a comic strip, *Dilbert*.

What Fun Do People Have on the Internet?

> **Really Curious?**
>
> As mentioned in Chapters 3 and 4, the corners of the mostly uncensored Internet hold a repository of X-rated stuff, including smutty newsgroup messages, filthy e-mail, computer files holding dirty pictures, and off-color online chats. One should note that although some of the material caters to pure adolescent prurience, other material qualifies as intelligent—even literate—adult erotica, including erotic fiction and poetry.
>
> Whether or not this hotly debated aspect of the Internet qualifies as fun depends on how often you tend to agree with Dan Quayle. Because some people do find it fun (not me! no sir!), it deserves a mention in this chapter.
>
> For more about newsgroups, e-mail, and chatting, see Chapter 6. For more about how files are copied, see Chapter 7.

They Listen to the Radio

Talk radio has invaded every corner of American life, and the Internet is not immune. The Internet has, however, its own, unique variant on the model—Internet Talk Radio.

As I pointed out earlier, advances in multimedia technology have made it possible to store pictures, video, and sound in computer files. Computers with the right multimedia hardware and software can "play" these files so that the user can see and hear their contents. The Internet Talk Radio program is a weekly radio show stored in computer files and made available on the Internet. Interested listeners copy the files (see Chapter 7 for more on copying files) and play them on their computers.

What's on? Internet Talk Radio offers interviews with important Internet folk and other technology movers and shakers, and news segments about Internet-related issues and events. The programs are mostly talk, but also they may feature music or sound effects. There are also messages from sponsors, who help pay for the program so it can be offered free on the Internet.

Did You Know...

At the moment, Internet Talk Radio is the subject of some controversy—not about its content, but about its technique. If you take a half-hour's worth of words, type them up, and send them out on the Internet in a text file, they can be copied quickly to a user's computer, they don't take much disk space on that computer, and the user doesn't need any special hardware or software to read them.

Word for word, however, a sound file is much bigger than a text file. Take the same words and record them as sound, and you have a monster computer file (a whole set of files, actually) that takes a long time to copy (straining Internet resources) and requires a ton of disk space and special equipment on the user's computer. Why not, critics ask, simply publish the words as text instead of sound so that everybody can read them and the network isn't bogged down by the extra demands of sound files?

What Fun Do People Have on the Internet? 181

It's a fair question, but it ignores the example of history. When people have access to new media for presenting old information, they gravitate to the new—we went from books to radio, radio to TV, black and white to color, mono to stereo. Once folks have the ability to play sound and show pictures on their computers, they quickly lose interest in ordinary text—never mind that the information may be the same. Multimedia is redefining what people expect from their computers, and the Internet will have to go along.

In time, even more sound and pictures will be on the Internet. In the meantime, emerging technology that shrinks files and speeds up networks will carve out some room for all the new material.

A companion show, the Internet Town Hall, works in the same way as Internet Talk Radio, but it features recordings of speeches and lectures given by politicians, scientists, and others. The speeches cover a variety of topics, including—but not limited to—technology. Users can select, copy, and listen to individual speeches from Internet Town Hall, whereas they have to copy whole programs from Internet Talk Radio.

Did You Know...

Some readers might wonder what is fun in Internet Talk Radio. Let me point out that, other than the fact that it's often a fun show, the Internet Talk Radio's unusual trick of squeezing an audio program through the Internet is a bit fun, in and of itself.

That's why Internet Talk Radio qualifies as fun, although the zillion other news and affairs resources on the Internet don't. In time, as sound becomes more common on the Internet and the novelty wears off, the criteria for "fun" will have to be redefined, and Internet Talk Radio will have to crank up its jollies to make the cut.

They Play Pretend in MUDs

MUDs are online role-playing games in which multiple users interact within an imaginary environment and situation created through messages that appear on the screen. The name originally derived from "Multi-User Dungeons," because the early MUDs borrowed their environment and rules from the Dungeons & Dragons role-playing games, and many MUDs still use D&D elements like knights and castles and sorcery. Lately, though, some users prefer the term "Multi-User Dialog" or "Multi-User Dimension" because the range of MUD environments has long since moved beyond D&D and into more contemporary and realistic scenarios.

MUDs and related MUD-like resources are increasingly used as virtual reality scenarios for serious research applications. Scientists are using the basic MUD method to hold meetings in which they jointly interact with scientific data, such as astronomical observations, to make discoveries. MUDs are also used in sociological research to study how people interact with one another under different virtual circumstances.

MUDs are related to Internet Relay Chats (see Chapter 6) in that they enable users from anywhere to join in an online conversation. As with chats, users access a computer running MUDs, then select a "room" where a specific MUD is underway. MUDs differ from chats in that the conversation must be carried out within the context of the game—a game with rules, strategies, and boundaries.

A player called the Wizard creates the environment through descriptive messages on-screen. Hundreds of MUDs are in action at any given time, and each has its own theme, set of circumstances, rules, and style.

Other players in the MUD respond to the situations and events the environment presents, and they interact with one another, commenting on the action, helping one another, or getting in each other's way. Mudders, as they're called, employ an elaborate code of words that allow them to manipulate the environment (*throw*, *look*, *eat*, *go*), interact with one another, move to other regions in the imaginary geography of the game (by typing compass directions), and even express emotions (*e-mote*). They also expand their range of expression with the "smiley" characters used in all Internet communication, such as the happy face **:-)** or the sad face **:-(**. To read the smileys, tilt your head to the left.

Most MUDs show text only. A few graphical MUDs do show pictures to users, but those are rare and users need special software to join in. There are also variations on the basic MUD. For example, there are MOOs (Multi-User Object-Oriented environments). MOOs are similar to MUDs except that the Mudders, not just the Wizard, can substantially modify the environment as they play. I've also seen MUSHes (Multi-User Shared Hallucinations), a real far-out MUD type in which the environments and the users operate on the far side of strange, which is how they like it.

> **Did You Know...**
>
> Internet Relay Chats (see Chapter 6) are more free-form than MUDs, and they don't typically involve rules and role playing. Even so, they often center around a theme, and enterprising users have turned chats into elaborate games.
>
> For example, a bunch of actors and others interested in Shakespeare set up a chat room for making fun of *Hamlet*, cleverly called "Hamnet." Participants in Hamnet join the chat at a scheduled time to give (or watch) an improvised performance in which they skewer the tale of the melancholy Dane by using the Bard's words sometimes and their own words at other times, depending on who has the funnier line. They jazz up performances with smileys and other Internet codes, make new jokes, and generally have a good time at Shakespeare's expense. Why not? Unlike most other butcherings of Shakespeare, this one's intentional.
>
> F.Y.I.: The name "Hamnet" is probably a play on "*Ham*let" (and *ham*my actors) and "*net*work," but you should also know that Shakespeare had a son named Hamnet, who according to some accounts died shortly before *Hamlet* was written. Drama scholars have speculated that Hamlet was named for Hamnet, and that the play's treatment of father-son love and loss arose from Shakespeare's own grief. (This is the stuff you can learn only in an Internet book whose writer has a Theatre degree.)

They Create Their Own WWW Home Pages

Using special software tools, Internet users can create their own *home pages* on the World Wide Web (WWW). The home page can show pictures and documents the user sets up, and can contain hypertext links that will take vistors to other pages in the WWW. Once the home page is set up, other WWW users can actually access a user's home page and check out what's there.

Many users apply this capability to serious purposes, such as making available the results of research they've done or creating handy lists of Internet resources for others to use. But other folks recognize that the same capability can be a source of good, goofy, exhibitionist fun. Users have set up home pages that show video of a tank of fish, animated clowns and priests, an animated robotic arm visitors can control, and more. As use of the WWW grows, more silliness is certain to follow.

So Now You Know...

The Internet has more than enough fun available to keep users entertained until somebody walks in and makes them work. Among the major sources of fun are

- Interactive games.
- Play-by-mail games.
- Computer files of cartoons, game software, and dirty pictures.
- Internet Talk Radio and Internet Town Hall.
- Role-playing games such as MUDs and MOOs.

Bear in mind that other areas of the Internet—particularly e-mail and newsgroups—are vehicles for people to communicate. Although it is possible to communicate and have no fun (ever communicate with an insurance company?), many folks try to make their Internet communications a ball. They like to bring a little electronic levity into the lives of those with whom they trade messages, and maybe get some giggles in return. Communication may represent the most important source of fun on the Internet.

9

Where Is the Internet Headed?

Read this chapter to satisfy your curiosity about where the Internet is going, and what that may mean for your own future. The answers include these:

- The Internet is headed down the information super-highway.
- The Internet is headed into business.
- The Internet is headed into the classroom.
- The Internet is headed into your TV.
- The Internet is headed into oblivion (maybe).

As you read, keep in mind that the record for predicting technology trends is lousy. In the mid 1960s, noted scientist and author Arthur C. Clarke thought we'd have a moon base before 2001. In the early 1980s, Microsoft founder Bill Gates predicted that there would be a PC in every American home by 1985. As of 1995, there's nothing on the moon but American flags, space junk, and Alan Shepherd's golf balls, and not even half of American homes are PC-equipped.

If Clarke and Gates—both rich and famous for their pre-science about technology—can't accurately predict the future, what do you want from me? I'm not rich or famous. I did win $18 once in the Indiana lottery, but that was luck, I think.

Take what you read in this chapter with a grain of salt. Even so, if these predictions turn out to be wrong, the material in this chapter will equip you to understand what actually does happen, whatever that may be.

The Internet Is Headed down the Highway

Governments have long loved to labor at infrastructure because an efficient infrastructure supports the growth and prosperity of the state and also because infrastructure development is one of the few things governments can do without some knucklehead complaining it's not the proper role of government.

Curious About the Word?

Infrastructure, according to Webster's New World Dictionary, is "the basic installations and facilities on which the continuance and growth of a community, state, etc. depend, as roads, schools, power plants, transportation, and communication systems, etc." Politicians who promise to "invest in the infrastructure" usually mean they will fill all the potholes. But they could also fix up the schools, the subway, and the snow removal system; they could even get the public library an Internet account.

Ancient Rome built roads so it could move goods (and armies) around its empire faster. The Greeks built piers so they could quickly move goods on and off ships, streamlining their lucrative international trade. Egypt built irrigation systems so people could eat better, which led inevitably to more people, hence more workers, hence more wealth for the Pharaohs. In the 1930s, Roosevelt's New Deal initiatives built hundreds of bridges and spread electricity and telephone service to rural America, in part to invent jobs but also to strengthen the national economy by making rural folks more active participants in it.

In the 1950s, a forward-thinking senator from Tennessee—Albert Gore, Sr.—was a big infrastructure fan. He championed the building of the federally funded interstate highway system, an investment that has returned its cost many times over by facilitating and encouraging interstate commerce, tourism, auto and gasoline sales, and many other economic windfalls in the 1950s, 1960s and 1970s. Gore and other promoters of the highway system saw that middle America was evolving from a farming economy into a manufacturing economy, and that more Americans were becoming aggressive consumers of mass-produced goods. An efficient interstate system could move more stuff to more people more quickly and accelerate the upward economic spiral already underway to benefit both manufacturers and consumers.

It's not surprising, then, that Big Al's son—Al Gore, Jr.—("Mr. Vice President" to you and me) has embraced the idea of a government-sponsored National Information Infrastructure, which he nicknamed "The Information Superhighway" to make sure everybody notices the historical precedent.

Just as proponents of the interstate system recognized and nurtured America's evolution to a consumer society populated by factory workers, Gore and others recognize an evolution to an *information-based* society, populated by *knowledge workers*—people who work with information rather than concrete think. They think government should encourage the creation of a new "highway" system to nurture that evolution—a high-speed highway for carrying electronic communication. The Internet may be an important part of making that happen.

Think about how people work today. More and more people spend their days at computer screens, performing desk-based, service-sector jobs, the fastest-growing type of job. The federal government says 60 percent of all U.S. workers are knowledge workers, and that 8 of 10 new jobs created in the next several years will be in information-intensive sectors of the economy. Feeding off that change is the rising number of "telecommuters," people who do their jobs at home on PCs and communicate with their bosses, clients, or customers through telephones, fax machines, and modems. Telecommuting is not only convenient for workers, but also may help society by reducing traffic, pollution, and fuel consumption.

Now consider how business is done today:

- Companies rely on telephones, fax machines, and e-mail for their very survival.

- They do their accounting on computers and file their tax returns by sending the information through a modem to the Internal Revenue Service.

- Their field personnel keep in touch though cellular phones and pagers, which rely on private satellite communications networks. More and more, they're also using notebook PCs and smaller hand-held computers that rely on the cellular phone networks to exchange orders, e-mail, and faxes with the home office, from anywhere.

- Companies make and receive payments through Electronic Funds Transfer, a system that allows one company to transfer money directly from its bank account to another company's bank account—no checks, no paper, and with instant verification. (Services such as Checkfree let consumers do the same thing—make payments directly from their bank accounts without writing checks.)

- When selling to customers, companies rely on the banking computer systems to verify and process credit card transactions—another type of electronic payment.

Although most businesses today depend on electronic communication for the operational needs I've just described, a growing number of businesses do their thing solely within the realm of cyberspace. They are in the business of supplying or manipulating electronic information, and little else. Among these are stock and commodities traders, bankers and other financial services providers, payroll processors, software companies, and companies that publish electronic information, like books on CD-ROM.

> **Did You Know...**
>
> Some point out—correctly, I think—that if our economy depends too heavily on moving information and money around and not enough on manufacturing stuff, we're headed for a fall. But that's another issue, for another book. The Information Superhighway isn't about choosing an economic direction—it's about supporting the one we've got, right or wrong.

Finally, think about how we live when we're not working. We do our banking at automated teller machines (ATMs). We order products by telephone, using credit card numbers. About 60 percent of us get our TV entertainment through cables that run into our homes. And of course, many of us have PCs in our homes for home-office work, entertainment and education, and even the Internet.

All these trends in business and personal activity have one thing in common: they depend on electronic communication. The intensity of that electronic communication has caught us off guard. Nobody planned for it, and as a result, it's running on a rickety, outdated infrastructure, full of redundancy and limitations.

Why, for example, do we have two sets of communications wires running into our homes: one for the telephone, another for cable TV? How come the telephone line allows two-way communication, whereas the cable goes one way—from them to us? How come it's so complicated to get an Internet account? Why can't you get an Internet account from the telephone company, just as you can get another telephone line or call-waiting? And where is this "video on demand" stuff we've been hearing about since the 1980s?

For businesses, the limitations are more serious. When communications lines are overloaded, communication slows down and becomes unreliable. The communications demands of business, however, have grown faster than anybody ever expected them to, and the infrastructure is perpetually overloaded. What's more, because our communications infrastructure was really built to carry telephone calls and not all this other stuff, there's a lack of standardization in the ways different computer devices, networks, companies, and countries communicate. That creates problems ranging from unreliable communication to no communication.

Looking ahead, it's obvious that we need to get our act together. We need a very fast, high-capacity, reliable, flexible, and affordable national communications network so that businesses can keep growing and so that new, communications-intensive products and services can be offered to a hooked-in public—products and services such as interactive TV, video on demand, home shopping, home schooling, and more. Ideally, there would be a single high-capacity line running to every home, carrying reliable telephone service, TV, shopping, banking, information services, and more. That's what the National Information Infrastructure (NII) hopes to supply.

Curious About the Word?

\, in/tər-'net\

The formal name for Gore's pet project is the *National Information Infrastructure (NII)*, and his nickname for it is *Information Superhighway*. You'll also hear the terms *Infobahn, Infohighway, Infopike, Digital Highway*, and others. It's all the same idea. Blame bored magazine writers.

Sounds great, right? There's only one problem: Nobody knows quite how to build it.

Creating the NII will take more than just better wires—although that's part of it. The NII will depend heavily on the high-speed, high-capacity fiber-optic cables that have been steadily replacing older copper telephone lines for more than a decade. Microwave and satellite networks will also play an important role.

Improved data compression technologies will be required to squeeze more information through the lines more quickly. Data will be compressed by the sender's computer, sent quickly across the network in its smaller state, then automatically decompressed on the receiver's computer. This will be especially important for transmitting video, which requires moving huge amounts of data very quickly. The methods used for compression will be standardized so that, for example, any brand of TV you can buy will know how to decompress and display the standard NII video signal.

Beyond providing the wires, there are other roadblocks. These are much more serious because getting through them requires people to agree with each another. The NII is being developed through two forces. First, the government has been incrementally legislating it into existence. The most important bill so far is the *High Performance Computing Act of 1991*, which created the National Research and Education Network (see Chapter 3), a corner of the Internet and a vehicle for experimenting with NII concepts on a small scale. There are many other bills also, some pending now, that together will define government's role in shaping the infrastructure.

The rest of the work is being done through cooperation among the major telephone and data communications companies, computer makers, cable TV providers, and other interested parties in the private sector. Together, they'll iron out the technical and operational issues governing how the NII will work: the rules for underlying communications technologies, the data compression techniques, the rules about how different types of data (voice, fax, video, sound) should be handled, and so on.

While working together on the infrastructure, they'll be working privately on the products that will take advantage of it. For example, the cable companies are developing video-on-demand and home-shopping systems that will allow cable subscribers to order a movie to watch immediately or, right from their TVs, to order products to be delivered by mail—after the two-way superhighway lines replace the one-way cable lines.

The problem is that the NII *partners* are also *competitors*. For example, the telephone companies would like to use the highway to supply the same services the cable companies are working on, in addition to other services, such as videoconferencing and videophones. Who gets the job? Both? If both are allowed to offer these services, how can they cooperate effectively on designing a medium that they'll later fight over?

Did You Know...

Designing the NII would be easier if companies were given monopolies on given types of services. Each company could independently design its own aspect of the NII its own way, and the whole thing would get built quicker.

That's been tried before. In the 1930s, the government gave AT&T a monopoly on telephone service so that the company would use its own money to expand the national telephone network. In the 1970s, the government gave cable companies regional monopolies so they'd use their own money to wire communities for cable TV. It then took the government half a century to reintroduce competition into the telephone industry, and even now Congress is fussing over how to introduce competitive forces into the cable industry.

It appears that government has learned that it can't have its cable and eat it too—so nobody's getting ownership of any portion of the NII. In fact, the recent National Communications and Information Infrastructure Act of 1993 lifted a 10-year-old law that forbade telephone companies from going into the video transmission business. The same act requires the telephone companies to let competitors use their video system to offer competing products.

The competition, in theory, is supposed to yield the best products at the best prices, and it may do that. It also slows progress on building the NII.

Still other problems exist, including questions about whether the NII should be regulated or censored (and who should do the regulating), how international business can participate, and yet more problems as they come up. Even though government and private industry are cooperating in the design of the NII, it's unclear who will control the finished product. People are understandably concerned about the government controlling such a vital system. But is the control of private enterprise really any safer? (It's the same question as in the health care debate, and it will be at least as difficult to answer.)

Thus, despite all the buzz, a specific blueprint for the NII has yet to emerge—the whole thing is a pipe dream, a good intention with few specifics to back it up. It's unlikely to be completed during the administration of Clinton and Gore, even if they serve two terms. Will the next administration grab the baton? Odds are, as long as companies like AT&T and IBM are interested in the NII, whoever is in the White House will be, too. (Presidents tend to bend over backwards when the Fortune 500 comes calling.) There's no guarantee, however, and incoming administrations have been known to pull the plug on the previous tenants' pet projects.

Because the NII is only half-baked, nobody knows whether it will ultimately build on the Internet, replace it, or ignore it. After all, the Internet did sort of happen by accident. It's a Frankenstein system, patched together out of the body parts of other networks. That's exactly what the NII folks want to move away from. They want to create a truly cohesive, elegant environment to maximize network performance, reliability, and efficiency. To accomplish that, the NII is likely to require that users (and their computers, TVs, telephones, and other devices) observe certain rules in their underlying technical communications. (The Internet has technical rules, too. But they're very broad, probably more broad than the NII's can afford to be.)

The NII will also effectively replace the traditional domestic telephone and data networks used by the Internet today. Gore is spearheading a campaign to get other nations to build a Global Information Infrastructure, so the international networks used by the Internet are likely to adopt technologies that match the NII's. We don't yet know what the technical requirements, costs, and limitations of the new networks will be. If they're built to accommodate a variety of communication methods and aren't too expensive, the Internet might go on as usual—same computers and services, just a different network technology between them. At the moment, this scenario seems like the Internet's most likely future.

In fact, the NII could be the best thing that ever happened to the Internet. The emerging multimedia Internet resources (see Chapter 7) are horribly slow, mainly because of the limitations of the existing networks. The NII could open the floodgates to speedy, reliable multimedia computing on the Internet.

> **Really Curious?**
>
> The NII may also enable you to use the Internet through your TV set. You'll learn about that later in this chapter.

Of course, if the NII is too restrictive or expensive, the Internet may crumble because it requires access to open, affordable communications. There's also the possibility that new commercial services offered on the NII will prove attractive enough to draw away enough users that the Internet simply dies of neglect.

Then again, some look to the Internet as a potential model for the NII's design. In the spring of 1994, the National Research Council (NRC) issued a report recommending that the NII be patterned after the Internet in several important respects. Most important was preserving the Internet quality of "openness": the ability to accommodate many different types of data and applications.

The report cautions that, when big companies build communications networks, they tend to build in limits that favor their own products. To prevent that from happening, says the report, the companies involved in the NII should be split into two independent groups—one responsible for building an open, flexible network suited to limitless applications, and another to develop services to be offered on that network. The report also recommends that the government keep a close eye on the developers to make sure they don't shut out important academic, research, and non-profit services—like those on the Internet—in the headlong rush to supply for-profit services.

Of course, whether the government really intends the NII as a tool for the public good or as a profit center for big business remains debatable. On the one hand, Gore's speeches stress NII's value to homes and schools (more about that later). On the other hand, in early 1994, President Clinton formed the Advisory Council on the National Information Infrastructure to help design and promote the NII. To whom does the council report? The Secretary of Commerce.

The Internet Is Headed into Business

Should the NII shape up as planned, it would be a boon to business. Gore has already labeled his highway project the most important and lucrative marketplace of the twenty-first century. Business will use the NII for improved interbusiness communications—videoconferencing, for example—and to offer profitable new products and services, such as online shopping and the others described in this chapter.

Some proponents also tout the many new jobs that will be created to build and manage the NII and its products; but that's a red herring. For all anybody knows, those jobs will be offset by jobs lost in other industries. For example, if online shopping catches on, traditional retail sales jobs may dwindle.

While they wait for the superhighway, businesses are cutting their electronic teeth on the Internet. As discussed in Chapters 2 and 3, business use of the Internet is a controversial subject. Some die-hard Internet people are dead-set against it. But the anti-commercial contingent is fighting a losing battle. More than half of the Internet's users are business people, and their proportion is growing. Whether the Old Guard likes it or not, the Internet is becoming a marketplace.

The types of Internet resources used by the greatest number of businesspeople are intercompany e-mail and business research, both of which are used with growing fervor. The e-mail and file transfer capabilities are increasingly applied to the formation of "virtual corporations," temporary business alliances put together for a given project (see Chapter 3). But the once restricted activities of online advertising and selling are growing even more rapidly. Companies advertise quietly on newsgroups as a way to efficiently target a specific interest group. Also, companies are taking advantage of the World Wide Web (WWW—see Chapter 7) and its multimedia power to advertise with pictures of their products.

This practice is becoming especially common on the computers of the companies that sell Internet access. Because their clients must "dial-in" (see Chapter 5) to the company's computer and branch from there to the Internet, the company has a chance to show the user ads before he or she even ventures out on the Internet. For example, consider what I see when I first fire up Mosaic (see Chapter 7) to venture out on the WWW. My Internet access provider shows me a screen like the one in Figure 9.1.

Where Is the Internet Headed?   201

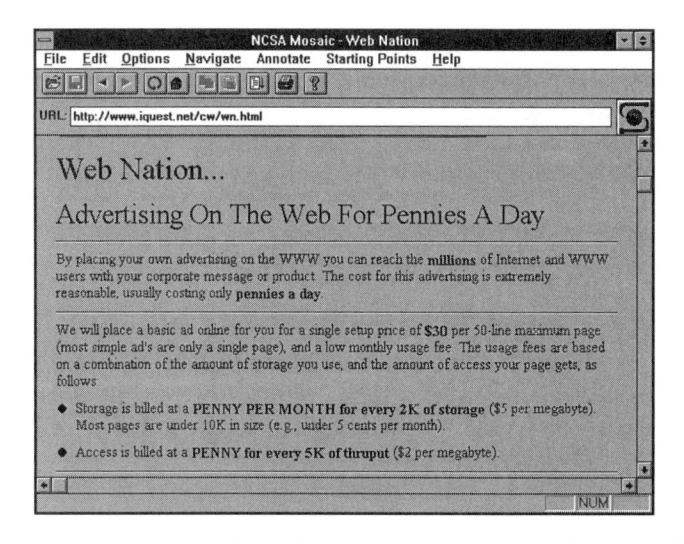

```
                    NCSA Mosaic - Web Nation
 File   Edit   Options   Navigate   Annotate   Starting Points   Help

 URL: http://www.iquest.net/cw/wn.html

   Web Nation...

   Advertising On The Web For Pennies A Day

   By placing your own advertising on the WWW you can reach the millions of Internet and WWW
   users with your corporate message or product. The cost for this advertising is extremely
   reasonable, usually costing only pennies a day.

   We will place a basic ad online for you for a single setup price of $30 per 50-line maximum page
   (most simple ad's are only a single page), and a low monthly usage fee. The usage fees are based
   on a combination of the amount of storage you use, and the amount of access your page gets, as
   follows:
   ◆ Storage is billed at a PENNY PER MONTH for every 2K of storage ($5 per megabyte).
     Most pages are under 10K in size (e.g., under 5 cents per month).
   ◆ Access is billed at a PENNY for every 5K of thruput ($2 per megabyte).
```

Figure 9.1. A screen shown by an Internet access provider who sells ad space on screens that its clients see before they jump into the Internet.

Did You Know...

Most Internet users have acquiesced to the inevitable expansion of commercial Internet applications. Nevertheless, they're quick to remind advertisers that Internet users have the power to combat excessive, saturation-type advertising practices.

The best illustration is the now infamous Green Card Incident. Attracted by the Internet's ability to broadcast cheaply a message to millions of users simultaneously, husband and wife law firm Canter and Siegel wrote a small computer program to post an ad automatically to nearly every Internet bulletin board. (The ad offered their legal services to help aliens get green cards). Mass-posting of this type is called "spamming" by Internet folk, a term meant to evoke an image of something that insidiously multiplies and spreads in all directions. Depending on whom you ask, "spamming" derives either from an old Monty Python routine in which the lads in drag sing the word *spam* repeatedly, or from the image of a hunk of Spam falling into a spinning fan.

Spamming is an Internet no-no under any circumstances, and a double no-no when you're selling something—it's the Internet equivalent of junk mail. Outraged Internet users responded to Canter and Siegel's ad with *flames*, vicious e-mailings meant to punish the spammers. Some users even spammed the spammers, dumping thousands of duplicate messages into Canter and Siegel's mailbox. The flames grew so hot that they overloaded the computer of the lawyers' Internet access provider, who was forced to cancel their account to keep the system running.

The message was received, to be sure, but although the Green Card Incident demonstrates the power of enraged Internet users, it also proves their impotence. Canter and Siegel told the *New York Times* that their ad still drummed up $100,000 in business, and their book about the experience is getting an initial 100,000-copy press run. The pair has promised they'll advertise on the Internet again. Checkmate.

Where Is the Internet Headed? 203

On the Internet, there is even a large network dedicated to commercial use, the Commercial Internet Exchange (CIX). Like a bizarre bazaar, CIX carries a range of ads and also offers online shopping services. Online shopping services (see Figure 9.2) provide on-screen descriptions or pictures of products that Internet users can purchase simply by supplying their names, addresses, and credit card numbers. As these services grow in popularity, they will ultimately shift over to the NII, where they will be offered through TV to reach an even larger consumer market (see more later in this chapter).

Figure 9.2. Online shopping.

Working now on how those services will operate is CommerceNet, a consortium of more than 40 computer companies, banks, retailers, and other companies. Funded by the federal, state, and local governments and by the member companies, CommerceNet is chartered to come up with better methods for performing online basic consumer tasks, such as finding products and services, ordering them, paying for them, and arranging for their delivery.

To ensure that the services catch on, CommerceNet is focusing on making these services easy-to-use and accessible to anyone. The companies are also trying to resolve the thorny issue of online privacy (see Chapter 4) to make sure that transactions and credit-card numbers remain confidential.

The Internet Is Headed into the Classroom

As described in Chapter 2, the Internet is already used by most universities to exchange information and offer enhanced resources—including actual online classroom sessions—to students and faculty. It's also making inroads in high schools and grade schools as an important teaching tool. Not only does the Internet offer access to people and information around the world, but also it makes students comfortable and proficient with computers. In his NII stumping, Gore has often stressed that our education system needs to emphasize computer skills in order to produce workers with the skills to keep America competitive in the twenty-first century.

Unfortunately, just as we've learned that our kids need better schooling, the resources to accomplish that are dwindling. The 1980s legacy of tax-consciousness has led many people to support cuts in education spending.

That leaves many school systems with the challenge of improving education without spending a lot of money. One way is to exploit computers and communications lines to provide *distance learning*, which means simply that students use their computers to participate in lessons actually going on somewhere else.

For years, educators have recognized the computer's value as a teaching tool. A computer has infinite patience and can repeat lessons as often as needed. Students pay attention to computers, in part because they enjoy the interactivity and in part because they've been conditioned to watch TV screens and have been raised on Nintendo.

Now consider the value of coupling that computer affinity with high-speed communications. Given the NII's ability to carry voice, video, and any other multimedia information, school kids in a Boston classroom can experience a lesson being given in Seattle or maybe London. Because the NII will support two-way communication, students will be able to ask questions and interact with their distant teachers and fellow students.

Not only does this open a way for schools to save money by sharing teachers and other resources, but also it improves education, allowing kids everywhere to benefit from the best teachers, wherever they may be. Imagine a high school Spanish class in Illinois getting a lesson from a teacher in San Juan or Madrid. Envision science classes all over the country interacting "live" with astronauts on the space shuttle or with archeologists in the field—it's like a daily field trip. The same technology may also allow homebound kids or those who live in remote areas to study from home.

Using the same technology, students can share not only teachers and lessons but also resources such as online textbooks. Some have cautioned that because distance learning requires computers, it will tend to be used first in the well-funded schools that need it least and won't be available in poorer school districts —widening an already unacceptable inequity in public education. With luck, public and private funds will be found to make sure everybody gets an equal chance to get online. The potential savings in staff, textbooks, and other resources may also help struggling schools get online.

All of these educational services are available today, in a limited fashion. The promise of the NII is that it will extend these benefits to millions of students. To the extent that they can be made affordable and accessible to schools, such services can save money and improve education at the same time.

The Internet Is Headed into Your TV

The more you look at all the proposed Superhighway benefits and services, the more you realize that the NII and its related projects are part of a move to unify all the ways we communicate electronically, cutting out the overlap.

Sooner or later, many people may realize that there's a wasteful redundancy in owning a PC and a TV. Why not just have one big screen where you can watch HBO, do your taxes, *and* play video games? Why can't the video cable double as a modem line, so your TV can go online?

That's the future some envision. Although not all visionaries think it will happen this way, others promote the concept of a PCTV—a PC and TV in one. It would probably look like a regular TV. Inside, however, it would have the "intelligent" processing power of a PC, and it would be accompanied by some kind of keyboard—maybe a fancy remote control or even a "voice interface" that would allow the user to control it by voice commands. At first, people would probably purchase "set-top boxes" that would convert a regular TV to a PCTV; but eventually, all new TVs would be built as PCTVs.

Using the household NII line as a combined, two-way cable TV and modem line, the PCTV would be the required end-user device for enjoying the following services:

Interactive TV: Like your telephone service today, your cable TV would be supplied by a two-way line. TV programs would come to you as before, but you could talk back to them by keying in responses or messages with your remote control. The favorite illustration for interactive TV is Interactive Jeopardy, in which you could press buttons on your remote control to send in your answers (or rather, your questions—"Alex, I'll take 'Homophones' for $100.") Other possible applications include interactive talk shows. As with some other NII plans, an early version of Interactive TV is already available in some places. The NII promises to greatly refine and expand what's available now, and extend it to everyone.

Shopping: Your two-way TV could become a shopping mall through which you order products and services. Unlike today's Home Shopping Club-type programs, interactive shopping would allow you to search actively for what you want, instead of waiting for the Home Shopping folks to show it. For example, to find that nice T-Fal cookware set, you might choose "cookware" from an on-screen menu, then choose "T-Fal" from the menu that appears next, after which you'd be shown pictures of sellers' wares and maybe even see a salesperson give a video pitch. When you're ready to buy, you do so by pressing a button or two on your remote. The video seller bills the item to your credit card or takes the money out of your bank account, then tosses your T-Fal in the mail.

Video-On-Demand: The NII is supposed to be able to accommodate 500 channels of TV programming. If you have cable, you know that you could have 1,000 channels and still find nothing to watch but infomercials, cheesy talk shows, and reruns of Congressional speeches. So, instead of going to the video store to rent a tape or laserdisc, you'd tap your remote to order a movie or other program to watch immediately. You might pick your movie from an on-screen menu or from a catalog. The video company would transmit the movie (or TV show, educational video, or other program) to your TV and charge your credit card or bill you for each movie. Early versions of this technology are already available through digital satellite systems. The NII versions, however, are likely to be more powerful, allowing you to pause, rewind, and fast-forward your program. NII-based cable is also expected to supply High-Definition Television (HDTV), a new video standard that will supply pictures that look as good as a movie screen on new HDTV sets.

Other Information Services: Remember, your PCTV will have many of the capabilities of a PC, some kind of remote keyboard control, and access to a high-speed, two-way communications line. That means it could be used to access the Internet or any of the other online services in use today. Because the PCTV would bring these services to many people who aren't Internet users (or even computer users), highly simplified services would soon appear. They would provide easy menus or voice prompts to lead users through simple tasks like looking up information in an online encyclopedia. Interactive banking is another likely service. You'll be able to check your balance, transfer money, and pay bills through your TV.

Other consumer-oriented, interactive consulting services are likely to appear, as well. You can dial up some personal tax advice or consult a lawyer, podiatrist, or psychic. You may be able to run software programs, but *how* you'll do it is up in the air. Your PCTV may have a disk or CD-ROM drive like a regular PC, or you may simply punch in a request to use software that's stored not on your TV but on the computer of the service provider, who would send it to your PCTV like an on-demand video.

Of course, some people doubt that the future will unfold exactly this way. Even after major portions of the NII are in place, most of us will still probably have separate telephone and cable lines for years. The difference is that the one-way cable lines will be switched to two-way, and the telephone lines will also offer video. The PCTV idea also may not happen all at once. Although most experts agree that the services I've described will be offered, PCTV scoffers say the more likely scenario has everyday consumers using a more simplified type of interactive TV set to use basic services like video-on-demand and shopping, whereas NII services involving more skill and more keyboard work will still require a PC of some kind.

The Internet Is Headed into Oblivion (Maybe)

If the information superhighway really shapes up, would it *replace* the Internet? That's not the goal of the NII by any means, but it could have that effect.

Whether the NII can or will replace the Internet is hard to say exactly, because as a formal organization the Internet doesn't actually exist. That is, given that an essential defining quality of the Internet is the fact that it *isn't* a formal organization, does the existence of a commercially or federally managed infrastructure make the Internet, as we know it, impossible?

Look at it this way:

- If you think of the Internet as the sum of its resources, it will probably survive in one form or another. Whatever the new networks are called, people will almost certainly still have access to newsgroups (or reasonable facsimiles), files to copy, e-mail, and the rest. These may be direct holdovers from the Internet, or they may be commercial or public descendants of those resources. Some of the specifics of the resources may change as well—but left alone, they'd still evolve, all by themselves.

- If you think of the Internet as a unique cultural and social phenomenon, your Internet may be disappearing. To the extent that Internet-type resources survive, there's no guarantee that any of them will be free. Charges would almost certainly skim off a proportion of current Internet users, whereas the easier access provided by interactive TV would bring in new users who wouldn't have touched the old Internet with a 10-foot modem cable. This would change—and perhaps limit—the spectrum of people and personalities on the network. It's possible that small, rebel networks would evolve to preserve the spirit of the Internet in the age of the NII, but these would lack the breadth that was an essential characteristic of the original Internet.

Although no one knows exactly what will happen, some fear that the involvement of government and business interests in the NII will—either by regulation or by market forces—effectively censor or skew the information exchange, as with other mass media, toward whatever conforms to the prejudices of the majority or the special interests of business and government.

So Now You Know...

Now you know the ropes, the lay of the land, the bottom line, the basic picture, the overall facts about the Internet. In this chapter, you've learned that the Internet is evolving into an Information Superhighway (or being replaced by it, depending on how you look at it). If it lives up to its promise, the Superhighway—formally called the National Information Infrastructure—will offer...

- Enhanced business communications services.
- Improved multimedia educational services.
- Interactive video and video on demand.
- New information services, such as home shopping and banking.

You also know that the National Information Infrastructure is far from a reality, and the open question of who would control it—government or private enterprise—is a source of much controversy. Internet aficionados would suggest a third alternative—an NII controlled by no one, just as the Internet is. But considering that government and private enterprise are building the NII out of their own pockets, they're extremely unlikely to turn it loose when they finish.

10

What If I'm Still Curious?

If you've read the preceding chapters, you're as well educated about the Internet as any non-Internet user can or should be. If you're still curious, that probably means you've decided to become a user—or you're leaning that way.

This final chapter offers suggestions for your next step. The sources described here provide information or services that can expand your Internet expertise. The sources include these:

- Internet organizations
- Online services
- Computer and Internet magazines
- Internet books

In keeping with the theme of this book, I have not included a directory of places *on* the Internet that can tell you more *about* the Internet. You should know, however, that they're there. In fact, you can find more information about the Internet on the Internet than anywhere else. It's a little hard to find, so we're caught in one of those chicken-egg paradoxes—to get to the resources that can help you understand the Internet, you must *already* understand the Internet. That's just one of the speedbumps that will have to be flattened out somewhere between today's Internet and tomorrow's superhighway.

True beginners will do best to move on to more advanced paper-based material before attempting to cruise the Internet. However, for those brave souls who want to jump right in and see what they can find, I've thrown in a few words about getting Internet access, to get you started, under the heading, "Hop Online."

Whatever you choose for the next step in your Internet education, I hope you'll discover that *Curious About the Internet?* prepared you well, enabling you to take on the more advanced material with ease.

Contact an Internet Organization

You can call or write the following organizations for more information about the Internet.

The Internet Society is the principle watchdog for the Internet's health and welfare. The all-volunteer organization doesn't control the Internet, but it helps keep the Internet running by determining technical standards for smooth network operation and recommending other policies. The Society publishes several newsletters and organizes conferences as well. It's the closest thing the Internet has to a central governing body, and it's the most authoritative source for up-to-the-minute Internet information.

> The Internet Society
> 1895 Preston White Drive, Suite 100
> Reston, VA 22091
> Voice: (703) 620-8990

The Electronic Frontier Foundation (EFF) is an activist group that works to keep the Internet free, open, and uncensored. In providing assistance to people whose online free speech or other civil rights may have been violated, the EFF plays an important advocacy role in shaping the Internet's culture and evolution. The EFF has come under fire at times for defending mischievous hackers whom others have considered troublemakers not worth protecting. But as the Internet equivalent of the American Civil Liberties Union, the EFF helps hold a line between a free Internet and those who would seek to abuse or limit that freedom.

> Electronic Frontier Foundation
> 155 Second St.
> Cambridge, MA 02141
> Voice: (617) 864-0665

Consult an Online Service

For some people, using a commercial online information service such as those in the following list provides a good stepping stone to the bigger, more complex Internet. Think of these services as the Internet with training wheels.

At this writing, they don't offer the entire breadth of Internet services (though CompuServe promises to by the end of 1995), and they may or may not be more expensive, depending on whether you'd have to pay for your Internet connection—see Chapter 5. But they're definitely easier to use. For a complete novice, a few months rooting around CompuServe or America Online is good preparation for Internet action. To the extent that they offer access to Internet services, they are an even better transition vehicle.

If you really think your future lies with the Internet and nothing but the Internet, you may be better off reading up and then taking the plunge into the Internet proper, forgetting the middlemen. If you're not sure, however, consider using an online service to break the ice. Be sure to investigate costs carefully, the amount of Internet access provided, and whether Internet services cost extra.

America Online
8619 Westwood Center Dr.
Vienna, VA 22182
Voice: (800) 827-6364

CompuServe
5000 Arlington Centre Blvd.
P.O. Box 20212
Columbus, OH 43220
Voice: (800) 848-8199

Prodigy
445 Hamilton Ave.
White Plains, NY 10601
Voice: (800) 284-5933

Read a Magazine

Increasingly, you'll find regular or semi-regular coverage of the Internet in many consumer computer magazines, including *PC/Computing*, *PC Magazine*, *MACWORLD*, *Computer*

What If I'm Still Curious?   217

Shopper, and even the relatively recent entry *Family Computing*. In their coverage, these magazines generally assume that you're familiar with the type of computers the magazine covers, but not especially familiar with the Internet.

If you already know your way around a computer, you may find insight in these publications and others like them. If you're a computer novice, though, you'll need to come up to speed on computers before you can appreciate what these publications say about the Internet.

At this writing, there are also two significant magazines that focus specifically on the Internet. In general, both require readers to possess an intermediate or better background in computers and online communication, although novices will find something interesting in either publication. The main difference between the two is that *Internet World* is more exclusively focused on the Internet and leans towards hands-on Internet information, whereas *Wired* covers the whole spectrum of electronic communications and is devoted mostly to issues and opinion pieces. *Wired* is also a hipper, slicker, snazzier publication than the more businesslike *Internet World*. Both publications regularly cover new or interesting resources on the Internet.

> *Internet World*
> Mecklermedia Corp.
> 20 Ketchum St.
> Westport, CN 06880
> Voice: (203) 226-6967
>
> *Wired*
> 544 Second St.
> San Francisco, CA 94107
> Voice: (415) 904-0660

Hop Online

Feeling brave? This book has not attempted to fully prepare you to use the Internet. That doesn't mean that you can't just damn the torpedoes and try it out. After all, you don't need a license. I'd recommend that you first check out one of the books listed later in this chapter—doing so would ensure a less frustrating learning curve. But you're the boss.

If you belong to a company or other organization that has its own Internet connection, you'll have to talk to your system administrator to find out how to get permission to use the organization's Internet account, which tools and facilities are available, and what your site's own Internet policies are. You may also want to ask a colleague who uses the Internet if you can peek over his or her shoulder for a lunch hour, to get a feel for how the Internet is used in your organization.

The fastest-growing type of Internet user is the individual or small business who acquires an Internet connection through an Internet access provider, as explained in Chapter 5. These providers typically supply either or both of the two types of "dial-in" service. The more powerful—and usually more expensive—option is a direct dial-in account, sometimes also described as an IP, SLIP (Serial Line Internet Protocol) or PPP (Point-to-Point Protocol) account. This type of connection lets you take full advantage of software tools (see Chapter 5) that can make your Internet journey easier. For example, the popular Mosaic (see Chapter 7) requires an IP account.

You can also subscribe to the more basic terminal accounts (also called command line or "shell" account) some providers offer. Typically, these don't give you the ability to take advantage of the Internet tools you can run on your own

What If I'm Still Curious? 219

computer—you're limited to the tools running on the access provider's computer. Depending on what tools the access provider has, a command line or shell connection could be more difficult to use for a novice. Then again, some people find these connections easier to use, because you don't have to deal with configuring your software. Command line or shell connections may also require less powerful (and less expensive) computers and modems than the direct dial-in accounts.

If you don't have access through your organization, your first step in getting on the Internet is to choose an access provider. You can use a local provider in your area, or others around the country. If your non-local options don't offer toll-free numbers for accessing their computers, you'll pay long-distance charges in addition to the access provider's charges—which is an important consideration.

> **Did You Know...**
>
> Don't forget to consider Free-Nets or online information services (both described in Chapter 5) as alternatives to a more straightforward Internet connection.

You may be able to find local access providers in the Yellow Pages or in local computer newsletters. If not, you can talk to your local computer club (ask them about Free-Nets, too) or society, or the folks at a local computer store. Lists of local and national providers and Free-Nets, and instructions for finding still more providers, appear in most of the books described later in this chapter.

When evaluating providers, consider the cost:

- How much is charged per minute, and is there a monthly minimum?

- Is there an option to pay a flat monthly fee for unlimited access time? Would you use the Internet for enough minutes each month to make the flat rate a better deal than per-minute charges? Are there special restrictions attached to the flat fee, such as resources you can't use unless you pay an additional per-minute charge?

- Are there other charges to consider, such as long-distance charges for using a non-local provider?

- Are extra-cost Internet resources, like the ClariNet news service (see Chapter 6), included in the cost?

You'll also want to carefully consider which tools the provider supplies, and how much, if any, software the provider gives you for an IP account. Usually, the software a provider supplies is shareware or freeware copied from the Internet anyway, but the provider is saving you the trouble of finding and configuring the stuff yourself. (Warning: If the provider gives you shareware, the software isn't really free. You're supposed to pay the programmer if you use it.) Find out how much telephone assistance the provider can supply, and whether it's free or not. Also, find out what type of computer hardware the provider requires or recommends for the type of account you're considering.

Once you find a provider, the next steps in gaining Internet access take place between you and the provider. Once you sign up, the access provider should give you complete instructions for getting onto the Internet through his or her service, and some instructions for any software supplied.

Bon voyage.

Read a Book

The following are recommended Sams titles for further study of the Internet. They can be found at your local bookstore or ordered directly from Sams with the form in the back of this book. You can also place orders by calling 800-428-5531.

Teach Yourself the Internet

>Subtitle: *Around the World in 21 Days*
>
>Author: Neil Randall
>
>Reader Level: Beginner/Intermediate
>
>Pages: 676
>
>Description: A step-by-step, day-by-day tour through a suite of Internet activities, starting with daily lessons on major Internet facilities (newsgroups, e-mail, Gopher, and so on) and branching out into Internet "excursions" to explore interesting resources. The object is to make you a strong Internet user in 21 days, and anyone who follows the directions closely is likely to achieve that.
>
>Special Features for *Curious About the Internet?* Readers: Provides well-rounded excursions for practical applications: using the Internet to learn the Internet, doing business, finding government information, job hunting, choosing a university, finding scientific research, and more. Offers clear, step-by-step instructions and a solid introduction to some of the best resources the Internet has to offer.

Your Internet Consultant

Subtitle: *The FAQs of Life Online*

Author: Kevin M. Savetz

Reader Level: All levels

Pages: 550

Description: A collection of more than 350 commonly asked (and not so commonly asked) questions and the same number of concise, clear answers. Questions range from the basic (How do I send e-mail to Congress?) to the issue-oriented (Should I worry about security?) to the simply curious (Are there recipes online?).

Special Features for *Curious About the Internet?* Readers: A good general-reference book to keep handy while using the Internet, and an excellent companion to *Curious About the Internet?* Not a step-by-step guide, but a great way to get straightforward answers in a hurry.

Navigating the Internet (Deluxe Edition)

Authors: Richard J. Smith and Mark Gibbs

Reader Level: Intermediate

Pages: 640

Description: A complete, detailed guide to using the Internet and everything that's on it. Features clear, step-by-step instructions for using the major Internet facilities and resources. An international bestseller, it's a bible for many Internet users.

What If I'm Still Curious? 223

Special Features for *Curious About the Internet?* Readers: More than 300 pages are dedicated to valuable reference listings: Internet access providers, Gopher sites, commands, popular newsgroups and mailing lists, and more. Also includes a PC disk containing access software, a suite of Internet software tools, and directories of newsgroups and mailing lists. Readers can order a Macintosh disk separately.

Internet Unleashed

Authors: Multiple.

Reader Level: Intermediate/Advanced

Pages: 1,387

Description: A detailed, comprehensive guide and reference book that doesn't simply cover the basic operation of the Internet, but offers advice on making the most of it.

Special Features for *Curious About the Internet?* Readers: The book was written by over 40 of the world's top Internet experts, each taking on the topics he or she knows best. Hundreds of specific (and sometimes little-known) tips and tricks are described to help readers master the Internet. Applications for business, research, education, government, and more are all included. A PC disk of Internet software and an offer for free Internet access time are included, as is a form for ordering Macintosh Internet software.

The Internet Business Guide

Subtitle: *Riding the Information Superhighway to Profit*

Authors: Rosalind Resnick and Dave Taylor

Reader Level: Beginning/Intermediate/Advanced

Pages: 418

Description: A complete guide to business uses of the Internet. Covers creating an Internet-based customer service center, online selling and advertising, security steps, and more.

Special Features for *Curious About the Internet?* Readers: Uses real-life business examples to illustrate business applications. Includes tips helpful to many users, such as how to find the best deal on Internet access.

Education on the Internet

Subtitle: *A Hands-On Book of Ideas, Resources, Projects, and Advice*

Author: Jill H. Ellsworth

Reader Level: Beginning-Intermediate

Pages: 591

Description: A complete guide to using the Internet in education—to learn and study, if you're a student; or to teach and perform research, if you're a teacher or professor.

Special Features for *Curious About the Internet?* Readers: In addition to listings of hundreds of education resources on the Internet, this book includes a nifty appendix called "Internet 101," which is probably one of the most concise, well-written guides to learning to use the various Internet tools available anywhere.

The World Wide Web Unleashed

Authors: John December and Neil Randall, and a team of experts

Reader Level: All levels

Pages: 1,100

Description: Like its big brother, *The Internet Unleashed*, this book includes in one big volume everything you need to know to master the World Wide Web, the part of the Internet that's attracting so much attention these days. It tells how to select and find a Web browser (such as Mosaic), it tells you how to explore the Web, and it even describes in great detail the process involved in designing and setting up Web pages of your own.

Special Features for *Curious About the Internet?* Readers: Although *The World Wide Web Unleashed* gets into some fairly detailed tech talk later on in the book, it includes one of the most comprehensive guides to all the various Web browsers—something that readers of all levels can make use of. And it takes the reader on a guided tour of the most interesting sites on the World Wide Web—something that even those without a Web connection can follow along and enjoy.

Plug-n-Play Mosaic

Subtitle: *The Instant Install Kit for Windows*

Authors: Angela Gunn

Reader Level: Beginning-Intermediate

Description: A book/disk set that promises to get you online and using Mosaic within minutes. The book is a complete guide to using Mosaic, the popular browser for the World Wide Web. The disk includes everything you need (other than a computer and Microsoft Windows) to install and configure a fully supported commercial version of Enhanced NCSA Mosaic.

Special Features for *Curious About the Internet?* Readers: This is the absolute easiest way to find out why everybody is talking about Mosaic and the World Wide Web. Just run the install program and the software takes care of everything for you.

Plug-n-Play Internet

Subtitle: *The Instant Install Kit for Windows*

Authors: Neil Randall

Reader Level: Beginning-Intermediate

Description: A book/disk set that promises to get you on the Internet within minutes. The disk includes easy-to-use Windows versions of all the important Internet tools—e-mail, Usenet news, Gopher, Mosaic, etc.—and then the book tells you how to use them and what to do with them.

What If I'm Still Curious? 227

Special Features for *Curious About the Internet?* Readers: The easiest way to get on the Internet with a complete suite of Windows Internet tools. The software automatically installs and configures everything for you.

So Now You Know...

Now you know everything I know (that's worth knowing). Thanks for entrusting your curiosity to me. Here's hoping you and I remain forever curious, no matter how much we may learn.

Glossary

account See **Internet account**.

address (also called *e-mail address*) A special code name that is a user's unique name on the Internet. Usually describing both the person and the place where the person works, the address is used to direct **e-mail** to its intended destination. See Chapter 6.

Archie A special facility that helps users locate a **file** on the Internet. See Chapter 7.

browse To wander around a portion of the Internet, screen by screen, looking for items of interest, as one would when shopping.

browser An Internet **software tool** that helps users browse. See Chapter 7.

bulletin board   A generic term for a computer system that enables users to read messages posted by others and to post messages for others. Many types of bulletin boards are available through **Telnet**. See Chapters 1 and 7.

Cello   A **software tool** for using the **World Wide Web**; similar in function to **Mosaic**. See Chapter 7.

commercial traffic   Internet messages or other **online** information created solely for commercial purposes, such as advertising. See Chapter 2.

compression   The process of making a computer **file** smaller so it can be copied more quickly between computers. Compressed files must be decompressed on the receiving computer before they can be used. See Chapter 7.

cyberspace   A broad expression used to describe the activity, communication, and culture happening on the Internet and other computer networks.

dial-in connection   A method that allows a computer lacking a **direct connection** to access the Internet. Using a **modem** and the telephone lines, the computer contacts another computer that *is* directly connected to the Internet and then uses that computer as an intermediary. See Chapters 5 and 10.

direct connection   A permanent, 24-hour link between a computer and the Internet. A computer with a direct connection can use the Internet at any time. See Chapter 5.

e-mail   Short for *electronic mail*, a system that enables a person to compose a message on a computer and transmit that message through a **network** to another user who reads the message on his or her computer screen. See Chapter 6.

FAQ file Short for Frequently Asked Questions *file*, a computer **file** containing the answers to frequently asked questions about a particular Internet resource. See Chapter 7.

file The unit in which a discrete block of information (a document, a picture, and so on) is stored in a computer. Files come in different types, each containing a different kind of information: text, graphics, sound, video, or mathematical data. See Chapter 7.

finger A facility that helps Internet users locate other Internet users and **resources**. See Chapter 6.

flame Hostile messages, often sent through **e-mail** or posted in **newsgroups,** from Internet users in reaction to breaches of **netiquette**.

freeware Software available to anyone, free of charge; unlike **shareware**, which requires payment. See Chapter 1.

FTP Short for *file transfer protocol*, the basic method for copying a **file** from one computer to another through the Internet. See Chapter 7.

Gopher A system of **menus** layered on top of existing **resources** that makes locating information and using services easier. See Chapter 7.

hypermedia and **hypertext** Methods for allowing users to jump spontaneously among on-screen documents and other **resources** by selecting highlighted keywords that appear on each screen. Hypermedia and hypertext appear most often on the **World Wide Web**. See Chapter 7.

Information Superhighway A public relations nickname for the **National Information Infrastructure**. See Chapter 9.

Internet   A large, loosely organized **internetwork** connecting universities, research institutions, governments, businesses, and other organizations so that they can exchange messages and share information. See Chapter 1.

Internet account   The name that describes a person's authorization to access the Internet. Everyone who uses the Internet has an Internet account, just as everyone who uses the bank has a bank account.

internetwork   A set of **networks** and individual computers that are connected so that they can communicate and share information. The Internet is a very large internetwork. See Chapter 1.

listserv   A special type of software that automatically handles the management of a **mailing list**. See Chapter 6.

Macintosh   A type of personal computer (**PC**) made by Apple Computer, Inc.

mailing list   An Internet **resource** that automatically sends **e-mail** messages related to a particular topic to people who have indicated an interest in that topic. See Chapter 6.

menu   A list of options that appear on the screen to make using computer systems easier. Users simply choose menu items to operate the system; they don't have to learn or remember special commands. See Chapter 7.

Microsoft Windows   A popular software program that provides a graphical computing environment for IBM-type **PC**s. Software programs that support the Windows environment (such as **Mosaic**) can display pictures and can be made easy to use through menus and on-screen pictures called *icons*.

modem   A device that allows a computer to communicate with another computer through telephone lines. **PC** users typically need a modem and a **dial-up connection** to use the Internet. See Chapter 5.

Mosaic   A **software tool** that helps users take advantage of the **multimedia** features of the **World Wide Web**. See Chapter 7.

mouse   A small, hand-operated device that, when moved, moves a pointer displayed on the computer screen. Using a mouse, a **PC** user can conveniently manipulate on-screen objects and select items from **menus**.

MUD   Short for *Multi-User Dungeon*, *Multi-User Dimension* or *Multi-User Dialog*, an Internet resource in which users role-play by interacting within an imagined environment created through on-screen messages. See Chapter 8.

multimedia   A description for systems capable of displaying or playing text, pictures, sound, video, and animation.

National Information Infrastructure   The formal name for the "Information Superhighway," a joint public-private initiative to revamp America's electronic communications system to support advanced business, educational, and consumer services. See Chapter 9.

netiquette   The code of proper conduct (etiquette) on the **Internet** ("the Net").

network   A set of computers interconnected so that they can communicate and share information. Connected networks together form an **internetwork**. See Chapter 1.

newsgroup   A Internet resource through which people post and read messages related to a specific topic. See Chapter 6.

NREN The National Research and Educational Network, a government-sponsored internetwork of academic and research computers. Now under construction, the NREN is a pilot for experiments in developing the **National Information Infrastructure**.

online An adjective describing things on a network. When a user is actually using the Internet, he or she is online (otherwise, he or she is *offline*).

password A secret code, known only to the user, that allows the user to access a computer that is protected by a security system. Used with a **user name**, passwords are needed most often for accessing computers through **Telnet**. See Chapter 7.

PC Short for *personal computer*, a term that can be used generically (as it is in this book) to refer to any type of single-user computer, including IBM-type PCs and **Macintosh**es.

PCTV An imaginary device combining the functions of a television and a **PC**. Some experts predict that PCTVs will be developed to replace TVs and PCs when new interactive services become available through the **National Information Infrastructure**. See Chapter 9.

resource A generic term to describe the varied information and activities available to Internet users.

shareware Software programs that users are permitted to acquire and evaluate for free. Shareware is different from **freeware** in that, if a person likes the program and plans to use it on a regular basis, he or she is expected to send a fee to the programmer. See Chapter 1.

sign on The act of accessing a computer system by typing a required **user name** and **password**. Internet users often must sign on to **Telnet** systems before they can use them.

Glossary 235

smileys Pictures created from typed characters (often punctuation marks), used by Internet people to express emotions or other abstract ideas in messages. To see what a smiley represents, you tilt your head to the left. Examples are the smile :-) and the frown :-(.

software tool Software programs that assist in using certain Internet resources. Examples are **Mosaic** and **e-mail** programs. See Chapter 5.

Spam The act of excessively or over-aggressively duplicating a message and broadcasting it all over the Internet; can incite **flames** in response. See Chapter 9.

Telnet A facility for accessing other computers on the Internet and for using the **resources** that are there. See Chapter 7.

user name Used with a **password** to gain access to a computer. A user name is a user's unique identifying name when using that computer. To access the computer, the user **signs on** by typing his or her user name and password. See Chapter 7.

Veronica A facility that helps users search for and locate information and **resources** available through **Gopher**. See Chapter 7.

Whois A facility that helps Internet users locate other Internet users and **resources**. See Chapter 6.

World Wide Web (WWW) A set of Internet computers and services that provide an easy-to-use system for finding information and moving among **resources**. WWW services feature **hypertext, hypermedia,** and **multimedia** information, which can be explored through **software tools** such as **Cello, Mosaic** and Lynx. See Chapter 7.

Windows See **Microsoft Windows**.

Index

Symbols

@ (ampersand), e-mail addresses, 130

A

Academy One (educational resources), 42
Acceptable Use Policies, 9
access
  providers, 219-220
  restriction (government files), 89
  tools, 122-124
  universal access, 97

accessing
  government resources via FedWorld, 52
  interactive games, 174
  resources, 147-156, 162-164
  Telnet, 152
accounts (Internet), 232
activist resources, 53-54
addresses (e-mail), 16, 130-131, 229
Adventurer's Guild game, 176
advertising via Internet, 48
agricultural resources, 46

alternative newsgroups, 141
America Online, 105, 216
ampersand (@), e-mail
 addresses, 130
antitrusts (telephone/cable
 services), 195
Archie (FTP aid), 117,
 161, 229
Arena game, 176
art via Internet, 67
AskERIC, *see* ERIC
astronomy resources, 38
Atlantis game, 176

B

billing information (online
 services), 106
biology resources, 38
Birkerts, Sven, 84
blind users, 69
board games on the
 Internet, 175
botany resources, 39
Broidy, Ellen, 87
browsers, 167, 229
 Mosaic, 119
 WWW tool, 114
browsing, 229
 menus, 163
 WWW, 165
bulletin boards, 230
business, *see* commercial
 business

C

cable service monopolies, 195
CARL (Colorado Association
 of Research Libraries), 45
Cello (WWW browser),
 167, 230
censoring (National Information Infrastructure), 196
Chat, 135-136
Checkfree, 191
chemistry resources, 39
CIA World Map, 39
CIX (Commercial Internet
 Exchange), 20, 203
ClariNet, 112, 141
Clear and Present Danger
 (technical accuracy), 151
CNN Headline News, 29
Colorado Association of
 Research Libraries), *see*
 CARL
comic strips, 178-179
command line accounts,
 115, 218
commands
 finger command, 143
 Help command, 153
 Whois command, 143
CommerceNet, 95, 203
commercial business, 18-21,
 48, 68-69
 NII (National Information
  Infrastructure), 199-204
 resources, 47-50
 telecommuting, 193

Commercial Internet exchange, *see* CIX
commercial
  providers (e-mail), 105
  software, 26, 117
  traffic, 230
communication
  hookups, 110-114
  networks, 83-84
  tools, 134-136
compressed files, 157, 230
CompuServe, 106, 216
computer science resources, 39
connections
  command line connections, 115
  cost, 112
  dial-in connections, 111, 230
  dial-in terminal connections, 111
  direct connections, 230
  direct dial-in connections, 111
  Free-Nets, 113
  mail connections, 112
  permanent connections, 111
Constituent Electronic Mail System, 53
conversational tools, 135-136
copying
  files, 156-162
  online files, 115
crackers, 82
creating National Information Infrastructure, 193-199
credit-card fraud, 94-96

The Cuckoo's Egg, 88
cyberpunks, 82
cyberspace, 230

D

data harvesting (e-mail), 91
databases, 38
decompressing files, 123, 157
demographic research (commercial business resources), 48
dial-in connection, 230
dial-in connections, 111
dial-in terminal connections, 111
direct connections, 230
direct dial-in connections, 111
directories
  FTP sites, 160
  resource directories, 104
disabled users, 69-70
discussion lists, 14, 137-139
domains (networks), 130
downloading files, 158
Duelmasters game, 176
Dungeons & Dragons via Internet, 176

E

e-mail, 15-18, 114, 126-134, 230
  address formats, 131
  commercial providers, 105

confidentiality, 90-94
data harvesting, 91
discussion lists, 137
emoticons, 133
Eudora shareware, 118
flames, 231
games, 176-177
intercompany e-mail, 200
mail connections, 112
mailing lists, 137
messages, 133
netiquette, 132
Education on the Internet, 224
education resources, 41-43, 204-206
EEF (Electronic Frontier Foundation), 215
electronic communication, 190
Electronic Funds Transfer, 191
electronic media (issues), 84-87
electronic newsletters, 103
electronic publications, 76
emoticons, 77, 133, 183, 235
employment opportunities via Internet, 87
encryption, 95
Engineering Task Force, 11
Environmental Activism Server, 54
environmental issues, 63-64
ERIC (Educational Information Resources Center), 41
erotica, 77-78
  see also pornography
Eudora shareware (e-mail), 118
external modems, 108

F

facilities
  Archie, 161
  Gopher, 162-164
  Veronica, 164-165
FAQ (Frequently Asked Questions) files, 154, 159, 231
faxes (e-mail transmission), 133
Federal Information Exchange, 41
FedWorld (government resources), 52
fee-based resources, 95
File Transfer Protocol, *see* FTP
files, 231
  compressed files, 157
  compressing, 230
  copying, 156-162
  decompressing, 123, 157
  downloading, 158
  FAQ files, 154, 159
  finding, 156-162
  sound files, 180
  text files, 160
  uploading, 158
financial research (commercial business), 49
finding files, 156-162
finger command, 143, 231
flames (e-mail), 231
forestry resources, 39
formats (e-mail addresses), 131
forward utility (e-mail), 129

fraud (credit-cards), 94-96
free items via Internet, 66-67
Free Software Foundation, 66
Free-Nets, 113, 219
free-speech environment,
    64-66, 86-87
freeware, 26, 116, 117,
    119, 231
Frequently Asked Question
    files, *see* FAQ
FTP (file transfer protocol),
    115, 158-159, 231

G

gag orders, 64
Galaxy game, 176
games
    e-mail games, 176-177
    interactive games, 174-176
    Internet Hunt, 177-178
    MUDs, 182-184
    Netrek, 175
    play-by-mail games, 176-177
    role-playing games, 182-184
Gates, Rick, 178
gateways (mailing lists/
    newsgroups), 142
gender ratios on the
    Internet, 86
geography resources, 39
Global Information Infrastructure, 197
Gonzo (electronic publications), 76

Gophers, 121, 162-164, 231
Gopherspace, 163-164
Gore, Al, 61, 65, 189
government resources,
    51-53, 89
grass-roots resources, 53-54
Green Card Incident
    (spamming), 201
GUI (graphical user
    interface), 110

H

hackers, 82-83, 89-90
Hamlet was a College Student, 76
hardware requirements,
    108-110
HDTV (High-Definition
    Television), 208
help (Telnet), 153
Help command, 153
High Performance Computing
    Act, 194
home pages (WWW), 185
hosts, 108
Humane Genome Project
    (scientific research), 62-63
humor newsgroups, 75-77
hypermedia, 119,
    167-171, 231
hypertext, 231
Hytelnet, 152

I

icons, 116
Information Superhighway, 192, 231
infrastructure, 188
interactive
  games, 174-176
  TV, 207
intercompany e-mail, 200
interlibrary networking, 21-24
internal modems, 108
International Discount Communications, 70
international issues via Internet, 64-66, 70-72
international users, 2-6
Internet
  accounts, 232
  addresses, 16, 130-131, 142
  connections, 110-114
  evolution, 29
  expansion, 55
  future security, 209-211
  legal issues, 92-94
  log on, 123
  magazine resources, 216-217
  navigating, 122-123
  organizations, 214-215
  personal necessity, 103-107
  published tutorials, 221-227
  resources, 109, 112
  subscriber population, 2
Internet Architecture Board, 11
The Internet Business Guide, 244
Internet Hunt, 177-178
Internet Shopping Network, 68
Internet Society, 2, 214-215
Internet Talk Radio, 179-182
Internet Town Hall, 181
Internet Unleashed, 223
Internet World, 217
Internet/TV interaction, 206-209
internetworks, 7, 232
IP links (dial-in connections), 111
IRCs (Internet Relay Chats), 184

J–K–L

JASON Project (educational resources), 42
jokes (humor newsgroups), 75-77
journalism resources, 44

Kelly, Kevin, 72
keywords (WWW), 166
KidLink (educational resources), 42
King of the Hill game, 177
Kuttner, Bob, 88

Learning Link (education resource), 41
legal
  issues, 92-94
  research (commercial business), 50
  resources, 43

Legends game, 176
libel (electronic media), 85
libraries, 21-24
library resources, 45
lists, 232
listservs, 137, 232
log on, 123
logging on Telnet, 151
Lynx (WWW browser), 167

M

Macintosh, 232
magazine resources, 216-217
magazines, 28
mail connections, 112
mailing lists, 12, 14, 137-139, 146-156, 232
main menu, 150
media (electronic), 84-85
medical resources, 40, 44
menus, 115, 150, 232
    Gopher menu, 163
    WWW menu, 166
messages (newsgroups vs. mailing lists), 140
meteorology resources, 39
Microsoft Windows, 232
Middle Earth game, 176
miscellaneous resources, 54-57
modems, 108-109, 233
moderators, 138
Moore, Cindy Tittle, 87
MOOs (Multi-User Object-Oriented environments), 183

Mosaic (WWW browser), 119, 167-168, 233
mouse, 233
MUDs (Multi-User Dungeons), 136, 182-184, 233
multimedia, 120, 233
MUSHes (Multi-User Shared Hallucinations), 183

N

National Center for Atmospheric Research, see NCAR
National Communications and Information Infrastructure Act, 196
National Information Infrastructure, 190, 233
National Information Infrastructure, see NII
National Research Council, see NRC
national security, 88-89
navigating
    Gopherspace, 164
    Internet, 122-123
Navigating the Internet (Deluxe Edition), 222
NCAR (National Center for Atmospheric Research), 37
netiquette, 132, 233
Netrek, 175
Network News, see newsgroups

networks, 7-8, 233
  communication, 83-84
  domains, 130
  internetworks, 232
  libraries, 21-24
  NFSnet, 30
  offline, 103
  online, 103
news resources, 27-29
newsgroups, 14, 114, 139-142, 146-156, 233
  humor newsgroups, 75-77
  NewsReader! shareware, 118
  searching, 118, 143-144
  topic ranges, 12
  unmoderated, 138
NewsReader! shareware, 118
newsreaders, 114
NFSnet, 30
nicknames (Chat), 136
NII (National Information Infrastructure), 193-199
  Advisory Council, 199
  commercial business, 199-204
  future development, 209-211
NRC (National Research Council), 198
NREN (National Research and Educational Network), 234
NSF (National Science Foundation), 18

O

OBI (Online Book Initiative), 24

oceanography resources, 39
online
  files, 109, 115
  resources, 103
  services, 103, 105, 215-216, 234
    billing information, 106
    e-mail messages, 133
  shopping services, 203
  opening menu, 150
Out of Control: The Rise of Neo-Biological Civilization, 72

P

passwords, 234
PCs (personal computers), 234
PCTVs (personal computer TVs), 206-209, 234
PeaceNet, 71
periodicals via Internet, 67
permanent connections, 111
personal ads, 72-73
play-by-mail games, 176-177
Plug-n-Play Internet, 226
Plug-n-Play Mosaic, 226
pornography, 96-97, 179
  see also erotica
PPP (Point-to-Point Protocol), 218
privacy (e-mail), 90
Prodigy, 216
professional consulting resources, 43-46
program viewers, 161
Project Gutenberg, 23

Q-R

QVT WinNet (multipurpose access tool), 122-124
receiving e-mail, 127-128
regulating NII, 196
remote login, 147
reply utility (e-mail), 129
Research Libraries Information Network, 45
resources, 234
    accessing, 147-156, 162-164
    activist resources, 53-54
    agricultural resources, 46
    astronomy resources, 38
    biology resources, 38
    botany resources, 39
    chemistry resources, 39
    ClariNet, 112
    commercial business resources, 47-50
    computer science resources, 39
    directories, 104
    education resources, 41-43, 204-206
    Environmental Activism Server, 54
    ERIC, 41
    erotica resources, 77-78
    FedWorld, 52
    forestry resources, 39
    geography resources, 39
    government resources, 51-53
    grass-roots resources, 53-54
    Internet, 109
    journalism resources, 44
    legal resources, 43
    libraries, 21-24, 45
    medical resources, 40, 44
    meteorology resources, 39
    miscellaneous resources, 54-57
    news resources, 27-29
    oceanography resources, 39
    online resources, 103
    professional consulting resources, 43-46
    Research Libraries Information Network, 45
    science resources, 35-41
    searching, 123
    software tools, 114-122
    Telnet resources, 147-156
    topic ranges, 12-13
    writing resources, 45
restricted access (government files), 89
role-playing games, 136, 182-184

S

science resources, 35-41
scientific research via Internet, 37, 62-63
screens (split), 134
search tools, 123
searching
    Gopherspace, 164
    government resources, 52
    Internet addresses, 142

newsgroups, 118, 141-144
  resources, 123
segregation, 97
selecting
  keywords (WWW), 166
  menu items, 150
sending e-mail, 127-128, 133
Serial Line Internet Protocol,
  see SLIP
servers
  Archie server, 117, 161
  WAIS (Wide Area Information Servers), 168
services (online),
  215-216, 234
sexism (electronic media), 86
shareware, 26, 116-118, 234
shell accounts (dial-in
  connections), 111, 218
signing on Telnet, 151, 234
sites (FTP), 159
SLIP (Serial Line Internet
  Protocol), 218
smileys, 77, 183, 235
  see also emoticons
social segregation, 97
software, 25-27
  commercial software, 117
  freeware, 117
  shareware, 117
  terminal emulation software, 153

tools, 114-122, 235
Gopher, 162-164
Veronica, 164-165
viewers, 161
WWW browsers, 167
sound files, 180
spamming, 202, 235
split screens in Talk, 134
Stoll, Cliff, 88
sysops, 91, 154
system administrators, 91
systems (Telnet), 155-156

T

Talk, 36, 134-135
Talk Radio program, 179
Teach Yourself the Internet, 221
telecommuting, 190-193
telephone service monopolies, 195
Telnet, 147-156, 235
terminal accounts, 218
terminal emulation software, 153
text files, 160
top menu, 150
tutorials, 221-227
TV interaction with Internet, 206-209

U

universal access, 97
unmoderated mailing lists, 138
unmoderated newsgroups, 138
uploading files, 158
Usenet newsgroups, *see* newsgroups
Usenet sites, 141
user name, 235
users (disabled), 69-70

V

VC (Virtual Corporation), 50, 68, 87
vending machine distribution status, 73-75
Veronica (Very Easy Rodent-Oriented Net-wide Index to Computerized Archives), 165, 235
video-on-demand (TV/Internet interaction), 208
viewers, 161
Virtual Communities, 71, 83
virtual communities, 83
viruses, 89

W

WAIS (Wide Area Information Servers), 168
WebLouvre, 67
Whois, 235
whois command, 143
WinGopher, 121
Wired, 217
writing resources, 45
The World Wide Web Unleashed, 225
WWW (World Wide Web), 165-171, 235
  Cello, 230
  home pages, 185
  Mosaic, 233
  software tools, 114

Y–Z

Your Internet Consultant, 222

GET CONNECTED
to the ultimate source of computer information!

The MCP Forum on CompuServe

Go online with the world's leading computer book publisher! Macmillan Computer Publishing offers everything you need for computer success!

Find the books that are right for you!
A complete online catalog, plus sample chapters and tables of contents give you an in-depth look at all our books. The best way to shop or browse!

- ➤ Get fast answers and technical support for MCP books and software
- ➤ Join discussion groups on major computer subjects
- ➤ Interact with our expert authors via e-mail and conferences
- ➤ Download software from our immense library:
  - ▷ Source code from books
  - ▷ Demos of hot software
  - ▷ The best shareware and freeware
  - ▷ Graphics files

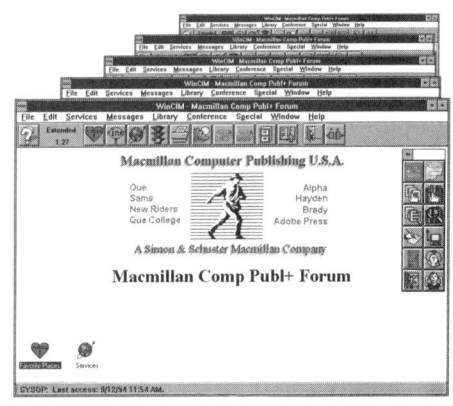

Join now and get a free CompuServe Starter Kit!

To receive your free CompuServe Introductory Membership, call **1-800-848-8199** and ask for representative #597.

The Starter Kit includes a personal ID number and password, a $15 credit on the system, and a subscription to *CompuServe Magazine!*

MACMILLAN COMPUTER PUBLISHING

CompuServe

Once on the CompuServe System, type:

GO MACMILLAN

for the most computer information anywhere!

Add to Your Sams Library Today with the Best Books for Programming, Operating Systems, and New Technologies

The easiest way to order is to pick up the phone and call

1-800-428-5331

between 9:00 a.m. and 5:00 p.m. EST.

For faster service please have your credit card available.

ISBN	Quantity	Description of Item	Unit Cost	Total Cost
0-672-30617-4		The World Wide Web Unleashed	$35.00	
0-672-30519-4		Teach Yourself the Internet: Around the World in 21 Days	$25.00	
0-672-30466-X		The Internet Unleashed	$39.95	
0-672-30485-6		Navigating the Internet, Deluxe Edition	$29.95	
0-672-30520-8		Your Internet Consultant: The FAQs of Life Online	$24.99	
0-672-30530-5		The Internet Business Guide: Riding the Information Superhighway to Profit	$25.00	
0-672-30595-X		Education on the Internet	$25.00	
0-672-30464-3		Teach Yourself UNIX in a Week	$28.00	
0-672-30457-0		Learning UNIX, Second Edition	$39.95	
0-672-30382-5		Understanding Local Area Networks, 4th Edition	$26.95	
0-672-30209-8		NetWare Unleashed	$45.00	
0-672-30173-3		Enterprise-Wide Networking	$39.95	
0-672-30501-1		Understanding Data Communications, 4th Edition	$29.99	
0-672-30119-9		International Telecommunications	$39.95	

❑ 3 ½" Disk

❑ 5 ¼" Disk

Shipping and Handling: See information below.	
TOTAL	

Shipping and Handling: $4.00 for the first book, and $1.75 for each additional book. Floppy disk: add $1.75 for shipping and handling. If you need to have it NOW, we can ship product to you in 24 hours for an additional charge of approximately $18.00, and you will receive your item overnight or in two days. Overseas shipping and handling adds $2.00 per book and $8.00 for up to three disks. Prices subject to change. Call for availability and pricing information on latest editions.

201 W. 103rd Street, Indianapolis, Indiana 46290

1-800-428-5331 — Orders   1-800-835-3202 — FAX   1-800-858-7674 — Customer Service

Book ISBN 0-672-30459-7